Emile Zola

The Joy of Life

Emile Zola

THE JOY OF LIFE

Edited, with a preface, by:
Ernest Alfred Vizetelly

Mondial

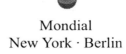

Mondial
New York · Berlin

Emile Zola: The Joy of Life (aka Zest for Life)
(French original title: "Le Joie de vivre")

Edited, with a preface, by:
Ernest Alfred Vizetelly

Copyright © 2006 Mondial
(for this edition of "The Joy of Life")
Editor (Mondial, 2006): Andrew Moore
All rights reserved.

ISBN 1595690476
ISBN 9781595690470

Library of Congress Control Number: 2006936660

Cover painting: Uday K. Dhar

www.mondialbooks.com

PREFACE

'LA JOIE DE VIVRE,' here translated as 'The Joy of Life,' was written by M. Zola in 1888, partly at his country house at Médan, and partly at Bénodet, a little seaside place in Brittany. The scene of the story is laid, however, on the coast of the neighbouring province of Normandy, between the mouth of the Orne and the rocks of Grandcamp, where the author had sojourned, more than once, in previous years. The title selected by him for this book is to be taken in an ironical or sarcastic sense. There is no joy at all in the lives of the characters whom he portrays in it. The story of the 'hero' is one of mental weakness, poisoned by a constantly recurring fear of death; whilst that of his father is one of intense physical suffering, blended with an eager desire to continue living, even at the cost of yet greater torture. Again, the story of the heroine is one of blighted affections, the wrecking of all which might have made her life worth living. And there is a great deal of truth in the various pictures of human existence which are thus presented to us; however much some people, in their egregious vanity, may recoil from the idea that life and love and talent and glory are all very poor and paltry things.

M. Zola is not usually a pessimist. One finds many of his darkest pictures relieved by a touch of hopefulness; but there is extremely little in the pages of 'La Joie de Vivre,' which is essentially an analysis of human suffering and misery. Nevertheless, the heroine, Pauline Quenu, the daughter of the Quenus who figure largely in 'Le Ventre de Paris' ('The Fat and the Thin'), is a beautiful, touching, and almost consolatory creature. She appears to the reader as the embodiment of human abnegation and devotion. Her guardians rob her, but she scarcely heeds it; her lover Lazare, their son, discards her for another woman, but she forgives him. It is she who infuses life into the lungs of her rival's puny babe; and when Lazare yields to his horrible fear of death it is she who tries to comfort him, who endeavours to dispel the gloomy thoughts which poison his hours. No sacrifice is too great for her—money, love, she relinquishes everything, in the vain hope of securing a transient happiness for the man to whom she has given her heart. At times, no doubt, she yearns for his affection, she experiences momentary weaknesses, but her spirit is strong, and it invariably triumphs over her rebellious flesh.

Lazare, on the other hand, is one of those wretched beings whose number seems to be constantly increasing in our midst, the product of our corrupt civilisation, our grotesque educational systems, our restlessness and thirst for wealth, our thousand vices and our blatant hypocrisy. At the same time he is a talented young fellow, as are so many of the wretched *décadents* of nowadays; and 'something more or something less' in his brain might have turned his talent into genius. In this respect, indeed, he suggests another of M. Zola's characters, Claude Lantier, the painter of 'L'Œuvre'; but he is far weaker than was Claude, whose insanity sprang from his passion for his art, whereas Lazare's mental disorder is the fruit of that lack, both of will-power and of the spirit of perseverance, which always becomes manifest in decaying races. Briefly, he is a type of the talented, versatile, erratic weakling—a variety of what Paris expressively calls the *arriviste,* who loomed so largely through the final years of the last century, and who by force of numbers, not of power, threatens to dominate the century which has just begun.

In one respect Lazare differs greatly from Claude Lantier. Claude's insanity drove him to suicide, but Lazare shrinks from the idea of annihilation. His whole life indeed is blighted by the unreasoning fear of death to which I have previously alluded. In the brightest moments of Lazare's existence, in the broad sunshine, amid the fairest scenes of Nature, in the very transports of love, as in moments of anxiety and bereavement, and as in the gloom, the silence, and the solitude of night, the terrible, ever-recurring thought flashes on him: 'My God, my God, so one must die!' In the course of years this dread is intensified by the death of his mother and his old dog; and neither of the women who love him—the devoted Pauline, whom he discards, and the puppet Louise, whom he marries—can dispel it. The pious may argue that this fear of death is only natural on the part of an unbeliever, and that the proper course for Lazare to have pursued was to have sought the consolation of religion. But they have only to visit a few lunatic asylums to find in them extremely devout patients, who, whilst believing in a resurrection and a future life, nevertheless dread death quite as keenly as Lazare Chanteau did. Indeed, this fear of dissolution constitutes a well-known and perfectly defined disorder of the brain, rebellious alike to scientific and to spiritual treatment.

By the side of Lazare and Pauline 'La Joie de Vivre' shows us the former's parents. There is Lazare's mother, who despoils and wrongs Pauline for his benefit, who lives a life of sour envy, and who dies a wretched death, fearful of punishment. And there is his father, whose only thought is his stomach, and who, as I have mentioned, clings despairingly to a semblance of life amid the direst physical anguish. Louise, whom Lazare marries, is a skilfully drawn type of the weak, pretty, scented, coquettish, frivolous woman, who seems to have been with us ever since the world began, the woman to whom men are drawn by a perversion of natural instincts, and whom they need, perhaps, in order that in their saner moments they may the better appreciate the qualities of those few who resemble Pauline. As for the subordinate characters of the story, the grumpy Norman servant, though of a type often met with in M. Zola's stories, is perhaps the best, the various changes in her disposition towards the heroine being described with great fidelity to human nature. Then the rough but kind-hearted old doctor, the sturdy, tolerant priest, the artful and vicious village children, are all admirably delineated by M. Zola, and grouped around the central figures in such wise as to add to the truth, interest, and impressiveness of his narrative. And, painful as the tale at times may be, it is perhaps as well, in these days of pride and vanity, that one should be recalled now and again to a sense of the abject grovelling which unhappily characterises such a vast number of human lives. It may slightly console one, no doubt, to remember that there are at least some Paulines among us. But then, how few they are, and how numerous on the other hand are the men like Lazare and the women like his mother! When all is considered, judging by what one sees around one every day, one is forced to the conclusion that this diseased world of ours makes extremely little progress towards real sanity and health.

E. A. V.
MERTON, SURREY.

III

EMILE ZOLA'S "LES ROUGON-MACQUART"

La Fortune des Rougon (1871) - The Fortune of the Rougons

La Curée (1871–72) - The Kill / La Curee

Le Ventre de Paris (1873) -
The Fat and the Thin / The Belly of Paris

La Conquête de Plassans (1874) - The Conquest of Plassans

La Faute de l'Abbé Mouret (1875) -
Abbé Mouret's Transgression / The Sin of the Abbé Mouret

Son Excellence Eugène Rougon (1876) - His Excellency

L'Assommoir (1877) - L'Assommoire / The Dram Shop

Une Page d'amour (1878) - A Love Episode / A Page of Love

Nana (1880) - Nana

Pot-Bouille (1882) - Pot-Bouille / Pot Luck

Au Bonheur des Dames (1883) - The Ladies' Paradise

La Joie de vivre (1884) - The Joy of Life / Zest for Life

Germinal (1885) - Germinal

L'Œuvre (1886) - The Masterpiece

La Terre (1887) - The Earth

Le Rêve (1888) - The Dream

La Bête humaine (1890) - The Human Beast / Beast in Man

L'Argent (1891) - Money

La Débâcle (1892) - The Debacle

Le Docteur Pascal (1893) - Doctor Pascal

I

WHEN the cuckoo-clock in the dining-room struck six, Chanteau lost all hope. He rose with a painful effort from the arm-chair in which he was sitting, warming his heavy, gouty legs before a coke fire. Ever since two o'clock he had been awaiting the arrival of Madame Chanteau, who, after five weeks' absence, was to-day expected to bring from Paris their little cousin, Pauline Quenu, an orphan girl, ten years of age, whose guardianship they had undertaken.

'I can't understand it at all, Véronique,' he said, opening the kitchen-door. 'Some accident must have happened to them.'

The cook, a tall stout woman of five-and-thirty, with hands like a man's and a face like a gendarme's, was just removing from the fire a leg of mutton, which seemed in imminent danger of being over-done. She did not express her irritation in words, but the pallor of her usually ruddy cheeks betokened her displeasure.

'Madame has, no doubt, stayed in Paris,' she said curtly, 'looking after that endless business which is putting us all topsy-turvy.'

'No! no!' answered Chanteau. 'The letter we had yesterday evening said that the little girl's affairs were completely settled. Madame was to arrive this morning at Caen, where she intended making a short stay to see Davoine. At one o'clock she was to take the train again; at two she would alight at Bayeux; at three, old Malivoire's coach would put her down at Arromanches. Even if Malivoire wasn't ready to start at once, Madame ought to have been here by four o'clock, or by half-past at the latest. There are scarcely six miles from Arromanches to Bonneville.'

The cook kept her eyes fixed on the joint, and only shook her head while these calculations were thrown at her. After some little hesitation Chanteau added: 'I think you had better go to the corner of the road and look if you can see anything of them, Véronique.'

She glared at him, growing still paler with suppressed anger.

'Why? What for? Monsieur Lazare is already out there, getting drenched in looking for them: and what's the good of my going and getting wet through also?'

'The truth is,' murmured Chanteau, softly, 'that I am beginning to feel a little uneasy about my son as well. He ought to have been back by this time. What can he have been doing out on the road for the last hour?'

Without vouchsafing any answer Véronique took from a nail an old black woollen shawl, which she threw over her head and shoulders. Then, as she saw her master following her into the passage, she said to him, rather snappishly: 'Go back to your fire, if you don't want to be bellowing with pain to-morrow.'

1

She shut the door with a bang, and put on her clogs while standing on the steps and crying out to the wind:

'The horrid little brat! Putting us to all this trouble!'

Chanteau's composure remained perfect. He was accustomed to Véronique's ebullitions of temper. She had entered his service in the first year of his married life, when she was but a girl of fifteen. As soon as the sound of her clogs had died away, he bolted off like a schoolboy, and planted himself at the other end of the passage, before a glass door which overlooked the sea. There he stood for a moment, gazing at the sky with his blue eyes. He was a short, stout man, with thick closely-cut white hair. He was scarcely fifty-six years old, but gout, to which he was a martyr, had prematurely aged him.

Just then he was feeling anxious and troubled, and hoped that little Pauline would be able to win Véronique's affection. But was it his fault that she was coming? When the Paris notary had written to tell him that his cousin Quenu, whose wife had died some six months previously, had just died also, charging him in his will with the guardianship of his little daughter, he had not felt able to refuse the trust.

It was true they had not seen much of one another, as the family had been dispersed. Chanteau's father, after leaving the South and wandering all over France as a journeyman carpenter, had established a timber-yard at Caen; while, on the other hand, Quenu, at his mother's death, had gone to Paris, where one of his uncles had subsequently given him a flourishing pork-butcher's business, in the very centre of the market district.[1] They had only met each other some two or three times, on occasions when Chanteau had been compelled by his gout to quit his business and repair to Paris for special medical advice. But the two men had ever had a genuine respect for one another, and the dying father had probably thought that the sea air would be beneficial to his daughter. The girl, too, as the heiress of the pork-butcher's business, would certainly be no charge upon them. Madame Chanteau, indeed, had fallen so heartily into the scheme that she had insisted upon saving her husband all the dangerous fatigue of the journey to Paris. Setting off alone and bustling about she had settled everything, in her perpetual craving for activity; and Chanteau was quite contented so long as his wife was pleased.

But what could be detaining the pair of them? Anxiety seized him again, as he looked out upon the dark sky, over which the west wind was driving huge masses of black clouds, like sooty rags whose tattered ends draggled far away into the sea. It was one of those March

[1] See 'The Fat and the Thin,' in which story already figures little Pauline, who becomes the heroine of 'The Joy of Life.'—ED.

2

gales, when the equinoctial tides beat furiously upon the shores. The flux was only just setting in, and all that could be seen of it was a thin white bar of foam, far away towards the horizon. The wide expanse of bare beach, a league of rocks and gloomy seaweed, its level surface blotched here and there with dark pools, had a weirdly melancholy aspect as it lay stretched out beneath the quickly increasing darkness that fell from the black clouds scudding across the skies.

'Perhaps the wind has overturned them into some ditch' murmured Chanteau.

He felt constrained to go out and look. He opened the glass door, and ventured in his list-slippers on to the gravelled terrace which commanded a view of the village. A few drops of rain were dashed against his face by the hurricane, and a terrific gust made his thick blue woollen dressing-jacket flap and sap again. But he struggled on, bareheaded and bending down, and at last reached the parapet, over which he leaned while glancing at the road that ran beneath. This road descended between two steep cliffs, and looked almost as though it had been hewn out of the solid rock to afford a resting-place for the twenty or thirty hovels of which Bonneville consisted. Every tide threatened to hurl the houses from their narrow shingle-strewn anchorage and crush them against the rocky cliff. To the left there was a little landing-place, a mere strip of sand, whither amid rhythmic calls men hoisted up some half-score boats. The inhabitants did not number more than a couple of hundred souls. They made a bare living out of the sea, clinging to their native rocks with all the unreasoning persistence of limpets. And on the cliffs above their miserable roofs, which every winter were battered by the storms, there was nothing to be seen except the church, standing about halfway up on the right, and the Chanteaus' house across the cleft on the other hand. Bonneville contained nothing more.

'What dreadful weather it is!' cried a voice.

Chanteau raised his head and recognised the priest, Abbé Horteur, a thick-set man of peasant-like build, whose red hair was still unsilvered by his fifty years. He used a plot of graveyard land in front of the church as a vegetable garden, and was now examining his early salad plants, tucking his cassock the while between his legs in order to prevent the wind from blowing it over his head. Chanteau, who could not make himself heard amidst the roaring of the gale, contented himself with waving his hand.

'They are doing right in getting their boats up, I think,' shouted the priest.

But just then a gust of wind caught hold of his cassock and wrapt it round his head, so he fled for refuge behind the church.

3

Chanteau turned round to escape the violence of the blast. With his eyes streaming with moisture he cast a glance at his garden, over which the spray was sweeping, and the brick-built two-storeyed house with five windows, whose shutters seemed in imminent danger of being torn away from their fastenings. When the sudden squall had subsided, he bent down again to look at the road; and just at that moment Véronique returned. She shook her hands at him.

'What! you have actually come out!—Be good enough to go into the house again at once, sir!'

She caught him up in the passage, and scolded him like a child detected in wrong-doing. Wouldn't she have all the trouble of looking after him in the morning when he suffered agonies of pain from his indiscretion?

'Have you seen nothing of them?' he asked, submissively.

'No, indeed, I have seen nothing—Madame is no doubt taking shelter somewhere.'

He dared not tell her that she should have gone further on. However, he was now beginning to feel especially anxious about his son.

'I saw that all the neighbourhood was being blown into the air,' continued the cook. 'They are quite afraid of being done for this time. Last September the Ouches' house was cracked from top to bottom, and Prouane, who was going up to the church to ring the *Angelus,* has just told me that he is sure it will topple over before morning.'

Just as she spoke a big lad of nineteen sprang up the three steps before the door. He had a spreading brow and sparkling eyes, and a fine chestnut down fringed his long oval face.

'Ah! here's Lazare at last!' said Chanteau, feeling much relieved. 'How wet you are, my poor boy!'

In the passage the young man hung his hooded cloak, which was quite saturated with sea-water.

'Well?' interrogated his father.

'I can see nothing of them,' replied Lazare. 'I have been as far as Verchemont, and waited under the shed at the inn there, and kept my eyes on the road, which is a river of mud. But I could see no signs of them. Then, as I began to feel afraid that you might get uneasy about me, I came back.'

The previous August Lazare had left the College of Caen, after gaining his Bachelor's degree; and for the last eight months he had been roaming about the cliffs, unable to make any choice of a profession, for he only felt enthusiastic about music, a predisposition which distressed his mother extremely. She had gone away very much displeased with him, as he had refused to accompany her to Paris, where

4

she had thought she might be able to place him in some advantageous position.

'Now that I have let you know I am all right,' the young man resumed, 'I should like to go on to Arromanches.'

'No, no! it is getting late,' said Chanteau. 'We shall be having some news of your mother presently. I am expecting a message every moment. Listen! Isn't that a carriage?'

Véronique had gone to open the door.

'It is Doctor Cazenove's gig,' she said. 'Shall I bring him in, sir? Why! good gracious! there's madame in it!'

They all three hurried down the steps. A huge dog, a cross between a sheep-dog and a Newfoundland, who had been lying asleep in a corner of the passage, sprang forward and began to bark furiously. Upon hearing this barking, a small white cat of delicate aspect made its way to the door, but, at the sight of the wet and dirt outside, it gave a slight wriggle of disgust with its tail, and sat down very sedately on the top step to see what was going to happen.

A lady about fifty years of age sprang from the gig with all the agility of a young girl. She was short and slight, her hair was still perfectly black, and her face would have been quite pleasant but for the largeness of her nose. The dog sprang forward and placed his big paws on her shoulders, as though he wanted to kiss her; but this displeased her.

'Down! down! Matthew. Get away, will you? Tiresome animal!'

Lazare ran across the yard behind the dog, calling as he went, 'All right, mother?'

'Yes, yes!' replied Madame Chanteau.

'We have been very anxious about you,' said Chanteau, who had followed his son, in spite of the wind. 'What has happened to make you so late?'

'Oh! we've had nothing but troubles,' she answered. 'To begin with, the roads are so bad that it has taken us nearly two hours to come from Bayeux. Then, at Arromanches, one of Malivoire's horses went lame and he couldn't let us have another. At one time I really thought we should have to stay with him all night. But the Doctor was kind enough to offer us his gig, and Martin here has driven us home.'

The driver, an old man with a wooden leg, who had formerly served in the navy, and had there had his limb amputated by Cazenove, then a naval surgeon, had afterwards taken service under the Doctor. He was tethering the horse when Madame Chanteau suddenly checked her flow of speech and called to him:

'Martin! help the little girl to get down!'

No one had yet given a thought to the child. The hood of the gig

5

fell very low, and only her black skirt and little black-gloved hands could be seen. She did not wait, however, for the coachman's assistance, but sprang lightly to the ground. Just then there came a fierce puff of wind, which whirled her clothes about her and sent the curls of her dark brown hair flying from under her crape-trimmed hat. She did not seem very strong for her ten years. Her lips were thick; and her face, if full, showed the pallor of the girls who are brought up in the back shops of Paris. The others stared at her. Véronique, who had just bustled up to welcome her mistress, checked herself, her face assuming an icy and jealous expression. But Matthew showed none of this reserve. He sprang up between the child's arms and licked her with his tongue.

'Don't be afraid of him!' cried Madame Chanteau. 'He won't hurt you.'

'Oh! I'm not at all afraid of him,' said Pauline quietly; 'I am very fond of dogs.'

Indeed, Matthew's boisterous welcome did not seem to disturb her in the slightest degree. Her grave little face broke out into a smile beneath her black hat, and she affectionately kissed the dog on his snout.

'Aren't you going to kiss your relations too?' exclaimed Madame Chanteau. 'See, this is your uncle, since you call me your aunt; and this is your cousin, a great strapping scapegrace, who isn't half as well behaved as you are.'

The child manifested no awkward shyness. She kissed everyone, and even found a word or two for each, with all the grace of a young Parisienne already schooled in politeness.

'I am very much obliged to you, uncle, for taking me to live with you—You will see that we shall get on very well together, cousin—'

'What a sweet little thing she is!' cried Chanteau, quite delighted.

Lazare looked at her in surprise, for he had pictured her as being much smaller and far more shy and childish.

'Yes, indeed, she is a sweet child,' said the lady, 'and you have no idea how brave she is! The wind blew straight in our faces as we drove along, and the rain quite blinded us. Fully a score of times I thought that the hood, which was flapping about like a veil, would be carried away altogether. Well, that child there, instead of being alarmed, was quite amused by it all and enjoyed it. But what are we stopping out here for? It is no use getting any wetter than we are; the rain is beginning to fall again.'

She turned round to see where Véronique was. When she saw her keeping aloof and looking very surly, she said to her sarcastically:

'Good evening, Véronique. How are you? While you are making up your mind to come and speak to me, you had better go and get a bottle of wine for Martin. We have not been able to bring our luggage with us, but Malivoire will bring it on early to-morrow.'

Then she suddenly checked herself and hastily returned to the gig. 'My bag! my bag! Ah, there it is! I was afraid it had slipped into the road.'

It was a large black leather bag, already whitened at the corners by wear. She would not trust it to her son, but persisted in carrying it herself. Just as they were at last about to enter the house, another violent squall made them halt, short of breath, near the door. The cat, sitting on the steps with an air of curiosity, watched them fighting their way onwards; and Madame Chanteau then inquired if Minouche had behaved properly during her absence. The name of Minouche again brought a smile to Pauline's serious little face. She stooped down and fondled the cat, which rubbed itself against her skirts, whilst holding its tail erect in the air. Matthew for his part, in proclamation of the return, began to bark again as he saw the family mounting the steps and entering the vestibule.

'Ah, it is pleasant to be home again!' said Madame Chanteau. 'I really thought that we should never get here. Yes, Matthew, you are a very good dog, but please be quiet—Lazare, do make him keep still. He is quite splitting my ears!'

However, the dog proved obstinate, and the entry of the Chanteaus into their dining-room was accompanied by this lively music. They pushed Pauline, the new daughter of the house, before them; Matthew came on behind, still barking loudly; and Minouche followed last, with her sensitive hair bristling amidst the uproar.

In the kitchen Martin had already drunk a couple of glasses of wine, one after the other, and was now hastening away, stamping over the floor with his wooden leg and calling 'good-night' to everybody. Véronique had just put the leg of mutton to the fire again, as it had got quite cold. She thrust her head into the room, and asked:

'Will you have dinner now?'

'Yes, indeed we will,' said Chanteau. 'It is seven o'clock. But, my good girl, we must wait till madame and the little one have changed their things.'

'But I haven't got Pauline's trunk here,' said Madame Chanteau. 'Fortunately, however, our underclothing is not wet. Take off your cloak and hat, my dear. There, take them away, Véronique. And take off her boots. I have some slippers here.'

The cook knelt down before the child, who had seated herself. Madame Chanteau took out of her bag a pair of small felt slippers and put them on the girl's feet. Then she took off her own boots, and, once more dipping her hand into the bag, brought out a pair of shoes for herself.

'Shall I bring dinner in now?' asked Véronique again.

'In a minute. Pauline, come into the kitchen and wash your hands and face. We will make more of a toilet later on, for, just now, we are dying of hunger.'

Pauline came back first, having left her aunt with her nose in a bowl of water. Chanteau had resumed his place in his big yellow velvet armchair before the fire. He was rubbing his legs mechanically, fearing another attack of pain; while Lazare stood cutting some bread in front of the table, on which four covers had been laid more than an hour before. The two men, who were scarcely at their ease, smiled at the child, without managing to find a word to say to her; while she calmly inspected the room, which was furnished in walnut-wood. Her glance wandered from the sideboard and the half-dozen chairs to the hanging lamp of polished brass, and then rested upon some framed lithographs which hung against the brown wall-paper. Four of them represented the seasons, and the fifth was a view of Vesuvius. Probably the imitation wainscotting of oak-coloured paint, scratched and showing the plaster underneath, the flooring soiled with old grease-spots, and the general shabbiness of this room, where the family lived, made her regret the beautiful marble-fitted shop which she had left the previous day, for her eyes assumed an expression of sadness, and she seemed to guess all the cares that lay concealed in this her new dwelling-place. Then, after curiously examining a very old barometer mounted in a case of gilded wood, her eyes turned to a strange-looking affair which monopolised the whole of the mantelpiece. It was enclosed in a glass box, secured at the edges by strips of blue paper. At first sight it looked like a toy, a miniature wooden bridge; but a bridge of extremely intricate design.

'That was made by your great-uncle,' explained Chanteau, who was delighted to find a subject of conversation. 'My father, you know, began life as a carpenter, and I have always preserved his masterpiece.'

He was not at all ashamed of his origin, and Madame Chanteau tolerated the presence of the bridge on the mantelpiece, in spite of the displeasure which this cumbersome curiosity always caused her by reminding her of her marriage with a working-man's son. But the little girl was no longer paying attention to her uncle's words, for through the window she had just caught sight of the far-reaching horizon, and she eagerly stepped forward and planted herself close to the panes, whose muslin curtains were held back by cotton loops. Since her departure from Paris her one continual thought had been the sea. She had dreamed of it and never ceased to question her aunt about it during their journey; inquiring at every hill they came to whether the sea lay at the other side of it. When at last they reached the beach at Arromanches, she had been struck silent with wonder, her eyes dilating and her heart heaving with a heavy sigh. From Arromanches to Bonneville she had every minute thrust her head out of the gig's hood, in spite of the violent wind, in order to look at the sea, which seemed to follow them. And now the sea was still there; it would always be there, as though it belonged to her. With her eyes she seemed to be slowly taking possession of it.

The night was falling from the grey sky, across which the wind drove the clouds at headlong speed. Amid the increasing darkness of that turbulent evening only the white line of the rising tide could be distinguished. It was a band of foam, which seemed to be ever widening, a succession of waves flowing up, pouring over the tracts of weed and covering the ridges of rock with a soft gliding motion, whose approach seemed like a caress. But far away the roar of the billows increased, huge crests arose, while at the foot of the cliff, where Bonneville had stowed itself away as securely as possible behind its doors, there hovered a death-like gloom. The boats, drawn up to the top of the shingle, lay there, alone and deserted, like huge stranded fish. The rain steeped the village in vaporous mist, and only the church still stood out plainly against a pale patch of sky.

Pauline stood by the window in silence. Her little heart was heaving anew. She seemed to be stifling, and as she drew a deep sigh all her breath appeared to drain from her lips.

'Well! it's a good deal bigger than the Seine, isn't it?' said Lazare, who had just taken his stand behind her.

The girl continued to be a source of much surprise to him; he felt all the shy awkwardness of a schoolboy in her presence.

'Yes, indeed,' she replied, in a very low voice, without turning her head.

'You are not frightened of it?'

At this she turned and looked at him with an expression of astonishment. 'No, indeed. Why should I be? The water won't come up so far as this!

'Ah! one never knows what it will do,' he said, yielding to an impulse to make fun of her. 'Sometimes the water rises over the church.'

She broke into a hearty laugh, an outburst of noisy, healthy gaiety, the merriment of a sensible person whom the absurd delights.

'Ah! cousin,' said she, playfully taking the young man's hand, 'I'm not so foolish as you think. You wouldn't stop here if the sea were likely to come up over the church.'

9

Lazare laughed in his turn, and clasped the child's hands. The pair were henceforth hearty friends. In the midst of their merriment Madame Chanteau returned into the room. She appeared quite delighted, and exclaimed as she rubbed her hands: 'Ah! you have got to know each other, then?—I felt quite sure you would get on well together.'

'Shall I bring in dinner, Madame?' asked Véronique, standing by the kitchen door.

'Yes, certainly, my girl. But you had better light the lamp first; it is getting too dark to see.'

The night, indeed, was falling so quickly that the dining-room would have been in darkness but for the red glow of the coke fire. Lighting the lamp caused a further delay, but at last the operation was satisfactorily performed, and the table lay illuminated beneath the lowered shade. They were all in their places, Pauline between her uncle and cousin, and opposite her aunt, when the latter rose from her chair again, with that restlessness of one who can never remain still.

'Where is my bag? Wait a moment, my dear; I am going to give you your mug. Take the glass away, Véronique. The little girl is used to having her own mug.'

She took a silver mug, already a little battered, out of her bag, and, having first wiped it with her napkin, placed it before Pauline. Then she put the bag away behind her, on a chair. The cook brought in some vermicelli soup, warning them, in her crabbed fashion, that it was much overcooked. No one dared complain, however. They were all very hungry, and the soup hissed in their spoons. Next came some soup-beef. Chanteau, fond of dainties, scarcely took any of it, reserving himself for the leg of mutton. But when this was placed upon the table there was a general outcry. It was like fried leather; surely they could not eat it!

'I knew very well how it would be,' said Véronique, placidly. 'You oughtn't to have kept it waiting.'

Pauline, with a laugh, cut her meat up into little bits, and managed to swallow it, in spite of its toughness. As for Lazare, he was quite unconscious of what he had upon his plate, and would have eaten slices of dry bread without knowing that they were not cut from a fowl's breast. Chanteau, however, gazed at the leg of mutton with a mournful expression.

'And what else have you got, Véronique?'

'Fried potatoes, sir.'

He made a gesture of despair and threw himself back in his chair.

'Shall I bring the beef back again, sir?' asked the cook.

But he answered her with a melancholy shake of his head. 'As well have bread as boiled beef. Oh, my gracious! what a dinner! and just in this bad weather, too, when we can't get any fish.'

Madame Chanteau, who was a very small eater, looked at him compassionately.

'My poor dear,' she said, suddenly, 'you quite distress me. I have brought a little present with me; I meant it for to-morrow, but as there seems to be a famine this evening—'

She had opened her bag as she spoke and drew out of it a pan of *foie gras.* Chanteau's eyes flashed brightly. *Foie gras!* Ah, it was forbidden fruit! A luxury which he adored, but which his doctor had absolutely forbidden him to touch.

'You know,' continued his wife, 'you must have only a very little. Don't be foolish, now, or you shall never have any more.'

Chanteau had caught hold of the pan, and he began to open it with trembling hands. There were frequently tremendous struggles between his greediness and his fear of gout; and almost invariably it was his greediness that got the upper hand. Never mind! it was too good to resist, and he would put up with the pain that would follow.

Véronique, who had watched him helping himself to a thick slice, took herself off to the kitchen, grumbling as she went:

'Well, well! how he will bellow to-morrow!'

The word 'bellow' was habitually on her tongue, and her master and mistress had grown quite used and reconciled to it, so naturally and simply did it come from her lips. When the master had an attack of gout he bellowed, according to Véronique, and she was never scolded for her want of respect in saying so. The dinner ended very merrily. Lazare jokingly dispossessed his father of the *foie gras.* When the cheese and biscuits were put upon the table, Matthew's sudden appearance caused a boisterous commotion. Until then he had been lying asleep under the table. But the arrival of the biscuits had awakened him. He seemed to have scented them in his sleep. Every evening, just at this stage of the meal, it was his custom to get up and shake himself and make the round of the table, questioning the faces of the diners to see if they were charitably disposed. Usually it was Lazare who first took pity upon him, but that evening Matthew, on his second circuit of the table, halted by Pauline's side and gazed up at her earnestly with his honest human-like eyes; and then, divining in her a friend both of man and beast, he laid his huge head on her little knee, without dropping his glance of mild supplication.

'Oh, what a shameful beggar you are!' said Madame Chanteau. 'Aren't you ashamed of yourself, Matthew, to be so greedy?'

The dog swallowed at a single gulp the piece of biscuit which

Pauline offered him, and then again laid his head on her little knee, asking for another piece, with his eyes constantly fixed on those of his new friend. She laughed at him and kissed him and found him very amusing, with his flattened ears and the black spot under his left eye, the only spot of colour that marked his rough white hairy coat. Then there came a diversion of another character. Minouche, growing jealous, leapt lightly upon the edge of the table, and began to purr and rub her head against the little girl's chin, swaying her supple body the while with all the grace of a young kid. To poke one with her cold nose and kiss one lightly with her sharp teeth, while she pounded about with her feet like a baker kneading dough, was her feline way of caressing. Pauline was now quite delighted between the two animals. The cat on her left, the dog on her right, took possession of her and worried her shamefully in order to secure all her biscuits.

'Send them away,' said her aunt. 'They will leave you nothing for yourself.'

'Oh! that doesn't matter,' she placidly replied, feeling quite happy in being despoiled.

They finished, and Véronique removed the dishes. The two animals, seeing the table quite bare, gave their lips a last lick and then took themselves off, without even saying 'thank you.'

Pauline rose from her chair, and went to stand by the window, straining her eyes to penetrate the darkness. Ever since the soup had been put upon the table she had been watching the window grow darker and darker, till it had gradually become as black as ink. Now it was like an impenetrable wall; the dense darkness had hidden everything—sky, sea, village, and even church itself. Nevertheless, without feeling in the least disturbed by her cousin's jests, she tried to distinguish the water, worrying to find out how far the tide was going to rise; but she could only hear its ever-increasing roar, its angry threatening voice, which seemed to grow louder every minute amidst the howling of the wind and the splashing of the rain. Not a glimmer, not even the whiteness of the foam, could be seen in that chaos; and nothing was heard but the rush of the waves, lashed on by the gale in the black depths.

'Dear me,' said Chanteau, 'it is coming up stiffly, and yet it won't be high-water for another couple of hours.'

'If the wind were to blow from the north,' put in Lazare, 'Bonneville would certainly be swept away. Fortunately for us here, it is coming slantwise.'

The little maid had turned and was listening to them, her big eyes full of an expression of anxious pity.

'Bah!' said Madame Chanteau, 'we are safe under shelter, and we must let other folks get out of their trouble as best they may—Tell me, my dear, would you like a cup of hot tea? And then, afterwards, we will go to bed.'

Véronique had laid an old red cloth, with a faded pattern of big bunches of flowers, over the dinner-table, around which the family generally spent the evening. They took their accustomed places. Lazare, who had left the room for a moment, came back carrying an inkstand, a pen, and a whole handful of papers, and, seating himself beneath the lamp-light, he began to copy some music. Madame Chanteau, whose eyes since her return had never ceased following her son with an affectionate glance, suddenly became very stiff and surly.

'That music of yours again! You can't devote an evening to us, then, even on the night of my return home?'

'But, mother, I am not going out of the room. I mean to stay with you. You know very well that this doesn't interfere with my talking. Fire away and talk to me, and I will answer you.'

He went on with his work, covering half the table with his papers. Chanteau had stretched himself out comfortably in his armchair, with his hands hanging listlessly at his sides. In front of the fire Matthew lay asleep, while Minouche, who had sprung upon the table again, was performing an elaborate toilet, carefully licking her stomach, with one leg cocked up in the air. The falling light from the hanging lamp seemed to make everything cosy and homelike, and Pauline, who with half-closed eyelids had been smiling upon her newly-found relatives, could no longer keep herself from sleep, worn out as she was with fatigue and rendered drowsy by the heat of the room. Her head slipped down upon her arm, which was resting on the table, and lay there, motionless, beneath the placid glow of the lamp. Her delicate eyelids looked like a silk veil cast over her eyes, and soft regular breath came gently from her pure lips.

'She must be tired out,' said Madame Chanteau, lowering her voice. 'We will just wake her up to give her some tea, and then I will take her to bed.'

Then silence reigned in the room. No sound broke upon the howling of the storm except the scratching of Lazare's pen. It was perfect quiet, the habitual sleepiness of life spent every evening in the same spot. For a long time the father and mother looked at each other without saying a word. At last Chanteau asked, in a hesitating voice:

'And is Davoine doing well at Caen?'

'Bah! Doing well, indeed! I told you that you were being taken in!'

Now that the child was fast asleep they could talk. They spoke in low tones, however, and at first seemed inclined to tell each other what there was to be told as briefly as possible. But presently passion got the better of them and carried them on, and, by degrees, all the worries of the household became manifest.

At the death of his father the former journeyman carpenter, who had carried on his timber-trade with ambitious audacity, Chanteau had found the business considerably compromised. A very inactive man himself, unaspiring and careful, he had contented himself with simply putting matters on a safe basis, by dint of good management, and living upon a moderate but sure profit. The one romance of his life was his marriage. He had married a governess whom he had met in a friend's family. Eugénie de la Vignière, the orphan daughter of one of the ruined squireens of the Cotentin, reckoned upon fanning his indolent nature into ambition. But he with his imperfect education, for he had been sent late to school, recoiled from vast schemes, and opposed his own natural inertness to the ambitious plans of his wife. When their son was born, she transferred to that child her hopes for the family's rise in life, sent him to college, and superintended his studies every evening herself. But a last disaster upset all her plans. Chanteau, who had suffered from gout from the time he was forty years of age, at last experienced such severe and painful attacks that he began to talk about selling his business. To Madame Chanteau this portended straitened means and mediocrity, the spending of their remaining days in retirement on their petty savings, and the casting of her son into the struggle for life, without the support of an income of twenty thousand francs, such as she had dreamed of for him.

Thereupon she had insisted upon having, at any rate, a hand in the sale. The profits were about ten thousand francs a year, on which the family made a considerable show, for Madame Chanteau was fond of giving parties. Having discovered a certain Davoine, she had worked out the following scheme. Davoine was to buy the timber business for a hundred thousand francs, but he was only to pay fifty thousand in money; in consideration of the other fifty thousand remaining unpaid, the Chanteaus were to become his partners in the business and share the profits. This man Davoine appeared to be a very bold fellow, and, even if he did not extend the business of the firm, they would still be sure of five thousand francs a year, which, added to the interest of the fifty thousand invested in stock, would give them altogether an income of eight thousand francs. And on this they would get on as well as they could, pending the time when their son should achieve some brilliant success and be able to extricate them from a life of mediocrity.

It was upon these principles that the business was sold. Two years previously Chanteau had bought a seaside house at Bonneville, which he had been able to get as a bargain through the bankruptcy of an insolvent debtor. Instead of selling it again at a profit, as for a time she had thought of doing, Madame Chanteau determined that the family should go and live there, at any rate until Lazare had achieved his first successes. To give up her parties and bury herself in such an out-of-the-way place was for her, indeed, almost suicide; but as she had agreed to surrender their entire house to Davoine, she would have had to rent another, and so she summoned up all her resolution to go in for a life of economy, with the firm hope of one day making a triumphal return to Caen, when her son should have gained a high position. Chanteau gave his consent to everything. His gout would have to accommodate itself to the sea air, and, besides, of three doctors whom he had consulted, two had been good enough to declare that the fresh breezes from the open would act as a splendid tonic on his system generally. So, one morning in May, the Chanteaus departed to settle at Bonneville, leaving Lazare, then fourteen years old, at the college at Caen.

Since this heroic exile, five years had passed, and the affairs of the family had gone from bad to worse. As Davoine was constantly launching out into fresh speculations, he was ever telling them that it was necessary he should have further advances; and the consequence was that all the profits were risked again and again, and the balance-sheet generally showed a loss. The Chanteaus were reduced to living at Bonneville on the three thousand francs a year derived from the money they had invested in stock, and they were so hardly pressed that they had been obliged to sell their horse, and get Véronique to undertake the management of the kitchen garden.

'At any rate, Eugénie,' said Chanteau, a little timorously, 'if I have been let in, it is partly your fault.'

But she repudiated the responsibility altogether. She always conveniently forgot that the partnership with Davoine was her own work.

'My fault indeed!' she replied drily. 'How can that be? Am I laid up? If you were not such an invalid, we might perhaps be millionaires.'

Whenever his wife attacked him in this bitter fashion, he always lowered his head with pain and shame at the thought that it was his illness that was ruining the family.

'We must wait and be patient,' he murmured. 'Davoine appears to be very confident of the success of his new scheme. If the price of deal goes up, we shall make a fortune.'

'And what good will that be?' interrupted Lazare, who was still copying out his music. 'We have enough to eat as it is. It is very foolish of you worrying yourselves in this way. I don't care a bit about money.'

Madame Chanteau shrugged her shoulders again.

'It would be a great deal better if you cared about it a little more, and didn't waste your time in foolish nonsense.'

It was she herself who had taught him to play the piano, though the mere sight of a score now sufficed to make her angry. Her last hope had fled. This son of hers, whom she had dreamed of seeing a prefect or a judge, talked of writing operas; and she foresaw that in the future he would be reduced to running about the streets giving lessons, as she herself had once done.

'Here is the balance-sheet for the last three months, which Davoine gave me,' she said. 'If things continue in this way, it will be we who shall owe him money by next July.'

She had put her bag upon the table, and she took out of it a paper, which she handed to Chanteau. He just turned it round, and then laid it down in front of him without opening it. At that moment Véronique brought in the tea. No one spoke for some time, and the cups remained empty. Minouche was dozing placidly beside the sugar-basin, and Matthew was snoring like a man before the fire. The roar of the sea continued outside like a mighty bass accompaniment to the peaceful echoes of the drowsy room.

'Won't you awaken her, mother?' said Lazare, at last. It can't be good for her to go on sleeping there.'

'Yes! yes!' murmured Madame Chanteau, who seemed buried in deep thought, with her eyes fixed upon Pauline.

They all three looked at the sleeping girl. Her breathing was very calm, and there was a flowery softness about her pale cheeks and rosy lips beneath the glow of the lamp-light. Her chestnut curls, which the wind had disarranged, cast a slight shadow over her delicate brow. Then Madame Chanteau's thoughts reverted to her visit to Paris, and all the bother she had met with there, and she felt quite astonished at the enthusiasm with which she had undertaken the child's guardianship, inspired with instinctive regard for a wealthy ward, though her intentions of course were scrupulously honourable, and quite without thought of benefiting by the fortune of which she would be trustee.

'When I alighted at the shop,' she began slowly, 'she was wearing a little black frock, and she came to kiss me, sobbing and crying. It is a very fine shop indeed; beautifully fitted up with marble and plate-glass, and just in front of the markets. There was such a servant there, about as big as a jackboot, with a fresh red face. It was she who had given information to the notary, and had brought him to put everything under seal. When I got there she was going on quietly selling sausages and black puddings. It was Adèle who told me about our poor cousin

Quenu's death. Ever since he had lost his wife, six months previously, his blood seemed to be suffocating him. He was constantly fidgeting about his neck with his hand to loosen his neckerchief; and at last they found him one evening lying with his face all purple in a bowl of dripping. His uncle Gradelle died in just the same way.'

She said no more, and silence fell again. Over Pauline's face, as she lay asleep, there played a passing smile, suggesting some pleasant dream.

'And the law business, was that all transacted satisfactorily?' asked Chanteau.

'Oh! quite so. But your lawyer was very right in leaving a blank for the name in the power-of-attorney; for it appears that I could not have acted in your stead, as women are not eligible in such matters. But, as I wrote and told you, on my arrival I went to consult the parish lawyer who sent us the extract from the will in which you were appointed guardian. He at once inserted his chief clerk's name in the power-of-attorney, which is quite a common course, he tells me. Then we were able to get along, I went before a justice of the peace and nominated as members of the family council three relations on Lisa's side: two young cousins, Octave Mouret and Claude Lantier, and a cousin by marriage, Monsieur Rambaud, who lives at Marseilles; then, on our side, that is Quenu's side, I chose his nephews, Naudet, Liardin, and Delorme. It is a very proper council, you see, and one which we can easily manage as we think best for the child's benefit. At their first meeting they nominated as surrogate-guardian Monsieur Saccard,[1] whom I had chosen, out of necessity, from among Lisa's relations.'

'Hush! hush! She is waking up,' interrupted Lazare.

Pauline had just opened her eyes widely. Without moving, she gazed with some astonishment at the people talking around her, and then, with a smile full of sleepiness, closed her eyes once more, being worn out with fatigue. Again did her motionless little face show a milky camellia-like transparency.

'Isn't that Saccard the speculator?' asked Chanteau.

'Yes,' answered his wife. 'I saw him, and we had a talk together. He is a charming man. He has so many things to look after, he told me, that I must not reckon much on his assistance. But, you know, we really don't want anybody's help. From the moment we take the child—well, we do take her; and we don't want anybody coming and interfering with us. All the other business was got through quickly. Your power-of-attorney conferred all the necessary authority. The seals were removed, an inventory of the property was made, and the business was sold by

---

[1] The chief character in, 'Money.'—ED.

auction. The sale went off splendidly, for there were two parties bidding hotly one against the other, and so we got ninety thousand francs, cash down. The notary had previously discovered scrip for sixty thousand francs in a desk. I begged him to buy more scrip, and so now we have a hundred and fifty thousand francs securely invested. I have brought the scrip along with me, having first given the chief clerk the full discharge and receipt, which I asked you to send me by return of post. See! here it is!'

She had thrust her hand into her bag and brought out a bulky packet. It was the scrip, tied up between two pieces of thick cardboard which had formed the binding of one of the shop account-books. The green marbled surface was speckled with grease-spots. Both father and son looked attentively at the fortune which lay upon the shabby table-cloth.

'The tea is getting cold, mother,' said Lazare, putting his pen down at last. 'Hadn't I better pour it out?'

He got up from his seat and filled the cups. His mother had returned no answer to his question. Her eyes were still fixed on the scrip.

'Of course,' she continued slowly, 'at a subsequent meeting of the family council which I summoned, I asked to have my travelling expenses reimbursed, and the sum that we are to receive for the child's maintenance was fixed at eight hundred francs a year. We are not so rich as she is, and we cannot afford to take her for nothing. None of us would desire to make a farthing profit out of the girl, but it would have pressed us too much to have kept her out of our own income. The interest of her fortune will be banked and invested, and her capital will be almost doubled by the time she comes of age. Well, it is only our duty that we are doing. We are bound to obey the wishes of the dead. And if it costs us something to do it, perhaps the sacrifice may bring us better fortune, of which, I am sure, we stand in great need—The poor little dear was so cut up, and sobbed so bitterly at leaving her nurse! I trust she will be happy with us here.'

The two men were quite affected.

'Most certainly I shall never be unkind to her,' said Chanteau.

'She is a charming little thing,' added Lazare. 'I love her already.'

Just then Matthew appeared to have smelt the tea in his dreams, for he gave himself a shake, and again came and thrust his big head upon the edge of the table. Minouche, too, got up and stretched herself and yawned, and, when she was quite awake, she craned out her neck to sniff at the packet of papers in the greasy covers. As the Chanteaus glanced at Pauline, they saw that her eyes were also open and fixed upon the scrip and the old ledger binding.

'Ah! she knows very well what is inside there,' said Madame Chanteau. 'Don't you, my dear? I showed them all to you in Paris. That is what your poor father and mother have left you.'

Tears trickled down the child's face. Her grief often recurred in April-like showers. But she soon smiled again through her tears, feeling amused at Minouche, who had for a long time smelt at the papers and was doubtless attracted by their odour, for she began to purr and rub her head against the corners of the ledger.

'Come away, Minouche!' cried Madame Chanteau. 'Money isn't to be made a plaything of!'

Chanteau laughed, and so did Lazare. With his head resting on the edge of the table, Matthew was becoming quite excited. Looking eagerly with his flaming eyes at the packet of papers which he must have taken for some great delicacy, he began to bark at the cat. Then all the family grew lively. Pauline caught up Minouche and fondled her in her arms as though she were a doll.

For fear the girl should drop off to sleep again, Madame Chanteau made her drink her tea at once. Then she called Véronique.

'Bring us our candles. Here we are sitting and talking and never going to bed. Why! it is actually ten o'clock, and I am so tired that I half fell asleep at dinner!'

But a man's voice sounded from the kitchen, and when the cook returned with four lighted candles her mistress asked her:

'Whom were you talking to?'

'It is Prouane, Madame. He came up to tell the master that things are in a very bad way down yonder. The sea is breaking everything to pieces apparently.'

Chanteau had been prevailed upon to accept office as mayor of Bonneville, and Prouane, the tipsy scamp, who acted as Abbé Horteur's beadle, likewise discharged the duties of mayor's clerk. He had been a non-commissioned officer in the navy, and wrote a copybook hand. When they called to him to come into the room, he made his appearance with his woollen cap in his hand and his jacket and boots streaming with water.

'Well! what's the matter, Prouane?'

'Sure, sir, the Cuches' house is completely flooded. And if it goes on like this much longer it will be the same with the Gonins'. We have all been down there, Tourmal, Houtelard, myself, and the others. But it is no use; we can't do anything against that thievish sea. It's written that it will carry off a slice of the land every year.'

Then they all became silent. The four candles burned with tall flames, and the rush of the devouring sea against the cliffs broke through the night air. It was now high tide, and the house shook as every wave dashed against the rocky barrier. It was like the roaring of giant artillery; thunderous consecutive reports arose amidst the rolling of shingle, which, as it swept over the rocks, sounded like the continuous crackling of a fusillade. And amidst all this uproar the wind raised its howling plaint, and the rain, every now and then increasing in violence, seemed to pelt the walls of the house with a hail of bullets.

'It is like the end of the world,' Madame Chanteau murmured. 'What will the Cuches do? Where are they going to take refuge?'

'They will have to be sheltered,' said Prouane. 'Meantime they are at the Gonins'. What a sight it was! There was a little lad, who is only three years old, perfectly drenched, and his mother with nothing on but a petticoat—begging your pardon for mentioning it—and the father, too, with his hand split open by a falling beam, while madly trying to save their few rags.'

Pauline had risen from the table and returned to the window. She listened to what was being said with all the serious demeanour of a grown-up person. Her expression indicated distressful sympathy and pity, and her full lips trembled with emotion.

'Oh, aunt!' she said, 'how very sad for the poor things!' Then her gaze wandered through the window into that inky darkness where nothing was visible. They could hear that the sea had reached the road, and was sweeping wildly and fiercely over it, but they could see nothing. The little village and the rocks and the whole neighbourhood seemed submerged beneath a flood of ink. For the young girl it was a painful experience and surprise. That sea which she had thought so beautiful hurled itself upon poor folks and ruined them!

'I will go down with you, Prouane,' cried Lazare. 'Perhaps something can be done.'

'Oh yes! do go, cousin!' said Pauline, with flashing eyes. But the man shook his head.

'It is no use troubling yourself, Monsieur Lazare; you couldn't do anything more than the others. We can only stand about and watch the sea work its will, and destroy what it likes; and when it gets tired of that we shall have to be grateful that it has done no worse. I merely came up to inform Monsieur Chanteau.'

Then Chanteau began to grow angry, bothered by this business, which would give him an uneasy night and demand all his attention in the morning.

'I don't believe there ever was a village built in such an idiotic position!' he cried. 'You have buried yourselves right under the waves, and it's no wonder if the sea swallows up your houses one by one. And

why ever in the world do you stop in such a place? You should leave it
and go elsewhere.'

'Where can we go?' asked Prouane, who listened with an expression of stupefaction. 'We are here, sir, and we have got to stop here. We
must be somewhere.'

'Yes, that's true,' said Madame Chanteau, bringing the discussion
to an end. 'And wherever you are, here or elsewhere, there will always
be trouble—We are just going to bed. Good-night. To-morrow it will
be light.'

The man went off bowing, and they heard Véronique bolt the door
behind him. They took their candles and gave a parting caress to Matthew and Minouche, who both slept in the kitchen. Lazare collected his
music together, and Madame Chanteau put the scrip in its greasy covers beneath her arm, and also took from the table Davoine's balance-
sheet, which her husband had forgotten. It was a heartbreaking paper,
and the sooner it was put out of sight the better.

'We are going to bed, Véronique,' she cried. 'You need not wander
up and down at this time of night.' But, hearing nothing save a grunt in
the kitchen, she added in lower tones:

'What is the matter with her? I haven't brought a baby home for
her to wean!'

'Leave her alone,' said Chanteau. 'She has her whims, you know.
Well! we are all four here: so good-night!'

He himself slept on the ground floor, in a room on the other side
of the passage. This arrangement had been made so that, when he was
suffering from an attack of gout, he might be readily wheeled in his
arm-chair either to table or to the terrace. He opened the door, and then
stood still for a moment. His legs were very heavy, as at the approach
of a fresh attack, of which, indeed, the stiffness of his joints had been
giving him warning since the previous day. Plainly enough, he had
acted very foolishly in eating that *foie gras*. The consciousness of his
error made him feel anything but happy.

'Good-night,' he repeated in a mournful voice. 'You others can
always sleep. Good-night, my little dear. Have a good long rest; you
want it at your age.'

'Good-night, uncle,' said Pauline in reply, as she kissed him. Then
the door closed. Madame Chanteau went upstairs fast with the little
girl. Lazare followed behind. 'Well, for my part, I shan't want anyone
to rock me to sleep to-night,' said the old lady, 'that's quite certain. And
I don't at all object to that uproar. I find it lulling. When I was in Paris
I quite missed the shaking of my bed.'

They all went up to the first floor. Pauline, who carefully held her candlestick straight, was somewhat amused by this procession in Indian file, each carrying a lighted candle, which set all their shadows dancing. When she reached the landing she paused, hesitating where to go, till her aunt gently pushed her forward.

'Straight on,' she said. 'That room there is kept for visitors, and this one opposite is mine. Come in for a minute; I want to show you something.'

The bedroom, hung with yellow cretonne with a pattern of green leaves, was very plainly furnished in mahogany. There was a bed, a wardrobe, and a secrétaire. In the middle stood a small table on a square of red carpet. When she had examined every corner carefully with her candle, Madame Chanteau went up to the secrétaire and opened it.

'Come and look!' she said.

She drew out one of the little drawers and placed Davoine's disastrous balance-sheet in it, with a sigh. Then she emptied the drawer above it, pulled it right out and shook it, to clear it of a few old scraps, and, with Pauline looking at her as she prepared to stow the scrip away in it, she said:

'I am going to put it in here, you see. There is nothing else in the drawer, and it will be all by itself. Would you like to put it there yourself?'

Pauline felt a slight sense of shame, which she could not have accounted for. She blushed as she answered, 'Oh! aunt dear, what difference does it make?'

But she had already taken the old ledger-binding in her hand, and she put it in the drawer, while Lazare threw the light of the candle he was holding upon the secrétaire.

'There!' said Madame Chanteau, 'you are quite sure about it now, and you may feel quite easy about it. The drawer is the top one on the left, remember. It will stop there till the day when you are old enough to come and take it out and do what you like with it. Minouche won't be able to come and eat it here, will she?'

The idea of Minouche opening the secrétaire and eating the papers quite tickled the child's fancy, and she broke into a merry laugh. Her momentary embarrassment altogether disappeared, and she began to joke with Lazare, who amused her by purring like a cat and pretending to make an attack upon the secrétaire. He, too, laughed gaily. His mother, however, very solemnly locked the flap, turning the key round twice.

'It is quite safe now,' she said. 'Come, Lazare, don't make yourself ridiculous. Now, Pauline, I will go up with you to your room to see if you have got everything you want.'

They all three filed out into the staircase. When they reached the second floor, Pauline with some hesitation opened the door of the room on her left, but her aunt immediately called out:

'No! no! not that one! That's your cousin's room. Yours is the one opposite.'

Pauline, however, stood where she was, lost in amazement at the size of the room and the state of confusion it was in. It contained a piano, a couch, and a huge table, besides a lot of books and pictures. And when at last she opened the opposite door, she was quite delighted to find that her own room was a very small one in comparison with the other. The wall-paper was of a creamy yellow, flowered with blue roses. The furniture consisted of an iron bedstead hung with muslin curtains, a dressing-table, a chest of drawers, and three chairs.

'Yes; you have everything here, I think,' said Madame Chanteau—'water, sugar, towels, and soap. I hope you will sleep well. Véronique has a little room beside you. If you feel at all frightened, knock on the wall.'

'And I am close to you as well,' added Lazare. 'If a ghost comes, I will fly at him with my sword.'

The doors of both rooms, which faced each other, were open; Pauline's eyes strayed from one to the other.

'There are no ghosts,' she said merrily. 'You must keep your sword for robbers. Good-night, aunt. Good-night, cousin.'

'Good-night, my dear. You know how to undress yourself?'

'Oh! yes. I am getting a big girl, you know, now. I always did everything for myself in Paris.'

They kissed her, and Madame Chanteau told her, as she went off, that she might lock her door. But the child had already sprung to the window, impatient to find out whether it overlooked the sea. The rain was streaming so violently down the panes that she dared not open it. All was pitchy dark outside, but she felt quite happy when she heard the waves beating beneath her. Then, in spite of her fatigue, which almost prevented her from keeping her eyes open, she walked round the room and examined the furniture. The thought that she was to have a room of her own, separate from anyone else, where she might shut herself up entirely alone, quite flattered and pleased her, and made her feel as though she were grown up already. Just as she was about to turn the key in the lock, however, she hesitated, and felt a little uneasy. How should she escape, if she should see anybody in the night? She trembled for a moment, and then, though she was in her petticoats, having taken off her dress, she opened the door. Opposite to her she saw Lazare, standing in the middle of his room and looking at her.

'Well?' he said. 'What's the matter? Do you want anything?'

She turned very red, and felt disposed to tell him a fib, but her natural frankness got the better of that inclination.

'No, nothing,' she replied. 'But I feel afraid, do you know, when the door is locked; so I am not going to fasten it; and if you hear me knock, it will be for you to come. You, mind, and not the cook!'

He had walked out of his room to her door, attracted by the charm of her child-like frankness and innocence.

'Good-night!' he repeated, stretching out his arms to her. She thereupon threw her puny little arms round his neck and pressed him to her, quite regardless of the scantiness of her attire.

'Good-night, cousin!'

Five minutes later she bravely blew her candle out, and buried herself in her muslin-curtained bed. For a long time her slumber was light and broken, from her very weariness. She heard Véronique come upstairs, without the least care to hush her footsteps, and then push her furniture about with noise enough to waken everybody. After a while, however, there was nothing to be heard save the tumult of the storm outside. The rain beat down upon the slates; the wind shook the windows and whistled under the doors, and the girl long listened to that cannonading, and trembled and quivered as each wave broke against the cliff. It seemed to her that the house, now silent and lifeless, was being carried out to sea like a ship, Then, as she grew warm and snug beneath her blankets, her wandering thoughts strayed, with sympathetic pity, to the poor people down in the village, whom the sea was driving from their beds. But at last everything faded from her mind, and she slept soundly, scarce breathing.

FROM the first week Pauline's presence in the house proved a source of joy and pleasure to the family. Her cheerful healthiness and her calm, tranquil smile spread a softening influence over the asperities of the Chanteau household. In her the father found a nurse, while the mother was made happy by the fact that her son now spent more of his time at home. It was only Véronique who went on grumbling and growling. The knowledge that there were a hundred and fifty thousand francs locked up in the secrétaire, although they were to remain scrupulously untouched, seemed also to give the family a semblance of wealth. There was a new influence in their midst, and fresh hopes arose, though what they were it would have been difficult to say.

On the third night after Pauline's arrival, the attack of gout, which Chanteau had foreseen, broke out in all its violence. For a week past he had been experiencing prickings in his joints, tremblings and quiverings in his legs, and an utter distaste for all exercise. He had gone to bed feeling somewhat easier, but about three o'clock in the morning had been seized with a frightful pain in the big toe of his left foot. Thence it had quickly spread to his heel, and then risen to his ankle. He endured the agony as well as he could till morning, sweating beneath his blankets, anxious as he was to disturb nobody. His attacks were the dread of the whole house, and he always put off calling for assistance till the last possible minute, feeling ashamed of his helplessness, and dreading the angry reception which awaited the announcement of each fresh attack. But when he heard Véronique go past his door, about eight o'clock in the morning, he could no longer restrain a groan, as a sharper spasm of pain than previously shot through his foot.

'There we are again!' growled the cook. 'Just listen to him bellowing!'

She came into the room and watched him as he lay moaning and tossing his head about. And her only attempt at consolation was to say: 'You don't suppose this will please Madame when she hears of it, do you?'

As soon as Madame Chanteau heard of her husband's fresh attack she bounced into the room, and, letting her hands drop by her sides in angry desperation, cried out: 'What, again! No sooner do I get back than this begin afresh!'

For the last fifteen years she had harboured intense hatred against gout. She cursed it as an enemy, a thief that had blighted her existence, ruined her son, blasted all her hopes. If it had not been for that gout, would they have all been living a life of exile in that forsaken hole? Thus, in spite of all her natural kindness, she always manifested a petulant, hostile disposition towards her husband in his attacks, declaring, too, that she was quite incapable of nursing him.

'Oh! what agony I suffer!' groaned the unhappy man. 'I know it is going to be much worse this time than it was the last. Don't stop there, as it puts you out so, but send for Doctor Cazenove at once.'

The house was immediately in a state of commotion. Lazare set off to Arromanches, though the family retained but little confidence in medical help. During the last fifteen years Chanteau had tried all sorts of medicines, and with each fresh kind he had only grown worse. His attacks, which at first had been slight and infrequent, had quickly multiplied and become much more violent. He was racked with pain in both feet, and one of his knees was threatened also. Three times already had he seen his system of treatment changed, and his wretched body had become a mere basis for experimenting with competing nostrums. After being copiously bled, he had been scoured with purgatives, and now they crammed him with colchicum and lithium. The draining-away of his blood and the weakening of his frame had turned what had been intermittent into chronic gout. Local treatment had been no more successful. Leeches had left his joints in a state of painful stiffness; opium only prolonged his attacks, and blisters brought on ulceration. Wiesbaden and Carlsbad had done him no good, and a season at Vichy had all but killed him.

'Oh dear! oh dear! what agony I am suffering!' repeated poor Chanteau. 'It is just as though a lot of dogs were gnawing at my feet.'

He was perpetually altering the position of his leg, hoping to gain some relief by the change, but he was still racked with agony, and each fresh movement drew another groan from him. Presently, as the paroxysms of his pain grew sharper, a continuous howl came from his lips. He shivered and grew quite feverish, and his throat was parched with a burning thirst.

Pauline had just glided into his room. She stood by his bed and gazed at him gravely, but did not give way to tears; though Madame Chanteau lost her head, distracted by her husband's cries and groans. Véronique wished to arrange the bedclothes differently, as the sufferer found their weight intolerable, but as she was about to lay hold of them with her big awkward hands he screamed yet more loudly and forbade her to touch him. He was quite frightened of her, and said that she shook him as roughly as though he were a bundle of linen.

'Don't call for me again then, sir,' she said as she bounced angrily out of the room. 'If you won't let anybody help you, you must attend to yourself!'

Thereupon Pauline gently glided up to the bedside, and with delicate skilfulness lightened the pressure of the bedclothes with her childish fingers. The sufferer felt a short respite from his agony, and accepted the girl's help with a smile.

'Thank you, my dear. Stay! stay! Ah! that fold there weighs five hundred pounds! Oh! not so quickly, my dear, you quite frightened me.'

Then his agony returned in full force again; and as his wife, trying to find some occupation in the room, first drew up the blinds and then bustled to his bedside and placed a cup on the little table, he grew still more querulous.

'Oh! do keep still; don't rush about so! You make everything shake and tremble. Every step you take is just like a blow on my head with a hammer.'

She made no attempt at apologising or soothing him. Matters always ended in this fashion, and he was left to suffer in solitude.

'Come along, Pauline,' she said, quite unconcernedly. 'You see that your uncle can't endure to have any of us near him.'

But Pauline stayed behind in the sick-room. She glided about with such a light step that her feet scarcely seemed to touch the floor. From that moment she installed herself there as the sick man's nurse, and she was the only person whose presence in the room he could endure. She seemed able to read his thoughts, and she anticipated all his wants, softening the light as occasion seemed to require, and giving him his gruel, which Véronique brought as far as the door. But what the poor man found especially soothing and comforting was to see her constantly before him, sitting thoughtfully and quietly on her chair, with her big sympathetic eyes ever fixed upon him. He tried to find some distraction from his weariness in telling her of his sufferings.

'Just now I feel as if someone were sawing away at the joints of my toes with a jagged knife, and at the same time I could almost swear that I was being drenched with warm water.'

Then the character of his agony changed. It seemed as though a steel wire were twisted tightly round his ankle, and he could feel his muscles being strained till they were on the point of breaking. Pauline listened with affectionate complaisance and seemed to fully understand all he told her, remaining ever placid amongst all his groanings, with no other thought than to do what she could to alleviate his pain. She even forced herself to appear gay, and actually succeeded in making him laugh between his paroxysms.

When Doctor Cazenove at last arrived, he was filled with admiration of the little nurse, and gave her a hearty kiss upon her head. The Doctor was a man of fifty-four, vigorous and lean, who, after thirty years' service in the navy, had just settled down at Arromanches, where an uncle had left him a house. He had been a friend of the Chanteaus ever since he had cured Madame Chanteau of an awkward sprain.

'Well! well! here I am again!' he said. 'I have just come in to shake hands; but, you know, I can do nothing more for you than the little girl is already doing. When one has inherited gout, and has got past one's fiftieth year, one must reconcile oneself to it. And then, you know, you ruined your constitution with the shopful of drugs you swallowed. The only remedies are patience and flannel!'

The Doctor affected utter scepticism of the power of medicine in such a case. In thirty years he had seen so many poor sufferers racked with pain and disease, in all sorts of climates and in all kinds of surroundings, that he had grown very modest about his power to afford any actual relief. He generally preferred to let Nature work out its own cure. However, he carefully examined Chanteau's swollen toe, whose gleaming skin had turned a deep red, went on to look at the knee which was threatened with inflammation, and finally took note of the presence of a little pearl-like deposit, white and hard, at the edge of the patient's right ear.

'But, Doctor,' groaned the sufferer, 'you are not going to leave me suffering like this?'

Cazenove's demeanour had become quite serious. That chalky bead interested him, and his faith in medical science returned at the sight of this new symptom. 'Dear me!' he murmured half to himself, 'I had better try what salts and alkalies will do. It is evidently becoming chronic.'

Then in a louder and angry tone he said: 'It is your own fault, you know. You won't follow the directions I have given you. You are always glued to your arm-chair, and you never think of taking any exercise. And then I dare say you have been drinking wine and eating too much meat. Eh! haven't you, now? Confess that you have been taking something heating!'

'Nothing but a tiny bit of *foie gras,*' murmured Chanteau, very humbly.

The Doctor raised both his arms, as though to call the elements to witness his patient's folly. Then he took some little phials from the pockets of his overcoat, and began to prepare a draught. By way of local treatment he simply wrapped the foot and knee in cotton-wool, which he kept in its place by twisting some waxed thread round it. When he went away, it was to Pauline that he gave his directions. The invalid was to have a tablespoonful of the draught every two hours, and as much gruel as he liked, but he must observe the greatest strictness in the matter of diet.

'If you suppose that anybody can keep him from eating anything he chooses, you are very much mistaken,' said Madame Chanteau, as she went with the Doctor to the door.

'No! no! aunt dear; he will be very good, you will see,' Pauline ventured to assert. 'I will make him do what is right.'

Cazenove looked at her, and was amused by her serious manner. He kissed her again, on both her cheeks this time.

'There's a good little girl,' he said, 'who came into the world on purpose to help others.'

For a whole week Chanteau lay groaning. Just when the attack seemed over, his right foot was seized by the foe, and all his agony returned with increased violence. The whole house rang with his cries.

Véronique kept in the depths of her kitchen so as to escape the sound of them, and Madame Chanteau and Lazare sometimes actually ran out of the house, quite overcome by nervous excitement. It was only Pauline who remained with the sick man, and she indeed never left his room. She was ever struggling with his foolish whims and fancies; as, for instance, when he furiously insisted upon having a cutlet cooked, saying that he was very hungry, and roundly declaring that Doctor Cazenove was an ass and didn't know what was good for him. The night was the worst time, for then the attacks seemed to come on with increased violence. Pauline could only snatch some two or three hours' sleep. But, in spite of it all, she retained her spirits, and her health did not seem in any way to suffer. Madame Chanteau readily accepted her services, until, when Chanteau was again convalescent, the girl at last regained her liberty; and then a close companionship sprang up between her and Lazare.

It took its rise in that by-room which the young man occupied upstairs. He had had a partition knocked down, and so this room of his covered half of the second storey. A little iron bedstead was hidden away behind a tattered old screen. Against the wall and on the bare floor-boards were piled a thousand volumes of books, classical works, largely imperfect sets, which had been discovered in a lumber-room at Caen and had been transported to Bonneville. Near the window there was a huge antique Norman wardrobe crammed with all kinds of out-of-the-way objects, specimens of minerals, old and useless tools, and broken toys. There was a piano, also, over which were hung a pair of foils and a fencing-mask: and there was an enormous table in the centre, an old high drawing-table, so completely littered with papers, engravings, tobacco-jars and pipes that it was difficult to find a hand's-breadth of space available for writing.

Pauline was delighted when she was given the freedom of this wild chaos. She spent a month in exploring it thoroughly, and every day she made some new discovery, such as an illustrated 'Robinson Crusoe' which she came upon in rummaging amongst the books, or a doll which she fished out of the miscellaneous collection in the cupboard. As soon as she was dressed of a morning, she sprang out of her own room into her cousin's and settled herself there; and in the afternoon she often returned thither again.

From the day of her first visit Lazare had received her as though she had been a boy, a younger brother, some nine years his junior, but so merry and amusing and with such big intelligent eyes as to be in no wise in his way; and as usual he went on smoking his pipe, lolling in his chair with his legs cocked up in the air, or reading, or writing long letters into which he slipped flowers. Sometimes they made a pretty riot between them, for Pauline had a habit of suddenly springing upon the table or bounding through the split folds of the old screen. One morning as Lazare wondered why he did not hear her, and turned to ascertain what she might be about, he saw her, foil in hand, with her face screened with the fencing-mask as she flourished away at space. Whenever he told her to be still or threatened to turn her out of the room, the result was a tremendous skirmish and a wild pursuit through the disorderly place. Then she would fly at him and throw her arms on his neck, and he twirled her round like a top, with her petticoats circling about her. As the room echoed with their merry childlike laughter, he felt quite a boy again himself.

Next the piano afforded them occupation. It was an old instrument of Érard's make, dating from the year 1810, and upon it, in former times, Mademoiselle Eugénie de la Vignière had given lessons for fifteen years. The strings in its mahogany case, from which most of the polish had departed, sighed out far-away tones of a muffled softness. Lazare, who had never been able to persuade his mother to get him a new piano, strummed away on the old instrument with all his might, without succeeding in eliciting from it the sonorous rhapsodies buzzing in his head; and he had got into the habit of adding the notes of his own voice to the instrument's in order to obtain the required volume of sound. His passion for music soon led him to abuse Pauline's easy complaisance. He had found a listener, and for whole afternoons he kept her there while he went through his *répertoire,* which comprised all that was most complicated in music, and notably the then unacknowledged scores of Berlioz and Wagner. He poured forth his vocal accompaniment, and, as his enthusiasm increased, rendered the piece quite as much with his throat as with his fingers. On these occasions the poor child used to feel dreadfully bored, but she went on listening with an air of rapt attention, so that she might not hurt her cousin's feelings.

Sometimes darkness would surprise them still at the piano, and then Lazare would leave off playing and tell Pauline of his dreams for the future. He would be a great musician in spite of his mother, in spite of everybody. At the college at Caen a professor of the violin, struck by his genius for music, had prophesied a glorious career for him. He had secretly taken private lessons in composition, and now he was working hard by himself. He already had in his head a vague outline of a symphony on the subject of the Earthly Paradise; and, indeed, he had actually written the score of one passage descriptive of Adam and Eve being driven away by the angels, a march of a solemn and mournful character, which he consented to play one evening to Pauline. The child quite approved of it and declared it delightful. Then, however, she began to talk to him; of course it must be very nice, she said, to compose pretty music, but wouldn't it be more prudent if he were to obey the wishes of his parents, who wanted to make him a prefect or a judge? The whole house was made unhappy by the quarrel between the mother and the son; he declaring that he would go to Paris to the Conservatoire, and she replying that she would just give him till next October to make up his mind to embrace some respectable profession. Pauline backed up her aunt's designs, and told her, with an air of tranquil conviction, that she would take upon herself to bring her cousin round to proper views. She indeed argued the matter with Lazare, who grew angry with her and violently closed the piano, telling her that she was 'a horrid *bourgeoise.*'

For three days they sulked with each other, and then made friends again. To win her over to his musical scheme, Lazare wished to teach her to play on the piano. He showed her how to place her fingers on the keys, and kept her for hours running up and down the scales. But she discouraged him very much by her lack of enthusiasm. She was always on the look-out for something to laugh at and make a joke of, and took great delight in making Minouche promenade along the key-board and execute barbaric symphonies with her paws, asserting that the cat was playing the famous banishment from the Earthly Paradise, whereat the composer himself smiled. Then they broke out into boisterous fun again, she threw her arms round his neck, and he spun her round like a top, while Minouche, joining in the merriment, sprang from the table to the top of the cupboard. As for Matthew, he was not admitted into the room, as he was apt to become over-riotous when he felt merry.

'You drive me crazy, you wretched little shopkeeper!' Lazare one day broke out, quite impatiently. 'You had better get my mother to teach you, if you can persuade her to do so.'

'All this music of yours will never do you any good, you know,' Pauline answered quite roundly. 'If I were you I would be a doctor.'

He stared at her fiercely. A doctor, indeed! What had put that idea into her head? He worked himself into a state of excitement that made him lose all self-control.

'Listen to me!' he cried. 'If they won't let me be a musician, I'll kill myself!'

The summer completed Chanteau's restoration to health, and Pauline was now able to follow Lazare in his rambles out of doors. The big room was deserted, and they set off on wild adventures together. For some days they confined themselves to the terrace, where vegetated tufts of tamarisks, which the salt winds had nipped and blighted. Then they invaded the yard, broke the chain belonging to the well, terrified the dozen skinny fowls that lived upon grasshoppers, and hid themselves in the empty stable and coach-house and knocked the plaster off the walls. Thence they slipped into the kitchen-garden, a bit of poor dry ground, which Véronique dug and hoed like a peasant. There were four beds sown with tough vegetables and planted with miserable stumps of pear-trees, which were all bent by the north-west gales. And while here, on pushing open a little door, they found themselves on the cliffs, under the broad sky, with the open sea in front of them. Pauline's absorbing interest in that mighty expanse of water, now so soft and pure under the bright July sun, had never diminished. It was always for the sea that she looked from every window in the house. But she had never yet been near it, and a new era in her life commenced when she found herself alone with Lazare in the solitude of the shore.

What happy times they had together! Madame Chanteau grumbled and wanted to keep them in the house, in spite of all her confidence in Pauline's discretion; and so they never went out through the yard, where Véronique would have seen them, but glided stealthily through the kitchen-garden, and so escaped, to appear no more till evening. They soon found their rambles round the church and the graveyard, with its shadowing yews and the priest's salad-beds, a trifle monotonous, and in a week they had quite exhausted the attractions of Bonneville, with its thirty cottages clinging to the side of the cliff and its strip of shingle where the fishermen drew up their boats. When the tide was low it was far more amusing to wander along at the foot of the cliffs. They walked over fine sand, frightening the little crabs that scudded away before them, or jumped from rock to rock among the thick seaweed and the sparkling pools where shrimps were skimming about; to say nothing of the fish they caught, of the mussels they ate, raw and even without bread, or the strange-looking creatures they carried away in their handkerchiefs, or the odd discoveries they sometimes made, such as that of a stranded dab or a little lobster lurking at the bottom of a hole. They would sometimes let themselves be overtaken by the rising tide and rush merrily for refuge to some big rock, to wait there till the ebb allowed them to go their way again. They were perfectly happy as they came back home in the evening wet through and with their hair all tossed about by the wind. And they grew so accustomed to this life in the fresh salt breezes that they found the atmosphere of the lamp-lighted room at night quite suffocating.

But their greatest pleasure of all was bathing. The beach was too rocky to attract the inhabitants of Caen and Bayeux, and, whereas every year new villas rose on the cliffs at Arromanches, never a single bather made his appearance at Bonneville. Lazare and Pauline had discovered, about half a mile from the village, over towards Port-en-Bessin, a delightful spot, a little bay shut in by two rocky cliffs and carpeted with soft glittering sand. They called it the Golden Bay, for its secluded waves seemed to wash up pieces of glittering gold. They were quite alone and undisturbed there, and undressed and slipped on their bathing things without any feeling of shame. Lazare in a week taught Pauline to swim. She was much more enthusiastic about this than she had been about the piano, and in her plucky attempts she often swallowed big mouthfuls of salt water. If a larger wave than usual sent them tottering one against the other, they laughed gleefully; and when they came out of the water, they went romping over the sand till the wind had dried them. This was much more amusing than fishing.

The days slipped away, however, and August came round, and as yet Lazare had come to no decision. In October Pauline was to go to a boarding-school at Bayeux. When bathing had tired them, they would sit on the sand and talk over the state of their affairs gravely and sensibly. Pauline had succeeded in interesting Lazare in medical matters by telling him that if she were a man she should think nothing nobler or more delightful than to be able to cure ailing people. Besides, for the last week or so, the Earthly Paradise had not been getting on satisfactorily, and Lazare was beginning to have doubts about his genius for music. At any rate, there had been great glory won in the practice of medicine, and he bethought him of many illustrious names, Hippocrates, Ambrose Paré, and others.

One afternoon, however, he burst out into a loud cry of delight. He had the score of his masterpiece in his hand at the time. It was all rubbish, he said, that Paradise of his, and could not be worked out. He would destroy it all, and write quite a new symphony on Grief, which should describe in sublime harmonies the hopeless despair of Humanity groaning beneath the skies. He retained the march of Adam and Eve, and boldly transferred it to his new work as the 'March of Death.' For a week his enthusiasm increased every hour, and the whole universe entered into the scheme of his symphony. But, when another week had passed away, Pauline was very much astonished to hear him say one evening that he was quite willing to go and study medicine in Paris. He was really thinking that by doing so he would be near the Conservatoire, and would then be able to see what could be done. Madame Chanteau, however, was delighted. She would certainly have preferred seeing her son hold some judicial or administrative office, but, at any rate, doctors were very respectable persons and sometimes made a good deal of money. 'You must be a little witch!' she said, kissing Pauline; 'you have more than repaid us, my dear, for taking you.' Everything was settled. Lazare was to leave on the 1st of October. During the month of September that remained to them they gave themselves up with greater fervour than ever to their romps and rambles, resolved to finish their term of freedom in a worthy manner. They sported about in the Golden Bay at times till darkness surprised them there.

One evening they were sitting on the beach, watching the stars appear like fiery beads in the paling sky. Pauline gazed at them with the placid admiration of a healthy child, whereas Lazare, who had become feverish ever since he had been preparing for his departure, blinked nervously, while in his mind revolved all kinds of schemes and ambitions for the future.

'How lovely the stars are!' said Pauline quietly, after a long interval of silence.

He made no reply. All his cheerfulness had left him; his gaze seemed disturbed by some inward anxiety. Up in the sky the stars were growing thicker every minute, as if sparks were being cast by the handful across the heavens.

'You have never learned anything about them, have you?' he said at last. 'Each star up yonder is a sun, round which there are planets wheeling like the earth. There are thousands and thousands of them; and far away beyond those you can see are legions of others. There is no end to them.' Then he became silent for a moment. By-and-by he resumed in a voice that quivered with emotion: 'I don't like to look at them; they make me feel afraid.'

The rising tide was raising a distant wail, like the mournful cry of a multitude lamenting its wretchedness. Over the horizon, black now with fallen night, glittered the gold-dust of wheeling worlds. And amid that sad wail that echoed round them from the world, pressed low beneath the countless stars, Pauline thought she detected a sound of bitter sobbing beside her.

'What is the matter with you? Are you ill?'

Lazare made no answer. He was indeed sobbing, with his face hidden in his convulsively twitching hands, as though he wanted to blot out the sight of everything. And as soon as he was able to speak, he gasped: 'Oh, to die! to die!'

The scene filled Pauline with long-lasting astonishment. Lazare rose to his feet with difficulty, and they went back to Bonneville through the darkness, the rising tide pressing closely upon them. Neither spoke a word to the other. As Pauline watched the young man go on in front of her, he seemed to grow shorter, to bend beneath the breeze from the west.

That evening they found a newcomer waiting for them in the dining-room, talking to Chanteau. For a week past they had been expecting the arrival of a young girl called Louise, who was eleven years and a half old, and came to spend a fortnight every year at Bonneville. They had twice gone to meet her at Arromanches, without finding her, and now, that evening, when no one was looking for her, she had turned up quite unexpectedly. Louise's mother had died in Madame Chanteau's arms, recommending her daughter to the other's care. Her father, Monsieur Thibaudier, a banker at Caen, had married again six months afterwards, and had already three children by his present wife. Absorbed by his new family and business matters, he had sent Louise to a boarding-school, and was only too glad when he could get her off his hands during the holidays by sending her upon a round of visits to her friends. He gave himself as little trouble about her as possible, and she had come to the Chanteaus' a week behind her time, in the charge of a servant. 'The master had so much to worry him,' said the latter, who returned home immediately she had deposited her charge at Bonneville, with an intimation that Mademoiselle's father would do his best to come and fetch her himself when her time was up.

'Come along, Lazare!' cried Chanteau. 'Here she is at last!'

Louise smiled and kissed the young man on both his cheeks, though the acquaintance between them was slight, for she had been constantly shut up in school, and it was barely a year since he had left college. Their knowledge of each other really dated from their last holidays, and Lazare had hitherto treated the girl somewhat ceremoniously, fancying that she already considered herself grown-up, and despised any youthful display of boisterousness.

'Well, Pauline, aren't you going to kiss her?' said Chanteau, entering the room. 'She is older than you by a year and a half, you know. You must be very fond of each other; it will please me very much to see you so.'

Pauline looked keenly at Louise, who was slight and delicate, with somewhat irregular though very pleasing features. Her hair was thick and fair, and was curled and arranged like that of a young woman. Pauline turned a little pale on seeing Louise kiss Lazare; and when she herself was kissed by her with a smile, it was with quivering lips that she returned the salute.

'What is the matter with you?' asked her aunt. 'Are you cold?'

'Yes, I think I am a little. The wind was rather chilly,' she answered, blushing at the falsehood she was telling.

When they sat down to dinner she ate nothing. Her eyes never strayed from the faces of those who were present, and became very black whenever her uncle or her cousin or even Véronique paid any attention to Louise. But she seemed to be especially pained when Matthew, making his customary round of the table, went and laid his huge head upon the newcomer's knee. It was quite in vain that she called him to her. He would not leave Louise, who gorged him with sugar.

When they rose from the table, Pauline immediately left the room. Véronique was clearing the things away, and as she came back from the kitchen for a fresh trayful she said, with a triumphant expression: 'Ah, Madame! I know you think your Pauline quite perfect, but just go and look at her now in the yard.'

They all went out to see. Hiding away behind the coachhouse, Pauline was holding Matthew against the wall, and, apparently mad with passion, was hitting his head with all the strength of her clenched fists. The poor dog seemed quite stupefied, and, instead of offering resistance to her blows, simply hung down his head. They rushed out at her, but even at their approach she did not desist from her cruel treatment, and they were obliged to carry her off. She was found to be in such a feverish, excited state that she was at once put to bed, and for the greater part of the night her aunt dared not leave her.

'Oh! yes, she's a dear little thing, a very dear little thing!' sneered Véronique, who was quite delighted at having discovered a flaw in the diamond.

'I remember, now,' said Madame Chanteau, 'that people spoke to me about her outbursts of temper when I was in Paris. She is quite jealous—what a nasty thing! I have noticed during the six months that she has been with us several trifling matters that haven't pleased me; but, really, to try to murder the poor dog beats everything!'

When Pauline saw Matthew the next day, she threw her trembling arms round him and, kissing him on the nose, burst into such a flood of tears that they feared she was going to have another hysterical attack. In spite of her repentance, she could not restrain these outbursts of mad passion. It was as though some sudden storm within her sent all her blood boiling and hissing into her head. She had doubtless inherited this jealous violence from some ancestor on her mother's side; yet she had a deal of common-sense for a child of ten years old, and used to say that she did all she could to struggle against those outbreaks, but without avail. They made her very miserable, as though they had been the symptoms of some shameful disease.

At times, when Madame Chanteau reproached her, she replied, hiding her head against her aunt's shoulder: 'I love you so much, why do you love others?'

Thus, in spite of all her efforts and struggles, Pauline suffered a great deal from Louise's presence in the house. Ever since the other had been expected, she had been looking forward to her coining with uneasy curiosity, and now she was impatiently counting the days of her stay, all eagerness for her departure. Yet she could not help remarking the charm of Louise's manner, the pretty seductiveness of her half-childish, half-womanish demeanour; but, perhaps, it was this very charm and seductiveness that troubled her and made her so angry when Lazare was present. For his part, the young man showed the greater preference for Pauline, and even made jokes about Louise, saying that she wearied him with her grand airs, and that Pauline and he had better leave her alone to play the fine lady by herself, while they went off somewhere to amuse themselves as they liked. All boisterous romping had ceased since Louise's arrival; indoors they remained looking at pictures, and when they went to the shore they walked about with irreproachable decorum. It was a fortnight utterly wasted.

One morning Lazare announced his intention of anticipating his departure by five days. He was anxious, he said, to get settled down in Paris, where he expected to find one of his old chums at the College of Caen. Pauline, whom the thought of the approaching separation had distressed for a month past, now strongly approved of her cousin's determination, and gleefully assisted her aunt to pack his trunk. But as soon as he had driven off in old Malivoire's ancient *berline* she rushed away to her room, locked herself in it, and gave herself up to weeping. Then, in the evening, she bore herself very kindly and affectionately towards Louise, and the remaining week which the latter spent at Bonneville passed away delightfully. When the maid came to fetch her home again, explaining that the banker had not been able to leave his business, the two girls rushed into each other's arms and swore eternal friendship.

A year slowly passed away. Madame Chanteau had changed her mind, and, instead of sending Pauline to a boarding-school, had kept her at home with herself, being chiefly moved to this course by the complaints of Chanteau, who had grown so used to the girl that he declared he could not possibly get on without her. But the good lady did not confess that any such reason of self-interest had anything to do with the alteration of her plans; she talked about undertaking the child's education herself, feeling quite youthful again at the thought of reverting to her old profession of tuition. Besides, in boarding-schools, said she, little girls became acquainted with all kinds of things, and she wished her young ward to be reared in perfect innocence and purity. They hunted out from among Lazare's miscellaneous books a Grammar, an Arithmetic, a Treatise on History, and even an Abridgment of the Greek Mythology; and Madame Chanteau resumed her functions of preceptress. Lazare's big room was turned into a schoolroom; Pauline had to resume her music lessons there, and was put through a severe course of deportment to rid her of all the unladylike, boyish ways into which she had fallen. She showed herself very docile and intelligent, and manifested a great willingness to learn, even when the subject-matter of her lessons was distasteful to her. There was only one thing which seemed to weary her, and that was the catechism. She had not as yet supposed that her aunt would take the trouble to conduct her to mass on Sundays. Why should she, indeed? When she lived in Paris, no one had ever taken her to Saint-Eustache, which was quite near their house. It was only with difficulty that abstract ideas found their way into her understanding, and her aunt had to explain to her that a well brought-up young lady's duty in the country was to set a proper example by showing herself to be on good terms with the priest. Religion, with her, had never been anything more than a matter of appearance and respectability, and she looked upon it as part of a polite education, standing upon very much the same footing as the art of deportment.

Twice every day the tide swept up to the cliffs of Bonneville, and Pauline's life passed on with the great expanse of surging water before her eyes. She had given over playing and romping, for she no longer had a companion. When she had run along the terrace with Matthew, or strolled to the end of the kitchen-garden with Minouche, her only pleasure was to go and gaze at the sea, which was full of changing life, dark and gloomy in the stormy days of winter, and gleaming with bright blues and greens beneath the summer sun. The beneficent influence which seemed to flow from the girl's presence in the house manifested itself in another form that year, for Chanteau received from Davoine a quite unlooked-for remittance of five thousand francs, which threats of a dissolution of partnership had extorted from him. Madame Chanteau never missed going to Caen each quarter to receive her niece's dividends, and when she had deducted her expenses and the sum which she was allowed for Pauline's board, she invested the balance in the purchase of further stock. On returning home she always took the girl into her room, and, opening the well-known drawer in the secrétaire, said to her: 'There, you see, I am putting this with the other. Isn't it getting a big heap? Don't be at all uneasy about it. You will find it all there when you want it. There won't be centime missing.'

One fine morning in August Lazare suddenly made his appearance, bringing with him the news of his complete success in his preliminary examinations. He had not been expected for another week, but he had wanted to take his mother by surprise. His arrival greatly delighted them all. In the letters which he had written home every fortnight he had shown an increasing interest in medicine, and, now that he was amongst them again, he appeared to be completely changed. He never spoke a word about music, but was perpetually chattering about his professors and his scientific studies, dragging them in *à propos* of everything, even of the dishes that were served at dinner and the direction in which the wind was blowing. He was, now, a prey to another wildly enthusiastic ambition, for he dreamed, day and night, of becoming a physician, whose wonderful skill would be trumpeted through the whole world. Pauline, when she had thrown her arms round his neck and kissed him with child-like frankness, was more surprised than the others at this change in him. It almost grieved her, indeed, that he should have dropped all his interest in music, even as a recreation. Could it be possible, she asked herself, that, when one had really loved anything, one could end by caring nothing at all about it? One day when she asked him about his symphony, he began to make fun of it, and told her that he had quite done with all such nonsense. She felt quite sad at those words. But he also seemed to be soon bored with her society, and laughed with an unpleasant laugh; while his eyes and his gestures spoke of a ten months' life which could not have been related in detail to little girls.

He had unpacked his trunk himself, so as to keep from view the books he had brought home with him, novels and medical works, some of them copiously illustrated. He no longer twirled his cousin like a top, as he had been wont to do, making her petticoats fly in a circle round her, and he even seemed quite confused at times when she persisted in coming into his room and staying there. However, she had scarcely grown at all during his absence, and she still looked him frankly in the face with her pure innocent eyes, in such wise that by the end of a week his appearance of uneasiness had vanished, and they reverted to their old intimacy and comradeship. The fresh sea-breezes had now swept the unhealthy influences of the students' quarter of Paris out of Lazare's brain, and he felt once more a child himself as he romped about with his little cousin, both of them full of vigorous health and gaiety. All the old life began anew; the racing round the table, the scampers with Matthew and Minouche through the garden, the rambles to the Golden Bay and the bathing in the open air. And that year, too, Louise, who had paid a visit to Bonneville in May, went to take her holidays with some other friends at Rouen; and so the others spent two very delightful months, without a single disagreement or misunderstanding to mar their enjoyment. When October came, Pauline watched Lazare pack his trunk for his return to Paris. He gathered together the books he had brought with him, which had remained stowed away in his cupboard without once being opened.

'Are you going to take them all back with you?' the girl asked in a melancholy voice.

'Yes, indeed,' he replied. 'I shall want them all for my studies. You have no notion how hard I am going to work. I shall want every one of them.'

The little house at Bonneville once more subsided into lifeless, monotonous quietude. Each day passed in precisely the same way as its predecessors, bringing the same round of incidents beside the ceaseless rhythm of the ocean. That year, however, was marked distinctly for Pauline. In the month of June she took her first communion, being then twelve and a half years old. By slow degrees a religious feeling had taken possession of her, but it was a religious feeling loftier than the one indicated in her catechism, whose answers she constantly repeated without understanding them. With her reflective young mind she had ended by picturing the Deity to herself as a very powerful and very wise ruler, who directed everything upon earth in accordance with principles of strict justice; and this simplified conception of hers sufficed to put her on a footing of understanding with Abbé Horteur. The Abbé was a peasant's son, and into his hard head nothing but the letter of the law had ever made its way. He had grown to be contented with the observance of outward ceremonies and the maintenance of religious practices. True, he bestowed the greatest care and thought upon his own salvation; and if his parishioners should finally be damned, well, it would be their own fault. For fifteen years he had been trying to terrify them without success, and now all that he asked of them was to come to church on the great feast days. And, in spite of the sinful state in which it rotted, Bonneville did come to church pretty regularly, drawn thither by the influence of old habit. But the priest's tolerance had degenerated into indifference as to the real spiritual condition of his flock. Every Saturday it was his custom to go and play draughts with Chanteau, although the mayor, making his gout an excuse, never set foot inside the church. But then Madame Chanteau did all that was necessary by attending the services regularly and taking Pauline with her. It was the priest's great simplicity and frankness which by degrees won Pauline over. While living in Paris, she had heard priests scoffed and sneered at as hypocrites, whose black robes concealed all manner of sins and wickedness. But the priest of that little sea-side hamlet seemed to her a thoroughly genuine, honest fellow, with his heavy boots and sun-browned neck and farmer-like speech and manner. One little fact especially impressed her. Abbé Horteur was strongly addicted to puffing away at a big meerschaum pipe, but he seemed to be disturbed by some slight scruples as to the propriety of such a habit, for whenever he wanted to smoke he always retired into his garden, and hid himself away in the solitude of his lettuce-beds. And it was the anxious air with which he hastily tried to put his pipe out of sight when he was taken unawares in his garden that touched the girl, though she could scarcely have told why. She took her first communion in a very serious and reverent frame of mind, in company with two other girls from the village and one boy. When the priest came to dine with the Chanteaus in the evening, he declared that never since he had been at Bonneville had he seen a communicant who had conducted herself with such reverence at the Holy Table.

Financially, the year was not so prosperous for the Chanteaus. The rise in the price of deal, for which Davoine had been hoping for a long time past, did not take place, and so only bad news came from Caen, for, being driven into selling at a loss, the business was in a bad way indeed. Thus the family lived in the most meagre fashion, and were only able to make their income of three thousand francs cover the necessary expenses by practising the most rigid economy. Lazare, whose letters to herself she kept strictly private, was Madame Chanteau's chief source of anxiety. He was apparently leading a life of extravagance and dissipation, for he constantly applied to her for money. When she went to Caen in July to receive Pauline's dividend, she made a fierce attack upon Davoine. Two thousand francs which he had previously given to her had been sent to Lazare, and now she succeeded in wringing another thousand francs out of him, and these she at once despatched to Paris. For Lazare had written to tell her that he would not be able to come home unless he was provided with the means of paying his debts. Every day during a whole week they expected his arrival amongst them, but each morning a letter came announcing that his departure had been put off till the morrow. When at last he did actually start for home, his mother and Pauline went as far as Verchemont to meet him. They met there, kissed each other on the high-road, and walked home together, followed by the unoccupied coach, which carried Lazare's luggage.

Lazare's return home that year was by no means so gay as his previous triumphal surprise. He had failed to pass an examination in July, and was embittered against all his professors, of whom he fell foul throughout the evening. The next morning, in Pauline's presence, he threw his books upon one of the shelves in the wardrobe, exclaiming that they might lie there and rot. This sudden disgust for his studies alarmed her. She heard him scoff bitterly at medicine, and deny its power to cure even a cold. One day when she was attempting to defend it from his attacks, in an impulse of youthful belief, he sneered so bitterly at her ignorance of what she was talking about that his remarks brought a hot blush to her cheeks. But, all the same, he said, he had resigned himself to being a doctor; as well that kind of humbug as any other: everything was equally stupid at bottom. Pauline grew quite indignant and angry at the new ideas which he had brought home with him. Where had he got them from? From those wicked books he read, she was quite sure; but she dared not discuss the matter fully, held back as she was by her own ignorance, and feeling ill at ease amidst her cousin's sneers and innuendoes and pretences that he could not tell her everything. The holidays glided away in perpetual misunderstandings and bickerings. In their walks together the young man seemed to be bored, and declared that the sea was wearisome and monotonous. As a means of killing time, however, he had taken to writing verses, and composed sonnets on the sea with great elaboration and fastidiousness of rhymes. He declined to bathe, saying that he had found that cold baths disagreed with his constitution, for, in spite of his denial of all value to medical science, he now indulged in the most sweeping and authoritative opinions, condemning or curing people with a word. About the middle of September, when they were expecting Louise's arrival, he suddenly expressed his intention of returning to Paris, saying that he wished to prepare for his examination again. He really thought that his life would be unbearable between two little girls, and wished to get back to the Latin Quarter. Pauline's manner to him, however, became gentler and more submissive the more he did to vex her. When he was rude and sought to distress her, she merely looked at him with those tender, smiling eyes of hers, whose soft influence was able to soothe even Chanteau when he groaned and moaned amidst one of his attacks of gout. She thought that her cousin was in some way out of health, for he looked upon life like a weary old man.

The day before his departure Lazare manifested such delight at the prospect of leaving Bonneville that Pauline burst into tears.

'You don't love me any more now!'

'Don't be a goose! Haven't I got to make my way in life? A big girl like you to be crying! The idea of it!'

Then she summoned up her courage again and smiled as she said to him: 'Work hard this year, so that when you come back again we may all be quite happy and satisfied.'

'Oh! there's no good in working hard! Their examinations are nothing but foolery. I didn't pass because I didn't care to. I am going to hurry through with it all now, since my lack of fortune prevents me from living a life of ease and leisure, which is the only satisfactory life a man can lead.'

In the early part of October, after Louise had returned to Caen, Pauline again resumed her lessons with her aunt. The curriculum of her third year's studies embraced bowdlerised French History, and Greek Mythology as 'adapted to the use of young persons.' But the girl, who had shown such diligence in the previous year, now seemed to have become quite sluggish and dull. Sometimes she even went to sleep over her tasks, and her face flushed with a hot surging of blood. A mad outburst of anger against Véronique, who didn't like her, she declared, made her so ill that she had to stop in bed for a couple of days. Then came changes in herself which disquieted and distressed her. About Christmas-time Pauline's health was such as to alarm Madame Chanteau. But that worthy woman, from ridiculous notions of her own, was largely to blame, as she refused to take Doctor Cazenove's advice and talk to the girl as she should have done. And in the result Pauline, at an important period in her youth, narrowly escaped being stricken with an attack of brain-fever.

When she was well again and resumed her studies, she began to affect an enthusiastic interest in the Greek Mythology. She shut herself up in Lazare's big room—which was still used as a schoolroom—and had to be sent for at meal-times. When she came down, she seemed buried in thought and quite indifferent to all that went on. Upstairs, however, the Mythology lay quite neglected on the table, for it was in poring over all the medical books which Lazare had left in the old wardrobe that she now spent her time. There were a good many of those works, and, though at first she failed to understand all the technical terms she met with, she plodded on through anatomy and physiology, and even pathology and clinical medicine. Thus she not only learnt—in all simplicity and purity of mind, saved from all vicious thought by a healthy craving for knowledge—many things of which girls of her age are usually ignorant; but her researches extended to the symptoms and treatment of all sorts of disease and ailment. Superfluous subjects she passed by unheeded. She seemed to know intuitively what knowledge was necessary to enable her to be of assistance to those who suffered. Her heart melted with pity as she read on, and she gave her-self up again to her old dream of learning everything so that she might be able to cure all that went amiss.

Knowledge rendered Pauline grave and thoughtful. She felt surprised and annoyed at her aunt's silence towards her, which had resulted in such terror and serious illness. And when one day Madame Chanteau did see fit to refer to the matter, the girl quietly intimated that she needed no information. At this the other was alarmed, and Pauline then told her all about Lazare's books. There was a scene, but the girl, with her outspoken frankness, quite routed her aunt. 'How can there be harm in knowledge of the normal conditions of life?' she asked. Her enthusiasm was perfectly mental, and never did a single wrong thought disturb the pure depths of her clear, child-like eyes. On the same shelf with the medical books she had found novels which had repelled her and bored her, so that she had thrown them aside after glancing at the first few pages. Her aunt, growing more and more disconcerted, though she had recovered a little from her first shock, contented herself with locking the wardrobe and taking away the key. But a week later it was there again, and Pauline indulged herself in reading at intervals, by way of recreation, either a chapter on neurosis, with her mind fixed the while upon her cousin, or one relating to the treatment of gout, with the idea of undertaking her uncle's cure.

Each day increasing love of life and its various manifestations displayed itself in Pauline and made of her, to use her aunt's phrase, a general mother. Everything that lived, everything that suffered, aroused in her a feeling of active tenderness and won from her abundant kindliness and thoughtful care. She had now forgotten all about Paris, and began to feel as though she had been born in that wild spot under the pure breezes from the sea, She had developed, too, into a well-formed young woman, and with her healthy mind and love of knowledge it was with delight that she found herself reaching full growth and sunny ripeness. On her part there was a full acceptance of life, life beloved in all its functions, welcomed with the triumphant greeting of vigorous health and soundness of nature.

That year Lazare remained for six months without writing home, with the exception, that is, of a very brief note now and then to tell them he was all right. Then all at once he began to deluge his mother with letters. He had again been plucked at the November examination, and had become more disgusted than ever with the study of medicine, which dealt with too gloomy matters for his taste, so that he had now enthusiastically turned to chemistry. He had chanced to make the acquaintance of the illustrious Herbelin, whose discoveries were then revolutionising the science, and had entered his laboratory as an assistant, without owning, however, that he was relinquishing medicine. But his letters were soon full of a new scheme, which he at first mentioned somewhat timidly, but gradually grew wildly enthusiastic about. It was a plan for turning sea-weed to wonderful profit, by the adoption of some new methods and reagents discovered by the illustrious Herbelin. Lazare dwelt upon the great probability of the scheme's success;

the great chemist's assistance; the ease with which raw material could be obtained, and the very small expense that would be incurred for plant. In the end he frankly expressed his disinclination to be a doctor, and jokingly declared that he should prefer to sell remedies to the sick rather than to kill them off himself. He finished all his letters by recapitulating the prospects of speedily acquiring a large fortune, and mentioned as an additional lure to his parents that, if they would consent to his new plans, he should remain with them, as he proposed setting up his works quite close to Bonneville.

The months slipped away, and Lazare did not come home for the vacation. All through the winter he continued to unfold the details of his new scheme in long closely-written letters, which Madame Chanteau used to read aloud in the evening after dinner. One night in May they resolved themselves into a solemn family council to discuss the matter seriously, for Lazare had written to ask for a categorical reply. Véronique was bustling about the room, taking off the dinner-cloth and putting the red one on the table in its place.

'He is his grandfather over again, always running after some fresh scheme and doing no good at anything,' declared Madame Chanteau, glancing up at the former journeyman-carpenter's masterpiece, whose presence on the mantel-shelf was a perpetual source of annoyance to her.

'Well, he certainly doesn't get his flighty disposition from me, for I detest all change,' sighed Chanteau between a couple of groans, as he lay back in his arm-chair, where he was just recovering from another attack of gout. 'But you yourself, my dear, you know you are a little given to restlessness.'

His wife shrugged her shoulders as though to imply that all her actions were dictated and carried out by reason and common-sense. Then she added slowly: 'Well, what are we to say? I suppose we shall have to write to him and tell him that he may have his own way. I wanted to see him in the magistracy, and I wasn't over well pleased at his being a doctor; but now he has got down to being an apothecary! Still, if he comes back home again and makes a lot of money, that will be better than nothing.'

It was really this hope of money-making which decided her. She began to indulge in new dreams for the son she was so fond of. She foresaw him very wealthy, the owner of a fine house at Caen, a councillor-general, perhaps even a deputy. Chanteau, who had no opinion either one way or the other, and was absorbed in his own sufferings, left his wife to see after all the interests of the family. Pauline, in spite of her surprise and silent disapprobation of her cousin's continual changes, thought that he had better be allowed to try his luck at the grand new scheme which he had got into his head.

'At any rate, we shall be all together,' she said.

'And it's precious little good that Monsieur Lazare seems to be doing in Paris,' Véronique ventured to add. 'It will be better for him to come and live quietly here with us.'

Madame Chanteau nodded assent. She again took up the letter which she had received that morning.

'He here goes into the financial side of his scheme,' she said. Then she read the letter, commenting on it as she proceeded. Sixty thousand francs would be required for erecting the works. In Paris Lazare had met one of his old Caen friends, Boutigny, who was now selling wine on commission there. Boutigny was very enthusiastic about the new scheme, and had offered to invest thirty thousand francs in the business. He would make an admirable partner, one whose practical business habits would ensure the success of the undertaking. There would, however, still remain thirty thousand francs to be borrowed somewhere, as Lazare was anxious to have half the business in his own hands.

'As you hear,' continued Madame Chanteau, 'he wants me to apply in his name to Thibaudier. It is a good idea, and I am sure Thibaudier will let him have the money. Louise is not very well just now, and I have thought of going to Caen to ask her to stay with us for a week. As I shall see her father, I will mention the matter to him.'

A cloud passed before Pauline's eyes, and her lips quivered as she drew them tightly together. Véronique was standing at the other side of the table, wiping a tea-cup and watching her closely.

'I had, indeed, thought of another way,' said Madame Chanteau in a low voice; 'but as there is always some risk in a business enterprise, I have come to the conclusion to say nothing about it.'

Then, turning to the young girl, she added: 'Yes, my dear, you might have lent the thirty thousand francs to your cousin yourself. You couldn't find a better investment, and you would very likely get twenty-five per cent interest, for your cousin would share his profits with you, and it quite grieves me to think of a lot of money going into an outsider's pocket. But I shouldn't like you to run any risk with your fortune. It is a sacred deposit. It is quite safe upstairs, and I will restore it to you unimpaired.'

Pauline grew pale as she listened to her aunt's words; and a struggle went on within her. She had inherited a somewhat avaricious disposition: Quenu's and Lisa's love of money. In the pork-butcher's shop she had been taught to reverence its power, and to guard against the want of it. Then, too, her aunt had so frequently called her attention to the drawer in the secrétaire where her little fortune was locked up, that the thought of seeing it gradually squandered by her erratic cousin irritated her. So she kept silent, though she was also troubled by a vision of Louise handing a great bag of money to Lazare.

'Even if you, my dear, should wish it, I shouldn't,' Madame Chanteau continued; and, addressing her husband, she added: 'It is quite a matter of conscience, isn't it?'

'Her money belongs to her,' said Chanteau with a deep groan as he tried to move his leg. 'If things were to turn out badly, we should be called upon to make good the loss. No! no! we mustn't do that. Thibaudier will be glad to lend it, I have no doubt.'

Then Pauline, in an impulse of affection, cried:

'No! no! please don't grieve me like this. I certainly ought to lend the money to Lazare myself. Isn't he my brother? It would be very unkind of me if I refused to let him have it. How could you suppose that I could have any objection? Give him the money at once, aunt; give him all of it!'

Her eyes filled with tears at the effort she had just made; then her face broke out into a smile, while she remained in a state of confusion between her regret at having hesitated for a moment and a miserable fear that the money would be lost. She had to struggle a little while against the protest of her relations, who were certainly honest enough to show her the risks she would run.

'Come and kiss me then, my dear,' her aunt finished by saying, yielding to the girl's tears. 'You are a very good girl, and you shall lend Lazare your money, since it would vex you so much if he did not take it.'

'Come and kiss me, too, dear, won't you?' added her uncle. They cried and kissed all round the table. Then, as Pauline went out of the room to call Matthew, and Véronique brought in the tea, Madame Chanteau exclaimed, wiping the tears from her eyes: 'It's a great consolation to find her generous-minded.'

'Of course!' growled the servant; 'why, she would strip her chemise off her back rather than let that other one have a chance of giving anything!'

It was a week later, on a Saturday, that Lazare returned to Bonneville. Doctor Cazenove, who had been invited to dine with the Chanteaus, brought the young man along with him in his gig. They found Abbé Horteur, who was also dining there that evening, playing draughts with Chanteau, who was lying back in his invalid's chair. He had been suffering for three months past from the attack from which he was now recovering. It had been more painful and violent than any previous one, and now, in spite of the terrible twinges he constantly felt in his feet, he considered himself in a state of Paradise. His skin was scaling, and the swellings had almost disappeared. Véronique was busy roasting some pigeons in the kitchen, and every time the door opened he sniffed the appetizing odour, overcome, again, by his irrepressible greediness, on which subject the priest began to remonstrate with him.

'You are not attending to the game, Monsieur Chanteau. Now, be advised by me, and be very careful about what you eat this evening. Rich food is bad for you in your present condition.'

Louise had arrived the previous day. When she and Pauline heard the Doctor's gig approaching, they both rushed wildly into the yard. But it was only his cousin whom Lazare appeared to notice, and he looked at her with an expression of amazement.

'What! can this really be Pauline?'

'Yes, indeed, it is!'

'But, good gracious, what a lot you must have eaten to have grown like that! Why, you are quite big enough to get married now!'

She blushed, and laughed gaily, her eyes glistening with pleasure at seeing him take such notice of her. He had left her a mere chit, a raw schoolgirl in a pinafore, and now he saw her again as a well-grown young woman, whose figure showed to advantage in her white rose-sprayed summer gown. However, she became quite serious as she examined him in turn. She thought he was looking much older, he stooped, his laugh no longer sounded young, and his face twitched nervously at times.

'By the way,' said Lazare, 'I must really treat you a little more ceremoniously now. How do you do, partner?'

Pauline's blush assumed a deeper tint; the word 'partner' made her feel intensely happy. When her cousin had kissed her, he might well kiss Louise afterwards. She experienced no feeling of jealousy now.

It was a delightful dinner. Chanteau, alarmed by the Doctor's threats, ate with moderation. Madame Chanteau and the priest discussed magnificent schemes for the aggrandizement of Bonneville when the sea-weed business should have enriched the neighbourhood. It was eleven o'clock before they separated. As Lazare and Pauline were about to quit each other, at the doors of their rooms, the young man said to her laughingly:

'So young ladies, when they have grown up, no longer wish one good-night?'

'Why, yes, they do,' she cried; and, throwing her arms round his neck, she kissed him full on the lips with all her old girlish impulsiveness.

Two days later a very low tide laid the rocks quite bare. Lazare, brimming over with the wild enthusiasm which always filled him at the outset of any of his new schemes, was impatient to be off to the sea-weed. So away he hurried, with bare legs and just a canvas jacket over his bathing-costume. Pauline went with him to share in his investigations. She, too, wore a bathing costume and the heavy shoes which she used when bound on shrimping expeditions. When they had got about half a mile from the cliffs, and had reached the centre of the spreading tract of sea-weed, still streaming with the water of the ebbing tide, the young man's enthusiasm burst forth as if he were only now discovering that immense crop of marine plants over which he and Pauline had rambled a hundred times before.

'Look! look!' he cried; 'what money we shall make out of it all; and nobody has ever thought of making any use of it before!'

Then he began to point out to her the different species with gleeful pedantry; the zosterias, of a delicate green and similar to long hair, stretching far away in spreading lawns; the ulvae, with large lettuce-like leaves of glaucous transparency; the serrated fuci and the bladder-bearing fuci, which grew in such thick profusion that they enveloped the rooks like thick moss. As they followed the tide, too, they came upon species of greater size and stranger forms, such as various kinds of laminaria, especially that known as Neptune's Belt, a girdle-like strip of greenish leather, with wrinkled edges, that looked as though it were made to circle some giant's waist.

'What wealth there is going to waste here!' exclaimed Lazare. 'How stupid people are! In Scotland folks are sensible enough to make some use of the ulvae at any rate, for they turn it into food and eat it. We here just use the fuci to pack fish with, and the zosteria to stuff mattresses; and as for the rest, it is simply turned into manure; and all that science does is to bum a few cartloads to extract soda from the residue.'

Pauline, in the water to her knees, felt perfectly happy amidst all the sharp saltness; and her cousin's explanations interested her extremely.

'So do you intend to distil all this?' she asked.

Lazare was very much amused with the word 'distil.'

'Yes; distil it, if you like to call it so. But the process is a very complicated one, as you'll see. However, mark my words. We have subjugated terrestrial vegetation to our use; we eat vegetables and fruit, and avail ourselves in other ways of trees and plants, don't we? Well, perhaps we shall find that we can turn marine vegetation to still greater profit when we seriously try to do so.'

Meantime they both enthusiastically gathered specimens, loading themselves and going so far out that they became drenched on their way back. Lazare went on pouring forth explanations, repeating all that his master, Herbelin, had told him. The ocean was a vast reservoir of chemical compounds, and the sea-weed was ever condensing in its tissues the salts contained in the water. The problem they had to solve was how to extract from the sea-weed all its useful components at small cost. He talked of taking the ashes which resulted from combustion—the impure soda of commerce—of sifting them, and finally extracting in a state of perfect purity the various iodides and bromides of sodium and potassium, the sulphate of soda, and the various salts of iron and manganese, so as to turn every particle of the material to profitable use. He waxed particularly enthusiastic over the fact that by the system which the illustrious Herbelin had devised nothing that could be of the slightest use would be lost. So there was an immense fortune before them.

'Good gracious! what a mess you're in!' cried Madame Chanteau, when they got home again.

'Never mind about that,' said Lazare gaily, as he flung his load of sea-weed on to the middle of the terrace. 'We are bringing you back five-franc pieces.'

The next day one of the Verchemont peasants was sent with a cart to bring back a whole load of weed, and the experiments were commenced in the big room on the second floor. Pauline was appointed assistant. For a month they went quite mad over the subject. The room was soon crammed with dried weeds, with jars containing floating sprays, and instruments of all sorts of odd shapes. There was a microscope on the table, and the piano was hidden beneath retorts and flasks; whilst the wardrobe groaned with the weight of technical works and collections that were perpetually being referred to. The experiments, made with small quantities of material with the most scrupulous care, gave encouraging results. Herbelin's cold system was based upon the discovery that certain bodies crystallise at very low temperatures, and the only thing required was to obtain the necessary lowness of temperature, whereupon each particular substance deposited itself in crystals successively, and thus separate from others. Lazare burned the weeds in a pit, mixed the ashes with water, and subjected them to the necessary temperature, which he obtained by a refrigerative method based upon the rapid evaporation of ammonia. He would afterwards have to carry out these operations on a large scale and transfer them from the laboratory to proper works, observing careful economy in the method of manufacture and the installation of the requisite plant.

On the day when he succeeded in extracting five distinct substances from his crude liquor, the room rang with cries of triumph. They had obtained quite a surprising proportion of bromide of potassium, and would be able to supply that popular remedy as plentifully as bread. Pauline danced wildly round the table; and then flew downstairs and burst into the dining-room, where her uncle was reading his newspaper and her aunt was marking table-napkins.

'There!' she cried, 'you can be as ill as you like now, and we can give you as much bromide of potassium as ever you'll want!'

Madame Chanteau, who had been suffering lately from nervous attacks, had been put upon a bromide *régime* by Doctor Cazenove. She smiled as she answered:

'Have you got enough to cure everyone?—for everyone seems to be out of sorts just now.'

The vigorous young girl, whose face beamed with robust health, spread out her arms as though she were casting the remedy to the four corners of the earth.

'Yes, yes!' said she, 'we shall make enough for the whole world. Neurosis is done for!'

After inspecting the coast Lazare decided that he would build his works near the Golden Bay. It answered all the necessary requirements. It had a wide spreading beach, flagged as it were with flat rocks, which facilitated the gathering of the weed; there was good communication from it by the Verchemont Road; land was cheap; the necessary materials were at hand; and it was sufficiently isolated without being remote. Pauline joked about the name which they had given to the bay on account of its gleaming sand. They did not think then, said she, that they would ever find real gold there, as they were going to do now. They made a capital beginning, bought about five acres of barren land at a low price, and obtained the Prefect's authorisation after only two months' delay. Then the building was commenced. Boutigny had already arrived on the scene. He was a little, ruddy-faced man of thirty, extremely common in appearance, and the Chanteaus did not take to him at all. He declined to live at Bonneville, saying that he had found a very convenient house at Verchemont; and the family's coldness towards him increased when they heard that he had brought there a woman whom he had probably picked up in some low haunt in Paris. Lazare shrugged his shoulders at what he called their provincial narrow-mindedness. She was a very pleasant sort of person, he thought, and had shown a good deal of devotion in consenting to bury herself in such a wilderness; but he made no further protest, on Pauline's account. What was expected from Boutigny was active surveillance and intelligent organisation of the work, and in this respect he showed himself to be all that could be desired. He was never idle, and had a perfect genius for management; under his direction the building soon sprang up.

For the next four months, while the work for the installation of the machinery was going on, the Golden Bay Factory, as they called it, became the goal of the young people's daily walk. Madame Chanteau sometimes went with them, but Matthew was more often their only companion. He soon grew tired, dragged his big feet along wearily till they reached the works, when he would lie down, with his tongue hanging out, panting like a blacksmith's bellows. The dog was the only one of the party who bathed now, and would rush into the sea whenever a stick was thrown for him to fetch, showing sufficient intelligence to turn his back to the waves when he seized the stick, so as to avoid swallowing the salt water. At each visit to the works Lazare used to hurry on the contractors, while Pauline made practical remarks which occasionally showed a good deal of common-sense.

The apparatus, constructed after designs made by Lazare himself, had been ordered at Caen, and workmen came thence to set it up. Boutigny was beginning to show a good deal of uneasiness at the rapid rate at which the estimates increased. Why couldn't they have commenced with as small a building as possible, and with merely the absolutely indispensable appliances, he asked. Why launch out into all those intricate workshops and rooms and all that elaborate machinery for a business which it would have been more prudent to have started on a small scale? They might gradually have extended it as they gained some experience of the conditions under which it ought to be carried on and the demand there might be for the output. But Lazare was carried away by his enthusiastic dreams, and, if he had been allowed to have his own way entirely, he would have added to the works a magnificent façade looking towards the sea and proclaiming the grandeur of his plans to the limitless horizon. Each visit only seemed to increase his feverish hopes. So, what was the use of being stingy, especially as they were going to make such a fortune out of the place? Thus the walk back was delightfully gay. Poor Matthew used to lag far behind them; and at times Pauline and Lazare would hide behind a wall, as delighted as little children when the dog, suddenly finding himself alone and fearing that he was lost, began hunting about for them in a state of comical alarm.

Every evening on their return they were greeted with the same question: 'Well, how's it all getting on? Are you well pleased?'

The answer, too, was always the same.

'Oh, yes; but it is not finished yet.'

This was a period of close intimacy between the two young people. Lazare showed a warm affection for Pauline, which a feeling of gratitude for the money she had advanced served to strengthen. Again, too, he gradually lost sight of her sex and regarded her as a boyish companion, a younger brother, whose good points became more manifest every day. She was so sensible and courageous, so cheerful and pleasant, that he could not refrain from looking on her with an unconfessed feeling of respect and esteem, which he tried to conceal even from himself by chaffing and teasing her. In the most unconcerned and casual way she had told him of her private studies and her aunt's horror, and he had experienced a moment's wonder and embarrassment as the girl, who knew so much already, turned her big candid eyes upon him. After that, however, a perfect understanding seemed to exist between them, and he talked freely and openly, as they worked together at their common studies. She was continually asking him questions, in which she appeared to have no other object than the simple acquisition of information, so that she might make herself useful to him. And she often amused him by the many gaps which she showed in her knowledge, by the extraordinary mixture of information with which she was crammed. When she showed herself to be labouring under some ludicrous misconception, Lazare broke out into such peals of laughter that she grew quite angry with him and told him that it would be much better if, instead of laughing at her, he would show her where she was wrong; and the matter generally terminated in a lesson.

Pauline, however, was changing; she often felt a vague uneasiness. At times, when Lazare pulled her about in his brotherly fashion, her heart would beat excitedly. The woman whom they had forgotten all about was awaking within her amid the pulsing of her blood. She often believed that she was on the point of falling into some serious illness, for she grew very feverish, and could not sleep. In the day-time, too, she felt weary and listless, but she made no complaints to her aunt.

One evening, after dinner, however, she began to talk about the absurdity and annoyance of dreams. How tiresome it was that one was compelled to lie on one's back, quite defenceless and helpless, a prey to all sorts of idiotic ideas and fancies! But what vexed her most, she said, was the absolute loss and annihilation both of the will and body power. Then her cousin, with his pessimistic views, also fell foul of dreams, as disturbing the happiness and serenity of utter unconsciousness. Her uncle, however, proceeded to distinguish between different sorts of dreams, saying that he liked to have pleasant ones, while he detested nightmares. Pauline spoke so strongly on the subject that Madame Chanteau, in surprise, began to question her. Then she stammered and hesitated, saying that her dreams were about all sorts of ridiculous things, trifles too vague to remember. And she was speaking the truth in this respect, for the incidents of her dreams remained obscure. She saw no one in them; and all she felt was like the kiss of the sea-breezes as they flew at her window in the summer-time. Every day Pauline's affection for Lazare seemed to increase. And this was not merely the instinctive awakening of womanhood after seven years' brotherly companionship; she also felt a need of devoting herself to somebody, and illusion showed him to her as the worthiest in intelligence and strength of all she knew. By slow degrees her old sisterly feeling was being transformed into love, with sweet touches of budding passion, secret thrills, furtive longings, all the fond delights that attend the heart's start upon its journey of affection, beneath the promptings of Nature. Lazare, protected by his former free-and-easy life in the students' quarter of Paris, had no curiosity to satisfy, and still looked upon her as a sister, never as an object of desire; while she, on the other hand, all virginal purity in this lonely spot where she knew no other young man, grew to worship him more and more, and to bestow herself upon him entirely. From morning till evening, when they were together, she seemed to derive life from his presence, and her eyes ever sought his, as she eagerly busied herself to serve him.

About this time Madame Chanteau became quite astonished at Pauline's piety. She saw her go twice to confession. Then all at once she seemed to take a dislike to Abbé Horteur, and for three Sundays even refused to go to mass, only resuming her attendance at the church subsequently in order that she might not displease her aunt. She gave no explanation of her conduct; but she had probably been offended and displeased by something the Abbé had said to her, for he was not a man of refined speech. It was at this period that Madame Chanteau, with her keen maternal instinct, discovered Pauline's growing love for Lazare; but she said nothing about it to anyone, not even to her husband. The knowledge of it came upon her as a surprise, for until now affection and possible marriage between the young people had not entered into her plans or thoughts. Like Lazare, she had gone on regarding her ward as a mere schoolgirl. Now, she told herself, it was her duty to look sharply after them; but she did not do so, really feeling very little interest or anxiety about a love which her son did not appear to return.

When the hot days of August came round, Lazare suggested one evening that they should have a bathe next day, on their way to the works. Madame Chanteau accompanied them on this occasion, in spite of the terrible heat. She sat down on the burning shingle, with Matthew by her side, sheltering herself beneath her sunshade, under which the dog tried to stretch his head.

'Hallo! where's she off to?' all at once cried Lazare, as he saw Pauline disappear behind a rock.

'She is going to get ready, of course!' said Madame Chanteau. 'Turn your head away. It isn't decorous; and she won't like it.'

He seemed quite astonished, then looked at his mother, and turned his back to the rock. Finally, he also began to undress, without saying a word.

'Are you ready?' he shouted, at last. 'What a time you are!'

Pauline ran lightly towards him, with a laugh which sounded a little forced. They had never bathed together since Lazare's return home. She wore a swimming-costume, made in a single piece and fastened about her waist by a belt. With her lissom figure she looked like a Florentine statue. Her arms and legs were bare, and her small feet, white as a child's, were shod with sandals.

'Well,' said Lazare, 'shall we go as far as the Picochets?'

'Yes, to the Picochets,' she answered.

'Don't go far!' cried Madame Chanteau. 'I shall feel so frightened if you do.'

But they were already in the water. The Picochets were a group of rocks which the high tide did not quite cover, and lay about half a mile off. The young people swam along leisurely, side by side, like a pair of friends out for a walk on some smooth straight road. Matthew followed them for a little way, but, when he saw them still going forward without sign of returning, he swam back to the shore and shook the water out of his coat, splashing the drops all over Madame Chanteau. Unnecessary exertion of this kind did not commend itself to his lazy nature.

'You are a sensible animal,' said the old lady. 'It is quite wicked of them to go risking their lives in this way.'

She could only just discern the heads of Pauline and Lazare bobbing up in the water like tufts of sea-weed moving with the waves. There was a pleasant swell, and they skimmed along with a gentle undulatory motion, talking quietly and examining the sea-weed that floated past them in the transparent water. Then Pauline, beginning to feel a little tired, turned herself upon her back and floated, gazing the while at the sky, like one lost amidst the blue immensity. She still retained all her old love for the sea that was now so softly cradling her. She loved its sharp fresh breath and its pure cold waves; and she yielded to it entirely, happy in its ceaseless rippling against her flesh, and revelling in the exertion of swimming, which kept down the throbbing of her heart. Suddenly, however, she gave a slight cry. Her cousin glanced towards her uneasily, and asked what was the matter.

'I'm afraid,' she said, 'that the bodice of my costume has split. I swung my left arm out too quickly.'

Then they both laughed. Pauline had begun to swim leisurely again, and was smiling a little uneasily as she contemplated the accident to her costume. A shoulder-strap had given way. Her cousin merrily told her to feel in her pocket, to see if she had not some pins about her. Soon afterwards, however, they reached the Picochets, whereupon Lazare mounted on a ledge of rock, as it was the custom to rest and draw breath before returning to the shore. But Pauline remained in the water and continued swimming round the rocks.

'Aren't you coming up?'

'No. I'd rather stay where I am.'

Lazare thought it was a mere whim of hers, and felt vexed with her. It was very foolish, he remarked. If she didn't come out of the water and rest a little, she would break down on the journey back. But she persisted in staying where she was, and did not even answer her cousin, as with the water up to her chin, she still swam on gently, seeking to hide the snowy whiteness of her naked shoulder, which shone, vague and milky, like the pearliness of a shell. Towards the open sea the rocks were hollowed out into a kind of grotto, where they had often played at being Robinson Crusoes. Far away on the other side Madame Chanteau, sitting on the beach, looked like a black insect.

'Take your own course, then, you foolish, obstinate girl!' cried Lazare, springing into the water again. 'I sha'n't help you, remember that.'

Then they slowly started on their return to the shore. They sulked with each other and would not speak. When Lazare heard Pauline beginning to pant, he told her that she had better turn upon her back again and float, but she did not appear to hear him. The rent in her costume was widening. At the slightest attempt to turn, her breast would have burst clear out of the water. Lazare, at last, apparently began to understand things, and, seeing how tired she was, and fearing that she would never be able to reach the shore without assistance, swam close to her, resolutely determined upon bearing her up. She tried to escape him, however, and to continue swimming by herself. But at last she was obliged to yield to him; and when they reached the shore again, Lazare was holding her in a close embrace.

Madame Chanteau had rushed down to the edge of the water in a terrible state of alarm, while Matthew stood in the sea up to his stomach, barking loudly.

'How wicked and foolish of you! I told you that you were going too far!'

Pauline had fainted. Lazare carried her on to the sand as though she were a child. And all at once she heaved a deep sigh and opened her eyes. As soon as she recognised her cousin, she burst out sobbing and nearly choked him with her hysterical embrace, as she kissed him full on the lips. She hardly knew what she was doing; she was acting under the influence of a sudden impulse of love, which the consciousness of her escape from death had sent thrilling through her.

'Oh! how good you are, Lazare! Oh! how I love you!'

He shook, almost unbalanced by the impetuosity of his cousin's kiss. While Madame Chanteau was dressing her, he went off of his own accord. The walk back to Bonneville was slow and painful, as both the young people were thoroughly worn out with fatigue. Madame Chanteau walked between them, thinking that the time had come for decisive action.

There were other causes for uneasiness in the family. The works at Golden Bay were now finished, and for the last week they had been testing the apparatus, with the most deplorable results. Lazare was obliged to confess that he had made some serious mistakes in several portions of it. He thereupon set off to Paris to consult his master, Herbelin, and came back in a very discouraged frame of mind. Everything would have to be made over again. The celebrated chemist had introduced great improvements into his method, which necessitated many alterations in the appliances. But then the sixty thousand francs were entirely spent, and Boutigny absolutely refused to advance another sou. From morning till night he talked sarcastically and bitterly of the foolish squandering of money over fads, with the pertinacity of a practical man whose warning has turned out correct. Lazare felt inclined to murder him. But what troubled him more than anything else was the thought of Pauline's thirty thousand francs lying lost in that abyss of disaster. His honour and pride revolted against the idea. It was impossible to think of it. More money must be got somewhere. They could not abandon an undertaking which would surely bring them millions eventually.

'Don't make yourself unhappy about it,' said his mother, as she saw him becoming quite ill with the worry of obtaining more capital. 'We haven't got so low yet as not to be able to raise a few thousand-franc notes.'

Madame Chanteau was working out a plan of her own. The idea of a marriage between Pauline and Lazare struck her as being very feasible and desirable. There was only some nine years' difference between their ages, and that was a thing one saw every day. A marriage, too, would be such a convenient way of settling matters. Lazare would be working for his wife, and need not trouble himself any further about the debt; moreover, he would be able to take from Pauline's fortune whatever further sums he wanted. At the bottom of her heart, it is true, Madame Chanteau felt some trifling scruples about the course she meditated, having a lurking fear of the possibility of an utter catastrophe, and the complete ruin of her ward. But she pooh-poohed the idea of such an ending to the great scheme. Wasn't it beyond doubt that Lazare was a very clever fellow who knew perfectly well what he was doing? He would make Pauline very wealthy one of these days, and it was really she who would benefit by the marriage. It mattered nothing that Lazare was without fortune at present. He was a fortune in himself.

The marriage was quickly agreed upon. One morning Madame Chanteau went into Pauline's room and sounded the young girl, who, with smiling tranquillity, confessed her love for her cousin. Then her aunt told her she must pretend to be tired, and in the afternoon went alone with her son to the works. As they came back she unfolded to him her scheme, telling him of his cousin's affection for him, the convenience and suitability of the proposed marriage, and the advantages to be derived from it. At first he was quite amazed. He had never entertained such a notion. The girl was quite a child, wasn't she? Then he became moved, and finally told his mother that he certainly liked Pauline very much, and would do all she wished.

As they came back into the house they found Pauline laying the table, for want of something else to do. Her uncle, with his newspaper laying on his knee, was watching Minouche, who was fastidiously licking her fur.

'Well, so there's a probability of a wedding, I hear,' said Lazare, concealing his emotion beneath an affectation of gaiety.

Pauline stood quite still, holding a plate in her hands, and blushed deeply, unable to say a word.

'Who is going to be married?' asked her uncle, suddenly, as though he had just awoke.

His wife had told him all about it in the morning, but the dainty way in which the cat was licking herself had absorbed his attention. However, he quickly remembered.

'Ah! yes, of course!' said he.

Then he looked at the young people mischievously, while a sudden painful twinge in his right foot made his lips twitch. Pauline had gently put the plate down, and, turning to Lazare, she said:

'If you are willing, I'm quite willing too.'

'There! that's settled, then. Give each other a kiss,' exclaimed Madame Chanteau, hanging up her straw hat.

The girl went up to Lazare, holding out her hands to him. He, laughing, took them within his own, and began to joke.

'You have deserted your doll, then? And this is why you hide yourself away so that one may not even see you washing your finger-tips! And it is poor Lazare that you have selected for your victim!'

'Oh! aunt, do make him give over, or I shall go away!' murmured Pauline, looking painfully confused and trying to make her escape. Little by little he drew her closer to him, playing with her as in the old days of their boy-like chumship. Then she suddenly planted a smacking kiss on his cheek, which he returned chancewise on her ear. But some secret thought seemed to cast a gloom over him, and he said sadly:

'It's a sorry bargain you are making, my poor child. You don't know what a very old man I am. Still, if you really wish it—'

The dinner was wildly gay. They all talked at once, and made all kinds of plans for the future, as though they were now meeting for the first time. Véronique, who had just come into the room as the engagement was being announced, went back into the kitchen and banged the door after her without saying a single word. When the dessert was laid upon the table, their noisy gaiety toned down a little and they began to talk about matters more seriously. Madame Chanteau said that the marriage could not take place for another two years, for she should prefer them to wait till Pauline was fully of age, so that there might be no risk of any suspicion that any advantage had been taken of her youth. Pauline looked aghast at this announcement of two years' delay, but her aunt's sense of honour touched her deeply, and she got up from her chair to go and kiss her. A date for the wedding was fixed; the two young people would have to learn to be patient, and meanwhile they would also be earning the first portion of their future millions. No doubt at all was felt as to their ultimate great wealth.

'Pull out the drawer, aunt dear,' said Pauline, 'and give him as much money as ever he wants. It is as much his as mine now.'

But Madame Chanteau would not hear of this.

'No, indeed. Not a single sou of it shall be spent unnecessarily. You know you can fully trust me for that, and I would rather have my right hand cut off than that you should be a loser. You want ten thousand francs for the works. Well, those ten thousand francs I will give you, and the rest I will keep tightly locked up. Not a sou of it shall be touched.'

'With ten thousand francs,' said Lazare, 'I am quite certain of success. All the heavy expenses are already paid, and it would really be wicked not to go on with it now. You will see presently. And you, my dear, I will have you dressed in a robe of cloth-of-gold like a queen on our wedding-day.'

Their happiness and gaiety were increased by the unexpected arrival of Doctor Cazenove. He had just been attending to the injuries of a fisherman, who had crushed his fingers underneath a boat, and the family insisted upon his remaining with them and having some tea. The great news did not appear to surprise him; but, as he heard the Chanteaus launching out enthusiastically in praise of the sea-weed scheme, he glanced uneasily at Pauline, and said:

'Yes, no doubt the idea is ingenious and worth a trial. But a safe investment in stock is better. If I were you, I should prefer being happy at once in a quiet sort of way—'

He stopped short on seeing a shadow pass over the young girl's face, and the warm affection which he felt for her induced him to speak against his own convictions.

'But money is very pleasant to have; so, perhaps, you had better make a lot of it. And I will certainly come and dance at the wedding. I will dance the Zambuco of the Caribbeans, a dance I don't suppose you ever heard of. You stretch out your arms like the sails of a windmill, and then keep striking your thighs as you dance round a captive, while he is being cut up and cooked by the women.'

The months flew past. Pauline regained all her old placid cheerfulness. Doubt and uncertainty were the only things that could seriously trouble her candid and frank nature. The confession of her love and the fixing of a date for her marriage with Lazare seemed to have put an end to the disturbing feelings that had assailed her. Her engagement caused little difference in her relations with Lazare; they both led their old life of familiar companionship; he ever busily engaged in the advancement of his great scheme, and quite protected from sudden passion by his former adventures in Paris, and she so simple and pure-minded in her virginity and knowledge that she was shielded as by a double wall of protection.

Sometimes, indeed, they would take each other by the hand, in that big disorderly room, and lovingly smile at one another; and while they read together some treatise on Marine Botany their heads would perhaps rest tenderly against each other; or, as they examined some flask brown with bromine or some purple specimen of iodine, Pauline would lean gently against Lazare, or bend down over the instruments that littered the table and piano and bring her face near to his, or ask him to lift her up so that she might reach the topmost shelf of the cupboard. But at those moments there was nothing beyond decorous permissible tenderness, such as might have been manifested openly before the members of their family. Madame Chanteau herself said that they behaved in an extremely proper and sensible manner; and when Louise arrived, with all her pretty airs and graces, Pauline did not exhibit the slightest jealousy.

A whole year passed away in this fashion. The works were now in operation, and the worries which arose kept Pauline and Lazare from thinking about anything else. The new appliances had been set up after considerable difficulty, and the first results seemed excellent. Certainly the yield was slight, but when the system should be brought to greater perfection, and all care and energy should be shown, there was no doubt that they would quickly reach an enormous output. Boutigny had already found great openings for their products; more than they could supply, indeed. Success and fortune seemed ensured, and this apparent certainty carried them off their heads. From their former despondency they now rushed to the other extreme, casting money by handfuls into extensions and alterations of the works, and never feeling the least doubt that they would find it all again, melted into a huge golden ingot. Every fresh outlay seemed only to urge them on to another.

On the first few occasions Madame Chanteau refused to take any money from the drawer without notifying Pauline.

'There are some payments to be made on Saturday, my dear,' she would say. 'Will you come with me upstairs, and settle what scrip we shall sell?'

'Oh! there's no occasion for that, aunt,' Pauline would reply. 'You can settle that yourself.'

'No, my dear, you know that I never do anything without consulting you. It is your money.'

In time, however, Madame Chanteau grew less rigid in this respect. One evening Lazare told her of a debt which he had concealed from Pauline, five thousand francs spent on copper pipes which had not even been used. She had only just returned from a visit to the drawer with her niece, so she went upstairs again by herself, on seeing the despair her son was in, and took out the extra five thousand francs, on a solemn promise that he would repay them out of the first profits.

But from that day her old strictness departed, and she began to take scrip out of the drawer without consulting Pauline. She found it a little unpleasant and humiliating, too, at her age, to be continually consulting a mere child, and she rebelled against doing so. The money would all be paid back to Pauline; and, even if it did belong to her, that was no reason why one should never be able to make the slightest move without obtaining her permission. So from this time she ceased to insist on Pauline accompanying her on her visits to the secrétaire. Pauline was really happier in consequence, for, in spite of her kind and generous heart, those constant withdrawals of money perturbed her. Her common-sense began to warn her of the probability of a catastrophe, and the feelings of prudence and economy which she had inherited from her mother were now roused in opposition to all the reckless expenditure. At first she was surprised at Madame Chanteau's silence, for she felt sure that the money was going the same way as before, with the one difference that she was not being consulted about it. After a little time, however, she felt that she preferred it to be so. It, at any rate, saved her the grief of seeing the bundle of papers grow smaller at each visit to the drawer. Between herself and her aunt there was but a quick exchange of glances at certain times; a steady anxious gaze on the girl's part, when she guessed some further abstraction, and a vacillating look from Madame Chanteau, who felt irritated that she should be obliged to turn away her head. Thus bitterness and dislike began to arise between them.

That year, unfortunately, Davoine became a bankrupt. Though the disaster had been foreseen, it was none the less a terrible blow for the Chanteaus. They still had their three thousand francs a year arising from their investments in stock; and all that they were able to save from the wreck of the timber business, some twelve thousand francs, was at once invested, so as to bring their total income up to three hundred francs a month. In the second fortnight Madame Chanteau was driven to take fifty francs of Pauline's money. The butcher from Verchemont was waiting with his bill, and she could not send him away without paying him. Then there were fifty francs wanted to pay for a washing-machine, and ten more for potatoes, and even fifty sous for fish. She came to the point of supplying the needs of Lazare and the works in wretched little sums, which she doled out day by day. Towards the end of each month she was often to be seen stealthily disappearing and then coming back again with her hand in her pocket, from which she reluctantly drew forth sou after sou, to make up the amount of a bill. The habit quickly grew upon her, and she soon depended entirely upon the contents of the drawer, helping herself to the money, whenever occasion required, without any hesitation. When she opened the lid of the secrétaire, however, that old piece of furniture would give a slight creak which used to affect her unpleasantly. The stupid old thing, she would say to herself. To think that during all those years she had never been able to buy a decent desk! The poor old secrétaire, which, when it had contained a fortune, had seemed to impart an air of wealth and gaiety to the house, now only irritated her, and she looked upon it as the abode of every evil, diffusing misfortune from every chink.

One evening Pauline ran into the house from the yard, crying, 'The baker's here! He says we owe him three days' bread, two francs and eighty-five centimes.'

Madame Chanteau began to fumble in her pockets.

'I shall have to go upstairs,' she murmured.

'Stay here,' said the young girl carelessly. 'I will go for you. Where's your money?'

'No, no, I'll go myself. You would never find it. It is put away.'

Madame Chanteau stammered out these words, and she and Pauline exchanged a silent glance, at which they both grew pale. There was a moment of painful hesitation, and then the aunt went upstairs, quite shivering with suppressed anger, and feeling sure that her ward knew perfectly well where she was going to get those two francs eighty-five centimes. Why, she asked herself, had she always insisted upon her presence when taking the money from the drawer? The memory of her old scrupulous probity quite angered her now, convinced as she was that her niece was following her in imagination, and watching her as she opened the drawer, took out the money, and then closed the secrétaire again. After she had come downstairs and paid the baker, her anger vented itself in an attack upon the girl.

'Good gracious! what a state your dress is in! What have you be doing with yourself? You have been drawing water for the kitchen, surely. Eh? Be good enough to let Véronique do her own work, if you please. Upon my word, I believe you have gone out of your way on purpose to make a mess of yourself. You seem to have no idea that your clothes cost money. I don't get so much for your keep that it is easy to make both ends meet!'

And so she went on. Pauline had at first made some slight attempt to defend herself, but she soon refrained, and listened to her aunt in silence, with an aching heart. She was quite conscious that the other's affection for her had been on the wane for some time, and when she was alone with Véronique she often gave way to tears. At those times the servant would rattle the saucepans and affect to be very busy, in order to excuse herself from taking notice or siding with one party or the other. Although she was continually growling at Pauline, she was now beginning to feel some qualms of conscience and to doubt whether the girl was receiving fair treatment.

When the winter came round again, Lazare grew quite despondent. Once again his whim had changed; he began to hate the works. There had been fresh pecuniary embarrassments in November, and he had fallen into a perfect state of panic. He had got over previous worries, but this one seemed to reduce him to despair, to render him hopeless of everything; and he began to revile science. The idea of making anything out of sea-weed was ridiculous! They might improve their system as much as they liked, but they would never be able to drag out of Nature anything that Nature didn't want them to have. He even fell foul of his master, the great Herbelin himself, who, having been good enough to visit the works at Golden Bay, had seemed quite distressed by all the elaborate appliances, which, he said, were perhaps on too large a scale to yield the results which had been obtained with careful small experiments in his own laboratory. The truth of the matter was, that, except in laboratory experiments on a small scale, no means was yet known of maintaining the low temperature which was necessary for the crystallisation of the various substances. Lazare had, indeed, succeeded in extracting a certain quantity of bromide of potassium from sea-weed, but, as he could not sufficiently isolate the four or five other bodies mingled with it, the result was failure. He felt quite sick of the whole business, and confessed himself beaten. One evening, when Madame Chanteau and Pauline besought him to be calm and to make one last effort, there came a very painful scene, when unkind recriminations were indulged in, bitter tears shed, and doors banged with such noisy violence that poor old Chanteau jumped up in his arm-chair in sheer fright.

'You will end by killing me!' the young man screamed, as he rushed away and locked himself up in his room, completely overcome by childish despair.

At breakfast-time the next morning he brought down with him a paper covered over with figures. Out of Pauline's hundred and eighty thousand francs, nearly a hundred thousand were already gone. Was there any sense in wasting more money? It would all be lost. He was still under the influence of the previous evening's alarm. His mother, too, now seemed inclined to back him up. She had never been able to go against him and vex him, even in his faults. It was only Pauline who still tried to discuss the matter. The announcement of the expenditure of those hundred thousand francs quite dazed her. What! they had taken more than half her fortune, and those hundred thousand francs would be utterly lost if they did not try to struggle on! But her arguments and persuasions were all in vain, and she went on talking to no purpose till Véronique had cleared the table. Then, to avoid breaking out into reproaches against them, she rushed off to her own room, quite sick at heart.

There was a short interval of silence while the embarrassed family lingered before the table.

'The girl is evidently avaricious,' said Madame Chanteau at last. 'It is a pitiful failing, but I won't have Lazare worried to death with all these bothers and vexations.'

Then Chanteau broke in timidly:

'I was never told that any such sum had been spent. It is dreadful to think of. A hundred thousand francs!'

'Well, what of it!' interrupted his wife sharply. 'It will be all repaid to her. If our son marries her, he is certainly capable of making a hundred thousand francs.'

Then they began to discuss the best way out of this difficulty. What had alarmed Lazare more than anything else was a statement given to him by Boutigny, which showed a most desperate condition of affairs. The debts amounted to about twenty thousand francs; and, when Boutigny saw that his partner was determined to retire, he expressed his intention of going to Algeria, where, said he, there was a splendid position awaiting him. But, afterwards, he came to the conclusion that his best coarse would be to get the works into his own possession. So he feigned such unwillingness, and so complicated the accounts, that in the end he managed to secure the site and buildings and apparatus against payment of the twenty thousand francs debts; and when, ultimately, Lazare succeeded in wringing out of him some bills for five thousand francs, to be paid at intervals of three months, he regarded it as quite a wonderful victory. On the very next day Boutigny sold off the apparatus and began to adapt the buildings for the manufacture of common commercial soda, to be made in the ordinary routine way, without any ultra-scientific process.

Pauline, who felt a little ashamed at her impulsive movement in favour of prudence and economy, became quite cheerful again and submissive, as though she recognised that she had done something for which she ought to seek pardon. When Lazare produced the bills for the five thousand francs, Madame Chanteau was quite triumphant, and insisted upon her niece going upstairs with her to see them put away in the drawer.

'There, my dear, that's five thousand francs we've got back. There they are: they are all for you. My son has refused to keep a single one of them to repay him for all the trouble he has had.'

Chanteau had been worried in mind for some time now. Although he dared not refuse his signature when it was asked of him, the way in which his wife was dealing with their ward's fortune filled him with alarm. That total of a hundred thousand francs was for ever ringing in his ears. How could they possibly make up such a deficiency by the time when the accounts would have to be examined? And the worst of it all was that Saccard, the surrogate-guardian, with the fame of whose speculations all Paris re-echoed, had just recalled Pauline's existence, after apparently forgetting all about her for nearly eight years. He had written to ask after her, and had even spoken of calling at Bonneville one day on his way to transact some business at Cherbourg. What explanation could they possibly give him, if he were to ask for an account of how matters stood, as he undoubtedly had the right to do? This sudden awaking after such a long period of utter indifference was very alarming.

When Chanteau at last spoke to his wife on the matter, he found that she was much more affected by curiosity than by alarm. For a moment, she felt sure that the truth of the matter was that Saccard, with his gigantic speculations, had suddenly found himself ruined, and had bethought himself of getting hold of Pauline's money to try and regain what he had lost. Then, directly afterwards, she began to wonder whether it was not the girl herself who had written to her surrogate-guardian out of some feeling of revenge. But, when she found that her husband expressed the deepest disgust at any such hypothesis, she began to indulge in complicated suppositions of the most unlikely kind. Perhaps, said she, that creature of Boutigny's, the hussy whom they had refused to receive at their house, and who was running them down in all the shops of Verchemont and Arromanches, had written anonymous letters to Saccard.

'But they may do what they like, for all that,' she said. 'The girl is not eighteen yet, but we have only to marry her straight off to Lazare, and the marriage will at once make her complete mistress of her fortune.'

'Are you quite sure of that?' asked Chanteau.

'Of course I am. I was only reading it in the Code this morning.'

Madame Chanteau had taken to studying the Code lately. Her conscientious scruples were not quite extinct, and she sought about her for reasons to allay them. Legal subtleties had a special interest for her just now in the growing decline of her honesty, which the temptation afforded by the large sum of money in her keeping was gradually and completely destroying.

However, she seemed to hesitate about actually bringing the marriage scheme to an immediate issue. After the financial disaster at the sea-weed works, Pauline herself had wished to hasten affairs. What was the good of waiting another six months till she should be eighteen? They had better get married at once, without waiting for Lazare to look out for other employment. She ventured to say as much to her aunt, who, put out by the girl's frankness, had recourse to a lie. She closed the door, and whispered that Lazare was really rendered very unhappy by secret trouble. He was extremely sensitive, and it would pain him very much to marry her before he was able to bring her a fortune, now that he had compromised her own. The girl listened to all this with great astonishment, quite unable to understand any such romantic delicacy. What did it matter? Even if he had been very rich, she would have married him all the same, because she loved him. Besides, how long would they have to wait? For ever, very likely. Then Madame Chanteau protested, saying she would do what she could to persuade him to overcome this exaggerated sense of honour, if Pauline would only keep quiet and not try to hurry matters; and, in conclusion, she made her niece swear to say nothing on the subject, as she feared that the young man might do something foolish, perhaps suddenly leave home, if he found that his secret had been discovered and discussed. Pauline, whom her aunt's remarks filled with uneasiness, then promised to remain silent and patient. Chanteau, however, continued to grow more and more afraid of Saccard, and one day he said to his wife: 'If it can be managed, Pauline and Lazare had much better be married at once.'

'There is no hurry,' she said. 'The danger is not at the door yet.'

'But as they are to be married some day—You haven't changed your mind about it, eh? It will kill them if they are separated.'

'Kill them, indeed! As long as a thing is not done, it need not be done at all, if it should turn out inadvisable. But they are quite free to do as they like, and we shall see if they continue in the same mind.'

Pauline and Lazare had resumed all their old comradeship, while the terribly severe winter kept them both confined to the house. During the first week Lazare seemed so melancholy, and so ashamed of himself and embittered by his ill-fortune, that Pauline lavished all her tenderness upon him and treated him as gently as though he were an invalid. She felt great pity for that big young man, whose whimsical, enthusiastic temperament, and mere nervous courage accounted for all his failures, and she gradually began to assume a sort of scolding mother-like authority over him. At first he entirely lost his head and vowed that he would go and work as a mere peasant; then he gave himself up to all kinds of wild projects for making an immediate fortune, and declared that he would not remain a burden on his family for another day. But time slipped on, and he continually deferred putting his plans into execution. Every morning he came down with some new scheme which would at once lead to the greatest wealth and honour. Pauline, frightened by her aunt's lying confidences, scolded him and asked him if he supposed that anyone wanted him to go bothering himself in that way. It would be soon enough for him to look out for something to do when the spring came, and, no doubt, he would speedily be successful; but, till then, it was necessary for him to rest. At the end of a month she seemed to have gained the better of him, and he fell into a state of dreamy idleness and cynical resignation beneath what he called the burdens of life.

Every day now Pauline found some new trouble in Lazare which upset her. His previous outbursts of temper and his will-o'-the-wisp enthusiasm were preferable to this moody cynicism and bitter profession of scepticism. Pessimism acquired in Paris among fellow-students was reviving in him. The girl could understand that angry disgust at his failure—the catastrophe of the sea-weed scheme—lay at the bottom of his railings against life. But she was not able to divine the other influences at work in him, and had to confine herself to indignant protests when he reverted to his old philosophy—the denial of all progress and the futility of science. Wasn't that beast of a Boutigny on the high road to fortune with his wretched commercial soda? said Lazare. What was the good, then, of ruining one's self to make something better, to discover new laws and systems, when empiricism won the day? This was his constant strain, and he would finish by saying, with a bitter smile on his lips, that the only good thing science could do would be to discover a way to blow the whole universe into atoms by means of some colossal cartridge. Then he frigidly jested on the will-power that directs the world and the blind folly of wishing to live. All life, he said, was pain and trouble, and he adopted the doctrine of the Hindoo fakirs, that annihilation was the supreme blessing. When Pauline heard him affecting a horror and disgust of all active motion, and predicting the ultimate self-extinction of the nations, who one day—when their intelligence was highly enough developed to enable them to realise the imbecile, miserable part which an unknown power made them play—would refuse to beget fresh generations, she became indignant and tried to find arguments to confute him; but all to no avail, for she was quite ignorant of these matters, and, as her cousin told her, did not possess a metaphysical head. Still, she would not allow she was beaten, and roundly sent Schopenhauer to the devil when Lazare wanted to read some extracts from his works to her. Schopenhauer, indeed! A man who had written such horrid lies about women! If he had not shown a little affection for animals she would have strangled him! Vigorous with robust health herself, and full of cheerfulness and hope for the morrow, she at last reduced her cousin to silence by her merry laughter and youthful freshness.

'Stop! stop!' she would cry. 'You are talking nonsense. We will think about dying when we have grown old.'

The idea of death, which she spoke of so lightly, always affected him very painfully, and he quickly turned the conversation, after murmuring:

'People die at all ages.'

Pauline at last understood that the thought of death was terrible to Lazare. She called to mind his fear-stricken cry that night as they lay on the beach gazing at the stars. At the mention of certain things she saw him turn sickly pale, shut himself up in moody silence, as though he were concealing some disease whose existence he dared not confess. She was greatly surprised at the fear of personal extinction felt by this pessimist, who talked about snuffing out the stars like so many candles amid the wreck of the whole universe. This mental disease of Lazare's was of old standing, and the girl did not guess the dangerous hold that it had obtained upon her cousin. As he grew older, Lazare had seen death rise before him. Till he was twenty years of age but a faint chill had touched him when he went to bed. But now he could not lay his head on his pillow without the thought of Nevermore freezing his very blood. He tossed about, a prey to sleeplessness, and could not resign himself to the fatal necessity which presented itself so lugubriously to his imagination.

And when, from sheer exhaustion, he had at last fallen asleep, he would awake with a start, and spring up in bed, his eyes staring wildly with terror and his hands clutching one another, as he gasped in the darkness: 'O my God! my God!' He would pant for breath and believe that he was dying; and it was not till he had struck a light and thoroughly awakened himself that he regained anything like calmness. After these outbreaks of panic he always retained a feeling of shame that he had allowed himself to cry out to a God whose existence he denied, that he had yielded to the hereditary weakness of the human race in calling amidst its powerlessness for help. But every night he suffered in this way, and even during the daytime a chance word or a momentary thought, arising from something he saw or read, sufficed to throw him into a state of terror. One evening, as Pauline was reading a newspaper to her uncle, Lazare hastily rushed from the room, completely upset by the fancies of some story-teller who pictured the skies of the twentieth century filled with troops of balloons conveying travellers from continent to continent. He had thought that he would no longer be living then, that his eyes would never gaze upon those balloons, which vanished into far-away centuries, the idea of whose revolution, after his own complete extinction, filled him with anguish. It was to no purpose that philosophers reminded him that not a spark of life is ever utterly lost; the *Ego* within him ragefully refused to accept its fate. These inward struggles had already deprived him of his former cheerfulness; and when Pauline, who could not always follow the twists and turns of his morbid mind, looked at him at those times when tormenting shame prompted him to conceal his anguish, her heart melted with compassion; she burned to show her love and do all she could to make him happier.

Their days were spent in the big room on the second floor, amidst a litter of sea-weed, bottles, jars, and instruments, which Lazare had never had the energy to clear away. The sea-weed was falling to pieces and the bottles were growing discoloured, while the instruments were getting damaged by neglect. But in all this disorder Pauline and Lazare were alone and warm. Frequently did the December rains beat upon the slates of the roof from morning till night, while the west wind roared organ-like through the crevices of the woodwork. Whole weeks passed without sight of the sun, and there was nothing for the eye to rest upon save the grey sea—a grey immensity, in which the earth seemed to be melting away. Pauline found amusement for her unoccupied hours in classifying a collection of *floridae* which she had gathered during the previous spring. At first Lazare, with his utter *ennui,* had just watched her as she mounted the delicate forms, whose soft blues and reds showed like water-colours; but afterwards, growing weary of his idleness, and forgetting his theory of inaction, he unearthed the piano from the litter of damaged appliances and dirty bottles beneath which it was buried. A week later his passion for music had resumed all its old sway over him. It was a revival of the artistic sense which lay beneath his failure as a scientist and a manufacturer. One morning, as he was playing his March of Death, the idea of the great symphony on Grief, which he had once thought of composing, excited him again. All that had been already written, except the March, was worthless, he thought; and the March was the only portion he would retain. But what a magnificent subject it was—what a task to perform! And how he might embody all his philosophy in it! He would commence with the creation of life by the selfish caprice of some superior power. Then would come the delusiveness of happiness and the mockery of life in striking passages, an embrace of lovers, a massacre of soldiers, and the death of a God upon the cross. Throughout everything a cry of woe should ascend; the groans of humankind should mount upwards to the skies, until came the final hymn of deliverance, a hymn whose melting sweetness should express all the happiness that came of universal annihilation.

The next morning he set enthusiastically to work, jingling, strumming on the piano, and covering sheets of paper with black bars. As the instrument was in a more feeble condition than ever, he sang the notes himself in a droning manner. Never had any of his previous fads taken such strong hold of him. He was so completely absorbed that he forgot his meals, and all but deafened poor Pauline, who, in her desire to please him, pretended that she liked it all very much, and neatly recopied portions of the score. This time he was quite sure that he had a masterpiece in hand.

But by-and-by his enthusiasm flagged. He had the whole score written except the introduction, and inspiration for that failed him. He would have to let it wait for a time, he said, and he smoked cigarettes, while his manuscript lay upon the table in front of him. Pauline played little bits from it on the piano, with all a beginner's clumsiness. It was now that the intimacy between the two young people began to assume a dangerous character. Lazare's brain was no longer occupied; and, shut up with Pauline in a state of idleness, he began to feel for her a warmer passion than before. She was so light-hearted and merry; so affectionate and devoted. At first he thought that all he felt was a mere impulse of gratitude, an amplification of that fraternal affection with which she had inspired him ever since childhood. But by degrees passion, hitherto dormant, awoke into life. In that younger brother he was at last beginning to recognise a woman; and he flushed as she did when he brushed against her. If their hands happened to meet, they both looked confused and their breath came quickly, while their cheeks crimsoned. And thus all the time they now spent alone together they felt troubled and ill at ease.

Sometimes, to relieve them from embarrassment, Pauline would begin to joke with all the frank boldness of her innocent, though well-read mind.

'By the way,' said she, one day, 'did I tell you that I dreamed that your favourite Schopenhauer had received tidings in the other world of our marriage, and that his ghost came to pay us a visit?'

Lazare laughed uneasily. He understood very well that she was poking fun at his inconsistencies, but his whole being was now thrilled with tenderness, which carried all his distaste for existence away.

'Don't be naughty, dear,' he said. 'You know that I love you.'

She assumed a chiding look.

'I am afraid you are inclined to put off the universal deliverance. You are grovelling in egotism and delusions again.'

'Hold your tongue, you wicked tease!'

He sprang up and chased her round the room, as she continued to hurl at him fragments of pessimistic philosophy with all the solemnity of a doctor of the Sorbonne. But when he caught hold of her, he no longer dared to keep her within his grasp, and pinch her for punishment as in olden time.

One day when he was chasing her round the room, and had succeeded in getting close, he clutched her by the waist. She broke into a ringing laugh, while he, holding her against the wardrobe, quivered with excitement as he felt her struggling.

'Ah! I have got you this time!' he cried.

Their faces were touching, and she still laughed, though in an uneasy manner.

'Please let me go,' she entreated. 'I won't be naughty any more.'

He roughly planted a kiss on her lips. Then the whole room appeared to swim round them and a hot feverish gust seemed to sweep them into space. She staggered, and then, with a sudden effort, released herself from her cousin's grasp. For a moment they both stood silent and confused, their cheeks crimson as they avoided each other's glance. At last Pauline dropped upon a chair to get her breath.

'You have hurt me, Lazare,' she said, speaking as though she were seriously displeased with him.

From that day he guarded himself from contact with her. His sense of honour rebelled against the thought of any disgraceful lapse; he was quite conscious that in heart and soul she was entirely his own; but he felt that respect and protection were her due, and that in dangerous dallying his would be the guilt alone. However, this very struggle on his part only served to increase his love. Everything lately had tended to fan its flame: the idleness of the first few weeks, his assumed indifference as to what became of him, his disgust with life, through which sprang a fresh passionate desire of life and love and even suffering, as occupation for his empty hours. And then music finally transported his mind, carrying him away to a land of dreams on spreading wings of melody. He began to believe that a mighty passion possessed him, and vowed to cultivate it for his genius' sake. He could no longer doubt it. He would be a great musician, for he need only hearken to the promptings of his heart. Everything then appeared to him purified; he felt content to worship Pauline on his knees, and did not even think of hurrying on their marriage.

'Come and read this letter I have just received,' said Chanteau in alarm one day to his wife, who had just come up from the village.

It was another letter from Saccard, and quite a threatening one. Ever since November he had been asking for a statement of the accounts of Pauline's fortune, and, as the Chanteaus had only replied by evasions and subterfuges, he now announced that he meant to lay the matter before the family council. Madame Chanteau, though she would not confess it, was quite as alarmed as her husband.

'The wretch!' she growled, when she had read the letter.

They looked at each other, quite pale and without finding a word to say. They already seemed to hear in that lifeless little dining-room the echoes of a disgraceful lawsuit.

'There must be no more dilly-dallying,' resumed Chanteau. 'We must marry the girl at once, since marriage releases her from all control.'

But to his wife this expedient seemed to grow more distasteful every day. She expressed various fears. Who could tell if the two young folks would get on well together? It is quite possible for people to agree as friends, and yet to make each other perfectly miserable as man and wife. Lately, she said, various unpleasant things had struck her.

'No,' she added; 'it would be wrong to sacrifice them for the sake of our own peace. Let us wait a little longer. And, besides, should we gain any advantage by marrying her now? She was eighteen last month, and we can apply for legal emancipation.'

She was beginning to feel quite confident again. She went upstairs to get the Code, and they both pored over it together. Article 478 tranquillised them, but they felt uneasy again as they read Article 480, for there it was enacted that the accounts of a ward's estate must be submitted to a curator appointed by the family council. It was true that she could easily manage all the members of the council, and make them do what she wanted, but whom could she choose as curator? The difficulty was to find some easy-going man, instead of Saccard, the surrogate-guardian.

Suddenly she had an inspiration.

'I've got it,' she cried, 'Doctor Cazenove! He is somewhat in our confidence, and he won't refuse.'

Chanteau nodded approval. He continued, however, to look at his wife, as though revolving some thought in his mind.

'And so,' he said at last, 'you will hand over the money? What is left of it, I mean?'

Madame Chanteau remained silent for a moment. Her eyes sought the Code, whose pages she turned with nervous excitement. Then with an effort she replied:

'Of course; and it will be a great relief to me to do so, after the accusations that have already been made against us. Upon my word, it is enough to make one suspect oneself! I would give something to see the tiresome papers removed from my secrétaire to-night. And, anyway, we should always have to give them up to her.'

The next day, when Doctor Cazenove made his usual Saturday round in Bonneville, she mentioned the great service they awaited from his friendship. She made an open breast of the situation, and told him how the money had been swallowed up in the sea-weed works, without the family council having been consulted in the matter, Then she dwelt upon the intended marriage and the sad possibility of the bonds of affection which united them all together being torn asunder by the scandal of a law-suit.

Before promising his assistance the doctor desired to have an interview with Pauline. He had long suspected that she was being taken advantage of, and that her fortune was being gradually frittered away; and, though he had hitherto said nothing for fear of causing her pain, he felt that now, as he was being invited to become an accomplice, it was his duty to warn her. The interview took place in the girl's own room. At the commencement of the conversation her aunt was present. She had accompanied the Doctor to declare that the marriage now depended entirely on Pauline's emancipation from the family council's control, as Lazare would never consent to marry as long as it was possible for others to accuse him of doing so for the mere purpose of avoiding an examination of the accounts. Then she left the room, saying that she did not wish to do anything to affect the decision of the dear girl whom she already regarded as her darling daughter. Pauline, quite overcome with emotion, immediately begged the Doctor to render them the delicate service the necessity of which had just been made clear to him. It was to no purpose that Cazenove tried to explain the exact position of affairs to her, to show her that she was despoiling herself, reducing herself to a condition of absolute dependence, or that he revealed his own fears for the future—perfect ruin, possible ingratitude and suffering. At every gloomy suggestion she uttered indignant protests, refused to listen further, and showed a feverish haste to complete the sacrifice.

'No! no! don't try to make me regret things. I am really very avaricious at heart, though I don't let it appear. It has given me a world of trouble to conquer myself. Let them have everything. If they will only give me their love, they may have all that belongs to me!'

'And so,' asked the Doctor, 'it is affection for your cousin that leads you to strip yourself of your fortune?'

She blushed and did not reply.

'But suppose that after a time your cousin should cease to love you?'

She stared at him with a frightened look. Her eyes filled with big tears, and a cry of protesting love burst from her heart. 'No! no! Why do you torture me like this?'

Then Doctor Cazenove consented to do as she wished.

He could not summon up the courage to amputate that generous heart of the illusions of love. Trouble would come to her soon enough.

Madame Chanteau conducted the campaign with astonishing brilliancy of intrigue. That struggle made her feel quite young again. She set off to Paris once more, taking along with her all the necessary powers and authorisations. She quickly won the members of the family council over to her own way of thinking. Those good people, indeed, had never troubled about their duties; they showed the indifference usual in such matters. The members of the council who came from Quenu's side of the family, cousins Naudet, Liardin, and Delorme, agreed with her at once; and as for the three on Lisa's side, it was only upon Octave Mouret that she had to expend any argument; the others, Claude Lantier and Rambaud, who were both then living at Marseilles, contented themselves with forwarding her their written consent. To all of them she poured out a moving, if somewhat confused, story, and spoke of the old Arromanches surgeon's affection for Pauline, and his manifest intention to leave her all his money should he be permitted to take her under his care. As for Saccard, he, too, acquiesced, as the others had done, after Madame Chanteau had paid him three visits and suggested a brilliant new idea to him, the formation of a ring in Normandy butter. Pauline's emancipation was formally pronounced by the family council, and the ex-naval surgeon Cazenove, of whom the Justice of the Peace had received the most satisfactory account, was nominated trustee.

A fortnight after Madame Chanteau's return to Bonneville the auditing of the guardianship accounts took place in the simplest manner. The Doctor had lunched with them, and they sat lingering round the table, discussing the latest news from Caen, whence Lazare had just returned after a two days' visit, taken thither by the threat of an action on the part of 'that scamp Boutigny.'

'By the way,' added the young man, 'Louise will give you all a surprise when you see her next week. When I saw her, I positively didn't recognise her. She is living with her father now, and has grown into quite a fashionable young lady. We had a very merry laugh over it.'

Pauline looked at him, feeling some surprise at the warmth of his tone.

'Talking of Louise,' interrupted Madame Chanteau, 'reminds me that I travelled with a lady from Caen who knew the Thibaudiers. I was quite thunderstruck when she told me that Thibaudier would give his daughter a dowry of a hundred thousand francs. With the other hundred thousand which she had from her mother the girl will have two hundred thousand. Two hundred thousand francs! She will be quite wealthy!'

'She could do very well without all that,' said Lazare, 'for she's quite charming. And so kittenish in her ways!'

A gloomy expression thereupon came into Pauline's eyes, and her lips twitched nervously. However, the Doctor, who had never ceased watching her, lifted up his little glass of rum, saying:

'Ah, we haven't clinked glasses yet! Here's to your health, my young friends! Get married quickly and have plenty of children.'

Without a smile Madame Chanteau slowly raised her glass; while her husband, to whom liqueurs were forbidden, contented himself with nodding his head approvingly. Lazare, however, had just caught hold of Pauline's hand with such an expression of affection that all the blood in her heart had come pulsing to her cheeks. Was she not, indeed, his good angel, whose love for him he would adorn with the brilliance of genius? She returned the pressure of his grasp. Then they all clinked glasses.

'To your hundredth birthday!' continued the Doctor, who considered that a hundred years was a good and proper age for a man to reach.

Lazare turned pale. The mention of those hundred years sent a painful thrill through him, reminding him of the time when he would have ceased to exist, the dread of which everlastingly lurked within his mind. In a hundred years where would he be, indeed? And what would he be? What stranger would be seated drinking wine at that table where he now sat? He raised his little glass with a trembling hand; while Pauline, who had grasped hold of the other, pressed it with a kind of maternal encouragement, as though she had seen the icy quiver of 'Nevermore!' passing over his pallid face. After a short interval of silence Madame Chanteau said very seriously, 'And now suppose we get our business over?'

She had settled that the formalities should be gone through in her own room. It would lend additional solemnity to them, she thought. Chanteau had been able to walk better since he had begun to take salicylic acid. With the help of the banisters he climbed the stairs behind his wife. Lazare talked about going on to the terrace to smoke a cigar there; but his mother called him back, and insisted upon his presence, which would only be seemly and proper, she said.

The Doctor and Pauline had already gone on before. Matthew, who looked at the procession with wondering eyes, followed in the rear.

'That dog is quite a nuisance!' cried Madame Chanteau, as she tried to shut the door. 'One can't go anywhere without being followed by him. Well! well! come in, then; I can't have you scratching outside. There! no one will come and disturb us now. Everything, you see, is quite ready.'

Some pens and an inkstand were all ready laid upon the table. In the room one found all the closeness and mournful silence that clings to places that are rarely occupied. Only Minouche spent her idle hours there, when she could manage to glide inside of a morning; and just now she happened to be lying asleep on the middle of the eider-down quilt. She raised her head, in surprise at the invasion, and stared at the new-comers with her green eyes.

'Sit down! Sit down!' said Chanteau. Then things were quickly settled. Madame Chanteau refrained from all share in the proceedings, leaving her husband to play the part in which she had been carefully coaching him since the day before. In conformity with the requirements of the law, the latter, ten days previously, had delivered to Pauline and the Doctor the accounts of his guardianship in a bulky volume, where the expenses were noted on one page and the receipts on the other. Everything was charged for, not only Pauline's board and lodging, but also the cost of the journeys to Paris and Caen. All that had to be done was to accept the accounts by a private deed. But Cazenove, taking his office of curator somewhat seriously, wanted an explanation about some of the expenses that had been incurred in connection with the sea-weed works, and compelled Chanteau to enter into details. Pauline cast a supplicating glance at the Doctor. What was the use of all this? She herself had assisted in the preparation of the accounts, which her aunt had copied out in her most elegant English—that is, angular—handwriting.

Meantime Minouche had sat up on the eider-down quilt, the better to view these strange proceedings. Matthew, after lying with his huge head stretched out on the carpet with an air of great wisdom, had just thrown himself on his back and was rolling and twisting about with noisy manifestations of joy.

'Oh, do make him be still, Lazare!' cried Madame Chanteau, quite impatient of the disturbance. 'One can't hear one's self speak!'

The young man was looking out of the window, following a far-off white sail with his eyes in order to conceal his embarrassment. He experienced a feeling of deep shame as he listened to his father, who was giving a detailed account of the money lost in the works.

'Make a little less noise, Matthew!' he cried, reaching out his foot.

The dog thought he was going to have his belly rubbed, a proceeding which he dearly loved, and he grew more demonstrative than ever. Happily, there was now nothing more to be done than to affix the signatures. Pauline, with a stroke of her pen, hastened to signify her approval of everything. Then the Doctor, as if regretfully, scrawled a huge flourish over the stamped paper. Painful silence fell.

'The assets,' said Madame Chanteau, breaking the silence, 'amount, then, to seventy-five thousand two hundred and ten francs thirty centimes. I will now hand that sum to Pauline.'

She stepped towards the secrétaire and lowered the lid, which gave out the creak that had so often distressed her. But just now she was very grave, and, when she opened the drawer, they saw the old ledger-binding inside. It was the same as before, with its green-marble pattern stained with grease spots, but it was not nearly so bulky; as the scrip was removed it had grown thinner and thinner.

'No! no! aunt,' exclaimed Pauline, 'keep it!'

Madame Chanteau protested:

'We are giving in our accounts,' she said, 'and we must give up the money as well. It is your property. You remember what I said to you when I put it there eight years ago? We don't want to take a copper of it for ourselves.'

She drew out the papers and insisted on her niece counting them. There was scrip for seventy-five thousand francs, and a small packet of gold, wrapped up in a piece of newspaper, completed the balance.

'But where am I to put it all?' asked Pauline, whose cheeks flushed at the handling of so much money.

'Lock it up in one of your drawers,' her aunt replied. 'You are now big enough to take care of your own money. I don't want to see it again myself. Stay! if you really find it so troublesome, give it to Minouche, who is looking very attentively at you.'

Now that the Chanteaus had settled their accounts, their cheerfulness returned. Lazare, quite at his ease, began playing with the dog, making him try to catch hold of his tail, in such wise that he bent and twisted his spine and spun round and round like a top. Doctor Cazenove, for his part, had already entered upon his duties as trustee, and was promising Pauline to receive her dividends for her and advise her on the question of investments.

And precisely at that moment Véronique was bustling about amongst her pans down below. She had crept upstairs, and, with her ear at the keyhole, had overheard the statement of accounts. For several weeks past a slowly growing feeling of pity and affection for Pauline had been driving away her remaining prejudices against the girl.

'Ton my word, they have swindled her out of half her money!' she angrily growled. 'It's not right! Although she had no business to come and settle herself down here, still that was no reason why they should strip her as bare as a worm. No! no! I know what is right, and I shall end by quite loving the poor child!'

IV

On the following Saturday, when Louise, who had come on a two months' visit to the Chanteaus, stepped on to the terrace, she found the family there. The hot August day was drawing to a close, and a cool breeze rose up from the sea. Abbé Horteur had already made his appearance, and was playing draughts with Chanteau. Madame Chanteau sat near them, embroidering a handkerchief; and, a few yards further away, Pauline stood in front of a stone seat on which she had placed four children from the village, two little lads and two little girls.

'What! you have got here already!' cried Madame Chanteau. 'I was just folding up my work to go and meet you at the cross-roads.'

Louise gaily explained that old Malivoire had flown along like the wind. She was all right, she said, and did not even want to change her dress; and, while her godmother went off to see about her room, she hung her hat on the hasp of a shutter. She kissed them all round, and then, all smiling and caressing, threw her arms round Pauline's waist.

'Now, look at me,' she said. 'Good gracious! how we have grown! I'm turned nineteen now, you know, and am getting quite an old maid.'

And after a moment's silence she added rapidly:

'By the way, I must congratulate you. Oh! don't look so shy! I hear it is settled for next month.'

Pauline had returned her caresses with the grave affection of an elder sister, although in reality she was the younger by some eighteen months. A slight blush rose to her cheeks at the reference to her marriage with Lazare.

'Oh, no! you have been misinformed, really,' she replied. 'Nothing is definitely fixed, but it will perhaps be some time in the autumn.'

Madame Chanteau, when pressed on the subject, had indeed spoken of the autumn, in spite of her unwillingness to commit herself to the match, an unwillingness which the two young people were beginning to notice. She was again beginning to harp upon her old excuse for delay, saying that she should much prefer them waiting till Lazare should have acquired some definite position.

'Ah! I see,' said Louise, 'you want to make a secret of it. Well, never mind; but you'll ask me to come, won't you? Where's Lazare? Isn't he here?'

Chanteau, who had just suffered a defeat at the hands of the priest, here joined in the conversation, saying:

'Haven't you seen anything of him, Louise? We were expecting you to get here together. He has gone to Bayeux to make an application to the Sub-Prefect, but he will be back again this evening—almost directly, I should think.'

Then he turned to the draught-board to commence a fresh game.

'I move first this time, Abbé. We shall manage to get those famous dykes made, I fancy; for the department surely can't refuse to make us a grant to help on the undertaking.'

He was referring to a new scheme which Lazare had taken up with his usual enthusiasm. During the spring-tides of the previous March the sea had again carried away a couple of houses at Bonneville. Devoured bit by bit on its narrow bed of shingle, the village, it was clear, would be driven to the very cliff unless some substantial protecting works were quickly built. But the little place, with its thirty cottages, was of such slight importance in the world that Chanteau, as Mayor, had for the last ten years been vainly calling the Sub-Prefect's attention to the perilous position of the villagers. At last Lazare, spurred on by Pauline, whose great wish was to see her cousin actively employed, had conceived a grand idea of a system of piles and breakwaters which would keep back the ravages of the sea. However, money was wanted, and at least twelve thousand francs would be necessary.

'Ah! I must huff you, my friend,' said the priest, taking one of Chanteau's pieces.

Then he launched out into details of old Bonneville.

'The old folks say that there was once a farm below the church, quite half a mile and more from the present shore. For five hundred years the sea has been gradually eating away the land. It is surely a punishment for the sins of their ancestors.'

Pauline, however, had now returned to the stone seat, where the four young ones were waiting, dirty, ragged, and open-mouthed.

'Who is it you've got there?' Louise asked her, not daring to venture too near them.

'Oh! they are some little friends of mine,' Pauline replied.

The girl's active charity now spread all over the neighbourhood. She had an instinctive affection for the wretched, and she was never repelled by their forlorn condition. She even carried this feeling so far as to patch up the broken legs of fowls with splinters of wood, and to set bowls of pap outside at night for homeless cats. Distress of every kind was a source of continual occupation to her, and to alleviate it was her great pleasure. So the poor flocked round her with outstretched hands, just as pilfering sparrows swarm round the open windows of a corn-loft. All Bonneville, with its handful of fishermen thrown into distress by the sweeping spring-tides, came up to see the 'young lady,' as they called her. But it was the children who were her especial favourites, the little things with ragged clothes, through which their pink flesh peeped, poor, frail-looking, half-fed creatures, whose eyes glistened wolfishly at the slices of bread and butter that she brought out for them. The cunning parents took advantage of Pauline's love for the children, making it a custom to send her the most sickly and ragged that they had, in order that they might increase her commiseration.

'You see,' she said, with a smile, 'I have my day at home, Saturday, just like a fashionable lady, and my friends come to see me. Now, now! little Gonin, just give over pinching that silly Houtelard. I shall be cross with you if you don't behave better. Now, we will begin in order.' Then the distribution commenced. She lectured them, and hustled them about in quite a maternal manner. The first she called up to her was young Houtelard, a lad of some ten years, with a sallow complexion and a gloomy timid expression. He began to show her his leg. A big strip of skin had been torn from the knee, and his father had sent him to let the young lady see it, so that she might give him something for it. It was Pauline who supplied arnica and liniments to all the country round. The pleasure she took in healing had resulted in the gradual acquisition of a complete collection of drugs, of which she was very proud. When she had attended to the lad's knee, she lowered her voice and proceeded to give Louise some particulars about his relations.

'They are quite well-to-do people, those Houtelards, you know; the only well-to-do fisher-folks in Bonneville. That big smack, you know, belongs to them. But they are frightfully avaricious, and live real dogs' lives in the midst of the most horrible filth. The worst of it all is that the father, after beating his wife to death, has married his servant, a dreadful woman, who is even harsher than himself, and between them they are gradually murdering the poor child.'

Then, without taking notice of her friend's repugnance, she raised her voice again, and called another of the children.

'Now, little one, you come here; have you drunk your bottle of quinine-wine?'

This child was the little daughter of Prouane, the verger. She looked like an infant Saint Theresa, marked all over with scrofula, flushed and frightfully thin, with big eyes, in which hysteria was already gleaming. She was eleven years old, but seemed to be scarcely seven.

'Yes, Mademoiselle,' she stammered; 'I have drunk it all.'

'You little story-teller!' cried the priest, without taking his eyes from the draught-board. 'Your father smelt strongly of wine last night.'

Pauline looked extremely annoyed. The Prouanes had no boat, but made their living by catching crabs and shrimps and gathering mussels. With the additional profits of the vergership they might have lived in decent comfort if it had not been for their drinking habite. The father and mother were often to be seen lying in their doorway stupefied by 'calvados,' the strong, raw, cyder-brandy of Normandy, while the little girl stepped over their legs to drain their glasses. When no 'calvados' was to be had, Prouane drank his daughter's quinine-wine.

'And to think I took so much trouble to make it for you!' said

Pauline. 'Well, for the future, I shall keep the bottle here, and you will have to come up every afternoon at five o'clock. And I will give you a little minced raw meat. The doctor has ordered it for you.'

It was next the turn of a big twelve-year-old boy, Cuche's son, a lean and scraggy stripling. Pauline gave him a loaf, some stewed meat, and also a five-franc piece. His was another wretched story. After the destruction of their house Cuche had deserted his wife, and gone to live with a female cousin, and the wife was now taking refuge in an old dilapidated Coastguard watch-house, where she led an immoral life. The lad, who kept with her and shared the little she had, was almost starving, but whenever any suggestion was made of rescuing him from that wretched den he bolted off like a wild goat. Louise turned her head away with an air of disgust when Pauline, without the slightest embarrassment, told her the boy's story. She, Pauline, had grown up in a free unrestrained way, and looked with charity's unflinching eye upon the vices of humanity. Louise, on the other hand, initiated into knowledge of life by ten years spent at boarding-schools, blushed at the ideas which Pauline's words suggested. In her estimation these were matters which people thought of, but should not mention.

'The other little girl there,' Pauline went on, 'that fair-haired little child, who is so rosy and bonny, is the daughter of the Gonins, with whom that rascal Cuche has taken up his quarters. She is nine years old. The Gonins were once very comfortably off, and had a smack of their own, but the father was attacked with paralysis in the legs, a very common complaint in our villages about here, and Cuche, who was only a common seaman to begin with, soon made himself the master. Now the whole house belongs to him, and he bullies the poor old man, who passes his days and nights inside an old coal-chest, while Cuche and the wife lord it over him. I look after the child myself, but I am sorry to say she comes in for a good many cuffings at home, and is unfortunately much too shrewd and noticing.'

Here Pauline stopped and turned to the child to question her.

'How are they all getting on at home?' she asked.

The child had watched Pauline while the latter was explaining matters in an undertone. Her pretty but vicious face smiled slyly at what she guessed was being said.

'Oh, they've beaten him again,' she said, still continuing to smile. 'Last night mother got up and caught hold of a log of wood. Ah! Mademoiselle, it would be very good of you to give father a little wine, for they have put an empty jug by the chest, telling him that he may drink till he bursts.'

Louise made a gesture of disgust. What horrible people! How could

Pauline take any interest in such dreadful things? Was it really possible that near a big town like Caen there existed such hideous places, where people lived in that utterly barbarous fashion?[1] For, surely, they could be nothing less than savages, to thus trample under foot all law, both divine and human.

'There! there! I have had quite enough of your young friends,' she said, in a low tone, as she went to sit down near Chanteau. 'I should not mourn for them very much if the sea were to sweep them all away.'

The Abbé had just crowned a king.

'Sodom and Gomorrah!' he cried. 'I have been warning them for the last twenty years. Well, it will be so much the worse for them.'

'I have asked to have a school built here,' said Chanteau, feeling a little distressed, as he saw the game going against him; 'but there aren't people enough. The children ought to go to Verchemont, but they don't like school, and only play about on the roads when they are sent there.'

Pauline looked up in surprise. If the poor things were clean, she was thinking, there would be no necessity to attempt to make them so. Wickedness and wretchedness went together, and she felt in no way repelled by suffering, even when it seemed to be the consequence of vice. But she confined herself to asserting her charitable tolerance with a gesture of protest. Then she went on to promise little Gonin that she would go to see her father; and while she was doing so Véronique appeared upon the scene, pushing another little girl in front of her.

'Here's another, Mademoiselle.'

The new-comer, who was very young, certainly not more than five years old, was completely in rags, with black face and matted hair. With all the readiness of one already accustomed to begging on the high-roads she at once began to whine and groan:

'Please take pity upon me. My poor father has broken his leg—'

'It's Tourmal's girl, isn't it?' asked Pauline of Véronique.

But before the servant could reply the priest broke out angrily:

'The little hussy! Don't take any notice of her. Her father has been pretending to break his leg for the last five-and-twenty years. They are a family of swindlers, who only live by thieving. The father helps the smugglers. The mother pilfers in all the fields about Verchemont, and the grandfather prowls about at night, stealing oysters from the Government beds at Roqueboise. You can see for yourselves what they are making of their daughter—a little thief and a beggar, whom they send

---

[1] The English tourist goes cycling and snap-shotting through the picturesque Norman villages, never dreaming, as a rule, that he is amongst the most sottish and vicious of all the French peasantry.—ED.

to people's houses to lay her hands upon anything that may happen to be lying about. Just look how she is glancing at my snuff-box!'

The child's eyes, indeed, after inquisitively examining every corner of the terrace, had flashed brightly on catching sight of the priest's old snuff-box. She was not in the slightest degree abashed by the Abbé's account of her family history, but repeated her petition as calmly as though he had not spoken a word.

'He has broken his leg. Please, kind young lady, help us with a trifle.'

This time Louise broke out into a laugh. That little five-year-old impostor, who was already as scampish as her parents, quite amused her. Pauline, however, remained perfectly grave and serious, and took a new five-franc piece from her purse.

'Now, listen to me,' she said; 'I will give you as much every Saturday if I hear a good account of you during the week.'

'Look after the spoons, then,' Abbé Horteur cried, 'or she will walk off with some of them.'

Pauline made no reply to this remark, but dismissed the children, who slouched off with exclamations of 'Thank you kindly 'and 'May God reward you!'

While this scene had been taking place Madame Chanteau, who had just come back from the house, whither she had gone to give a glance at Louise's room, was muttering with vexation at Véronique. It was quite intolerable that the servant should take upon herself to introduce those wretched beggars. Mademoiselle herself brought quite sufficient of them to the house. A lot of scum, who robbed her of her money and then laughed at her! Of course the money was her own, and she could play ducks and drakes with it if she were so disposed, but it was really becoming quite immoral to encourage vice in this way. She had heard Pauline promise a hundred sous a week to the little Tourmal girl. Another twenty francs a month! The fortune of an emperor would not suffice for such perpetual extravagance!

'You know very well,' she said to Pauline, 'that I hate to see that little thief here. Though you are now the mistress of your fortune, I cannot allow you to ruin yourself so foolishly. I am morally responsible. Yes, my dear, I repeat that you are ruining yourself, and more quickly than you have any notion of.'

Véronique, who had gone back to her kitchen, fuming with anger at Madame Chanteau's reprimand, now reappeared.

'The butcher's here!' she cried roughly. 'He wants his bill settled; forty-six francs ten centimes.'

A pang of vexation curtailed Madame Chanteau's remarks. She

fumbled in her pocket, and then, assuming an expression of surprise, she whispered to Pauline:

'Have you got as much about you, my dear? I have no change here, and I shall have to go upstairs. I will give it you back very shortly.'

Pauline went off with the servant to pay the butcher. Since she had begun to keep her money in her chest of drawers the same old comedy had been enacted each time a bill was presented for payment. It was a systematic levy of small amounts which had grown to be quite a matter of course. Her aunt no longer troubled to go and withdraw the money herself, but asked Pauline for it, and thus made the girl rob herself with her own hands. At first there had been a pretence of settling accounts, and sums of ten and fifteen francs had been repaid to her, but afterwards matters got so complicated that a settlement was deferred till later on, when the marriage should take place. Yet, in spite of all this, they took care that she should pay for her board with the greatest punctuality on the first day of every month, the sum due in this respect being now raised to ninety francs.

'There's some more of your money making itself scarce!' growled Véronique in the passage. 'If I had been you, I would have told her to go and find her change. It is abominable that you should be plundered in this way!'

When Pauline came back with the receipted account, which she handed to her aunt, the priest was radiant with triumph. Chanteau was vanquished; he had not a piece which he could move. The sun was setting, and the sea was crimsoned by its oblique rays, while the tide lazily rose. Louise, with a far-off look in her eyes, smiled at the bright and wide-stretching horizon.

'There's our little Louise up in the clouds,' said Madame Chanteau. 'I have had your trunk taken upstairs, Louisette. We are next-door neighbours again.'

Lazare did not return home till the following day. After his visit to the Sub-Prefect at Bayeux he had taken it into his head to go on to Caen and see the Prefect. And, though he was not bringing an actual subvention back in his pocket, he was convinced, he said, that the General Council[1] would vote at the least a sum of twelve thousand francs. The Prefect had accompanied him to the door and had bound himself by formal promises, saying that it was impossible Bonneville should be left to its fate, and that the authorities were quite prepared to back up the efforts of the inhabitants. Lazare, however, could not help feeling despondent, for he foresaw all sorts of delays, and the least delay in the carrying-out of one of his schemes proved agony to him.

---

[1] The equivalent of the English County Council.—ED.

'Upon my word of honour,' he cried, 'if I had the twelve thousand francs myself, I should be delighted to advance them! For the first experimental proceedings, indeed, so much would not be necessary. When we do get the money voted, you will see what a heap of worries and delays we shall have to go through. We shall have all the engineers in the department down here on our backs. But if we could make a start without them, they would be obliged to acquiesce in what had actually been done. The Prefect, to whom I briefly explained our plans, was quite struck with their advantage and simplicity.'

The hope of overpowering the sea now thrilled him feverishly. He had felt bitter rancour against it ever since he had considered it responsible for his failure with the seaweed scheme; and, though he did not venture to openly revile it, he harboured the thought of coming vengeance. And what revenge could be better than to stay it in its course of blind destruction, and call out to it, like its master, 'Thus far and no farther'?

There was, also, in this enterprise an element of philanthropy which, joined to the grandeur of the contemplated struggle, brought his excitement to a climax. When his mother saw him spending his days cutting out pieces of wood and burying his nose in treatises on mechanics, she thought, with trembling, of his grandfather, the enterprising but blundering carpenter, whose useless masterpiece lay slumbering in its glass ease on the mantelshelf. Was the old man going to live over again in his grandson to consummate the ruin of the family? Then she gradually allowed herself to be convinced and won over by the son whom she worshipped. If he were successful, and, of course, he would be successful, this would be the first step to fame, glorious and disinterested work which would make him celebrated. With this as a starting-point he might easily soar as high as ambition might prompt him. Henceforth the whole family dreamt of nothing but conquering the sea and of chaining it to the foot of the terrace, submissive like a whipped dog.

Lazare's scheme was, as he had said, one of great simplicity. He proposed to drive big piles into the sand, and to cover them with planks. Behind these the shingle, swept up by the tide, would form a sort of impregnable wall against which the waves would break powerlessly, and, by this means, the sea itself would build the barrier which was to keep it back. A number of groynes, built of long beams carried upon strong rafters forming a breakwater in front of the wall of shingle, would complete the works. Afterwards, if they had the necessary funds, they might construct two or three big stockades, whose solid mass would restrain the very highest tides. Lazare had found the first idea of his scheme in a 'Carpenter's Complete Handbook,' a little volume with quaint engravings, which had probably been bought long ago by his grandfather. He elaborated and perfected the idea, and went into the matter pretty deeply, studying the theory of forces and the resistance of which the different materials were capable, and manifesting considerable pride in a certain disposition and inclination of the beams, which, said he, could not fail to insure absolute success.

Pauline once more showed great interest in her cousin's studies. Like the young man's, her curiosity was always aroused by experiments in strange things. But, with her more calculating nature, she did not deceive herself as to the possibility of failure. When she saw the tide mount up, her eyes wandered with an expression of doubt to the models which Lazare had made, the miniature piles and groynes and stockades. The big room was now quite full of them.

One night the girl lingered till very late at her window. For the last two days her cousin had been talking of burning all his models; and one evening, as they all sat round the table, he had exclaimed in a sudden outburst that he was going off to Australia, as there was no room for him in France. Pauline was meditating over all this by her window, while the flood-tide dashed against Bonneville in the darkness. Each shock of the waves made her quiver, and she seemed to hear, at regular intervals, the cries of poor creatures whom the sea was swallowing up. Then the struggle which was still waging within her between love of money and natural kindliness became unendurable, and she closed the window, that she might no longer hear. But the distant blows still seemed to shake her as she lay in bed. Why not try to attempt even what seemed impossible? What would it matter, throwing all this money into the sea, if there were yet a single chance of saving the village? And she fell asleep at daybreak dreaming of the joy her cousin would feel when he should find himself released from all his brooding melancholy, set at last perhaps on the right path, happy through her, indebted to her for everything.

In the morning, before going downstairs, she called him. She was laughing.

'Do you know that last night I dreamt that I had lent you those twelve thousand francs? "

But Lazare became angry and refused in violent words: 'Do you want to make me set off and never come back again? No! we lost quite enough over the sea-weed works. I am really dying of shame about it, though I told you nothing.'

Two hours later, however, he accepted Pauline's offer, and pressed her hands in a passionate outburst of gratitude. It was to be an advance and nothing more. Her money would be running no risk, for there was not the least doubt that the subvention would be voted by the Council, the more especially if operations were actually commenced. That very evening the Arromanches carpenter was called in. There were endless consultations and walks along the coast, with a perpetual discussion of estimates. The whole family went wild over the scheme.

Madame Chanteau, however, had first flown into a tantrum on hearing of the loan of the twelve thousand francs. Lazare was astonished, unable to understand. His mother overwhelmed him with strange arguments. No doubt, said she, Pauline advanced small sums to them from time to time, but, if this kind of thing were to go on, she would begin to think herself indispensable. It would have been better to have asked Louise's father for an advance. Louise herself, who would have a dowry of two hundred thousand francs, did not make nearly so much fuss about her money. Those two hundred thousand francs of Louise's were ever on Madame Chanteau's lips, and seemed to fill her with angry contempt for the remnants of that other fortune which had dwindled away in the secrétaire and was still dwindling in the chest of drawers.

Chanteau, too, instigated by his wife, pretended to be greatly vexed. Pauline felt very much hurt. She recognised that they loved her less now, even though she was giving them her money. There seemed to be a bitter feeling against her, which increased day by day, though she could not even guess the cause of it. As for Doctor Cazenove, he found fault with her, too, when she mentioned the subject to him as a matter of form, but he had been obliged to acquiesce in all the loans, the large as well as the small ones. His office of trustee was a mere fiction; he found himself quite disarmed in that house, where he was always received as an old friend. On the day when the twelve thousand francs were lent to Lazare he renounced all further responsibility.

'My dear,' he said, as he took Pauline aside, 'I cannot go on being your accomplice. Don't consult me any more; ruin yourself just as you like. You know very well that I can never resist your entreaties; but I am really very much troubled about them afterwards. I would rather remain ignorant of what I cannot approve.'

Pauline looked at him, deeply moved. After a moment's silence she replied:

'Thank you, my dear friend. But am I not really taking the right course? If it makes me happy, what does anything else matter?'

He took her hands within his own and pressed them in a fatherly manner, with an expression of affection that was tinged with sadness.

'Well! if it does make you happy! After all, one has to pay quite as much sometimes to make one's self miserable.'

As might have been expected, in the enthusiasm of his approaching struggle with the sea Lazare had entirely abandoned his music. There was a coating of dust upon the piano, and the score of his great symphony was put away at the bottom of a drawer; a service which he owed to Pauline, who collected the different sheets together, finding some of them hidden even behind the furniture. With certain portions of the work he had grown much dissatisfied, and had begun to think that the celestial joy of final annihilation, which he had expressed in a somewhat commonplace fashion in waltz time, would be better rendered by a very slow march. One evening, indeed, he had declared that he would re-write the whole work when he had the leisure.

His flash of desire and feeling of uneasiness in the society of his young cousin seemed to disappear when his musical enthusiasm drooped. His masterpiece must be deferred to a more suitable time, and his passion, which he also seemed able to advance or retard, must be similarly postponed. He again began to treat Pauline as an old friend or long since wedded wife, who would fall into his arms as soon as ever he chose to open them. Since April they had not shut themselves up in the house so much, and the fresh air brought life and colour to their cheeks. The big room was deserted, while they rambled about the rocky shore of Bonneville, studying the best situations for the piles and stockades. And, after dabbling about in the water, they came home as tired and as easy in mind as in the far-away days of childhood. When Pauline sometimes played the famous March of Death to tease him, Lazare would cry out:

'Do be quiet! What a lot of rubbish!'

On the evening of the carpenter's visit, however, Chanteau was seized with another attack of gout. He now had a fresh attack almost every month. The salicylic treatment, which at first had given him some relief, seemed in the end to add to the violence of his seizures. For a fortnight Pauline remained a close prisoner at her uncle's bedside. Lazare, who was continuing his investigations on the beach, then invited Louise to go with him, by way of freeing her from the cries of the sick man, which quite frightened her. As she occupied the guests' bedroom, the one just above Chanteau's, she had to stuff her fingers into her ears and bury her head in the pillows at night-time in order to get some sleep. But when she was out of doors she became radiant again, enjoying the walk immensely and forgetting all about the poor man groaning in the house.

They had a delightful fortnight. The young man had at first gazed on his companion with surprise. She was a great change from Pauline; she cried out whenever a crab scuttled past her shoe, and was so frightened of the sea that she thought she was going to be drowned whenever she had to jump over a pool. The shingle hurt her little feet, she never relinquished her sunshade, and was for ever gloved up to her elbows, being in a constant state of fear lest her delicate skin should be exposed to the sun's rays. After his first astonishment, however, Lazare allowed himself to be attracted by her pretty airs of timidity, and her weakness, that ever seemed to be appealing to him for assistance. She did not smell simply of the breezy air, like Pauline; she intoxicated him with a warm odour of heliotrope, and he no longer had a boy-like companion at his side, but a young woman, whose presence now and then sent his blood pulsing hotly through his veins. True, she was not as pretty as Pauline; she was older, and seemed already a little faded, but there was a bewitching charm about her; her small limbs moved with easy supple motion, and her whole coquettish figure seemed instinct with promises of bliss. She appeared to Lazare to be quite a discovery on his part; he could recognise in her no trace of the scraggy little girl he had formerly known. Was it really possible that long years at boarding-school had turned that very ordinary-looking child into such a disquieting young woman, who, maiden though she was, seemed by no means shy? Little by little Lazare found himself possessed by growing admiration, disturbing passion, in which the mere friendship of childhood disappeared.

When Pauline was able to leave her uncle's bedroom and resume companionship with Lazare, she immediately noticed a change between him and Louise, unaccustomed glances and laughs, in which she had no share. For the first few days she maintained a sort of maternal attitude, treating the pair as foolish young things whom a mere nothing was sufficient to amuse. But she soon grew low-spirited, and the walks they all took abroad seemed to weary her. She never made any complaint, she simply spoke of persistent headaches; but, later on, when her cousin advised her to stay at home, she became vexed, and would not quit him even in the house. On one occasion, about two o'clock in the morning, Lazare, who had sat up in his room working at a plan, thought he heard some steps outside, and opened his door to look. Thereupon he was astonished to see Pauline in her petticoats leaning over the banisters in the dark, and listening. She declared that she thought she had heard a cry downstairs. But she blushed as she told this fib, and Lazare did the same, for a suspicion flashed through his mind. From that night forward, without anything being said, friendly relations suffered. Lazare considered that Pauline made herself very ridiculous by pouting and sulking about mere nothings, while she, continually growing more gloomy, never once left her cousin alone with Louise, but kept a strict watch over them, and tortured herself with fancies at night if she had caught them speaking softly to each other as they walked home from the shore.

However, the work had begun. A body of carpenters, after nailing a number of heavy planks across a framework of piles, succeeded in completing a first buttress against the sea's attack. This was simply meant as a trial, which they hurried along with, in expectation of a flood tide. If the timbers should be able to resist the sea's approach, then the system of defence would be completed. It unfortunately happened that the weather was execrable. Rain fell continually, and all Bonneville got soaked to the skin in going out to see the piles rammed into the sand. Then, on the morning when the high tide was expected, an inky pall hung over the sea, and, from eight o'clock the rain fell with redoubled violence, hiding the horizon with a dense cold mist. There was immense disappointment, for the Chanteaus had been planning to go in a family party to watch the victory which their beams and piles would win over the attacking flood.

Madame Chanteau determined to remain at home with her husband, who was still far from well. Great efforts, too, were made to induce Pauline to stay indoors, as she had been suffering from a sore throat for a week past, and always grew a little feverish towards the evening. But she rejected all the prudent advice that was offered her, resolving to go down to the beach, since Lazare and Louise were going. Louise, fragile as she appeared to be, ever, so it seemed, on the verge of fainting, really proved a girl of great physical endurance, particularly when any kind of pleasure made her excited.

They all three set off after breakfast. A sudden breeze had swept away the clouds, and glad smiles hailed the unexpected change. The patches of blue sky overhead were so large, though they still mingled with black masses, that the girls refused to take any other protection than their sunshades. Lazare alone carried an umbrella. He would see that they came to no harm, he said, and would place them under shelter somewhere should the rain begin to fall again.

Pauline and Louise walked on in front. However, on the steep slope leading down towards Bonneville, the latter stumbled on the wet and slippery soil, and Lazare rushed up to support her. Pauline then followed behind them. Her high spirits quickly fell, as with a jealous glance she noticed her cousin's arm pressed closely against Louise's waist. The contact of the two soon absorbed her; all else disappeared— the beach, where the fishermen of the neighbourhood stood waiting in a somewhat scoffing mood, and the rising tide, and the stockade already white with foam. Away on the right arose a mass of dark clouds, lashed on by the gale.

'What a nuisance!' said the young man; 'we are going to have more rain. But we shall have time to see things before it comes on, I think, and then we can take refuge close at hand with the Houtelards.'

The tide, which had the wind against it, was rising with irritating slowness. The wind would certainly keep it from mounting as high as had been expected. Still no one left the shore. The new groyne, which was now half covered, seemed to work very satisfactorily, parting the waves, whose diverted waters foamed up to the very feet of the spectators. But the greatest triumph was the successful resistance of the piles. As each wave dashed against them, sweeping the shingle with it, they heard the stones falling and collecting on the other side of the beams with a noise like the sudden discharge of a cartload of pebbles; and this wall which was thus gradually building itself up seemed to guarantee success.

'Didn't I tell you so?' cried Lazare. 'You won't make any more jokes about it now, I think!'

Prouane, who was standing near him, and had not been sober for the last three days, shook his head, however, as he stammered: 'We shall see about that when the wind blows against it.'

The other fishermen kept silent. But the expression on the faces of Cuche and Houtelard plainly showed that they felt little confidence in all such contrivances; indeed, they would scarcely have felt pleased to see their enemy the sea, which crushed them so victoriously, beaten back by that stripling of a landsman. How they would laugh when the waves some day carried off those beams like so many straws! The very village might be dashed to pieces at the same time; it would be rare fun all the same!

Suddenly the rain began to fall; great drops poured from the lurid clouds, which had covered three-quarters of the sky.

'Oh! this is nothing!' cried Lazare in a state of wild enthusiasm. 'Let's stay a little longer. Just look! not a single pile moves!' While speaking he set his umbrella over Louise's head. She pressed to his side with the air of a frightened turtle-dove. Pauline, whom they seemed to have forgotten, never ceased to watch them. She felt enraged; the warmth of their clasp seemed to set her cheeks on fire. But the rain was now coming down in a perfect torrent, and Lazare suddenly turned round and called to her: 'What are you thinking of? Are you mad? At all events, open your sunshade!'

She was standing stiffly erect beneath the downpour, which she did not seem to notice. And she simply answered in a hoarse voice: 'Leave me alone. I am all right.'

'Oh! Lazare!' cried Louise, quite distressed, 'make her come here!

There is room under the umbrella for all three of us.'

But Pauline, in her angry obstinacy, did not condescend to notice the invitation. She was all right; why couldn't they let her alone? And when Lazare, at the conclusion of his fruitless entreaties, finished by saying: 'It's folly! Let's run to the Houtelards'!' she answered rudely, 'Run wherever you like. I came here to see, and I mean to stop.'

The fishermen had fled. Pauline remained alone beneath the pouring rain, with her eyes turned towards the piles, which were now covered by the waves. The spectacle seemed to absorb all her attention, in spite of the grey mist which was rising from the rain-beaten sea, obscuring everything. Big black marks appeared on her streaming dress, about her shoulders and arms, but she would not leave her place till the west wind had swept the storm-cloud away.

They all three returned home in silence. Not a word of what had happened was mentioned to Madame Chanteau. Pauline hurried off to change her clothes, while Lazare recounted the complete success of the experiment. In the evening, as they sat at table, Pauline became feverish, but she pretended there was nothing the matter with her, in spite of the evident difficulty she had in swallowing her food; and she even ended by speaking very roughly to Louise, who evinced solicitude in her caressing way, and perpetually asked her how she felt.

'The girl is really growing quite unbearable with her bad disposition,' murmured Madame Chanteau behind Pauline's back. 'We had better give over speaking to her.'

About one o'clock in the morning Lazare was roused by a hoarse cough, which sounded so distressingly that he sat up in bed to listen. At first he thought it came from his mother; then, as he went on straining his ear, he heard a noise as of something falling, and his floor shook. Forthwith he jumped out of bed and hastily put on his clothes. It could only be Pauline, who must have fallen on the other side of the wall.

He broke several matches with his trembling hands, but, at last, when he had succeeded in lighting his candle and came out of his room, he found the door opposite wide open, and the young girl lying on her side and barring the entrance.

'What is the matter?' Lazare cried in amazement. 'Have you fallen?'

It had just flashed through his mind that she was prowling about again, playing the spy. But she made no reply, and never even stirred; in fact, with her closed eyes, she seemed to him to be dead. There could be no doubt that just as she was leaving her room to seek assistance a fainting-fit had thrown her on the ground.

'Pauline, speak to me, I beg you! What is the matter with you?'

He had bent down and was holding the light to her face. She was extremely flushed, and seemed a prey to violent fever. Then all hesitation on his part vanished, and he took her up in his arms and carried her to her bed full of fraternal anxiety. When he had placed her in bed again, he began to question her once more, 'For goodness' sake, do speak to me! Have you hurt yourself?'

She had just opened her eyes, but she could not yet speak, and merely looked at him with a fixed gaze. Then, as he still continued to press her with questions, she carried her hand to her throat.

'It is your throat that hurts you, is it?'

At last, in a strange voice, that seemed to come with immense difficulty, she gasped:

'Don't make me speak, please. It hurts me so.'

As she said this she was seized with another attack of coughing, the same hoarse guttural cough that he had heard from his bedroom. Her face turned bluish, and her distress became so great that her eyes filled with tears. She lifted her hands to her poor trembling brow, which was quivering with the hammer-like throbs of a frightful headache.

'You caught that to-day!' he stammered, quite distracted. 'It was very foolish of you to act as you did, when you were already far from well!' But he checked himself, as he saw her looking up at him with a gaze of entreaty.

'Just open your mouth and let me look at your throat.'

It was all she could do to open her jaws. Lazare brought the candle close to her, and was with difficulty able to espy the back of her throat, which was dry, and gleamed with a bright crimson. It was evidently a case of angina, and her burning fever and terrible headache filled him with alarm as to its precise nature. The poor girl's face wore such an agonised expression of choking that he was seized with a horrible fear of seeing her suffocated before his very eyes. She was not able to swallow; every attempt to do so made her whole body quiver. At last a fresh attack of coughing threw her into another fainting-fit; and thereupon in a state of complete panic he flew off to thump at Véronique's door.

'Véronique! Véronique! Get up! Pauline is dying.'

When Véronique, half-dressed and scared, entered the girl's room, she found Lazare excitedly talking to himself in the middle of it.

'What a forsaken hole to be in! One might die here like a dog! There is no help to be had nearer than a couple of miles!'

He strode up to Véronique.

'Try and get someone to go for the Doctor immediately,' he said.

The servant stepped up to the bed and looked at the sick girl. She was quite alarmed at seeing her so flushed, and in her increasing affection for Pauline, whom she had at first so cordially detested, she felt a painful shock.

'I'll go myself,' she said quietly. 'That will be the quickest way. Madame will be quite able to light a fire downstairs, if you want one.'

Then, scarcely yet fully awake, she put on her heavy boots and wrapped a shawl round her; and, after telling Madame Chanteau what the matter was as she went downstairs, she set off, striding along the muddy road. Two o'clock rang out from the church, and the night was so dark that she stumbled every now and then against heaps of stones.

'What is it, then?' asked Madame Chanteau, as she came upstairs.

Lazare scarcely answered her. He had just been ferreting about in the cupboard for his old medical treatises, and was now bending down before the chest of drawers, turning over the pages of one of his books with trembling fingers, while trying to remember something of what he had formerly learnt. But he grew more and more confused, and perpetually turned to the index without being able to find what he wanted.

'It's only a bad sick headache,' said Madame Chanteau, who had sat down. 'The best thing we can do is to leave her to sleep.'

At this Lazare burst out angrily:

'A sick headache! A sick headache indeed! You will drive me quite mad, mother, by standing there so unconcernedly. Go down stairs and get some water to boil.'

'There is no necessity to disturb Louise, is there?' she asked.

'No, indeed, not the least. I don't require anybody's assistance. If I want anything I will call you.'

When he was alone again, he went and took hold of Pauline's wrist to try her pulse. He counted one hundred and fifteen pulsations; and he felt the girl's burning hand cling closely and lingeringly to his own. Her heavy eyelids remained closed, but she was thanking him and forgiving him with that pressure of her hand. Though she was unable to smile, she still wanted to let him understand that she had heard and was pleased to know that he was there alone with her, without a thought for anybody else. Generally, he had a horror of all suffering, and took himself off at the slightest appearance of indisposition in any of his relatives, for he was a shockingly bad nurse, and was so unable to control his nerves that he ever feared lest he should burst out crying. And so it was a pleasant surprise to Pauline to see him now so anxious and devoted. He himself could not have explained the warmth of feeling that was upbuoying him, or the necessity he felt of relying on himself alone to give her relief. The pressure of her little hand upset him, and he tried to cheer her.

'It's nothing at all, my dear. I am expecting Cazenove directly; but we needn't feel the least alarm.'

She still kept her eyes closed as she murmured, apparently still in pain: 'Oh! I'm not at all frightened. What troubles me most is to see you so much disturbed.'

Then, in a still lower voice, barely a whisper, she added: 'Have you forgiven me yet? I behaved very wickedly this morning.'

He bent down and kissed her brow as though she were his wife. Then he stepped aside, for his tears were blinding him. The idea occurred to him that he might as well prepare a sleeping-draught while waiting for the doctor's arrival. Pauline's little medicine-chest was in a small cupboard in the room. He felt a little afraid lest he should make some mistake, and he looked closely at the different phials; finally he poured a few drops of morphia into a glass of sugared water. When she swallowed a spoonful of it, the pain in her throat became so great that he hesitated about giving her a second. There was nothing else he could do. That spell of inactive waiting was becoming terribly painful to him. When he could no longer endure to stand beside her bed and see her suffering, he turned to his books again, hoping to find therein an account of her malady and its remedy. Could it be a case of diphtheritic angina? He had certainly not seen any malignant growth on the roof of her mouth, but he plunged into the perusal of a description of that complaint and its treatment, losing himself in a maze of long sentences whose meaning he could not gather, and striving to grope through superfluous details, like a child battling with some lesson he cannot understand. By-and-by a sigh brought him hurrying back to the bedside, with his head buzzing with scientific terms, whose uncouth syllables only served to increase his anxiety.

'Well, how is she getting on?' inquired Madame Chanteau, who had come softly upstairs again.

'Oh! she keeps just the same,' Lazare replied.

Then, in a burst of impatience, he added:

'It is terrible, this delay on the Doctor's part! The girl might die twenty times over!'

The doors had been left open, and Matthew, who slept under the table in the kitchen, had also just come up the stairs, for it was his habit to follow people into every room of the house. His big paws pattered over the floor like old woollen slippers. He seemed quite gay at all this commotion in the middle of the night, and wanted to jump up to Pauline, and even tried to wheel round after his tail, like an animal unconscious of his master's trouble. But Lazare, irritated by his inopportune gaiety, gave him a kick.

'Be off with you, or I'll choke you! Can't you understand, you idiot?'

The dog, afraid of a beating, and, it may be, suddenly grasping the situation, went to lie down under the bed. But Lazare's rough behaviour had aroused Madame Chanteau's indignation. Without waiting any longer she went down to the kitchen again, saying drily: 'The water will be ready whenever you want it.'

As she descended the stairs Lazare heard her muttering that it was abominable to kick an animal like that, and that he would probably have kicked her also if she had remained in the room. Every moment he went to the bedside to glance at Pauline. She now seemed to be quite overcome with fever, utterly prostrate; the only sign of life that came from her was the wheezing of her breath amidst the mournful silence of the room, a wheezing that began to sound like a death-rattle. Then wild unreasoning fear again seized upon Lazare. He felt quite certain that the girl would soon choke if help did not arrive. He fidgeted about the room on tip-toes, glancing perpetually at the timepiece. It was not three o'clock, and Véronique could hardly have got to the Doctor's yet. He followed her in imagination through the black night all along the road to Arromanches. By this time she would be passing the oak-wood; then she would cross the little bridge, and then she would save five minutes by running down the hill. At last a longing for tidings of some sort led him to throw open the window, though it was quite impossible for him to distinguish anything amidst the profound darkness. Down in the depths of Bonneville only a single light was gleaming, the lantern, probably, of some fisherman preparing to put out to sea. Everything was wrapped in mournful sadness, far-reaching abandonment, in which all life appeared to die away. He closed the window and then opened it again, only to close it quickly once more. He began to lose all idea of the flight of time, and was startled when he heard three o'clock strike. By this time the Doctor must have got his horse harnessed, and his gig would be spinning along the road, transpiercing the darkness with the yellow glare of its lamp. Lazare grew so distracted with impatience as he watched the sick girl's increasing suffocation that he started up as from a dream, when, at about four o'clock, he finally heard some rapid footsteps on the stairs.

'Ah! here you are at last!' he cried.

Doctor Cazenove at once ordered a second candle to be lighted, in order that he might examine Pauline properly.

Lazare held one of the candles, while Véronique, whose hair the wind had thrown into wild disorder, and who was splashed with mud to the waist, stood at the head of the bed with the other. Madame Chanteau looked on. The sick girl was in a state of semi-somnolence, and could not open her mouth without a groan of pain. When the Doctor had laid her back in bed again, he, who upon his first entrance had shown signs of great uneasiness, stepped into the middle of the room with an expression of relief.

'That Véronique of yours put me into a pretty fright,' said he. 'She told me such a lot of terrible things that I thought the girl must have got poisoned, and you see that I have come with my pockets crammed full of drugs.'

'It is angina, is it not?' Lazare asked.

'Yes, simple angina. There is no occasion for alarm at present.'

Madame Chanteau indulged in a little gesture of triumph, as much as to say that she had known that from the first.

'"No occasion for alarm at present"!' repeated Lazare, his fears rising again. 'Are you afraid of complications?'

'No,' answered the Doctor, after some slight hesitation; 'but with these tiresome throat complaints one can never feel quite sure of anything.'

He added that nothing more could be done just then, and that he would prefer waiting till the morrow to bleed the patient. But as the young man pressed him to attempt at any rate some alleviating measures, he expressed his readiness to apply some sinapisms. Véronique brought up a bowl of warm water, and the Doctor himself placed the damped mustard-leaves in position, slipping them along the girl's legs from her ankles to her knees. But they only increased her discomfort, for the fever continued unabated and her head was still throbbing frightfully. Emollient gargles were also-suggested, and Madame Chanteau prepared a decoction of nettle-leaves, which had to be laid aside, however, after a first attempt to administer it, for pain rendered Pauline unable to swallow. It was nearly six o'clock, and dawn was breaking when the Doctor went away.

'I will come back about noon,' he said to Lazare on the landing. 'Be quite easy. She is all right, except for the pain.'

'And is the pain nothing?' cried the young man. 'One never ought to suffer like that!'

Cazenove glanced at him, and then raised his hands to heaven at such an extraordinary pretension.

When Lazare returned to Pauline's room, he sent his mother and Véronique to get a little sleep. He himself could not have slept if he had tried. He watched the day breaking in that disorderly room: the mournful dawn it was that follows a night of agony. With his brow pressed to the window-pane, he was looking out hopelessly at the gloomy sky, when a sudden noise made him turn. He thought it was Pauline getting up in bed, but it was Matthew, who had been forgotten by everybody, and who had at last crept from under the bed to go to the girl, whose hand hung down over the counterpane. And the dog began licking that hand with such affectionate gentleness that Lazare, quite touched at the sight, put his arm round his neck, and said:

'Ah! my poor fellow, your mistress is ill, you see; but she'll soon be all right, and then we'll all three go on our rambles once more.'

Pauline had opened her eyes, and, though it pained her, she smiled.

A period of suffering and sadness followed. Lazare, acting upon an impulse of wild affection, almost refused to let the others enter the sick-room. He would barely allow his mother and Louise there in the morning to inquire after Pauline; Véronique, in whom he now recognised a genuine affection for his cousin, was the only one whose presence he tolerated. At the outset of Pauline's illness Madame Chanteau tried to make him understand the impropriety of a young man thus nursing a girl; but he retorted by asking if he were not her husband, and by saying that doctors attended women equally with men. Between the young people themselves there was never the slightest embarrassment. Suffering and, it might be, the approach of death obliterated all other considerations. The world ceased to have any existence for them. The chief matters of interest were that the draughts should be taken at the proper times, and such little details, whilst they waited hour by hour for the illness to take a more favourable turn. Thus minor matters of mere physical life suddenly assumed enormous importance, as on them depended joy or sorrow. The nights followed the days, and Lazare's existence seemed to hang in the balance over a deep abyss into whose black darkness he ever feared to fall.

Doctor Cazenove came to see Pauline each morning, and sometimes called again in the evening after dinner. Upon his second visit he had determined to bleed her freely. The fever, however, though checked for a time, reappeared. Two days passed, and the Doctor was evidently disturbed in his mind, unable to understand the tenacity with which the fever clung to his patient. As the girl felt ever-increasing pain in opening her mouth, he could not make any proper examination of the back of her throat, which seemed to him to be much swollen and of a livid hue. At last, as Pauline complained of increasing tightness, which made her throat feel as though it would burst, the Doctor one morning remarked to Lazare:

'I am beginning to suspect the presence of a phlegmon.'

The young man then drew him into his own room. The previous evening, while turning over the pages of an old Manual of Pathology, he had read the chapter on retro-pharyngeal abscesses which project into the œsophagus, and are apt to cause death by suffocation from compressing the windpipe.

He turned very pale as he asked:

'Then she is going to die?'

'I trust not,' the Doctor answered. 'We must wait and see what happens.'

But Cazenove himself could not conceal his uneasiness. He confessed that he was almost powerless in the present circumstances of the case. How could they search for an abscess at the back of a contracted mouth? And, besides, to open the abscess too soon would be attended with grave danger. The best thing they could do was to leave the matter in the hands of Nature, though the illness would probably prove very protracted and painful.

'Well, I am not the Divinity,' he exclaimed, when Lazare reproached him with the uselessness of his science.

The affection which Doctor Cazenove felt for Pauline showed itself in an increased assumption of brusque carelessness. That tall old man, who seemed as dry as a branch of brier, was really much affected. For more than thirty years he had knocked about the world, changing from vessel to vessel, and working in hospitals all over the colonies. He had treated epidemics on board ship, frightful diseases in tropical climes, elephantiasis at Cayenne, serpent bites in India; and he had killed men of every colour; had studied the effects of poison on Chinese, and risked the lives of Negroes in delicate experiments in vivisection. But now this girl, with a soreness in her throat, so wrought upon his feelings that he could not sleep. His iron hands trembled, and his callousness to death failed him, fearful as he was of a fatal issue. And so, wishing to conceal an emotion which he considered unworthy of him, he made a pretence contempt for suffering. 'People were born to suffer,' said he, 'so why make a fuss about it?'

Every morning Lazare said to him:

'Do try something else, Doctor, I beg you. It is terrible. She cannot get a moment's rest. She has been crying out all the night.'

'Well, but, dash it all, it isn't my fault!' the Doctor replied, working himself up to a high pitch of indignation. 'I can't cut off her neck to cure her.'

Thereupon the young man grew vexed in his turn, and exclaimed:

'So medicine is worth nothing?'

'Nothing at all when the human machine is out of order. Quinine arrests fever, and purgatives act on the bowels, and bleeding is useful in apoplexy, but it's a happy-go-lucky business with almost everything else. We must leave the case to Nature.'

These remarks were wrung from him by his anger at being unable to discover what course of treatment to adopt. It was not his ordinary custom to deny the power of medicine so roundly, for he had practised it too much to be sceptical or modest as to its merits. For whole hours he would sit by the girl's bedside, watching her and studying her, and then he would go off without even leaving a single instruction behind him, for indeed he knew not what to do, and was compelled to leave the abscess developing, though he recognised that a hair's breadth more or less in its size might make all the difference between life and death. For a whole week Lazare gave himself up to the most terrible alarm. He, too, was in perpetual fear of seeing Nature's work suddenly cease. At every painful, difficult gasp that the girl gave he thought that all was over. He formed in his mind a vivid picture of the phlegmon, he fancied he could see it blocking Pauline's windpipe; if it were only to swell a little more her breath would no longer be able to pass. His two years of imperfect medical study served to increase his alarm. His fears made him lose his head, and he broke out into nervous mutiny, excited protest against life. Why was such frightful suffering permitted? Was not all such bodily torture, all such writhing and burning pain cruelly purposeless when disease fell on a poor weak girl? He was for ever at her bedside, questioning her, even at the risk of fatiguing her. Was she still in pain? How was she feeling now?

Sometimes he would take her hand and lay it upon his neck. It felt like an intolerable weight there, like a ball of molten lead, which throbbed till he almost choked. Her headache never left her. She did not know where or how to rest her head, and she was tortured by sleeplessness. During the ten days that the fever racked her she scarcely slept for a couple of hours. One evening, to make things still worse, she experienced a frightful pain in her ears, and fainted from sheer suffering. But she did not confess to Lazare all the agony she endured. She showed great courage and fortitude, recognising that he was almost as ill as she herself was, his own blood hot with fever, and his throat choked as by an abscess. She frequently even told fibs, and forced a smile to her lips when racked by the keenest suffering. She felt easier, she would say, and she would beg him to go and take a little rest. One of the most painful features of her illness was that she could not even swallow her saliva without giving a cry, at which Lazare would start up in alarm, and begin to question her afresh. What was the matter, and where did she feel pain? Then, with her eyes closed, and her face distorted by agony, she would try to deceive him and whisper that it was a mere nothing, that something had tickled her, and that was all.

'Go to sleep and don't be uneasy. I am going to sleep myself now.'

Every evening she went through this pretence of going to sleep, in order to induce him to lie down, but he persisted in watching over her from his arm-chair. The nights were so full of anguish that they never saw the evening fall without a sort of superstitious terror. Would they ever see the sun again?

One night Lazare was leaning against the bed, holding Pauline's hand in his own, as he often did, to let her know that he was there and was not deserting her. Doctor Cazenove had gone off at ten o'clock, angrily exclaiming that he could answer for nothing more. The young man derived some consolation from the thought that Pauline herself was not aware that she was in any imminent danger. In her hearing, only a mere inflammation of the throat was spoken of, which, though very painful, would pass away as easily as a cold in the head. The girl seemed quite tranquil as to the outcome, and bravely retained a cheerful countenance in spite of her sufferings. She smiled as she heard them forming plans for the time when she would be well again. That very night she had once more listened to Lazare arranging a stroll along the shore for the first day that she might be able to go out. Then they grew silent, and she seemed to sleep, but after an interval of a quarter of an hour or so she said distinctly:

'You will have to marry some other girl, I think, my dear.'

He stared at her in amazement, feeling chilled to his bones.

'Why do you say that?' he asked.

She had opened her eyes, and was looking at him with an expression of brave resignation.

'Ah! I know what is the matter with me, and I am glad that I do, for I shall be able to kiss you all before I go.'

Then Lazare grew quite angry. It was insane to think such things. Before a week was over she would be walking about. But he dropped her hand and made an excuse for hurrying to his own room, for sobs were choking him; and he threw himself down in the darkness upon his bed, on which he had not slept for a long time now. A frightful conviction suddenly wrung his heart. Pauline was going to die, perhaps that very night. And the thought that she knew it, and that her silence on the subject hitherto had been due to courageous consideration for the feelings of others, even in the imminent presence of death, completed his despair. She knew the truth; she would see her death agony approach, and he would be there powerless! Already he saw them saying their last good-bye. The whole mournful scene unfolded itself before his eyes with heartrending detail in the darkness of his room. It was the end of everything, and he grasped his pillow in his arms convulsively, and buried his head in it to drown the sound of his sobs.

The night, however, passed away without any misfortune. Then two days went by without any noticeable change in the patient's condition. Between her and Lazare a new bond had sprung up; the thought of death was with them. Pauline made no further allusion to her critical condition; she even forced herself to look cheerful; and Lazare, too, succeeded in feigning perfect tranquillity, complete confidence in seeing her leave her bed in a few days' time; yet both knew that they were ever bidding each other good-bye in the long, loving glances which their eyes exchanged. At night-time especially, as Lazare sat watching by the girl's bedside, they recognised that each other's thoughts were of that threatened eternal separation which kept them so reflective and silent. Never before had they experienced such melting sadness or felt such a complete blending of their beings.

One morning, as the sun was rising, Lazare felt quite astonished at the calmness with which he was able to contemplate the idea of death. He ransacked his memory, and he could only recall one occasion since the commencement of Pauline's illness when he had felt a cold shudder at the thought of ceasing to be. He had trembled, indeed, at the idea of losing his companion; but that was another kind of fear, into which no thought of the destruction of his own personality entered. His heart bled within him, indeed, but it seemed as though this combat which he was waging with death put him upon an equality with the foe, and gave him courage to look it calmly in the face. Perhaps, too, his fatigue and anxiety filled him with a drowsiness and weariness which numbed his personal fears. He closed his eyes so that he might not see the rising sun, and tried to recall all his old thrills of horror, by telling himself that he, too, would have to die some day. But no reply came; all that seemed to have become quite indifferent to him and to have ceased to have any power to affect him. Even his pessimism seemed to disappear in the presence of that sick-bed; and, far from plunging him into hatred and contempt of the world, his mutinous outburst against suffering was but a passionate longing for robust health, a wild love of life. He no longer talked of blowing the earth into bits, as a worn-out and uninhabitable planet. The one image which ever haunted his mind was Pauline, hearty once more and walking with him arm in arm beneath the bright sunshine; the only craving he felt was to lead her, gay and firm of step, along the paths through which they had once rambled together.

Yet it was that same day that Lazare felt sure of death's approach. At eight o'clock in the morning Pauline was seized with attacks of nausea, and each brought on dangerous symptoms of suffocation. Soon trembling fits supervened, and the poor girl shook so terribly that her teeth could be heard chattering. Lazare, in a state of frightful alarm, shouted from the window that a lad should be sent to Arromanches at once, although the doctor was expected, as usual, at eleven o'clock. The house had fallen into mournful silence, and there had been a sad void since Pauline's gay activity had no longer animated it. Chanteau spent his days downstairs in moody silence, with his eyes fixed on his legs, fearing lest he should be seized with another attack of gout while there was no one to nurse him. Madame Chanteau usually forced Louise to go out, and the pair of them, spending most of their time in the open air, had by this time become very intimate and familiar. Only Véronique's heavy step came and went everlastingly up and down the stairs, breaking the silence of the landings and empty rooms. Lazare had gone three times to lean over the banisters in his impatience to learn whether the servant had been able to get anybody to take a message to the doctor. He had just returned to Pauline's room and was looking at the girl, who appeared to be a little easier, when the door, which he had left ajar, creaked slightly.

'Well, Véronique?' he said.

But it was not Véronique; it was his mother. She had that day intended to take Louise to see some of her friends in the neighbourhood of Verchemont.

'Little Cuche has just gone," she said. 'He can run fast.'

Then, after a short interval of silence, she asked:

'Is she no better?'

Lazare made no answer, but with a hopeless gesture pointed to Pauline, who was lying motionless, as though she were quite dead, with her pale face bathed in cold perspiration.

'Ah! we won't go to Verchemont, then,' his mother continued. 'It seems very tenacious, this mysterious illness which no one seems to understand. The poor girl has been sorely tried.'

She sat down and went on chattering in the same subdued monotonous voice.

'We had meant to start at seven o'clock, but it happened that Louise overslept herself. Everything seems to be falling on one this morning; it almost looks as though it were done on purpose. The grocer from Arromanches has just called with his bill, and I have been obliged to pay him, and now the baker is downstairs. We spent forty francs on bread again last month. I can't imagine where it all goes to!'

Lazare was not paying the least attention to what she said; he was too much absorbed in his fears of a return of the shivering-fits. But that monotonous flood of talk irritated him, and he tried to get his mother to leave the room.

'Will you give Véronique a couple of towels and tell her to bring them up to me?' he said.

'Of course I shall have to pay the baker,' his mother resumed, as though she had not heard him. 'He has spoken to me, and so Véronique can't tell him that I have gone out. Upon my word, I've had quite enough of this house. It is becoming quite a burden. If Pauline were not unfortunately so ill, she would advance me the ninety francs for her board. It is the 20th to-day, so that there are only ten days to wait before it will be due. The poor child seems so very weak—'

Lazare suddenly turned towards her.

'Well, what is it you want?' he asked.

'You don't happen to know where she keeps her money, do you?'

'No!'

'I dare say it's in her chest of drawers. You might just look.'

He refused with an angry gesture, and his hands quivered.

'I beseech you, mother, for pity's sake, do go away.'

These last remarks had been hurriedly exchanged at the far end of the room. There was a moment's painful silence, which was broken by a clear voice speaking from the bed:

'Lazare, just come and take the key from under my pillow, and give my aunt what she wants."

They were both quite startled. Lazare began to protest, for he was very unwilling to open the drawer; but he was obliged to give way in order that he might not distress Pauline. When he had given his mother a hundred-franc note, and had slipped the key under Pauline's pillow again, he saw that the girl was taken with another trembling-fit, which shook her like a young aspen, and seemed likely to rend her in twain. Two big tears trickled from her closed eyes and rolled down her cheeks.

Doctor Cazenove did not arrive before his usual time. He had seen nothing of little Cuche, who was probably larking about amongst the hedges. As soon as he heard what Lazare had to say and cast a hasty glance at Pauline, he cried out: 'She is saved!'

That sickness and those alarming fits of trembling were simply indications that the abscess had at last broken. There was no more occasion to fear suffocation; the complaint would now gradually go off of itself. Their joy was great; Lazare accompanied the Doctor out of the room; and as Martin, the old sailor who had taken service with the Doctor, drank a bumper of wine in the kitchen, everyone wanted to clink glasses with him. Madame Chanteau and Louise drank some walnut liqueur.

'I never felt really alarmed,' said the former. 'I was sure there could be nothing serious the matter with her.'

'That didn't prevent the poor dear from having an awful time of it!'

exclaimed Véronique. 'I'm more pleased than if some one had given me a hundred sous.'

Just at that moment Abbé Horteur came in. He had called to make inquiries, and he drank a glass of wine by way of doing like the rest. Every day he had come in this way like a kindly neighbour; for, on his first visit, Lazare had told him that he could not see the patient for fear of alarming her, whereupon the priest had quietly replied that he understood it, and had contented himself with mentioning the poor girl's name when saying his masses. Chanteau, as he clinked glasses with him, complimented him upon his spirit of tolerance.

'Well, you see, she is coming round nicely, without the help of an *Oremus!*'

'Everyone is saved after his own fashion,' the priest declared sententiously, as he drained his glass.

When the Doctor had left, Louise wanted to go upstairs to kiss Pauline. The poor girl was still suffering much pain, but this was not now regarded as of much account. Lazare gaily bade her take courage, and, quite dropping all pretence, began even to exaggerate the danger through which she had passed, telling her that three times already he had believed that she was lying dead in his arms. Pauline, however, manifested no exuberant delight at being saved; but she was conscious of the joy of life, after having found the courage to look calmly upon death's approach. An expression of loving emotion passed over her worn, sad face as she pressed her cousin's hand and murmured to him, smiling:

'Ah! my dear, you can't escape after all, you see. I shall be your wife yet.'

Her convalescence was heralded in by long slumbers. She slept for whole days, quite calmly, breathing easily and regularly, steeped in a strength-restoring torpor. Minouche, who had been banished from the room during her period of prostration, took advantage of this quietness to slip in again. She jumped lightly upon the bed, and immediately lay down there, nestling beside her mistress. Indeed, she spent whole days on it, revelling in the warmth of the blankets, or making an interminable toilet, wearing away her fur by constant licking, but performing each operation with such supple lightness that Pauline could not even tell she was moving. At the same time Matthew, who, equally with Minouche, was now granted free access to the room, snored like a human being on the carpet by the side of the bed.

One of Pauline's first fancies was to have her young friends from the village brought up to her room on the following Saturday. They had just begun to allow her to eat boiled eggs after the very spare diet to which she had been subjected for three weeks. Though she was still very weak, she was able to sit up to receive the children. Lazare had to go to the drawer again to find her some five-franc pieces. After she had questioned her pensioners and had insisted on paying off what she called her arrears, she became so thoroughly exhausted that she lay back in a fainting condition. But she manifested great interest in the piles, groynes, and stockades, and every day inquired if they still remained firmly in position. Some of the timbers had already weakened, and her cousin told a falsehood when he asserted that only the nailing of a plank or two had ceased to hold. One morning, when she was alone, she slipped out of bed, wishing to see the high tide dash against the stockades in the distance; and this time again her budding strength failed her, and she would have fallen to the ground if Véronique had not come into the room in time to catch her in her arms.

'Ah! you naughty girl! I shall have to fasten you down in bed if you don't behave more sensibly!' said Lazare with a smile.

He still persisted in watching over her, but he was completely worn out with fatigue, and would drop asleep in his arm-chair. At first he had felt a lively joy in seeing her drink her broth. The young girl's restored health became a source of exquisite pleasure to him; it was a renewal of life of which he himself partook. But afterwards, when he had grown accustomed to it, and all the girl's suffering had passed away, he ceased to rejoice as over some unhoped-for blessing. All that was left to him was a sort of hebetation, a slackening of the nerves now that the struggle was over, a confused notion that the hollowness and mockery of everything was becoming manifest again.

One night when he had been sleeping soundly Pauline heard him awake with a sigh of agony. By the feeble glimmer of the night-light she caught a glimpse of his terror-stricken face, his eyes staring wildly with horror, and his hands clasped together in an attitude of entreaty. He stammered out some incoherent words: 'O God! O God!'

She leant towards him with hasty anxiety, and called: 'What is the matter with you, Lazare? Are you in pain?'

The sound of her voice made him start. He had been seen, then. He sat silent and vexed, and could only contrive to tell a clumsy fib.

'There's nothing the matter with me. It was you yourself who were crying out just now.'

But in reality the horror of death had just come back to him in his sleep—a horror without cause, born of blank nothingness—a horror whose icy breath had awakened him with a great shudder. O God! he thought, so he would have to die some day. And that thought took possession of him, and choked him; while Pauline, who had laid her head back again on her pillow, watched him with an air of motherly compassion.

V

EVERY evening, in the dining-room, when Véronique had cleared the table, Madame Chanteau and Louise chatted together; while Chanteau, buried in his newspaper, gave brief replies to his wife's few questions. During the fortnight when he had thought Pauline in danger, Lazare had never joined the family at dinner; but he now dined down-stairs again, though, directly the meal was over, he returned to his post at the invalid's bedside. He scarcely closed the door behind him before Madame Chanteau began with her old complaints.

At first she affected loving anxiety.

'Poor boy!' she said, 'he is quite wearing himself out. It is really foolish of him to go on endangering his health in this way. He has scarcely had any sleep for the last three weeks. He is paler than ever to-day.'

Then she would have a word or two of pity for Pauline. The poor dear seemed to suffer so much that it was impossible to stay in her room without a heartache. But she soon began to harp upon the manner in which that illness upset the house. Everything remained in a state of confusion; their meals were always cold, and there was no relying upon anything. Then she broke off suddenly, and, turning to her husband, asked him:

'Has Véronique found time to give you your marshmallow water?'

'Yes, yes,' he replied from behind his newspaper.

Then she lowered her voice and addressed herself to Louise.

'It is very peculiar, but that poor Pauline seems to have brought us nothing but misfortune. And yet some people persist in looking upon her as our good angel! I know the stories that are floating about. At Caen, they say—don't they, Louise?—that we have grown quite rich through her. Rich, indeed! I should just think so! You may speak to me quite frankly, for I am above taking any notice of their slanderous gossip.'

'Well, indeed, they do talk about you, just as they talk about every-body else,' the girl murmured. 'Only last month I was obliged to snub a notary's wife, who dared to speak on the subject, without knowing anything at all about it. You can't prevent people talking, you know.'

After that, Madame Chanteau made no attempt to veil her real feel-ings. There was no doubt, she said, that they were suffering from their own generosity. Had they wanted anyone's assistance before Pauline came? And where would she have been now, in what Paris slum, if they had not consented to take her into their house? It was all very fine for people to talk about her money, but that money had never been anything but a source of trouble to them; indeed, it seemed to have brought ruin with it. The facts spoke clearly enough for themselves. Her son would never have launched out into those idiotic speculations in seaweed, nor have wasted his time in trying to prevent the sea from sweeping Bonneville away, if that unlucky Pauline had not turned his head. If she had lost her money, well, it was her own fault. The poor young fellow had wrecked both his health and his future. Madame Chanteau could hardly find words strong enough with which to inveigh against those hundred and fifty thousand francs of which her secrétaire still reeked. It was, indeed, all the large sums which had been swallowed up, and the small amounts which were still being daily abstracted and thus increasing the deficit, that embittered her, as though therein lay the ferment in which her honesty had rotted away. By this time putrefaction was complete, and she hated Pauline for all the money she owed her.

'What is the good of talking to such an obstinate creature?' she resumed bitterly. 'She is horribly miserly at heart, and, at the same time, she is recklessness itself. She will toss twelve thousand francs to the bottom of the sea for the Bonneville fishermen, who only laugh at us, and feed all the filthy brats in the neighbourhood; while I perfectly tremble, upon my word of honour I do, if I have to ask her for only forty sous. What do you think of that? With all her pretence of charity to others, she has got a heart of stone.'

During all the talk of this kind Véronique was often in and out of the room, clearing away the dinner things or bringing in the tea, and she loitered to listen to what was being said, and sometimes even ventured on a remark.

'Mademoiselle Pauline got a heart of stone! Oh, Madame! how can you say so?'

Madame Chanteau reduced her to silence by a stern look. Then, resting her elbows on the table, she entered into a series of complicated calculations, talking as to herself.

'I've nothing more to do with her money now, thank goodness, but I should like to know how much of it there's left. Not more than seventy thousand francs, I'll be bound. Just let us reckon it up a little. Three thousand have gone already in that experimental stockade; then there are, at least, two hundred francs going every month in charity, and ninety francs for her board here. All that mounts up quickly. Will you take a bet, Louise, that she'll ruin herself? You will see her reduced to a pallet one of these days. And when she has quite ruined herself, who will take her in?—how will she manage to live?'

At this Véronique could not restrain herself, but broke out: 'I'm sure Madame could never think of turning her out of doors?'

'What do you mean? What are you speaking about?' her mistress demanded angrily. 'There's no question of anyone being turned out of doors. I never turned anybody out of doors. What I said was that nothing can be more foolish, when one has had a fortune of one's own, to go frittering it all away and becoming dependent upon other people. Go off to your kitchen.'

The servant went off, grinding out muttered protests from between her teeth. Then there came an interval of silence, while Louise poured out the tea. The only sound in the room was the slight rustling of the newspaper, which Chanteau read from end to end, not missing even the advertisements. Now and then he spoke a word or two to the young girl.

'You might give me another piece of sugar, please. Have you had a letter from your father yet?'

'No, indeed,' she answered with a smile. 'But if I am in the way I can leave at any time, you know. You have quite sufficient trouble with Pauline's illness. I would rather have gone away before, but you insisted upon my staying.'

'You mustn't talk like that,' he interrupted. 'It is only too kind of you to give us the pleasure of your society till poor Pauline can get downstairs again.'

'I can go to Arromanches till my father comes, if I am in the way,' she continued, as though she had not heard him, merely by way of teasing. 'My aunt Léonie has taken a châlet there, and there are plenty of people there, and a good beach where one can bathe at any rate. But she is very wearisome is my aunt Léonie.'

Chanteau laughed at the girl's playful, fondling ways. Though he dare not confess it to his wife, he was entirely on the side of Pauline, who nursed him so kindly and carefully. He buried himself in his newspaper again; while Madame Chanteau, who had been immersed in deep reflections, suddenly started up, as though awaking from a dream.

'There's one thing which I can't forgive her. She has completely taken possession of my son. He scarcely stops at the table for a quarter of an hour, and I can hardly get a single word with him.'

'That will soon be over,' said Louise. 'She must have someone with her.'

Madame Chanteau shook her head and tightened her lips but the words which she seemed trying to keep back broke out, apparently in spite of herself.

'It's all very well to say that, but it's a little peculiar for a young man to be always shut up with a sick girl. There! I've said what I mean and haven't kept it back, and if it doesn't please others I can't help it.'

Then, noticing Louise's embarrassed look, she added:

'It isn't healthy to breathe the atmosphere of a sickroom. She may easily infect him with her sore throat. Those girls who seem so vigorous have sometimes all sorts of impurities in their blood. Well, I don't know why I shouldn't say it, but I don't think she is quite sound and healthy.'

Louise then feebly defended her friend. She had always found her so nice and kind; that was the only argument which she contrived to bring forward in reply to the accusation of a stony heart and ill-health. An instinctive desire for tranquil peace and quietness induced her to try to mitigate Madame Chanteau's rough ill-feeling, although every day she listened to her trying to excel her bitterness of the day before. While making some kind of protest against the harshness of Madame Chanteau's language, Louise indeed flushed with secret pleasure at finding herself preferred to Pauline, promoted to the position of favourite. She was like Minouche in this respect, content to be caressing so long as her own enjoyment was not interfered with.

Every evening the conversation, after flowing along the same channels, ended invariably in the same way, Madame Chanteau slowly saying:

'No, Louisette, the girl that my son ought to marry—'

And from that starting-point she would launch out into a disquisition upon the qualities of an ideal daughter-in-law, while her eyes all the time remained fixed upon Louise, trying to make her understand more than she was willing to actually say. It was the girl's own self that was gradually being described. A young person who had been well brought up and educated, who had acquired a knowledge of society, and who was fit to play the part of a hostess, who was graceful rather than beautiful, and, what was especially desirable, who was truly feminine and lady-like; for a boy-like girl, a hoyden who made frankness a pretence for being rough and rude, was, said she, her detestation. Then there was the question of money—which was really the only one that influenced her—and this she made a pretence of dismissing with a word, saying that, though she made no account of a dowry, her son had great schemes and aims for the future, and could not, of course, afford to contract a marriage that would be likely to lead to ruin.

'I may tell you, my dear, that if Pauline had come here penniless, with nothing but the chemise she wore, the marriage would probably have taken place years ago. But you can't be surprised at my hesitation and distrust, when I see money slipping through her hands like water. The sixty thousand francs she still has left won't trouble her much longer, I fancy. No! Lazare deserves a better fate than that, and I will never consent to his marrying a mad creature who would stint the house in food so that she might ruin herself with idiotic follies.'

'Ah, no! money's nothing,' said Louise, lowering her eyes; 'still one needs some.'

Although Louise's dowry was not directly referred to, her two hundred thousand francs seemed to be lying there upon the table, glistening beneath the glow of the hanging lamp. It was because Madame Chanteau felt and saw them there that she became thus excited, and swept aside Pauline's paltry sixty thousand in her dream of winning for her son that other girl whose big fortune was still intact. She had noticed how Lazare had been drawn towards Louise before all this tiresome business, which now kept him in seclusion upstairs. If the girl was equally attracted towards him, why shouldn't they make a match of it? Her husband would give his consent, and that the more readily when he saw it was a case of mutual affection. Thus she did all she could to fan Louise's love into life, spending the rest of the evening in making such remarks as she thought likely to excite the girl's passion.

'My Lazare is so good! No one knows half how good he is. You yourself, Louisette, have no notion how affectionate is his nature. Nobody will pity the girl who gets him for a husband. She will be quite certain of being passionately loved. And he is such a handsome vigorous fellow, too! His skin is as white as a chicken's. My grandfather, the Chevalier de la Vignière, had such a white skin that he used to wear his clothes cut quite low like a woman's when he went to masked balls.'

Louise blushed and smiled, and was much amused with Madame Chanteau's details. The mother's advocacy of her son, and the confidences which she poured out to Louise with the object of inclining her to a union with Lazare, might have kept her there all night if Chanteau had not begun to feel very drowsy over his newspaper.

'Isn't it about time for us all to go to bed?' he asked with a yawn.

Then, as though he had been quite unconscious for some time of what had been going on, and was taking up the thread of Madame Chanteau's earlier conversation, he added:

'You are quite mistaken. She is a good girl, and I shall be very glad when she is able to come downstairs again and eat her soup beside me.'

'We shall all be glad,' cried his wife, with considerable bitterness. 'We may speak and say what we think, without ceasing to be fond of those of whom we talk.'

'The poor little dear!' exclaimed Louise, in her turn; 'I should be very glad to bear half the pain for her, if such a thing were possible. She is so amiable!'

Véronique, who was just bringing them their candles, once more put in her word.

'You are quite right to be her friend, Mademoiselle Louise, for no one, unless she had a paving-stone for a heart, could ever wish her unkindly.'

'That will do,' said Madame Chanteau. 'We didn't ask for your opinion. It would be very much better if you cleaned the candlesticks. This one here is quite filthy.'

They all rose from their seats. Chanteau lost no time in escaping from his wife's snappishness, and shut himself up in his room on the ground floor. But when the two women reached the landing upstairs, where their rooms adjoined each other, they did not at once go to bed. Madame Chanteau almost always took Louise into her own room for a little time and there resumed her remarks about Lazare, showing the girl one and another portrait of him, and even exhibiting little memorials and souvenirs, such as a tooth which had been extracted when he was quite young, or a lock of the pale hair of his infancy, or even some of his old clothes; for instance, the bow he had worn at his first communion, or his first pair of trousers.

'See!' she said, one night, 'these are some locks of his hair. I have a number, cut at all stages of his life.'

Thus, when Louise got to bed she could not sleep for thinking of the young man whom his mother was trying to force on her.

Up above, Pauline's convalescence was progressing gradually. Although the patient was now out of danger, she still remained very feeble, worn out and exhausted by feverish attacks which astonished the doctor. As Lazare said, doctors were always being astonished. He himself was growing more irritable every hour. The sudden lassitude which had fallen upon him when the crisis was over seemed to be turning into a kind of uneasy restlessness. Now that he was no longer wrestling against death, he began to feel distressed by the close atmosphere of the apartment and the spoonfuls of physic which had to be administered at regular hours, and all the other little duties of a sick-room, which he had so enthusiastically taken upon himself at first. Pauline was able to do without him now, and he sank back into the boredom of an aimless empty existence—a boredom which kept him fidgeting from chair to chair, with his hands hanging listlessly by his side, or wandering about the room, staring hopelessly at the walls, or deep in gloomy abstraction in front of the window, looking out, but seeing nothing.

'Lazare,' Pauline said to him one day, 'you must go out. Véronique will be quite able to do everything.'

But he hotly refused. 'Couldn't she bear his presence any longer,' he asked, 'that she wanted to send him away? It would be very nice of him, wouldn't it, if he were to desert her like that before she was quite strong again?'

But he grew calm as she gently explained to him:

'You wouldn't be deserting me by just going out to get a little fresh air. Go out in the afternoon. We should be in a pretty way if you were to fall ill too.'

Then, however, she unfortunately added:

'I have seen you yawning all the morning.'

'You've seen me yawning!' he cried. 'Say at once that I have no heart! This is a nice way to thank me!'

The next morning Pauline was more diplomatic. She pretended that she was very anxious that the construction of the stockades should be proceeded with; the high winter tides were coming on, and the experimental works would be swept away if the system of defence was not completed. But Lazare no longer glowed with his early enthusiasm; he was dissatisfied with the resistance of the timbers as he had arranged them, and fresh study would be necessary. Then, too, the estimate would be exceeded, and the authorities had not yet voted a single sou. For two days Pauline tried to fan his inventive *amour-propre* into fresh life. She asked him if he was going to let himself be beaten by the sea, with all the neighbourhood looking on and smiling; as for the money, it would certainly be paid back, if she advanced it, as they had settled she should. By degrees Lazare then seemed to work himself up to his old pitch of enthusiasm. He made fresh designs and again called in the carpenter from Arromanches, and had long consultations with him in his own room, the door of which he left open so that he might be ready to go to Pauline at the first summons.

'Now,' said he one morning as he kissed the girl, 'the sea won't be able to break anything. I am quite sure we shall be successful. As soon as you are able to walk, you must go and see how the works are getting on.'

Louise had just come up into the room to inquire after Pauline's health, and as she, too, kissed her, the patient whispered to her:

'Take him away with you.'

Lazare at first refused to go. He was expecting the doctor, he said. But Louise laughed and told him that she was sure he was much too gallant to let her go alone to the Gonins, where she was going to choose Borne lobsters to send to Caen. Besides, he could give a look at the works on the way.

'Yes, do go,' said Pauline. 'It will please me if you do. Take his arm, Louise. There, now, don't let him get away again.'

She grew quite merry as the two others jokingly pushed each other about; but when they had left the room she became very thoughtful, and leaned over the edge of her bed to listen to their laughter and footsteps dying away down the stairs.

A quarter of an hour later Véronique came in with the doctor. By-and-by she installed herself at Pauline's bedside, but without abandoning her saucepans, for she kept perpetually running to and fro between the kitchen and the bedroom, spending an hour or so there, as she was able, in the intervals of her work. She did not, however, take over all the duties of nurse at once. Lazare came back in the evening after going out with Louise, but he set off again the next morning; and each succeeding day, carried away as he was, absorbed more and more in outdoor life, his visits to Pauline grew shorter and shorter, till he soon stayed only long enough to inquire after her. Pauline, too, always told him to run off, if he merely spoke of sitting down; and when he and Louise returned together she made them tell her all about their walk, and grew quite bright amidst their animation and the touch of the fresh breezes which still seemed to cling to their hair. They seemed such good friends, and nothing else, that all her old suspicions of them had vanished. And when she saw Véronique coming towards her, with her draught in her hand, she cried out to her gaily:

'Oh! be off! You worry me! "

Sometimes she called Lazare to her to tell him to look after Louise, as though she had been a child.

'See that she doesn't get bored. She wants amusing. Take her for a good long walk; I shall get on very well without you for the rest of the day."

When she was left alone, her eyes seemed to be following them from a distance. She spent her time in reading, waiting till she should be strong again, for she was still so weak that it quite exhausted her to sit up for two or three hours in an easy-chair. She would often let her book slip on to her lap, while her thoughts dreamily wandered off after her cousin and her friend. She wondered whether they were walking along the beach, and had got to the caves, where it was so pleasant on the sands amidst the fresh breezes and rising tide. In those long reveries she fancied that the feeling of sorrow which depressed her came merely from the fact that she was unable to be with them. She soon grew weary of reading. The novels which lay about the house, love-stories abounding in romantic falsity and treason, had always offended her sense of honour, for she felt how impossible it would be, after once giving her heart, to withdraw it again. Was it true, then, that people's hearts could lie so, and that, after having once loved, they could ever cease to love? She threw the books from her in disgust; and with her wandering gaze saw, in imagination, her cousin bringing her friend home, he supporting her weary steps, as they came along side by side, whispering and laughing.

'Here is your draught, Mademoiselle,' suddenly said Véronique, whose deep voice, coming from behind, aroused Pauline from her reverie with a start.

By the end of the first week Lazare never came to her room without first knocking. One morning as he opened the door he caught sight of her, combing her hair as she sat up in bed, with her arms bare.

'Oh! I beg your pardon!' he cried, stepping back.

'What's the matter?' said she. 'Are you frightened of me?' Then he took courage, but he was afraid lest he should embarrass her, and turned his head aside until she had finished fastening up her hair.

A fortnight before, when he had thought that she was dying, he had lifted her in his arms as though she had been a child, without even noticing her nakedness. But now the very disorder of the room disquieted him. And the girl herself, catching his feeling of uneasiness, soon refrained from asking of him any of the little services that he had lately been accustomed to render her.

'Shut the door, Véronique'!' she cried one morning, as she heard the young man's step on the landing. 'Put all those things out of sight and give me that fichu.'

She was gradually growing stronger, and her great pleasure, when she was able to stand up and lean against the window, was to watch the progress that was being made with the defensive works. She could distinctly hear the blows of the hammers, and see the gang of seven or eight men, who bustled about like big ants over the yellowish shingle on the beach. Between the tides they worked away energetically, but they were obliged to retire before the rising water. It was with special interest, too, that Pauline's eyes followed Lazare's white jacket and Louise's pink gown, both of which glittered conspicuously in the sun. She followed them constantly with her gaze, and could have told their every action, almost their every gesture, throughout the day. Now that the operations were being pushed so vigorously forward they could no longer wander off together, or ramble to the caves inside the cliffs; and thus Pauline constantly had them within half a mile of her, always plainly visible beneath the wide expanse of sky, though their stature was reduced by distance to that of dolls. Quite unknown to herself, this jealous pleasure of accompanying them in fancy did much to cheer her convalescence and recruit her strength.

'It amuses you, eh, to watch the workmen?' Véronique used to repeat every day as she dusted the room. 'Well, it's much better for you than reading. Whenever I try to read I get a headache. And, besides, when one wants to get back strength, one must go and open one's mouth in the sunshine like the turkeys do, and drink in great mouthfuls of it.'

Véronique was not naturally of a talkative nature; she was even considered a little morose and taciturn; but with Pauline she chatted freely from a friendly impulse, believing that she did the girl good.

'It's a funny piece of business all the same! But it seems to please Monsieur Lazare. Though, indeed, he does not appear to be quite so full of it just now as he was. But he is so proud and obstinate that he will go on persisting in a thing, even if he is really sick to death of it. And if he just leaves those drunken fellows for a minute, they drive the nails in all crooked.'

After she had swept the floor under the bed she added:

'And as for the duchess—'

Pauline, who was scarcely listening to the woman, caught this word with surprise.

'The duchess! Whom are you talking of?'

'Mademoiselle Louise, of course! Wouldn't anyone say that she had sprung straight from Jupiter's thigh? If you were to go and look in her room and see all her little pots and pomades and scents—Why, as soon as ever you open the door, it all catches you at the throat, the place smells so! But she can't match you in good looks, for all that!'

'Oh, nonsense! I'm a mere country girl,' Pauline said with a smile; 'Louise is very graceful and refined.'

'Well, she may be all that; but she hasn't got a pretty face, all the same. I have had a good look at her when she has been washing herself; and I know that, if I were a man, I shouldn't be long in making up my mind between you.'

Carried off by her feeling of enthusiastic conviction, she came and leaned against the window, close to Pauline.

'Just glance at her there on the beach! Doesn't she look a mere shrimp? She is certainly a long way off, and one can't expect her to appear as big as a church, but she ought to show a figure of some sort! Ah! there's Monsieur Lazare lifting her up, so that she mayn't wet her pretty little shoes. She can't weigh very much in his arms, that's certain! But there are some men who seem to prefer bones!'

Véronique checked herself suddenly, as she felt Pauline quivering by her side. She was ever harping on this subject, as if she itched to talk of it. All that she heard and all that she saw—the conversations in the evening when Pauline was calumniated, the furtive smiles of Lazare and Louise, and the utter ingratitude of the whole family, which was rapidly growing into treason—stuck in her throat and made her choke. If she had gone up to the sick girl's room at the times when her honest heart glowed with a sense of some fresh injustice, she could not have restrained herself from revealing everything to Pauline, but her fear of making her ill kept her stamping about her kitchen, knocking her pots and pans about, and swearing that she could not go on much longer in that way, but would soon be driven into telling them all very roundly what she thought about them. However, when she got upstairs into Pauline's room, and a word that might vex or disturb the girl escaped her lips, she tried to recall it or explain it away with a touching awkwardness.

'But, thank goodness, Monsieur Lazare isn't the kind to fall in love with a bag of bones. He has been in Paris, and knows what's what. He has too much good taste. Look! he has set her on the ground again just as if he were throwing a match away!'

Then Véronique, in fear of letting her tongue slip again, began to flourish her feather brush once more; while Pauline, buried in deep thought, watched till evening Louise's pink gown and Lazare's white jacket both gleaming in the distance amidst the dark forms of the workmen. When she was beginning to feel fairly well again, Chanteau was seized with another violent attack of the gout; and this induced the young girl to come downstairs at once. The first time that she left her room it was to go and sit by the sick man's bedside. As Madame Chanteau said, very bitterly, the house was becoming quite a hospital. For some time her husband had not left his chair. After repeated seizures his whole body was now attacked by his foe; the disease mounted from his feet to his knees, and then to his elbows and hands. The little white pearl on his ear had fallen away, but others, of larger size, had appeared. All his joints became swollen, and spots of chalky tophus showed whitely, like lobster's eyes, through his skin in all parts. It was from chronic gout that he now suffered, chronic and incurable; the kind of gout which stiffens and deforms the body.

'Good heavens! what agony I'm in!' Chanteau kept repeating. 'My left knee is as stiff as a log; I can't move either my foot or my knee; and my elbow burns as though it were on fire. Just look at it!'

Pauline looked, and observed an inflamed swelling on his left elbow. He complained bitterly of the agony he was suffering there; indeed, it very soon became unendurable. He kept his arm stiffly stretched, as he sighed and groaned, with his eyes constantly fixed upon his hand, which was a pitiable sight, with all the finger-joints knotted and swollen, and the thumb warped as though it had been beaten with a hammer.

'I cannot keep like this. You must come and help me to move. I thought just now that I had got myself fairly comfortable, but I am as bad again as ever I was. It is just as though my bones were being scraped with a saw. Try to raise me a little.'

Twenty times in an hour did he have to be helped to change his position. He was in a continual state of anxious restlessness, always hoping to find relief in some new change. But Pauline still felt too weak to venture to move him without assistance.

'Véronique,' she would say softly, 'take hold of him very gently and help me to move him.'

'No, no! not Véronique!' Chanteau would cry out, 'she shakes me so!'

Then Pauline was obliged to make the effort herself, and her shoulders gave way under the strain. And, however gently she turned him round, he groaned and screamed so terribly that Véronique rushed hastily out of the room. She said that one needed to be a saint, like Mademoiselle Pauline, to be able to do such work, for the good God Himself would run away if He were to hear her master bellowing.

The paroxysms, however, became less acute, though they did not cease, but recurred frequently both day and night, keeping the sick man in a state of perpetual exasperation. It was no longer merely in his feet that he felt as though sharp teeth were gnawing at him, his whole body seemed bruised, as though it were being crushed beneath a millstone. It was impossible to afford him any relief; all that Pauline could do was to remain by his side and yield submissively to his caprices, ever changing his position for him, though without succeeding in giving him any lasting ease. The worst of he matter was that pain made him unjust and violent, and he spoke to her harshly, as though she were a very clumsy servant.

'Oh, stop! stop! you are as awkward as Véronique! Can't you manage it without digging your fingers into my body like that? Your hands are as clumsy as a gendarme's. Go away and leave me alone. I don't want you to touch me any more.'

But Pauline, without a word of self-defence, showing a submissive resignation nothing could ruffle, resumed her efforts with increased gentleness. When she imagined he was getting irritated with her she would conceal herself for a moment behind the curtains, hoping that his anger would cool when he no longer saw her. And often she would give way to silent tears in her hiding-place, not for the poor man's harshness towards her, but for the frightful martyrdom which made him so hasty and violent. She listened to him as he talked to himself amidst his sighing and groaning.

'She has gone away, the heartless girl! Ah! if I were to die, there would only be Minouche left to close my eyes. It is abominable to desert a human being in this way! I'll be bound she's gone off to the kitchen to have some broth!'

Then, after a little wrestling and struggling, he groaned more loudly, and ended by calling: 'Pauline, are you there? Come and raise me a little. I can't get easy as I am. Shall we try how the left side will do—shall we?'

Every now and then he would be suddenly seized with deep regret, and would beg the girl's pardon for having treated her unkindly. Sometimes he would tell her to fetch Matthew, for the sake of having another companion, fancying that the dog's presence would somehow or other alleviate his pain. But it was in Minouche rather than in Matthew that he found a faithful associate, for the cat revelled in the close, warm atmosphere of sick rooms, and spent her days lying on a couch near the bed. However, when the patient gave a more than usually loud cry she seemed surprised, and turned upon him, sitting on her tail, and staring at him with her big round eyes, in which glistened the indignant astonishment of a sober philosophic nature whose tranquillity had been deeply disturbed. What could possess him to make all that disagreeable and useless noise?

Every time that Pauline went out of the room with Doctor Cazenove she preferred the same request.

'Can't you inject a little morphia? It makes my heart bleed to hear him.'

But the doctor refused. It would do no good; the paroxysms would return again with increased violence. Since the salicylic treatment appeared only to have aggravated the disease, he preferred not to try any other drug. He spoke, however, of seeing what a milk diet might do as soon as the violence of the attack was over. Until then the patient was to keep to the most sparing diet and diuretic drinks, and nothing else.

'The truth is,' said Cazenove, 'that your uncle is a gourmand who is now paying dearly for all his fine dishes. He has been eating game; I know he has, for I saw the feathers in the yard. It will be much the worse for him in the end. I have warned him over and over again that the reason of his suffering is that, instead of denying himself such things, he prefers to yield to his appetite and take the consequences. But you yourself will act still more foolishly, my dear, if you over-exert yourself and make yourself ill again. Do be careful! You will, won't you? Your health still requires looking after.'

But she looked after it very little; she devoted herself to her uncle entirely, and all notion of time and even of life itself seemed to depart from her during the long days and nights that she passed by his bedside, with her ears buzzing with the groans and cries which ever filled the room. Her devotion and self-sacrifice were so complete that she actually forgot all about Louise and Lazare. She just exchanged a few words with them now and then, when she ran across them as she passed through the dining-room. By this time the work on the shore was finished, and heavy rains had kept the young people in the house for a week past; and, when the idea that they were together once suddenly occurred to Pauline, she felt quite happy to know that they were near her. Never before had Madame Chanteau appeared so busy. She was taking advantage, she said, of the confusion into which her husband's illness threw the household to go through her papers, make up her accounts, and clear off arrears of correspondence. So in the afternoons she shut herself up in her bedroom, leaving Louise to her own resources; and the girl immediately went upstairs to Lazare, for she detested being alone. They thus got into the way of being together, remaining undisturbed till dinner-time in the big room on the second floor, that room which had so long served Pauline both for study and amusement. The young man's little iron bedstead was still there, hidden away behind the screen. The piano was covered with dust, and the table buried beneath an accumulation of papers, books, and pamphlets. In the middle of it, between two piles of dry seaweed, was a little model of a stockade, cut out of deal with a knife, and recalling the grandfather's masterpiece, the bridge which, in its glass case, adorned the mantelpiece in the dining-room.

For some time Lazare had been falling into a nervous condition. His workmen had irritated him, and he had just rid himself of the works on the shore as of a burden beyond his strength, without tasting the pleasure of seeing his work accomplished. Other plans now filled his head—vague projects for the future, appointments at Caen, operations which would bring him great fame. Yet he never took any definite active steps, but relapsed into a state of idleness which seemed to render him weaker, less courageous, every hour. The great shock which he had received from Pauline's illness added to mental disquietude a perpetual craving for the open air, a peculiar physical longing, as though he felt some imperious necessity of recouping himself after his struggle against pain and sorrow. The presence of Louise still further excited his feverishness. She did not seem able to speak to him without leaning upon his shoulder; she smiled close to his face, and her cat-like graces, the warmth that came from her person, and all the disturbing freedom of her manner quite turned his head. He was seized with a feeling against which his conscience struggled. With a friend of his childhood, in his mother's house, any idea of the sort, he told himself, was not to be thought of for a moment; and his sense of honour made his arms tingle with pain whenever he caught hold of Louise as they played together, and a thrill sent his blood surging through his veins. It was no thought of Pauline that kept him back. She would never have known anything about the matter. Amidst all his strange fancies he began to indulge in ferocious, pessimistic sallies respecting women and love. Every evil originated in women, who were, said he, foolish and fickle, and perpetuated grief by desire; while love was nothing but delusion, the onslaught of future generations which wished to come into existence. He thus retailed all Schopenhauer's views, over which the blushing girl grew very merry.

By degrees Lazare became more deeply enamoured of her, genuine passion arose from amidst his disdainful prejudices, and he threw himself into that fresh love with all his early enthusiasm, which was still straining after a happiness that ever seemed to evade him.

On Louise's side there had long been nothing but everyday coquetry. She delighted in receiving attentions and compliments, and flirting with pleasant men; and when one of them ceased to appear interested in her she seemed quite melancholy and out of her element. If Lazare neglected her for a moment or two, to write a letter, or to plunge into one of his sudden apparently groundless fits of melancholy, she felt so unhappy that she began to tease and provoke him, preferring danger to neglect. Later on, however, she experienced some alarm as she felt the young man's burning breath fanning her neck like a flame. But though aware of the danger, she seemed unable to change her ways.

On the day when Chanteau's attack reached its worst point the whole house shook with his bellowing: prolonged heart-rending plaints, like the death-cries of a beast in the hands of the slaughterer. After breakfast, of which she had hastily partaken in a state of nervous irritation, Madame Chanteau rushed from the room, saying:

'I can't endure it any longer; I shall begin to scream myself if I stop here. If anyone wants me, I shall be in my own room writing. And you, Lazare, take Louise upstairs with you and try to amuse her, for the poor girl is not having a very gay time here.'

They heard her bang her door on the first floor, while her son and the girl climbed to the one above.

Pauline had gone back to her uncle. She, in her pity for so much suffering, was the only one who retained her calmness. If she could do nothing but just sit with him, she wished, at any rate, to afford the poor man whatever comfort could be derived from not being left to suffer in solitude. She fancied that he bore up more bravely against his pain when she looked at him, even if she did not speak a single word. For hours she would sit in this way by his bedside, and the gaze of her big compassionate eyes indeed soothed him somewhat. But that day, with his head hanging over the bolster, his arm stretched out, and his elbow racked with agony, he did not even recognise her, and screamed yet more loudly whenever she approached him.

About four o'clock Pauline, in a state of desperation, went into the kitchen to speak to Véronique, leaving the door open behind her, as she intended returning immediately.

'Something must really be done,' she said. 'I should like to try some cold compresses. The doctor says they are dangerous, though they are successful sometimes. Can you give me some linen?'

Véronique was in a frightfully bad temper.

'Linen? I've just been upstairs to get some dusters, and a nice reception I got! I had no business to come disturbing them up there! Oh, it's a nice state of things!'

'But you might ask Lazare for some,' Pauline continued, without yet understanding Véronique's remarks.

Then the servant, carried away by her anger, set her arms a-kimbo, and, without taking time to think of what she was saying, burst out: 'Yes, I should think so, indeed! They are much too busy gallivanting up there!'

'What do you mean?' the girl stammered, growing very pale.

Véronique, alarmed, at what she had said, attempted to recall those words which she had so long been keeping to herself. She tried to think of some explanation, some fib to tell Pauline, but she could hit upon nothing that seemed of any service. By way of precaution she had grasped the girl's wrists, but Pauline freed herself with a sudden jerk, and bounded wildly up the staircase, so choked, so convulsed by anger that Véronique dared not follow her, trembling as she did with fear at the sight of that pallid face, which she could scarcely recognise. The house seemed to be asleep; the upper floors were wrapped in silence, and nothing but Chanteau's yell came from below to disturb the perfect quietude. The girl sprang with a bound to the landing of the first floor, where she jostled against her aunt, who stood there, like a sentinel, barring any further advance. She had probably been keeping guard in this way for some little time.

'Where are you going?' she asked.

Pauline, still choking with emotion, and exasperated at this hindrance to her progress, could not at first answer.

'Let me pass!' she at last managed to stammer, making an angry gesture, before which Madame Chanteau quailed.

Then, with another bound she rushed up to the second floor, while her aunt, rooted to the spot, threw up her arms, but spoke no word. Pauline was possessed by one of those stormy fits of rebellion which broke out amidst all the gentle gaiety of her nature, and which, even when she was a mere child, had afterwards left her in a prostrate fainting condition. For some years past she believed that she had cured herself of them. But an impulse of jealousy had just thrilled her so violently that she could not have restrained herself without shattering herself entirely.

When she reached Lazare's door on the top floor, she threw herself against it. The key was bent by her impetuous onset, and the door clattered back against the wall. And the sight she then beheld brought her indignation to a climax. Lazare was clasping Louise in his arms against the wardrobe and raining kisses on her chin and neck, she passive, half-fainting, unable to resist his embrace. They had begun, no doubt, in mere sport, but the sport seemed likely to have a disastrous ending. At Pauline's appearance there was a moment of stupefaction. They all three looked at each other. Then, at last, Pauline burst out:

'Oh! you hussy! you hussy!'

It was the girl's treason that angered her more than anything. With a scornful gesture she pushed Lazare aside, as though he were a child of whose pitiful weakness she was well aware. But this girl, her own familiar friend, had stolen her husband from her while she was busy nursing a sick man down below! She caught her by the shoulders, shook her, and was scarcely able to keep from striking her.

'What do you mean by this? Tell me! You have been behaving infamously, shamelessly! Do you hear me?'

Then Louise, still in a state of stupor, and with her eyes wandering vacantly, stammered:

'He held me; I could not get away.'

'He! Why, he would have burst into tears if you had simply pushed him with your little finger!'

The sight of the room itself increased her anger—that room where she and Lazare had loved each other, where she, too, had felt her blood pulse more quickly through her veins at the warm touch of the young man's breath. What should she do to this girl to satisfy her vengeance?

Lazare, dazed, overcome with embarrassment, had just resolved to attempt some interference, when Pauline dashed Louise from her so violently that the girl's shoulders struck the wardrobe.

'Ah! I'm afraid of myself. Be off!'

And that was all she could now find to say. She chased the other through the room, drove her out upon the landing and down the stair-case, crying after her perpetually:

'Be off! be off! Get your things together and be off!'

Madame Chanteau was still standing on the landing of the first floor. The rapidity of the scene had given her no opportunity to inter-fere. But she now recovered her power of speech and signed to Lazare to shut himself in his own room, while she tried to soothe Pauline, pretending at first to be very much surprised at what had happened. Meantime Pauline, having driven Louise into her bedroom, still kept on repeating:

'Be off! be off!'

'What do you mean?' her aunt asked her. 'Why is she to be off? Are you losing your head?'

Then the young girl stammered out the whole story. She was over-come with disgust. To her frank, honourable nature such conduct ap-peared utterly shameless and incapable of either excuse or pardon. The more she thought about it the more indignant she felt, rebelling against it all in her horror of deceit and her faithfulness of heart. When one had once bestowed one's self, one could not withdraw the gift.

'Be off! Pack up your things at once and be off!' she repeated.

Louise, completely overcome, unable to find a word to say in her own defence, had already opened her drawers to get her clothes to-gether. But Madame Chanteau was growing angry.

'Stay where you are, Louisette. Am I the mistress of my own house? Who is it that presumes to give orders here and allows herself to send my guests away? Such behaviour is infamous! We are not liv-ing in a slum here!'

'Didn't you hear me, then?' cried Pauline. 'I caught her up there with Lazare. He had her in his arms, and was kissing her!'

Madame Chanteau shrugged her shoulders. All her stored-up bitter-ness broke out in words of base suspicion.

'They were only playing; where was the harm of it? When he was nursing you in your room, did we ever interfere?'

The young girl's excitement suddenly subsided. She stood quite motionless, pale, astounded at the accusation which was thus launched against her. It was she who was now being arraigned as guilty; her aunt appeared to suspect her of disgraceful conduct.

'What do you mean?' she cried. 'If you had really thought anything wrong you would not have allowed it for a moment!'

'Well, you are not children! But I don't want my son to lead a whole life of misconduct. And you had better leave off harassing those who still remain honest women.'

For a moment Pauline continued silent, with her big pure eyes fixed upon Madame Chanteau, who turned her own away. Then she went up the stairs to her room, saying curtly:

'Very well, it is I who will leave.'

Then silence fell again, a heavy silence, in which the whole house seemed to collapse. Athwart that sudden quietude Chanteau's groans suddenly rose once more like those of an agonized deserted animal. They seemed to grow louder and louder; they made themselves distinctly heard till they drowned all other sound.

And now Madame Chanteau began to regret the words which had escaped her. She recognised the irreparable nature of the insult, and felt much disturbed in mind lest Pauline should actually carry out her threat of immediate departure. With such a girl everything was possible, and what would people say of herself and her husband if their ward should set off scouring the country and telling the story of their rupture? Perhaps she would take refuge with Doctor Cazenove, which would certainly give rise to a dreadful scandal in the district. At the bottom of Madame Chanteau's embarrassment there lurked a fear of the past; of all the money which had been lost—a loss which might suddenly be brought up against them.

'Don't cry, Louisette,' she said, feeling angry with Pauline again. 'Here we are, in a bother again all through her folly. She's always going on in this mad, violent way. It's impossible to live quietly with her. But I will try to make matters comfortable.'

'Oh no, let me go away, I beg you,' Louise cried. 'It would be too painful for me to stop here. She is right; I had better go.'

'Not to-night, at any rate. I must see you safely to your father's house. Just wait a moment, and I will go upstairs and see if she is really packing her things.'

Madame Chanteau gently went upstairs and listened at Pauline's door. She heard her walking hurriedly about the room, opening and shutting her drawers. For a moment she thought of entering, provoking an explanation, and bringing the affair to an end with a flood of tears. But she was afraid; she felt that she would stammer and blush before the girl, and this feeling served to increase her hatred of her. So, instead of knocking at the door, she went downstairs to the kitchen, treading as silently as she could. An idea had just occurred to her.

'Have you heard the row to which Mademoiselle Pauline has just been treating us?' she asked Véronique, who had begun furiously polishing her brass-ware.

The servant, with her head bent over the polish, made no answer.

'She is getting quite unbearable! I can do nothing with her. Would you believe that she is actually talking about leaving us at once? She is packing her things at this moment. I wish you would go upstairs and try to reason with her.'

Then, as she still got no answer, she added:

'Are you deaf?'

'If I don't answer, it's because I don't choose,' Véronique cried snappishly, bursting with angry excitement, and rubbing a candlestick violently enough to hurt her fingers. 'She is quite right in going away. If I had been in her place, I would have taken myself off long ago.'

Madame Chanteau listened with gaping lips, quite stupefied by this mutinous outburst of loquacity.

'I'm not talkative,' Véronique continued, 'but you mustn't press me too far or I shall let out all I think. I should have liked to fling Mademoiselle Pauline into the sea on the day you first brought her here as a little girl, but I can't bear to see anyone ill-treated, and you have all of you treated her so abominably that one of these days I shall give anyone who hurts her a swinging box on the ears. You can give me warning, if you like; I don't care a button; but I will let her into some nice secrets. Yes, she shall know all about how you have treated her, with all your fine pretences to honour and honesty.'

'Hold your tongue! You are quite mad!' cried Madame Chanteau, much disquieted by this fresh explosion.

'No, I will not hold my tongue! It is all too shameful! Shameful, I say! Do you hear me? I have been choking with it all for years and years! Wasn't it bad enough of you to rob her of her money? Couldn't you have been content with that, without tearing her poor little heart to shreds? Oh yes! I know all about it; I have seen through all your underhand plottings. Monsieur Lazare is perhaps not quite so calculating as you are; but in other respects he's not much better than you, for he wouldn't much mind giving her her death-blow out of mere selfishness, just to save himself from feeling bored! Ah, me! there are some people who come into this world only to be preyed upon and devoured by others.'

She flourished the candlestick about, and then caught hold of a pan, which rumbled like a drum under the violent rubbing she gave it. Madame Chanteau had been sorely tempted to turn her out of the house at once, but she succeeded in restraining herself and said to her icily:

'So you won't go up and speak to the girl? It would be for her own good, to prevent her from committing a piece of folly.'

Véronique became silent again, but at last she growled out:

'I'll go up to her. Reason is reason, after all, and an inconsiderate act never does any good.'

She stayed for a minute or two to wash her hands, and then took off her dirty apron. When she opened the door in the passage to make her way to the stairs a loud wail rushed in. It was the ceaseless heart-rending wail of Chanteau. Madame Chanteau, who was following Véronique, thereupon seemed struck with an idea, and exclaimed in an undertone, emphasising her words:

'Tell her that she can't think of leaving her uncle in the dreadful state in which he is. Do you hear?'

'Well, he certainly is bellowing hard; there's no doubt of that,' Véronique replied.

She went up the stairs, while her mistress, who had stretched out her hand towards her husband's room, purposely refrained from closing the door. The sick man's groans ascended the staircase, increasing in volume at every fresh storey. When Véronique reached Pauline's room she found her just on the point of leaving, having fastened up in a bundle what little linen she would absolutely require, and intending to send old Malivoire to fetch the rest in the morning. She had calmed down again, and, though very pale and low-spirited, was simply obeying the dictates of her reason without any feeling of anger.

'Either she or I,' was the only answer she returned to all that Véronique said, and she sedulously avoided mentioning Louise's name.

When Véronique conveyed this reply to Madame Chanteau, she found the latter in Louise's room, where the girl, having dressed herself—for on her side she was determined to go away—stood trembling, alarmed at the slightest creaking of the door. Madame Chanteau was obliged to yield, and sent to Verchemont for the baker's trap, saying that she would take Louise to her Aunt Léonie at Arromanches. They would invent some story to tell this lady; they would make the violence of Chanteau's attack a pretext, alleging that his screams had become quite unendurable.

After the departure of the two ladies, whom Lazare safely seated in the baker's trap, Véronique shouted in the passage at the top of her voice:

'You can come downstairs now, Mademoiselle Pauline; there is nobody here.'

The house seemed empty; the heavy gloomy silence was broken only by Chanteau's perpetual groans, which became louder and louder. As Pauline came down the last step Lazare, returning to the house from the yard, met her face to face. His whole body shook with a nervous trembling; he paused for a moment, as though anxious to confess his fault and implore forgiveness, but a rush of tears choked his voice, and he hurried up to his own room, without having been able to say a word.

Chanteau was still lying with his head across the bolster and his arm rigidly outstretched. He no longer dared make the slightest movement; doubtless he had not even been aware of Pauline's absence, as he lay there with his eyes closed and his mouth open to yell and groan. None of the sounds of the house reached him; and all he thought of was to complain as long and as loudly as his breath would let him. His cries grew more and more desperate, till they at last seriously disturbed Minouche, who had had a family of four kittens thrown away that morning, and who, already quite forgetful of them, had been purring lazily on an armchair.

When Pauline took her place again, her uncle howled so loudly that the cat got up, unable to endure the din. She fixed her eyes steadily on the sick man, with the indignation of a well-behaved person whose serenity is disturbed. If she could not be allowed to purr in peace, it would be impossible for her to stop there. And she took herself off, with her tail in the air.

VI

W<small>HEN</small> Madame Chanteau returned home again in the evening, a few minutes before dinner, no further mention was made of Louise. She merely called to Véronique to come and take her boots off. Her left foot was paining her.

'Little wonder of that!' the servant murmured. 'It's quite swollen.'

The seams of the leather had indeed left crimson marks on the soft white skin. Lazare, who had just come downstairs, looked at his mother's foot and said:

'You have been walking too much.'

But she had really only walked through Arromanches. Besides the pain in her foot, she that day experienced a difficulty in breathing, such as had been increasingly affecting her at intervals for some months past. Presently she began to blame her boots for the pain she was enduring.

'Those tiresome bootmakers don't ever seem to make the instep high enough! As soon as ever I get my boots on I'm in a state of torture.'

However, as she felt no further pain after she had put on her slippers, nothing more was thought of the matter. Next morning the swelling had extended to her ankle, but by the following night it disappeared altogether.

A week passed. From the very first dinner at which Pauline had again found herself in the presence of Madame Chanteau and Lazare they had all forced themselves to resume their ordinary demeanour towards each other. No allusion was made to what had occurred; everything seemed to be just the same as usual. The family life went on in the old mechanical way, with the same customary expressions of affection, the same good-mornings and good-nights, and the same lifeless kisses given at fixed hours. A feeling of great relief came, however, that they were at last able to wheel Chanteau to his place at table. This time his knees had remained stiff with ankylosis, and he could not stand upright. But none the less he enjoyed his freedom from actual pain, and was so entirely wrapped up in egotistical satisfaction at his own well-being that he never gave a thought to the joys or cares of the other members of the family. When Madame Chanteau ventured to mention Louise's sudden departure, he begged her not to speak to him of such melancholy matters. Pauline, now freed from her attendance in her uncle's room, tried to find some other means of occupying herself, but she could not conceal the grief oppressing her. She found the evenings especially painful, and her distress was plainly visible despite all her affectation of calmness. Ostensibly everything was just the same as usual, and the old every-day routine was gone through; but every now and then a nervous gesture or even a momentary pause would make them all conscious of the hidden breach, the rift of which they never spoke, but which was, all the same, always widening.

At first Lazare had felt contempt for himself. The moral superiority of Pauline, who was so upright and just, had filled him with shame and vexation. Why had he lacked the courage to go to her, confess his fault, and ask her pardon? He might have told her the whole truth, how he had suddenly been excited and carried away by the presence of Louise, whose glamour had intoxicated him; and his cousin was too generous and large-hearted not to understand and make allowances. But insurmountable embarrassment had kept him back; he felt afraid of cutting a still more contemptible figure in the girl's eyes by entering upon an explanation in which he would very likely stammer and hesitate like a child. Beneath his hesitation, too, there lurked the fear of telling another falsehood, for his thoughts were still full of Louise, her image was perpetually haunting him. In spite of himself, his long walks always seemed to lead him into the neighbourhood of Arromanches. One evening he went right on to Aunt Léonie's little house and prowled round it, hurriedly taking flight as he heard a shutter move, all confusion at the baseness he had contemplated. It was the sense of his own unworthiness that doubled his feeling of shame in Pauline's presence; and he freely condemned himself, though he could not quench his passion. The struggle was perpetually going on within his mind, and never before had his natural irresolution proved such a source of pain to him. He only had sufficient honesty and strength of purpose left him to avoid Pauline and thus escape the last dishonour of perjuring himself. It was possible that he still loved his cousin, but the alluring image of her friend was ever before him, blotting out the past and barring the future.

Pauline, on her side, waited for his defence and apology. In her first outburst of indignation she had sworn that she would never forgive him. Then she had begun to suffer secretly at finding that her forgiveness had not been asked. Why did he keep silence, and seem so feverish and restless, spending all his time out of doors, as though he were afraid to find himself alone with her? She was quite ready to listen to him and to forget everything, if only he would show a little repentance. As the hoped-for explanation failed to come, she racked her mind to find reasons for her cousin's silence. Her own pride kept her from making the first advance; and, as the days painfully and slowly passed, she succeeded in conquering herself so far as to resume all her old cheerful activity. But beneath that brave show of calmness there lurked everlasting unhappiness, and in her own room at night she burst into fits of tears, and had to stifle the sound of her sobs by burying her head in her pillow. Nobody spoke about the wedding, though it was evident that they all thought of it. The autumn was coming on; what was to be done? Nobody seemed to care to say anything on the matter; they all avoided coming to a decision till they should feel able to discuss it again.

It was about this time that Madame Chanteau completely lost her head. She had always been excitable and restless, but the dim causes which had undermined all her good principles had now reached a period of great destructiveness. Never before had she found herself so completely off her balance, so nervously feverish as now. The necessity for restraint exasperated her torment. She suffered from her rageful longing for money, which grew stronger day by day and ended by carrying off her reason and her heart. She was continually attacking Pauline, whom she now began to blame for Louise's departure, accusing her of it as of an act of robbery that had despoiled her son. She felt an ever-open wound which would not close; the smallest trifles assumed monstrous proportions; she remembered the slightest incidents of the horrid scene; she could still hear Pauline crying, 'Be off! Be off!' And she began to imagine that she herself was being driven away, that all the joy and the fortune of the family was being flung into the streets. At night-time, as she rolled about in bed in a restless semi-somnolent state, she even regretted that death had not freed them from that accursed Pauline. Intricate schemes and calculations sprang up in wild confusion in her brain, but she was never able to hit upon any practicable means of getting rid of the girl.

At the same time a kind of reaction seemed to increase her affection for her own son, and she worshipped him now almost more than she had done when she had held him in her arms as an infant and had possessed his undivided love. From morning till night she followed him with her anxious eyes; and when they were alone together she would throw her arms around him and kiss him, and beg him not to distress himself. She swore to him that everything should be put right, that she would strangle those who opposed her rather than have him unhappy. After a fortnight of this continual struggling, her face had become as pale as wax, though she grew no thinner. The swelling in her feet had twice appeared again, and had then subsided.

One morning she rang for Véronique, to whom she showed her legs, which had swollen to the thighs during the night.

'Just look at the state I'm in! Isn't it provoking? I wanted to go out so much to-day, and now I shall be obliged to stay in bed! Don't say anything about it for fear of alarming Lazare.'

She did not seem to be at all alarmed herself. She merely remarked that she felt a little tired, and the members of the family simply supposed that she was suffering from a slight attack of lumbago. As Lazare had gone off on one of his rambles along the shore, and Pauline refrained from entering her aunt's room, knowing that her presence there would be unwelcome, the sick woman occupied herself by dinning furious charges against her niece into the servant's ears. She seemed to have lost all control of herself. The immobility to which she was condemned and the palpitations of the heart which stifled her at the slightest movement goaded her into ever-increasing exasperation.

'What's she doing downstairs? Up to some fresh wickedness, I'm sure! She'll never think of bringing me even a glass of water, you'll see!'

'But, Madame,' urged Véronique, 'it is you who drive her from you.'

'Ah! you don't know her! There never was such a hypocrite as she is. Before other people she pretends to be kind and generous, but there's nothing she wouldn't do or say when your back's turned. Yes, my good girl, you were the only one who saw things clearly on the day I first brought her here. If she had never come, we shouldn't now be in the state we are. She will prove the ruin of us all. Your master has suffered all the agonies of the damned since she has been in this house, and she has worried and distressed me till she has quite undermined my health; while as for my son, she made him lose his head entirely.'

'Oh, Madame! how can you say that when she is so kind and good to you all?'

Eight up to the evening Madame Chanteau thus unburdened herself of her anger. She raved about everything, particularly about the abominable way in which Louise had been turned out of the house, though it was the money question that aroused her greatest anger. When Véronique, after dinner, was able to go down to the kitchen again she found Pauline there, occupying herself by putting the crockery away; and so the servant, in her turn, took the opportunity of unburdening herself of the angry indignation which was choking her.

'Ah! Mademoiselle, it is very good of you to bother about their plates. If I were you, I should smash the whole lot to bits!'

'What for?' the girl asked in astonishment.

'Because, whatever you were to do, you couldn't come up to half of what they accuse you of!'

Then she broke out angrily, raking up everything from the day of Pauline's arrival there.

'It would put God Almighty Himself into a rage to see such things! She has drained your money away sou by sou, and she has done it in the most shameless manner imaginable. Upon my word, to hear her talk one would suppose that it was she who had been keeping you. When she had your money in her secrétaire she made ever so much fuss about keeping it safe and untouched, but all that didn't prevent her greedy hands from digging pretty big holes in it. It's a nice piece of play-acting that she's been keeping up all this time, contriving to make you pay for those salt workshops and then keeping the pot boiling with what was left! Ah! I daresay you don't know, but if it hadn't been for you they would all have starved! She got into a pretty flurry when the people in Paris began to worry her about the accounts! Yes, indeed, you could have had her sent right off to the assize court if you had liked. But that didn't teach her any lesson; she's still robbing you, and she'll end by stripping you of your very last copper. I daresay you think I'm not speaking the truth, but I swear that I am! I have seen it all with my eyes and heard it with my ears; and I have too much respect for you, Mademoiselle, to tell you the worst things, such as how she went on when you were ill and she couldn't go rummaging in your chest of drawers.'

Pauline listened without finding a single word with which to interrupt the narrative. The thought that the family were actually living upon her and rapaciously plundering her had, indeed, frequently cast a gloom over her happiest days. But she had always refused to allow her mind to dwell on the subject; she had preferred to go on living in ignorance and accusing herself secretly of avarice. To-day, however, she had to hear the whole truth of the matter, and Véronique's outspokenness seemed to make facts worse than she had believed. At each fresh sentence the young girl's memory awoke within her; she recalled old incidents, the exact meaning of which she had not at the time understood, and she now saw clearly through all Madame Chanteau's machinations to get hold of her money. Whilst listening she had slowly dropped upon a chair, as though suddenly overcome with great fatigue, and an expression of grief and pain appeared upon her lips.

'You are exaggerating!' she murmured.

'Exaggerating! I!' Véronique continued violently. « It isn't so much the money part of the business that makes me so angry. But what I can't forgive her is for having taken Monsieur Lazare from you after once having given him to you. Oh yes! it was very nice of her to rob you of your money and then to turn against you because you were no longer rich enough, and Monsieur Lazare must needs marry an heiress! Yes, indeed; what do you think of it? They first pillage you, and then toss you aside because you are no longer rich enough for them! No, Mademoiselle, I will not give over! There is no need to tear people's hearts to shreds after emptying their pockets. As you loved your cousin, and it was his duty to pay you back with affection and kindness, why, it was abominable of your aunt to steal him from you! She did everything. I saw through it all! Yes, every evening she excited the girl; she made her fall in love with the young man by all her talk about him. As certainly as that lamp is shining, it was she who threw them into each other's arms. Bah! she would have been only too glad to have seen them compelled to marry; and it isn't her fault if that didn't take place. Try and defend her if you can, she who trampled you under foot and caused you so much grief, for you sob in the night like a Magdalene! I can hear you from my room! I feel beside myself with all that cruelty and injustice!'

'Don't say any more, I beseech you!' stammered Pauline, whose courage failed her. 'You are giving me too great pain.'

Big tears rolled down her cheeks. She felt quite conscious that Véronique was only telling her the truth, and her heart bled within her. All the past sprang up before her eyes in lively reality, and she again saw Lazare pressing Louise to his breast, while Madame Chanteau kept guard on the landing. Ah, God! what had she done that everyone should join in deceiving her, when she herself had kept faith with all?

'I beg you, say no more! I am choking with it all!'

Then Véronique, seeing that she was painfully overcome, contented herself with adding:

'Well, it's for your sake and not for hers that I don't go on. She's been spitting out a string of abominations about you ever since the morning. She quite exhausts my patience and makes my blood boil when I hear her turning all the kindnesses you've done her into evil. Yes, indeed! She pretends that you have been the ruin of the family, and that now you are killing her son! Go and listen at the door, if you don't believe me!'

Then, as Pauline burst into a fit of sobbing, Véronique, quite unnerved, flung her arms round her neck and kissed her hair, saying:

'There, there, Mademoiselle, I'll say no more. But it's only right that you should know. It's too shameful for you to be treated in such a way. But there, I won't say another word, so don't take on so!'

They were silent for a time, while the servant raked out the embers still burning in the grate, but she could not refrain from growling:

'I know very well why she's swelling out! All her wickedness has gathered in her knees!'

Pauline, who was looking intently at the tiled floor, her mind upset and heavy with grief, raised her eyes and asked Véronique what she meant. Had the swelling, then, come back again? The servant showed some embarrassment, as she had to break the promise of silence which she had given to Madame Chanteau. Though she allowed herself full liberty to judge her mistress, she still obeyed her orders. Now, however, she was obliged to admit that her legs had again swollen badly during the night, though Monsieur Lazare was not to know it. While the servant gave details of Madame Chanteau's condition the expression of Pauline's face changed—depression gave place to anxiety. In spite of all that she had just learned of the old lady's conduct, she was painfully alarmed by the appearance of symptoms which she knew betokened grave danger.

'But she mustn't be left alone like this!' she exclaimed, springing up. 'She is in danger!'

'In danger, indeed?' cried Véronique, unfeelingly. 'She doesn't at all look like it, and she certainly doesn't think so herself, for she's far too busy befouling other folks and giving herself airs in her bed like a Pasha. Besides, she's asleep just now, and we must wait till to-morrow, which is just the day when the Doctor always comes to Bonneville.'

The next day it was no longer possible to conceal from Lazare his mother's condition. All night long had Pauline listened, constantly awakened from brief dozes, and ever believing that she heard groans ascending through the floor. Then in the morning she fell into so deep a sleep that it was only at nine o'clock she was roused by the slamming of a door. When, after hastily dressing herself, she went downstairs to make inquiries, she encountered Lazare on the landing of the first floor. He had just left his mother's room. The swelling was reaching her stomach, and Véronique had come to the conclusion that the young man must be warned.

'Well?' asked Pauline.

At first Lazare, who looked utterly upset, made no reply. Yielding to a habit that had grown upon him, he grasped his chin with his trembling fingers, and when at last he tried to speak he could scarcely stammer:

'It is all over with her!'

He went upstairs to his own room with a dazed air. Pauline followed him. When they reached that big room on the second floor, which she had never entered since the day she had surprised Louise there in her cousin's arms, Pauline closed the door and tried to reassure the young man.

'You don't even know what is the matter with her. Wait till the Doctor comes, at any rate, before you begin to alarm yourself. She is very strong, and we may always hope for the best.'

But he was possessed by a sudden presentiment, and repeated obstinately:

'It is all over with her; all over.'

It was a perfectly unexpected blow, and quite overcame him. When he had risen that morning, he had looked at the sea, as he always did, yawning with boredom and complaining of the idiotic emptiness of life. Then, his mother having shown him her knees, the sight of her poor swollen limbs, puffed out by oedema, huge and pallid, looking already like lifeless trunks, had thrilled him with panic-stricken tenderness. It was always like this. At every moment fresh trouble came. Even now, as he sat upon the edge of his big table, trembling from head to foot, he did not dare to give the name of the disease whose symptoms he had recognised. He had ever been haunted by a dread of heart disease seizing upon himself and his relations, for his two years of medical study had not sufficed to show him that all diseases were liable to lead to death. To be stricken at the heart, at the very source of life, that to him seemed the all-terrible, pitiless cause of death. And it was this death that his mother was going to die, and which he himself would infallibly die also in his own turn!

'Why should you distress yourself in this way?' Pauline asked him. 'Plenty of dropsical people live for a very long time. Don't you remember Madame Simonnot? She died in the end of inflammation of the lungs.'

But Lazare only shook his head. He was not a child, to be deceived in that manner. His feet went on swinging to and fro, and he still continued trembling, while he kept his eyes fixed persistently on the window. Then, for the first time since their rupture, Pauline kissed him on the brow in her old manner. They were together again, side by side, in that big room, where they had grown up, and all their feeling against one another had died away before the great grief which was threatening them. The girl wiped the tears from her eyes, but Lazare could not cry, and simply went on repeating, mechanically, as it were: 'It is all over with her; all over.'

When Doctor Cazenove called, about eleven o'clock, as he generally did every week after his round through Bonneville, he appeared very much astonished at finding Madame Chanteau in bed. 'What was the matter with the dear lady?' he asked. He even grew jocular, and declared that they were quite turning the house into an ambulance. But when he had examined and sounded the patient, he became more serious, and, indeed, needed all his great experience to conceal the fact that he was much alarmed.

Madame Chanteau herself had no idea of the gravity of her condition.

'I hope you are going to get me out of this, Doctor,' she said gaily. 'There's only one thing I'm frightened about, and that is that this swelling may stifle me if it goes on mounting higher and higher.'

'Oh! keep yourself easy about that,' he replied, smiling in turn. 'It won't go any higher, and if it does we shall know how to stop it.'

Lazare, who had come into the room after the Doctor's examination, listened to him trembling, burning to take him aside and question him, so that he might know the worst.

'Now, my dear Madame,' Doctor Cazenove resumed, 'don't worry yourself. I will come and have a little chat with you again to-morrow. Good-morning; I will write my prescription downstairs.'

When they got down, Pauline prevented the Doctor and Lazare from entering the dining-room, for in Chanteau's presence nothing more serious than ordinary lumbago had ever been mentioned. The girl had already put ink and paper on the table in the kitchen. And, noticing their impatient anxiety, Doctor Cazenove confessed that the case was a grave one; but he spoke in long and involved sentences, and avoided telling them anything definite.

'You mean that it is all over with her, eh?' Lazare cried at last, in a kind of irritation. 'It's the heart, isn't it?'

Pauline gave the Doctor a glance full of entreaty, which he understood.

'The heart? Well, I'm not quite so sure about that,' he replied. 'But, at any rate, even if we can't quite cure her, she may go on for a long time yet, with care.'

The young man shrugged his shoulders in the angry fashion of a child who is not to be taken in by fine stories. Then he exclaimed: 'And you never gave me any warning, Doctor, though you attended her quite recently! These dreadful diseases never come on all at once. Had you no idea of it?'

'Well, yes,' Cazenove murmured, 'I had indeed noticed some faint indications.'

Then, as Lazare broke out into a sneering laugh, he added:

'Listen to me, my fine fellow. I don't think that I'm a greater fool than others, and yet this is not the first time when it has happened to me to have had no inkling of what was coming, and to find myself taken by surprise. It is absurd of you to expect us to be able to know everything; it is already a great deal to be able to spell out the first few lines of what is going on in that intricate piece of mechanism—the human body.'

He seemed vexed, and dashed his pen about angrily as he wrote his prescription, tearing the thin paper provided for him. The naval surgeon cropped up once more in the brusque movements of his big frame. However, when he stood up again, with his old face tanned brown with the sea air, he softened as he saw both Pauline and Lazare hanging their heads hopelessly in front of him.

'My poor children,' he said, 'we will try our best to bring her round. You know that I never put on grand airs before you. So I tell you frankly that I can say nothing. But it seems to me that there is, at any rate, no immediate danger.'

Then he left the house, having ascertained that Lazare had a supply of tincture of digitalis. The prescription simply ordered some applications of this tincture to the patient's legs, and a few drops of it to be taken in a glass of sugar and water. This treatment, said the Doctor, would suffice for the moment; he would bring some pills with him in the morning. It was possible, too, that he might make up his mind to bleed her. Pauline went out with him to his gig in order to ask him to tell her the real truth, but the real truth was that he did not dare to say one thing or the other. When she returned into the kitchen the girl found Lazare re-perusing the prescription. The mere word digitalis had made him turn pale once more.

'Don't distress yourself so much,' said Véronique, who had begun to pare some potatoes, as an excuse for remaining where they were and hearing what was said. 'The doctors are all croakers. And surely there can't be much the matter when they can't tell you what it is.'

They began to discuss the question round the bowl into which the cook was cutting the potatoes, and Pauline appeared to grow a little easier in her mind. She had gone that morning to kiss her aunt, and had found her looking well. A person with cheeks like here could not surely be dying. But Lazare went on twisting the prescription with his feverish fingers. The word digitalis blazed before his eyes. His mother was doomed.

'I am going up again,' he said at last.

As he reached the door he seemed to hesitate, and turned to his cousin and asked:

'Won't you come, just for a minute?'

Pauline then seemed to hesitate in her turn, and finally murmured:

'I'm afraid she mightn't be pleased if I did.'

And so, after a moment of silent embarrassment, Lazare went upstairs by himself, without saying another word.

When Lazare, for fear lest his father should be disquieted by his absence, appeared again at luncheon, he was very pale. From time to time during the day a ring of the bell summoned Véronique, who ran up with platefuls of soup, which the patient could scarcely be induced to taste; and when she came downstairs again she told Pauline that the poor young man was growing perfectly distracted. It was heart-breaking, she said, to see him shivering with fever by his mother's bedside, wringing his hands and with his face racked by grief, as though he every moment feared that he should see her torn from him. About three o'clock, as the servant came downstairs once more, she leant over the balustrade and called to Pauline; and as the girl reached the first-floor landing she said to her:

'You ought to go in, Mademoiselle, and help him a little. So much the worse if it displeases her. She wants Monsieur Lazare to turn her round, and he can only groan, without daring to touch her. And she won't let me go near her!'

Pauline entered the room. Madame Chanteau lay back, propped up by three pillows, and, as far as mere appearances went, if it had not been for the quick, distressful breathing which set her shoulders heaving, she might have been keeping her bed from sheer idleness. Lazare stood before her, stammering:

'It's on your right side, then, that you want me to turn you?'

'Yes; just turn me a little. Ah! my poor boy, how difficult it seems to make you understand!'

But Pauline had already taken hold gently of her aunt and turned her, saying:

'Let me do it! I am used to doing it for my uncle. There! Are you comfortable now?'

But Madame Chanteau irritably exclaimed that they were shaking her to pieces. She seemed unable to make the slightest movement without being almost suffocated, and for a moment, indeed, she lay panting, with her face quite livid. Lazare had stepped behind the bed-curtains to conceal his expression of despair; still, he remained present while Pauline rubbed her aunt's legs with the tincture of digitalis. At first he turned his head aside, but some fascination ever made his eyes return to those swollen limbs, those inert masses of pale flesh, the sight of which made him almost choke with agony. When his cousin saw how utterly upset he was she thought it safer to send him out of the room. She went up to him, and, as Madame Chanteau dozed off, tired out by the mere changing of her position, she whispered to him softly:

'You would do better to go away.'

For a moment or two he resisted; his tears blinded him. Then he yielded and went down, ashamed, and sobbing:

'Oh, God! God! I cannot endure it! I cannot endure it!'

When the sick woman again awoke, she did not at first notice her son's absence. She seemed to be in a state of stupor, and as if egotistically seeking to make sure that she was really alive. Pauline's presence alone appeared to disquiet her, although the girl sat far away and neither spoke nor moved. As her aunt bent forward, however, she felt that she must just say a word to let her know why Lazare was absent.

'It is I. Don't worry. Lazare has gone to Verchemont, where he has to see the carpenter.'

'All right,' Madame Chanteau murmured.

'You are not so ill that he should neglect his business, are you?'

'Oh! certainly not.'

From that moment she spoke but seldom of her son, notwithstanding the adoration she had manifested for him only the previous night. He became obliterated from the rest of her life, after being so long the sole reason and object of her existence. The softening of her brain, which was now beginning, merely left her a physical anxiety about her own health. She accepted her niece's care and attendance, without apparently being conscious of the change, merely following her constantly with her eyes, as though she were troubled by increasing suspicions as she saw the girl pass to and fro before the bed.

Lazare had gone down into the kitchen, where he remained nerveless, beside himself. The whole house frightened him. He could not stay in his own room, the emptiness of which oppressed him, and he dared not cross the dining-room, where the sight of his father, quietly reading a newspaper, threw him into sobs. So it was to the kitchen that he constantly betook himself, as being the one warm, cheerful spot in the house—one where he was comforted by the sight of Véronique, bustling about amongst her pans, as in the old tranquil times. As she saw him seat himself near the fireplace on a rush-bottomed chair, which he made his own, she frankly told him what she thought of his lack of courage.

'It's not much use you are, Monsieur Lazare. It's poor Mademoiselle Pauline who will have everything to do again. Anyone would suppose, to see you, that there had never been a sick woman in the house before, and yet, when your cousin nearly died of her sore throat, you nursed her so attentively. Yes, you know you did, and you stayed with her for a whole fortnight helping her to change her position whenever it was necessary.'

Lazare listened to Véronique with a feeling of surprise. This inconsistency of his had not struck him before, and he could not understand his own illogical and varying feelings and thoughts.

'Yes; that is quite true,' he said, 'quite true.'

'You would not let anybody enter the room,' the servant continued, 'and Mademoiselle was even a more distressing sight than Madame is, her suffering was so great. Whenever I came away from her room I felt completely upset, and couldn't have eaten a mouthful of anything. But now the mere sight of your mother in bed makes your heart faint. You can't even take her a cup of gruel. Whatever your mother may be, you ought to remember that she's still your mother.'

Lazare no longer heard her; he was gazing before him into space. At last he said:

'I can't help it; I really can't. It's perhaps because it is my mother, but I can't do anything. When I see her and those poor legs of hers, and think that she is dying, something seems to be snapping inside me, and I should burst out crying if I did not rush from the room.'

He began to tremble all over again. He had picked up a knife which had fallen from the table, and gazed at it with his tear-dimmed eyes without seeing it. For some time neither spoke. Véronique busied herself over her soup, which was cooking, to conceal the emotion which choked her. At last she resumed:

'You had better go down to the beach for a little while, Monsieur Lazare. You bother me by always being here in my way. And take Matthew with you. He is very tiresome, and no more knows what to do with himself than you do. I have no end of trouble to keep him from going upstairs to Madame's room.'

The next morning Doctor Cazenove was still doubtful. A sudden catastrophe was possible, he said, or the patient might recover for a longer or shorter time, if the swelling could be reduced. He gave up the idea of bleeding her, and confined himself to ordering her to take some pills which he brought, and to continue the use of the tincture of digitalis. His air of vexation showed that he felt little confidence in those remedies in a case of organic disorder, when the successive derangement of every organ renders a physician's skill of no avail. However, he was able to assure them that the sick woman suffered no pain; and, indeed, Madame Chanteau made no complaint of actual suffering. Her legs felt as heavy as lead, and she breathed with constantly increasing difficulty whenever she moved; but, whilst she lay there quietly on her back, her voice remained so firm and strong, and her eyes so bright and clear, that even she herself was deceived as to the gravity of her condition. Her son was the only one of those around her who did not venture to be hopeful at seeing her looking so calm. When the Doctor went away in his gig, he told them not to grieve too much, for that it was a great mercy both for herself and for them that she was quite unaware of her danger.

The first night had been a very hard one for Pauline. Reclining in an easy chair, she had not been able to get any sleep, for the heavy breathing of the sick woman constantly filled her ears. Whenever she was on the point of dropping off, her aunt's breath seemed to shake the house; and then, when she opened her eyes again, she felt sad and oppressed; all the troubles which had been marring her life for the last few months sprang up in her mind with fresh force. Even by the side of that deathbed she could not feel at peace, she could not constrain herself to forgive. Amidst her nightmare-like vigil during the mournful night hours Véronique's assertions caused her great torture. Old outbursts of anger and bitter jealousy surged up in her again, as she mentally recapitulated the painful details. To be loved no more! To find herself deceived, betrayed by those she had loved! And to find herself all alone, full of contempt and revolt! Her heart's wound opened and bled afresh, and never before had she experienced such bitter pain from Lazare's insulting faithlessness. Since they had, so to say, murdered her, it mattered little to her now who died! And, amidst her aunt's heavy breathing, she went on brooding ceaselessly over the robbery of her money and her affections.

The next morning she still felt contrary influences at work within her; she experienced no return of affection; it was a sense of duty alone which kept her in her aunt's room. The consciousness of this made her unhappy, and she wondered if she too were growing as wicked as the others. In this troubled state the day passed away, and, discontented with herself, repelled by her aunt's suspicions, she forced herself into attentive activity. Madame Chanteau received her ministrations snappishly, and followed her movements with suspicious eyes, carefully watching her every action. If she asked her niece for a handkerchief, she always sniffed it before using it, and when she saw the girl bring her a hot-water bottle she wanted to examine the jug.

'What's the matter with her?' Pauline whispered very softly to Véronique. 'Does she think me capable of trying to do her harm?'

When Véronique gave her a dose of her draught after the Doctor had gone away, Madame Chanteau, not noticing her niece, who was looking for some linen in the wardrobe, inquired of the servant: 'Did the Doctor prepare this?'

'No, Madame, it was Mademoiselle Pauline.'

Then the sick woman just sipped it with her lips, and made a grimace.

'Ah! it tastes of copper. I don't know what she has been making me take, but I've never had the taste of copper out of my mouth since yesterday.'

And suddenly she tossed the spoon away behind the bed. Véronique looked on in amazement.

'Whatever's the matter? What an idea to get into your head!'

'I don't want to go away before my time,' replied Madame Chanteau, as she laid her head back again upon her pillow. 'Listen! my lungs are quite sound; and it's not impossible that she may go before I do, for she isn't very healthy.'

Pauline had heard her. She turned with a heart-pang and looked at Véronique; and instead of coming any nearer she stepped further away, feeling quite ashamed of her aunt for her abominable suspicions. A sudden change came over her feelings. The idea of that unhappy woman, consumed by fear and hatred, moved her to the deepest pity; far from feeling any increase of bitterness, it was sorrowful emotion that she experienced as her eyes caught sight of all the medicine which her aunt had thrown away under the bed, from a fear of being poisoned. Until the evening she evinced persevering gentleness, and did not appear to notice the distrustful glances with which her aunt followed every motion of her hands. Her one ardent desire was to overcome the dying woman's fears by affectionate attentions, in order that she might not carry such frightful suspicions to the grave. And she forbade Véronique to distress Lazare further by telling him the truth.

Only once since morning had Madame Chanteau asked for her son, and she had appeared quite content with the first excuse made for his absence, evincing no surprise at not seeing him again. She said nothing about her husband, expressed no uneasiness whatever about his being left alone in the dining-room. All the world was gradually disappearing for her, and, minute by minute, the icy coldness of her limbs seemed to mount higher till it chilled her very heart. Whenever meal-time came round, Pauline had to go downstairs and tell some fib to her uncle. In the evening she told one to Lazare as well, assuring him that the swelling was subsiding.

In the night, however, the disease made alarming progress, and the next morning, soon after daybreak, when Pauline and the servant beheld the sick woman they were terrified by the wandering look in her eyes. Her face was not changed, and there was no feverishness, but her mind appeared to be failing her, a fixed idea seemed to be destroying her reason. She had reached the last phase; her brain, gradually wrought upon by a single absorbing passion, had now become a prey to insanity.

That morning, before Doctor Cazenove's arrival, they had a terrible time. Madame Chanteau would not even let her niece come near her.

'Do let me nurse you, I beg you!' Pauline said. 'Just let me raise you a little, as you are lying so uncomfortably.'

But her aunt began to struggle as though they were trying to suffocate her.

'No, no! You have got a pair of scissors there! Ah! you are sticking them into me! I can feel them! I can feel them! I'm bleeding all over!'

The heart-broken girl was obliged to keep at a distance from her aunt. She was quite overcome with fatigue and distress, breaking down with her useless kindly endeavours. She was obliged to put up with insults and accusations which made her burst into tears before she could induce her aunt to accept the slightest service from her. Sometimes all her efforts were in vain, and she fell weeping upon a chair, despairing of ever winning back again that affection of former days, which was now replaced by insane animosity. Still she would become all resignation once more, and strive to find some way of making her assistance acceptable by manifesting even greater care and tenderness. That morning, however, her persistent entreaties ended by provoking a paroxysm which long left her trembling.

'Aunt,' she said, as she was preparing a dose of medicine, 'it's time for you to take your draught. The Doctor, you know particularly said that you were to take it regularly.'

Madame Chanteau insisted upon seeing the bottle, and then smelt its contents.

'Is it the same as I had yesterday?'

'Yes, aunt.'

'Then I won't have any of it!'

However, by much affectionate wheedling and entreaties, her niece

prevailed on her to take just one spoonful. The sick woman's face wore an expression of deep suspicion, and no sooner was the spoonful of physio in her mouth than she spat it out again upon the floor, torn by a violent fit of coughing, and screaming out between her hiccoughs:
'It's vitriol! It is burning me!'

Amidst this supreme paroxysm her hatred and terror of Pauline, which had gradually increased ever since the day when she had first abstracted a twenty-franc piece of the other's money, now found vent in a flood of wild words, to which the poor girl listened, quite thunderstruck, unable to say a single syllable in her defence.

'Ah! you fancied I shouldn't detect it! You put verdigris and vitriol into everything! It's that which is killing me! There was nothing the matter with me, and I should have been able to get up this morning if you hadn't mixed some verdigris with my broth yesterday evening. Yes, you are tired of me, and want to get me buried and done with. But I'm very tough, and it is I who will bury you yet.'

Her speech became thicker, she choked, and her lips turned so black that an immediate catastrophe seemed probable.

'Oh! aunt, aunt!' cried Pauline, overcome with terror, 'you are making yourself so much worse by going on like this!'

'Well, that's what you want, I'm sure! Oh! I know you. You have been planning it for a long time; ever since you have been here your only thought has been how to kill us off and get hold of our money. You want to have the house for your own, and I am in your way. Ah! hussy, I ought to have choked you the first day you came here! I hate you! I hate you!'

Pauline stood there motionless, weeping in silence. Only one word rose to her lips, as though in involuntary protest against her aunt's accusations. 'Oh God! God!'

But Madame Chanteau was completely exhausted by the violence of her fury, and her mad outburst gave place to a childish terror. She fell back on her pillow, crying:

'Don't come near me! Don't touch me! If you do I shall scream out for help! No, no! I won't drink it; it's poison!'

She pulled the bed-clothes over her with her twitching hands, buried her head amongst the pillows, and kept her mouth tightly closed. When her niece, who was terribly alarmed, came to her bedside to try to calm her, she broke out into frightful screams.

'Aunt dear, be reasonable. I won't make you take any against your will.'

'Yes, you will! You've got the bottle! Oh! I'm terrified! I'm terrified!'

She was almost at the last gasp; her head had got too low, and purple blotches appeared upon her face. Pauline, imagining that her aunt was dying, rang the bell for Véronique; and it was as much as the two of them could do to raise her up and lay her properly on her pillows. Then Pauline's own personal sufferings and heartaches disappeared amidst her intense grief. She thought no more about the last wound which her heart had received; all her passion and jealousy vanished in presence of that great wretchedness. Every other feeling became lost in one of deep pity, and she would have gladly endured injustice and insult and have sacrificed herself still more if by so doing she could only have given comfort and consolation to the others. She set herself bravely to bear the principal share of life's woes; and from that moment she never once gave way, but manifested beside her aunt's death-bed all the quiet resignation which she had shown when threatened by death herself. She was always ready; she never recoiled from anything. Even her old gentle affection came back to her; she forgave her aunt for all her mad violence during her paroxysms, and wept with pity at finding that she had gradually become insane; forcing herself to think of her as she had been in earlier years, loving her as she had done on that stormy evening when she had first come with her to Bonneville.

That day Doctor Cazenove did not call till after luncheon. An accident had detained him at Verchemont; a farmer there had broken his arm, and the Doctor had stayed to set it. After seeing Madame Chanteau he came down into the kitchen, and made no attempt to conceal his alarm. Lazare was sitting there by the fire, in that feverish idleness which preyed upon him.

'There is no more hope, is there?' he asked. 'I was reading Bouillaud's Treatise on the Diseases of the Heart again last night.'

Pauline, who had come downstairs with the Doctor, once more gave him an entreating look, which prompted him to interrupt the young man in his usual brusque fashion. Whenever an illness turned out badly, he always showed a little anger.

'Ah! the heart, my good fellow, the heart seems to be the only idea you have got! One can't be certain of anything. For my own part, I believe it's rather the liver that is affected. But, of course, when the machine gets out of order, everything in turn is more or less affected—the lungs, the stomach, and the heart itself. Instead of reading Bouillaud last night, which has only upset you, you would have done much better to go to sleep.'

This dictum of the Doctor's was like an order given to the house. In Lazare's presence it was always said that his mother was dying from a diseased liver; but he refused to believe it, and spent his sleepless hours in turning over the pages of his old books. He grew quite confused over the different symptoms, and the remark made by the Doctor that the various organs of the human body became successively deranged only served to increase his alarm.

'Well,' he said with difficulty, 'how long, then, do you think she will last?'

Cazenove made a gesture of doubt.

'A fortnight; perhaps a month. You had better not question me, for I might make a mistake, and then you would be right in saying that we know nothing and can do nothing. But the progress that the disease has made since yesterday is terrible.'

Véronique, who was washing some glasses, looked at him in alarm. Could it really be true, then, that Madame was so very ill and was going to die? Until then she had been unable to believe there was any actual danger, and had gone about her work muttering to herself of people who tried to frighten folks out of pure malice. But she now seemed stupefied, and when Pauline told her to go upstairs to Madame Chanteau, that there might be some one with her, she wiped her hands on her apron and left the kitchen, ejaculating:

'Oh, well, in that case—in that case—'

'We must not forget my uncle, Doctor,' said Pauline, who seemed to be the only one who retained self-possession. 'Don't you think we ought to warn him? Will you see him before you go?'

Just at that moment Abbé Horteur came in. He had only heard that morning of what he called 'Madame Chanteau's indisposition.' When he learned how seriously ill she really was, an expression of genuine sorrow passed over his tanned face, so cheerful a moment before as he came in from the fresh air. The poor lady! Could it be possible? She who had seemed so well and strong only three days ago!

Then after a moment's silence he asked if he could see her; at the same time glancing anxiously at Lazare, whom he knew to be little given to religion. On that account he seemed to anticipate a refusal. But the young man, who was quite broken down, did not appear to have noticed the priest's question, and it was Pauline who answered it.

'No, not to-day, your reverence. She does not know the danger she is in, and your presence might have an alarming effect upon her. We will see to-morrow.'

'Very well,' the priest at once replied; 'there is no great urgency, I hope. But we must all do our duty, you know. And as the Doctor here refuses to believe in God—'

For the last moment or two the Doctor had been gazing earnestly at the table, absorbed in thought, lost in a maze of doubt, as was always the case when he could not overcome illness. He had just caught the Abbé's last words, however, and he interrupted him, saying:

'Who told you that I didn't believe in God? God is not an impossibility; one sees very strange things! And, after all, who can be sure?' Then he shook his head and roused himself from his reverie.

'Stay!' he went on, 'you shall come with me and shake hands with our good friend Monsieur Chanteau. He will soon stand in need of all the courage he can muster.'

'If you think it will cheer him at all,' the priest obligingly replied, 'I shall be glad to stay and play a few games of draughts with him.'

Then they both went off to the dining-room, while Pauline hastened back to her aunt. Lazare, when he was left alone, rose and hesitated for a moment as to whether he also should not go upstairs; then he went to the dining-room door to listen to his father's voice, without mustering enough courage to enter; and finally he came back to the kitchen again, and sank down upon the same chair as before, surrendering himself to his despair.

The priest and the Doctor had found Chanteau rolling a paper ball across the table—a ball formed of a prospectus discovered inside a newspaper. Minouche, who was lying near, looked on with her green eyes. She appeared to disdain such an elementary plaything, for she had her paws stowed away beneath her, never deigning to strike out at it with her claws, though it had rolled close to her nose.

'Hallo! is it you?' cried Chanteau. 'It is very good of you to come and see me. I'm very dull—all by myself. Well, Doctor, she's getting on all right, I hope? Oh! I don't feel at all uneasy about her; she's by far the strongest of all of us; she will see us all buried.'

It occurred to the Doctor that this would be a good opportunity for informing Chanteau of the real state of affairs.

'Well, certainly, there's nothing very alarming in her condition, but she seems to me to be very weak.'

'Ah! Doctor,' Chanteau exclaimed, 'you don't know her. She has an incredible fund of strength; you will see her on her feet again in a day or two!'

In his complete belief in his wife's vigorous constitution, he quite failed to understand the Doctor's hints; and the latter, not wishing to tell him the dreadful truth in plain words, could say no more. Besides, he thought that it would be as well to wait a little longer; for just then Chanteau was free from pain, his gout only troubling him in his legs, though these were sufficiently incapacitated to make it necessary to wheel him to bed in his chair.

'If it were not for these wretched legs of mine,' he said, 'I would go upstairs and see her myself.'

'Resign yourself, my friend,' said Abbé Horteur, who in his turn now tried to carry out his office of consoler. 'We each have our own cross to bear, and we are all in the hands of God—'

But he did not fail to notice that these words, so far from consoling Chanteau, only appeared to bore and even disquiet him, so he cut his exhortation short and substituted for it something more efficacious.

'Would you like to have a game at draughts? It will do you good.'

He went in person to take the draught-board from the cupboard. Chanteau was delighted, and shook hands with the Doctor, who then took his departure. The two others were soon deep in their game, quite forgetful of all else in the world, when all at once Minouche, who had probably got tired of seeing the paper ball under her nose, sprang forward, sent it spinning away, and bounded in wild antics after it all round the room.

'What a capricious creature!' cried Chanteau, put out in his play. 'She wouldn't have a game with me on any account a little while ago, and now she prevents one from thinking by playing all by herself.'

'Never mind her,' said the priest mildly: 'cats have their own way of amusing themselves.'

Meantime, passing through the kitchen, Doctor Cazenove had experienced sudden emotion on seeing Lazare still sorrowfully brooding on the same chair; and he caught the young man in his big arms and kissed him paternally without saying a word. Just at that moment Véronique came downstairs, driving Matthew before her. The dog was perpetually prowling about the staircase, making a sort of hissing sound, which somewhat resembled the plaint of a bird; and, whenever he found the door of the sick woman's room open, he went in and there vented those sharp notes of his, which were ear-piercing in their persistency.

'Get away with you, do! Be off!' the servant cried. 'That noise of yours isn't likely to do her any good.'

And as she caught sight of Lazare she added: 'Take him for a walk somewhere. He will be out of our way, and it will do you good too.'

It was really an order of Pauline's that Véronique was conveying. The girl had told her to get Lazare to go out and take some long walks. But he refused to go; it even seemed to require an effort on his part to get upon his feet. However, the dog came and stood before him, and began wailing again.

'That poor Matthew isn't as young as he was once,' said the Doctor, who was watching him.

'No indeed!' said Véronique. 'He is fourteen years old now, but that doesn't prevent him from being as wild as ever after mice. Look how he has rubbed the skin off his nose, and how red his eyes are!

He scented a mouse under the grate last night, and never closed his eyes afterwards; he turned my kitchen upside down, poking about everywhere. And such a great big dog, too, to worry about such tiny creatures, it's quite ridiculous! But it isn't only mice that he runs after. Anything that's little or crawls, newly hatched chickens or Minouche's kittens, anything of that sort, excites him to such a point that he even forgets to eat and drink. Just now I'm sure he scents something out of the common in the house—'

She checked herself as she caught sight of Lazare's eyes filling with tears.

'Go out for a walk, my lad,' the Doctor said to him. 'You can't be of any use here, and it will do you good to go out a little.'

The young man at last rose painfully to his feet. 'Well, we'll go,' he said. 'Come along, my poor old Matthew.'

When he had accompanied the Doctor to his gig, he set off along the cliffs with the dog. From time to time he had to stop and wait for Matthew, for the dog was really ageing quickly. His hindquarters were becoming paralysed, and his heavy paws sounded like slippers as he dragged them along. He was now unable to go scooping out holes in the kitchen-garden, and quickly rolled over with dizziness when he set himself spinning after his tail. He had fits of coughing, too, whenever he plunged into the water, and after a quarter of an hour's walk he wanted to lie down and snore. He trudged along the beach just in front of his master's legs.

Lazare stood for a moment watching a fishing-smack coming from Port-au-Bessin, with its sail skimming over the sea like the wing of a gull. Then he went his way. The thought that his mother was dying kept on thrilling him painfully; if ever it left him for a moment, it was only to come back and rack him more violently than before. And it brought him perpetual surprise; it was an idea to which he could not grow reconciled, and which prevented him from thinking of anything else. If at times it lost distinctness he felt the vague oppression of a nightmare, in which he remained conscious of some great impending misfortune. Everything around him then seemed to disappear, and when he again beheld the sands and seaweed, the distant sea and far-reaching horizon, he started as if they were all new and strange to him. Could they be the objects that were so familiar to his eyes? Everything seemed to have changed; never before had he thus been struck by varying forms and hues. His mother was dying! And he walked on and on, trying to escape from that buzzing refrain which was ever sounding in his ears.

Suddenly he heard a deep sigh behind him. He turned and saw the dog completely exhausted, with his tongue hanging from his mouth.

'Ah! my poor old Matthew,' he said to him, 'you can't get on any farther. Well, we'll go back again. However far I may go, I shan't rid myself of my thoughts.'

That evening they hurried over dinner. Lazare, who could only swallow a few mouthfuls of bread, hastened away upstairs to his own room, excusing himself to his father by alleging some pressing work. When he reached the first floor, he went into his mother's room, where he forced himself to sit for some five minutes before kissing her and wishing her good-night. She seemed to be forgetting all about him, and never expressed the least anxiety as to what he might be doing during the day. When he bent over her, she offered him her cheek and seemed to consider his hasty good-night quite natural, absorbed as she was in the instinctive egotism which attends the approach of death. And Pauline took care to cut his visit as short as possible by inventing an excuse for sending him out of the room.

But in his own big room on the second floor his mental torment increased. It was in the night, the long weary night, that his anguish weighed heaviest upon him. He took up a supply of candles, so that he might never be without a light, and he kept them burning, one after another, till morning, terror-stricken by the thought of darkness. When he got into bed he tried in vain to read. His old medical treatises were the only books that had now any interest for him; but they filled him with fear, and he ended by throwing them away. Then he remained lying upon his back, with his eyes wide open, solely conscious of the fact that close to him, on the other side of the wall, there was an awful presence which weighed upon him and suffocated him. His dying mother's panting breath was for ever in his ears, that panting breath which had become so loud that for the last two days he had heard it whenever he climbed the staircase, which he never ascended now without hastening his steps.

The whole house seemed full of that plaint, which thrilled him as he lay in bed; the occasional intervals of quiet inspiring him with such alarm that he would run barefooted to the landing and lean over the banisters to listen. Pauline and Véronique, who kept watch together below, left the door of the room open for the sake of ventilation, and Lazare could see the pale patch of sleepy light which the night lamp threw upon the tiled floor, and could again hear his mother's heavy panting, which became louder and more prolonged in the darkness. When he went back to bed he, too, left his door open, and so intently did he listen to his mother's breathing that even in the snatches of sleep into which he fell towards morning he was still pursued by it. His personal horror of death had vanished again as at the time of his cousin's illness. His mother was going to die; everything was going to die! He abandoned himself to the contemplation of that collapse of life without any other feeling than one of exasperation at his powerlessness to prevent it.

The next morning saw the commencement of Madame Chanteau's death agony, a loquacious agony which lasted for twenty-four hours. She was calm, the dread of poison no longer terrified her, but she rambled on rapidly in a clear voice, without raising her head from her pillow. What she said was in no way conversation; she did not address herself to anyone; it was as though, in the general derangement of her faculties, her brain hastened to finish its work like a clock running down. That flood of rapid words seemed to be indeed the last tick-tack of the unwound chain of her mind. The events of her past life defiled before her; but she never said a word about the present, about her husband, or her son, or her niece, or her home at Bonneville, where, with her ambitious nature, she had suffered for ten long years. She was still Mademoiselle de la Vignière, giving music-lessons in the most distinguished families in Caen, and she familiarly spoke of people whom neither Pauline nor Véronique had ever heard of. She broke out into long rambling stories, whose details were incomprehensible even to the servant who had grown old in her service. She seemed to be emptying her brain of the recollections of her youth before she died; just as one may turn the faded letters of former days out of a desk in which they have long been lying.

In spite of her courage, Pauline could not help shuddering slightly as all those little involuntary confessions were poured out in the very throes of death. It was no longer difficult, panting breathing that filled the room, but a weird, rambling babble, of which Lazare caught fragments as he passed the door. But, however much he might turn them over in his mind, he was unable to understand them, and grew full of alarm, as though his mother were already speaking from the other side of the grave amidst invisible beings to whom she was relating those strange stories.

When Doctor Cazenove arrived he found Chanteau and Abbé Horteur playing draughts in the dining-room. From all appearances, they might still have been engaged on the game which they had commenced the day before, and have never stirred from the room since the Doctor's previous visit. Minouche sat near them, intently studying the draught-board. The priest had arrived at an early hour to resume his duties as consoler. Pauline no longer felt that his proposed visit to her aunt would be attended with inconvenience; and so, when the Doctor went upstairs to see her, the priest accompanied him to the sick woman's bedside, presenting himself simply as a friend anxious to know how she was getting on.

Madame Chanteau recognised them both, and, having been raised up on her pillows, she smilingly welcomed them with all the airs of a Caen lady holding a reception. The dear Doctor was surely quite satisfied with her, she said; she would soon be able to leave her bed. Then she questioned the Abbé about his own health. The latter, who had come upstairs with the intention of fulfilling his priestly duties, was so overcome by the dying woman's rambling chatter that he could not open his mouth; and, besides, Pauline, who was in the room, would have stopped him if he had mentioned certain subjects. The girl had sufficient control over herself to feign confident cheerfulness. When the two men went away, she accompanied them to the landing, where the Doctor, in low tones, gave her instructions as to what she should do at the last moment. Such words as 'rapid decomposition 'and 'carbolic acid' were frequently mentioned, while the ceaseless chatter from the dying woman still buzzed through the open doorway.

'You think, then, that she will see the day out?' the girl inquired.

'Yes, I feel sure that she will live till to-morrow,' Cazenove answered. 'But don't lift her up any more, or she might die in your arms. I shall come again this evening.'

It was settled that Abbé Horteur should remain with Chanteau and gradually prepare him for the fatal issue. Véronique stood listening near the door while this was being agreed upon, and her face assumed a scared expression. Ever since the probability of her mistress's death had become clear to her she had scarcely opened her lips, but sought to render all possible service with the silent devotion of a faithful animal. But the conversation was hushed, for Lazare, wandering over the house, now came up the staircase; he had lacked the courage to be present at the Doctor's visit and to inquire the truth as to his mother's danger. However, the mournful silence with which he was greeted forced the knowledge upon him in spite of himself, and he turned very pale.

'My dear boy,' said the Doctor, 'you had better come along with me. I will give you some lunch and bring you back with me in the evening.'

The young man turned yet more pallid and replied: 'No, thank you; I would rather not go away.'

From that moment Lazare waited, feeling a terrible pressure upon his breast, as if an iron band were drawn tightly round him. The day seemed as though it would never end, and yet it passed away without any consciousness on his part of how the hours went by. He had no recollection of how he had spent them, wandering restlessly up and down the stairs, and gazing out upon the distant sea, the sight of whose ceaseless rocking dazed him yet more. At certain moments the irresistible flight of the minutes seemed to be materialised, and to become the onslaught of a mass of granite driving everything into the abyss of nothingness. Then he grew exasperated and longed for the end, in order that he might be released from the strain of that terrible waiting. About four o'clock, as he was once more weeping up to his own room, he turned suddenly aside and entered his mother's chamber. He felt a desire to see her and kiss her once again. But, as he bent over her, she went on pouring out her incoherent talk, and did not even turn her cheek towards him in that weary manner with which she had received him ever since the beginning of her illness. Perhaps she did not see him, he thought; indeed, it was no longer his mother who lay there with that livid face and lips already blackened.

'Go away,' Pauline said to him gently. 'Go out for a little while. I assure you that the hour has not yet come.'

And then, instead of going up to his room, Lazare rushed downstairs and out of the house, ever with the sight of that woeful face, which he could no longer recognise, before him. He told himself that his cousin had lied, that the hour was really at hand; but then he was stifling, and needed space and air, and so he rushed on like a madman. The thought that he would never, never again see his mother tortured him terribly. But he fancied he heard some one running after him, and when he turned and saw Matthew, who was trying to overtake him at a heavy run, he flew without cause into a violent passion, and picked up stones and hurled them at the dog, storming at him the while, to drive him back to the house. Matthew, amazed at this reception, trotted back some distance, and then turned and gazed at his master with his gentle eyes, in which tears seemed to glisten. He persisted in following Lazare from a distance, as though to keep watch over his despair, and the young man found it impossible to drive him away. But the immensity of the sea had an irritating effect upon Lazare, and he fled into the fields and wandered about them, looking for out-of-the-way corners where he could feel alone and concealed. He prowled up and down till night fell, tramping over ploughed land, breaking his way through hedges. At last, worn out, he was returning homewards, when he beheld a sight which thrilled him with superstitious terror. At the edge of a lonely road there stood a lofty poplar, black and solitary, over which the rising moon showed like a yellow flame; and the tree suggested a gigantic taper burning in the dusk at the bedside of some giantess lying out there across the open country.

'Come, Matthew! Come!' he cried in a choking voice. Let us get on!'

He reached the house running, as he had left it. The dog had ventured to draw near, and licked his hands.

Although the night had now fallen, there was no light in the kitchen. It was empty and dark, with only the glow of the charcoal embers reddening the ceiling. The gloom weighed upon Lazare, and he lacked the courage to go further. Overcome with fear and emotion, he remained standing amidst the litter of pots and dusters, and strained his ears to catch the sounds with which the house was quivering. On one side he heard a slight cough; it came from his father, to whom Abbé Horteur was talking in low continuous tones. But what most frightened the young man was the sound of hushed voices and hasty steps on the stairs, and a muffled noise on the upper floor, which he could not account for, though it suggested something being hurriedly accomplished with as little noise as possible. He did not dare to go and see what it meant. Could it be all was over? He was still standing there perfectly motionless, without courage enough to go and inquire the truth, when he saw Véronique come down. She rushed into the kitchen, lighted a candle, and carried it away with her so hurriedly that she neither spoke to the young man nor looked at him. The kitchen, after being lighted for a moment, relapsed into darkness. Up above the stir was ceasing. Once more did the servant come down, this time to get a bowl, and again she displayed silent, desperate haste. Lazare no longer felt any doubt. All must be over. Then, overcome, he sank down upon the edge of the table, and waited amidst that darkness, without knowing for what he was waiting, his ears buzzing the while in the deep silence that had just fallen.

Upstairs, for two hours past, Madame Chanteau's last agony—an agony so awful that it thrilled Pauline and Véronique with horror—had been following its course. Her dread of poison having reappeared, she raised herself up in bed, still wildly rambling on, gradually mastered by furious delirium. She wished to jump out of bed and escape from the house, where someone wanted to kill her; and it was all that the young girl and the servant could do to restrain her.

'Let me go! I shall be murdered! I must escape at once, at once!'

Véronique tried to calm her.

'Oh! Madame, don't you see us? You can't suppose that we should let any harm come to you.'

The dying woman, exhausted by her violent struggles, lay for a moment panting. Her dim eyes wandered anxiously round the room, as though she were looking for something. Then she resumed:

'Shut up the secrétaire! It is in the drawer. Ah! there she is coming up-stairs! Oh! I am afraid! I tell you that I can hear her! Don't give her the key. Let me go, at once, at once!'

Then again she began to struggle, while Pauline held her in her arms.

'Aunt, there is no one here. There are only ourselves.'

'No! no! Listen! There she is! Oh, God! God! I shall die! The hussy has made me drink it all—I am going to die! I am going to die!'

Her teeth chattered, and she sought protection in the arms of her niece, whom she did not recognise. Pauline mournfully strained her to her heart, no longer fighting against that horrible suspicion, but resigning herself to the knowledge that her aunt would carry it to her grave.

Fortunately Véronique was watching, and threw her arms forward crying:

'Take care, Mademoiselle! Take care!'

It was the supreme convulsive struggle. By a violent effort Madame Chanteau had succeeded in throwing her swollen legs out of bed, and, but for the servant's presence, she would have fallen on the floor. Her whole body was shaken by delirium; she broke into incoherent spasmodic cries, while her fists clenched as though she were engaging in a close struggle, defending herself against some phantom that clutched her by the throat. At that supreme moment she must have understood that she was dying; there was an expression of intelligence in her eyes which horror dilated. For a moment a frightful spasm of pain made her press her hands to her breast. Then she fell back on her pillow and turned black. She was dead.

Deep silence fell. Pauline closed her aunt's eyes, but she was exhausted, and incapable of doing anything further. When she left the room, leaving there both Véronique and Prouane's wife, whom she had sent for after the Doctor's visit, her strength gave way; she was obliged to sit down for a moment on the stairs, and no longer felt the courage to go and tell Lazare and Chanteau the truth. The walls seemed to be turning round her. A few minutes went by; then she again laid her hand upon the banister, but on hearing Abbé Horteur's voice in the dining-room she preferred to enter the kitchen. And there she found Lazare, whose gloomy face showed against the red glow of the embers in the grate. Without speaking a word she stepped towards him and opened her arms. He understood, and threw himself upon the young girl's shoulder, while she pressed him to her in a long embrace. They kissed each other on the face, while she wept silently; but he was unable to shed a single tear; emotion was stifling him, he could scarcely breathe. At last the girl unclasped her arms, saying the first words that came to her lips:

'Why are you here without a light?'

He made a gesture, as though to signify that he had no need of any light in his great sorrow.

'We must light a candle,' she said.

Lazare had fallen upon a chair again, incapable, as he was, of keeping on his feet. Matthew restlessly wandered about the yard, sniffing the damp night air. At last he came back into the kitchen and looked keenly at them in turn, and then went and rested his head on his master's knee, remaining there and silently questioning him, with his eyes fixed upon the young man's. Lazare began to tremble at the dog's persistent gaze, and suddenly the tears gushed from his eyes and he burst into sobs, throwing his arms the while round the neck of the old dog which his mother had loved for fourteen years. And he began to stammer in broken words:

'Ah! my poor old fellow! my poor old fellow! We shall never see her again!'

Notwithstanding her emotion, Pauline had succeeded in finding and lighting a candle. She made no attempt to console Lazare; she was glad to find him able to shed tears. There was still a painful task before her, that of informing her uncle of his wife's death. Just as she was making up her mind to go into the dining-room, whither Véronique had taken a lamp at the beginning of the evening, Abbé Horteur had managed to explain to Chanteau, in long ecclesiastical phrases, that there was no chance of his wife's recovery, and that her death was only a question of hours. And so when the old man saw his niece enter the room, overcome with emotion and her eyes red from weeping, he knew what had happened, and his first words were:

'*Mon Dieu!* there was only one thing that I would have asked for: I should have liked to see her once more while she lived!—But, ah, these wretched legs of mine! These wretched legs!'

He said scarcely anything else. He shed a few bitter tears which quickly dried, and vented a few sighs, but he speedily returned to the subject of his legs, falling foul of them and ending by pitying himself. For a few moments they discussed the possibility of carrying him to the first floor in order that he might give the dead woman a last kiss; but, apart from the difficulties of the task, they considered that the emotion of such a farewell might have a dangerous effect on him; and, besides, he did not seem very anxious about the matter himself. So he remained in the dining-room near the draught-board, without knowing how to occupy his poor weak hands, and not even having his head clear enough, he said, to be able to read and understand the newspaper. When they carried him to bed, old memories seemed to awaken in him, for he shed many tears.

Then came two long nights and a day that seemed endless: those terrible hours during which death dwells in the house. Cazenove had only returned to certify the death, once more surprised by the rapidity with which the end had come. Lazare did not go to bed the first night, but spent his time till morning in writing to his relations at a distance. The body was to be taken to the cemetery at Caen and buried in the family vault there. The Doctor had kindly promised to see to all the formalities, and the only painful matter in connection with them was the necessity for Chanteau, as Mayor of Bonneville, to receive the declaration of his wife's death. As Pauline had no suitable black dress, she hastened to make one out of an old skirt and a merino shawl, which she cut into a bodice. In the midst of these occupations the first night and the following day passed; but the second night seemed endless, rendered the more interminable by the mournful prospect of the morrow. No one was able to get any sleep; the doors remained open, and lighted candles were left upon the stairs and tables, while even the most distant rooms reeked of carbolic acid. They were all in the grasp of grief, and went about with blurred eyes and clammy lips, feeling but one dim need, that of clutching hold of life once more.

At last, about ten o'clock the next morning, the bell of the little church on the other side of the road began to toll. Out of respect to Abbé Horteur, who had behaved so well and kindly under the sad circumstances, the family had determined that the religious ceremony should be performed at Bonneville, before the body was removed to the cemetery at Caen. As soon as Chanteau heard the bell toll, he began to wriggle about in his chair.

'I must see her go away, at any rate,' he repeated, 'Oh! these wretched legs of mine! What a misery it is to have such wretched legs as mine are!'

It was to no purpose that they tried to keep him from beholding the mournful spectacle. As the bell began to toll more quickly, he grew angry and exclaimed: 'Wheel me out into the passage. I can hear them bringing her down. Be quick! be quick! I must see her go away!'

Pauline and Lazare, who were in full mourning and had already put on their gloves, were obliged to do as he bade them. Standing, the one on his right and the other on his left, they wheeled the arm-chair to the foot of the staircase. Four men were just bringing the corpse downstairs, bending beneath its great weight. As Chanteau caught sight of the coffin, with its new wood and glittering handles and large brass name-plate, he made an instinctive effort to rise, but his leaden legs kept him down, and he was obliged to remain seated in his chair, shaken by such a convulsive trembling that his very jaws chattered. The narrowness of the staircase made the descent difficult, and he gazed at the big yellow box as it slowly came towards him, and, as it passed his feet, he bent over to read the inscription on the plate. There was more room in the passage, whence the bearers moved quickly towards the bier, which was standing before the door. Chanteau's eyes were still fixed on the coffin, and with it he saw forty years of his life depart, happy years and unhappy years, which he sadly regretted, as one ever does regret one's youth. Pauline and Lazare were weeping behind his chair.

'No, no! Leave me here!' he said to them, as he saw them prepare to wheel him back again to his place in the dining-room. 'You go along; I will stay here and watch.'

The bearers had laid the coffin on the bier, which was lifted by some other attendants. The little procession was formed in the yard, which was full of people of the neighbourhood, Matthew, who had been shut up since early morning, was whining from under the door of the coach-house amidst the profound silence; while Minouche, seated on the kitchen window-sill, examined with an air of surprise both the concourse of people and the box that was being carried away. As they still continued to linger, the cat grew tired of watching and began to lick her stomach.

'You are not going, then?' Chanteau said to Véronique, whom he had just perceived near him.

'No, sir,' she replied in a choking voice. 'Mademoiselle told me to stay with you.'

The church-bell was still tolling, and at last the coffin left the yard, followed by Pauline and Lazare, whose blackness seemed intensified by the sunlight. And, sitting in his invalid's chair in the open doorway of the hall, Chanteau watched his wife's body being borne away.

VII

THE funeral matters and certain business affairs that had to be attended to detained Lazare and Pauline in Caen for a couple of days. When they set out on their journey home, after paying a farewell visit to the cemetery, the weather had broken up and there was a strong gale blowing. They left Arromanches in a storm of rain, and the wind blew so strongly that it threatened to carry the hood of their trap away. Pauline thought of her first journey when Madame Chanteau had brought her from Paris. It was just such a stormy day as this, and her poor aunt had kept warning her not to lean out of the conveyance, while perpetually refastening a muffler that she wore round her neck. Lazare, too, in his corner of the trap, sat thinking of the past, and in his mind's eye saw his mother waiting to welcome him after each of his journeys along that road as she had ever done. One December, he remembered, she had walked a couple of leagues to meet him, and he had found her seated on yonder milestone. Thus reflecting, amidst the rain which poured unceasingly, the girl and her cousin did not exchange a single word between Arromanches and Bonneville.

Just as they were reaching home, however, the downpour stopped, but the wind's violence increased, and the driver was obliged to alight from his seat and take hold of the horse's bridle. At the moment of reaching the house Houtelard, the fisherman, ran past them.

'Ah! Monsieur Lazare!' he cried; 'it's all done for this time! The sea's breaking all your timbers to bits down yonder!'

The sea was not visible from that bend of the road. The young man, who had raised his head, had just caught sight of Véronique standing on the terrace and gazing towards the shore. On the other side, sheltering himself behind his garden wall, for fear lest the wind should rend his cassock, Abbé Horteur stood straining his eyes in the same direction. He bent forward and cried: 'It's washing your piles away!'

Thereupon Lazare walked down the hill, followed by Pauline, in spite of the storminess of the weather. When they came to the foot of the cliff they were amazed by the sight which they beheld. It was one of the September flood-tides, and the sea was rushing up in wild commotion. No warning had been issued of any probable danger, but the gale, which had been blowing from the north since the previous day, had thrown the sea into such tumult that mountains of water towered up in the distance and, rolling onward, broke with a mighty roar over the rocks. In the far distance the sea looked black beneath the shadow of the clouds which raced over the livid sky.

'Get into the trap again,' said the young man to his cousin. 'I will just see how things look, and come back directly.'

Pauline made no reply, but followed Lazare as far as the shore. There the piles and a great stockade which had been recently constructed were being subjected to a frightful assault. The waves, which ever seemed to be growing larger, rushed against them in quick succession, like so many battering-rams. They came on like an innumerable army; fresh masses sprang forward without a moment's cessation. Their huge green backs, crested with foam, curved on every side, and sped forward with giant strength; and, as these monsters dashed against the stockades, they burst into a mighty rain of drops, then fell in a mass of white boiling foam, which the sea seemed to suck in and carry away. The timbers cracked beneath the violence of each of those furious onsets. The supports of one groyne were already broken, and a great central beam, still secured at one end, swayed hopelessly like the dead trunk of a tree whose branches had been stripped off by grape-shot. Two others offered more resistance, but they were shaking in their fixings, as though gradually overpowered in that surging grasp, which seemed bent on wearing out their strength in order to dash them to pieces.

'I told you how it would be! " repeated Prouane, who was very drunk, and stood leaning against the broken shell of an old boat. 'I told you how it would be when the wind blew like this. A lot the sea cares about that young man and his bits of sticks!'

Jeers greeted these words. All Bonneville was there, men, women, and children; and they were all very much amused at seeing the thundering slaps which fell upon the stockades. The sea might smash their hovels to fragments; they still loved it with an admiring awe, and they would have felt it a personal insult if the first young man who tried had been able to conquer it with a few beams and a couple of dozen bolts. And they grew excited as with a feeling of individual triumph as they saw the sea at last awake, unmuzzle itself, and throw its great jaws forward.

'Look! look!' cried Houtelard. 'That's a smasher! It has swept a couple of beams away!'

They called to each other, and Cuche tried to reckon up the waves.

'It will take three more, and then you'll see! There's one! That's loosened it! There's two! Ah! that's swept it away! Two have sufficed to do it, you see! Ah, the old hussy she is!'

He referred to the sea, uttering the word 'hussy' as if it were a term of endearment. Affectionate oaths arose, children began to dance whenever a heavier wave than usual crashed and snapped another of the timbers. Yet another broke, and yet another; there would soon be not one left, they would all be crushed like fleas. But though the tide still rose, the great stockade still remained firm. It was the sea's struggle against this which was most anxiously awaited, for it would be the decisive contest. At last the mounting waves dashed between the timbers, and the spectators prepared themselves to laugh.

'It's a pity the young man isn't here,' said that rascal Tourmal in a jeering voice, 'or he might lean against it and try to keep it up.'

A 'Hush!' made him silent, for some of the fishermen had just caught sight of Lazare and Pauline. The latter, who were very pale, had heard Tourmal's sneer, and they continued to gaze at the disaster in silence. It was a mere trifle, the smashing of those beams, but the tide would go on rising for another two hours, and the village would certainly suffer if the stockade did not hold out. Lazare had passed his arm round his cousin's waist, and was holding her close to him to protect her from the squalls which, as cutting as scythe-blades, blew against them. A mournful gloom fell from the black sky and the waves howled, and the two young people, in their deep mourning, remained motionless amidst the flying foam and the clamour that was ever growing louder. Around them the fishermen were now waiting, still with a jeering expression on their lips, but feeling increasing anxiety.

'It won't last much longer now!' Houtelard murmured. The stockade still resisted, however. At each wave that struck it its black, pitch-coated timbers still showed forth amidst the white waters. But as soon as one of the beams was broken, the adjoining ones began to fall away, piece by piece. For fifty years past the oldest men there had not known such a heavy sea. Soon they had to retire, the beams which had been torn away were dashed violently against the others, and gradually wrought the complete destruction of the stockade, whose fragments were furiously hurled ashore. There was but one left upright, standing there like a post marking a sandbank. The Bonneville folks had given over laughing now; the women were carrying off their crying children. The 'hussy' had fallen upon them again, and the stupor that came of despairing resignation to the ruin which was certainly at hand now fell on that little spot, nestling so closely to the sea which both supported and destroyed it. There was a hasty retreat, a gallop of heavy boots. Everyone took refuge behind the walls of shingle, by which alone the houses were now protected. Some of the piles here were already yielding, planks had been knocked out, and enormous waves swept right over the walls which were too low to stay their course. Soon there was nothing left to offer resistance, and a mass of water, dashing against Houtelard's house, smashed the windows and deluged the kitchen. Then there came perfect rout, and only the victorious sea remained dashing unimpeded up the beach.

'Don't go inside!' the men shouted to Houtelard. 'The roof will fall in.'

Lazare and Pauline had slowly retired before the flood. It was impossible to render any assistance, and, climbing the hill homewards, they were about half-way up it when the girl turned, and gave a last look at the threatened village.

'Poor people!' she murmured.

But Lazare could not pardon them for their idiotic laughter. He was wounded to the heart by that disaster, which for him was a personal defeat; and, making an angry gesture, he at last opened his mouth and growled:

'Let the sea lie in their beds, since they're so fond of it! I certainly won't try to prevent it!'

Véronique came to meet them with an umbrella, for the rain had begun falling heavily again. Abbé Horteur, who was still sheltering himself behind his wall, called a few words to them which they could not catch. The frightful weather, the destruction of the stockade, and the woe and danger in which they were leaving the village, cast additional sadness upon their return home. The house seemed cold and bare as they entered it; nothing but the wind, with its ceaseless moaning, disturbed the silence of the mournful rooms. Chanteau, who was dozing before a coke-fire, began to cry as soon as they appeared. They refrained from going upstairs to change their clothes, in order that they might escape the terrible associations of the staircase. The table was already laid and the lamp lighted, so they sat down to dinner immediately.

It was a sinister night; the deafening shocks of the waves, which made the walls tremble, broke in upon the few words that were spoken. When Véronique brought the tea into the room she announced that Houtelard's house and five others were already swept away, and that half the village would certainly share the same fate this time. Chanteau, in despair at not yet having recovered his mental equilibrium after the sufferings he had gone through, silenced her by saying that he had enough troubles of his own, and didn't want to hear about those of other people. When they had put him to bed, the others went off to rest also, worn out as they were with fatigue. Lazare kept a light burning till morning; and half a score times at least during the night Pauline anxiously slipped out of bed and gently opened her door to listen; but only death-like silence now ascended from the first floor.

The next day there commenced for the young man a succession of those lingering, poignant hours which come in the train of great sorrows. He awoke with the sensation of recovering from unconsciousness after some painful fall, from which his body was still stiff and bruised. Now that the troubled dreams which had oppressed him had passed away, his mind vividly recalled the past. Each little detail presented itself clearly before him, and he lived all his griefs again. The reality of death, which had never been within his personal experience, was brought home to him by the loss of his poor mother, who had been so suddenly carried off after a few days' illness. His horror of ceasing to be seemed to assume a more tangible form. There had been four of them, but now there was a yawning gap in their midst, and three of them were left behind to shiver painfully in their wretchedness, and cling desperately to each other in their attempts to regain some fragment of lost vital warmth. This, then, was death: this was the 'Nevermore'—a circling of trembling arms around a shadow, of which naught remained save a wild regret.

Every hour, as the image of his mother arose before him, Lazare seemed to be losing her over again. At first he had not suffered so much, not even when his cousin had come down-stairs and thrown herself into his arms, nor during the prolonged misery of the funeral. It was only since his return to the empty house that he had felt the full weight of his loss; and he grew wild with remorse that he had not wept more and manifested greater grief while there yet remained in the house something of her who was now for ever gone.

Sometimes he would almost choke with sobs as he reproached himself with not having loved his mother sufficiently. He was perpetually recalling her; and her form was ever before his eyes. When he went up the stairs he half expected to see her come out of her room with the quick, short steps with which she had been wont to hurry along the landing. He often turned, fancying he heard her behind him, and he was so absorbed in thinking of her that sometimes he even felt sure that he heard the rustling of her dress behind the door. At night he did not dare to extinguish his candle, and in the dim light he fancied that he heard furtive sounds approaching his bed, and a faint breath hovering over his brow. His grief, instead of being assuaged, grew keener; at the least recollection came a nervous shock, a vivid but fugitive apparition, which, as it faded away, left him in all the anguish which the thought of death inspired.

Everything in the house reminded him of his mother. Her room remained untouched; nothing had been changed, a thimble was still lying upon the table beside a piece of embroidery. The clock on the mantelpiece had been stopped at twenty-three minutes to eight, the time of her death. He usually shunned the room, though sometimes, as he was hastily rushing upstairs, a sudden impulse constrained him to enter it; and then, as his heart throbbed wildly within him, it seemed to him that the old familiar furniture—the secrétaire, the table, and especially the bed—had acquired an awe-inspiring aspect, which made them different from what they had formerly been. Through the shutters, which were kept closed, there filtered a pale light, whose vague glimmer added to his distress as he went to kiss the pillow on which his mother's head had lain in the icy cold of death. One morning when he went into the room he paused astounded. The shutters had been thrown wide open and the full light of day poured into the chamber. A bright sheet of sunshine streamed over the bed to the very pillow, and the room was decked with flowers, placed in all the vases that the house possessed. Then he recollected that it was an anniversary, the birthday of her who had departed; a day which had been observed every year, and which his cousin had remembered. There were only the flowers of autumn there—some asters, marguerites, and the last lingering roses, already touched by frost—but they were sweetly redolent of life, and they set joyous colours round the lifeless dial, which seemed to mark the arrest of time's progress. That pious womanly observance filled Lazare with emotion, and for a long time he remained there weeping.

The dining-room, the kitchen, and the terrace, too, equally reminded him of his mother. All the little objects he saw lying about suggested her to him. He was quite beset by his mother's image, though he never spoke of it, and indeed, with a feeling of uneasy shame, tried to conceal the constant torture which he experienced. He even avoided mentioning his mother's name, so that it might have been supposed that he had already forgotten her, whereas all the time never a moment passed without memory bringing a bitter pang to his heart. It was only his cousin who penetrated his secret, and when she spoke to him about it he took refuge in falsehoods, protesting that he had put out his light at midnight, and had been very busy over some work or other. And he almost worked himself into an angry passion if he were further pressed. He took refuge in his room, and there abandoned himself to his reflections, feeling calmer in that retreat where he had grown up, free from the fear of revealing to others the secret of his distress.

At first he had tried to force himself to go out and resume his long walks, thinking that by doing so he would at any rate escape Véronique's grumpy taciturnity and the painful sight of his father, who lay listlessly in his chair, not knowing how to occupy himself. But he now felt an invincible distaste for walking; out of doors he grew weary with a weariness that almost amounted to discomfort. The sea with its perpetual surging, its stubborn waves that broke against the cliffs twice a day, irritated him as being a mere senseless force that recked nothing of his grief, and had gone on wearing the same rocks away for centuries, without ever shedding a single tear for the death of a human being. It was too vast, too cold; and he hurried back home again and shut himself up in his room, that he might feel less conscious of his own littleness, less crushed between the boundlessness of sea and sky. There was only one spot that had any attraction for him, and that was the graveyard which surrounded the church. His mother was not there, but he could think of her there with a melting tenderness; and, despite his horror of death, the place had a singularly calming effect upon him. The tombs lay asleep, as it were, amongst the grass; there were yew-trees which had sprung up in the protecting shade of the church, and not a sound was to be heard save the call of the curlews, hovering in the wind from the open. There he forgot himself for hours amongst the old tombstones, whence the very names of those who had long since passed away had been obliterated by the heavy rains from the west.

If Lazare had felt any belief in another world, if he had been able to think that he would one day again meet those he loved at the other side of the grave's black wall, he would have been far happier; but this consolation was denied him, he felt no doubt as to death being the end and extinction of individual life. And yet his own individuality, which ill-brooked the thought of being snuffed out, rose up in mutiny against his convictions. What joy there would have been in entering upon a fresh life elsewhere, far away amongst the stars, a new existence in which he would have been once again surrounded by all he loved! Ah! if he could only believe in that, how the agony he now suffered would be turned to sweetness, in looking forward to rejoin lost loved ones! How thrilling would be their kisses at meeting, and what blessedness it would be to live all together again in some realm where there would be no more death! He was racked with agony at the thought of the charitable falsehoods of creeds compassionately designed to hide the terrible truth from those too weak to bear it. No! Death was the end of everything; nothing that we had loved could ever bud into fresh life, the good-bye was said for ever. Oh! those awful words—'for ever'! It was they that carried his brain into the dizzy vertigo of empty nothingness.

One morning, as Lazare was brooding beneath the shadow of the yews, he caught sight of Abbé Horteur at the bottom of his vegetable garden, which was only separated from the graveyard by a low wall. Wearing an old grey blouse and a pair of wooden shoes, the priest was digging a cabbage-bed; and, with his face browned by the keen sea air and the back of his neck scorched by the sun, he looked like an old peasant bending over his work. With a miserable stipend, and without any casual remuneration in the shape of fees in that little out-of-the-way parish, he would have died of sheer starvation if he had not been able to eke out his livelihood by growing a few vegetables. What little money he had went in charity, and he lived quite alone, assisted only by a young girl from the village, and often obliged to cook his own meals. To make matters worse, the soil of that rocky spot was scarcely good for anything, and the wind withered the young plants, so that it was scarcely worth while to cultivate the atony ground for the sake of the meagre return he got. When he put his blouse on, he always tried to keep himself from notice, for fear lest it should give anyone cause to scoff at religion; and Lazare, knowing this, was about to withdraw when he saw him take his pipe out of his pocket, fill it with tobacco, and then light it with a loud smacking of his lips. Just as he was enjoying his first puffs, however, the Abbé caught sight of the young man. He then made a hasty movement, as though he wished to hide his pipe, but finally broke into a laugh, and called:

'Ah! you are enjoying the fresh air. Come in and have a look at my garden.'

And, as Lazare came up to him, he added gaily:

'Well, you see, you find me in the midst of a debauch. It is the only pleasure I get, my friend, and I'm sure that it will not offend God.'

Thereupon he put his pipe in his mouth again, and puffed away freely, only taking it out at times to make a short remark. For instance, the priest of Verchemont worried him. That priest was a happy man, possessing a really fine garden with a good and fruitful soil; but he never so much as touched a garden tool. And next the Abbé complained to Lazare about his potatoes, which had been falling off for the last two years, though the soil, he said, was exactly suited to them.

'Don't let me disturb you,' Lazare replied. 'Please go on with what you were doing.'

The Abbé then resumed his digging.

'Yes, indeed, I must get on,' he said. 'The youngsters will be here for the catechism class presently, and I want to get this bed finished before they come.'

Lazare had seated himself on a slab of granite, some ancient tombstone, placed against the low wall of the churchyard. He watched Abbé Horteur struggling with the stones and listened to him while he talked on in a shrill voice that suggested a child's; and, as the young fellow watched and listened, he wished that he could be as poor and as simple-minded as the priest, with a brain as empty and a body as tranquil. The mere fact that the Bishop had allowed Abbé Horteur to grow old in that wretched cure showed how innocent and guileless the good man had the reputation of being. Besides, he was one of those who never complain, and whose ambition is satisfied so long as they have bread to eat and water to drink.

'It isn't very cheerful living amongst all these tombs,' the young man remarked, thinking aloud.

The priest stopped digging in surprise.

'What! not cheerful?'

'Well, you have got death perpetually before your eyes. I should think you must dream about it at nights.'

The priest took his pipe out of his mouth and spat upon the ground.

'No, indeed, I never dream about it at all. We are all in the hands of God.'

Then he began to dig again, driving his spade into the ground with a blow of his heel. His faith kept him free from fear, and his imagination never strayed beyond what was revealed in the catechism. Good folks died and went to heaven. Nothing could be simpler and more encouraging. He smiled in a convinced sort of way; that stolid, unwavering theory of salvation sufficed for his narrow brain.

From that time forward Lazare visited the priest almost every morning in his garden. He would sit down on the old tombstone and forget his thoughts as he watched the Abbé cultivating his vegetables; he even gained a temporary tranquillity by the contemplation of the other's blind faith which enabled him to live in the midst of death without disquiet. Why couldn't he himself, he thought, become a simple child again, like that old man? In the depths of his heart he harboured some lurking hope that his dead faith might be fanned into life again by his converse with the guileless, simple-minded priest, whose tranquil ignorance had such a charm for him. He began to bring a pipe with him, and the pair of them smoked together while they chatted about the slugs that devoured the salad plants, or the manure that was too expensive, for it was seldom that the priest spoke of God. With his spirit of tolerance and long experience he reserved the Divinity for his own personal salvation. Other people looked after their affairs in their way and he looked after his in his fashion. After thirty years of unavailing preaching and warning he now strictly confined himself to the observance of his ministerial duties. It was very kind of that young man, he thought, to come and see him every day, and as, with his tolerant and charitable disposition, he did not want to cavil with him nor to inveigh against the theories which he must have brought back from Paris, he preferred to keep on talking with him about the garden; and thus Lazare, with his head buzzing with all the priest's simple gossip, sometimes thought that he was really on the point of relapsing into that happy age of ignorance when fear is unknown.

But though the mornings thus glided away, Lazare every night, up in his room, still brooded over the memory of his mother, without being able to summon up enough courage to put out his candle. His faith was dead. One day, as he sat smoking with Abbé Horteur, the latter hastily put his pipe out of sight on hearing the sound of footsteps behind the pear-trees. It was Pauline, who had come to look for her cousin.

'The Doctor is in the house,' said she, 'and I have asked him to stay to lunch. You'll come in soon, won't you?'

She was smiling, for she had caught sight of the Abbé's, pipe beneath his blouse. The priest quickly pulled it out again, with that cheerful laugh to which he was addicted whenever he was discovered smoking.

'It's very silly of me,' he said. 'People would think I had been committing a crime. See! I am going to light it again before you!'

'I tell you what, your reverence!' Pauline exclaimed gaily; 'come and lunch with us and the Doctor, and you can smoke your pipe afterwards.'

The priest was delighted, and immediately replied:

'Well yes, I accept. I will follow you directly. I must just put my cassock on. And I will bring my pipe with me; I promise I will.'

It was the first luncheon, since Madame Chanteau's death, at which the dining-room had re-echoed with the sound of laughter. Abbé Horteur smoked his pipe after dessert, and this made them all merry, but he evinced such genial humour over this indulgence that it at once seemed quite natural. Chanteau, who had eaten heartily, grew quite lively under the cheering influence of this fresh stir of life in the house. Doctor Cazenove told stories about savages, while Pauline beamed with pleasure at hearing all the noise, hoping that it might perhaps draw Lazare from his moody despondency.

After that luncheon, Pauline determined to revert to the Saturday dinners, which had been broken off by her aunt's death. The Abbé and the Doctor came regularly to these repasts, and the family life was resumed on its old lines once more. They jested together, and the widower would clap his hands on his legs and protest that, if it wasn't for that confounded gout, he would get up and dance, so jovial did he feel. It was only Lazare who still remained in an unsettled state; his gaiety was forced, and he often shook with a sudden shudder while he was noisily chattering.

One Saturday evening, in the middle of dinner, Abbé Horteur was summoned to the bedside of a dying man. He did not even wait to empty his glass, but set off at once, without paying any heed to the Doctor, who had visited the man before coming to dine and had told the Abbé he would find him already dead. The priest had shown himself so weak in intellect that evening that as soon as his back was turned Chanteau remarked:

'There are times when there seems to be very little in him.'

'I would willingly change places with him,' Lazare roughly rejoined. 'He is much happier than we are.'

The Doctor laughed.

'That may be so. Matthew and Minouche are also happier than we are. Ah! I recognise in that remark of yours the young man of to-day, who has nibbled at the sciences and filled himself with discontent because they have not enabled him to satisfy his old ideas of the absolute, ideas which he sucked in with his mother's milk. At the very first attempt you want to discover every truth in the sciences, whereas we can barely decipher them, when, maybe, the inquiry will go on for ever.

Then you begin to say that there is nothing in them, and you try to fall back upon your old faith, which will have nothing more to do with you, and so you drop into pessimism. Yes! pessimism is the disease of the end of the century. You are a set of Werthers turned upside down!'

This was the Doctor's favourite subject, and he grew quite animated over it. Lazare, on his side, exaggerated his denial of all certainty, and his belief in final and universal evil.

'How can we live,' he asked, 'when at every moment things give way beneath our feet?'

The old man yielded to an impulse of youthful passion as he retorted:

'Why, just go on living! Isn't life itself sufficient? Happiness consists in action.'

Then he abruptly addressed himself to Pauline, who was listening with a smile on her face.

'Come now!' he said, 'tell us what you do to be always cheerful!'

'Oh!' she replied, in a joking tone, 'I try to forget all about myself, for fear lest I should grow melancholy, and I think about others; that occupies my mind, and makes me bear my troubles patiently.'

This reply seemed to irritate Lazare, who, prompted by a spirit of malicious contradiction, asserted that women ought to be religious; and he pretended that he could not understand why Pauline had ceased to fulfil her duties for so long a time. Thereupon the girl gave her reasons in her tranquil manner.

'It is very easily explained,' she said. 'Confession proved very distasteful to me and hurt my feelings, and it affects many women, I think, in the same way. Then, again, I can't bring myself to believe things that seem contrary to reason. And, that being so, why should I tell a lie by pretending that I do believe them? And, besides, the unknown in no way disquiets me; it can only be a logical outcome of life, and it seems to me best to await it as tranquilly as possible.'

'Hush! Here's the Abbé!' interrupted Chanteau, whom this conversation was beginning to bore.

The man was dead, and the Abbé placidly finished his dinner, after which they each drank a little glass of chartreuse.

Pauline had now assumed the management of the household. All the purchases and every detail of the establishment came under her inspection, and a big bunch of keys dangled from her waist. She took over the control as a matter of course, and Véronique showed no sign of displeasure at it. The servant had been very morose, however, since Madame Chanteau's death, and almost appeared to be in a state of stupor. Her affection for the dead woman seemed to revive, and she once more began to treat Pauline with suspicious surliness. It was to no purpose that the latter spoke softly and soothingly to her; she took offence at a word, and could often be heard muttering and grumbling to herself in the kitchen. And whenever, after intervals of obstinate silence, she indulged in those muttered soliloquies, she always appeared to be overwhelmed by stupefaction at Madame Chanteau's death. Had she known that her mistress was going to die, she moaned to herself? If she had had any notion of such a thing, she would never have thought of saying what she had said. Justice before everything! It wasn't right to kill people, even if they had their faults. But she washed her hands of it all, she growled; it would be so much the worse for the person who was the real cause of the misfortune. Still, this assurance did not seem to calm her, for she went on growling and struggling against imaginary transgressions.

'What's the matter that you are perpetually worrying yourself like this?' Pauline asked her one day. 'We both did all we could; but we can do nothing against death.'

Véronique shook her head.

'Ah! people don't usually die like that. Madame Chanteau was what she was, but she took me in when I was quite a little girl, and I could cut my tongue out if I thought that anything I ever said had aught to do with her death. Don't let us talk about it any more; it would end badly.'

No further reference had been made by Pauline and Lazare to their marriage. Chanteau, who was desirous of bringing the matter to a conclusion, now that the main obstacle to it had disappeared, had ventured to allude to it one day when Pauline came and sat near him with her sewing to keep him company. He felt a keen desire to retain her beside him and a great horror of again falling into the hands of Véronique should his niece ever leave him. Pauline, however, gave him to understand that nothing could be settled until the completion of the period of mourning. It was not a feeling of propriety alone that prompted her to make that vague reply, but she was also looking to time to answer a question which she dared not attempt to answer herself. The suddenness of her aunt's death, that terrible blow from which neither she nor her cousin had yet recovered, had brought about a kind of truce between their wounded affections, from which they were gradually awaking, only to suffer the more on finding themselves, amidst their irreparable loss, face to face with their own distressful story: Louise driven out of the house; their love shattered, and, perhaps, the whole course of their existences modified. What was to be done now? Did they still love each other? Was their marriage possible or advisable?

Questions like these floated through their minds, amidst the stupor in which they were left by the sudden blow that had fallen upon them, and neither the one nor the other seemed anxious to force on a solution.

With Pauline, however, the recollection of the insult offered to her had lost much of its bitterness. She had long ago forgiven Lazare, and was quite ready to place her hand in his whenever he should show repentance. She had not the least jealous desire to see him humiliate himself before her; her only thought was for him, so that she might give him back his promise if he no longer loved her. Her whole anguish lay in that doubt: did he still love Louise?—or had he forgotten her and returned to the old affections of his early youth? However, as she thus thought of giving Lazare up rather than make him unhappy her heart sank, for, though she trusted she would have the courage to do so, if necessary, she hoped she would die soon afterwards.

Ever since her aunt's death an impulse of generosity had moved her to bring about a reconciliation between herself and Louise. Chanteau might write to Louise, and she herself would just add a line to say that she had forgotten what had happened. They all felt so lonely and dull that the other's presence would distract them from their gloomy thoughts. Since the terrible shock of her aunt's death, all that had happened previously seemed very far away, and Pauline had often regretted that she had behaved so violently. Yet, whenever she thought of speaking to her uncle on the subject, a feeling of repugnance held her back. Wouldn't it mean imperilling the future, tempting Lazare, and perhaps losing him altogether? However, perhaps she might still have found courage and pride enough to subject him to this risk, if her sense of justice had not risen in revolt against it. It was the treason alone that seemed to her so unpardonable. And then, again, was she not capable of restoring happiness and life to the house? Why call in a stranger, when she was conscious that she herself was brimming over with willing devotion and affection? Without being aware of it, there was a touch of pride in her abnegation, and she was a little jealous in her devotion. She yearned to be her relatives' one and only solace.

From this time all Pauline's endeavours were turned in that direction. She laid herself out in every way to make those about her cheerful and happy. Never before had she shown herself so persistently cheerful and kindly. Every morning she came down with a bright smile and a fixed determination to conceal her own griefs in order that she might do nothing to add to those of others. Her gentle amiability seemed to set all troubles at defiance, and she possessed a sweet evenness of disposition which disarmed all feeling against her. She was now in perfect health again, strong and sound as a young tree, and the happiness that she spread around her was the emanation of her own healthy brightness. The arrival of each fresh day delighted her, and she found a pleasure in doing what she had done the day before, perfectly contented and quiet in mind, and looking forward to the morrow without any touch of feverish expectation. Though Véronique went on muttering in her kitchen, and indulged in strange and inexplicable caprices, a fresh burst of life was driving all mournfulness from the house; the merry laughter of former days rang through the rooms and echoed up the staircase. Chanteau himself seemed particularly delighted by the change, for the gloominess of the house had always weighed on him. Existence, in his case, had really become abominable, yet he clung to it with the desperate clutch of a sick man who holds dearly to life, though it be but pain to him. Every day that he managed to live seemed to be a victory achieved, and his niece appeared to him to brighten and warm the house like a beam of sunlight, beneath whose rays death could not lay its chilly touch upon him.

Pauline, however, had one source of trouble. Lazare seemed proof against all her attempts to console him, and she grew distressed as she saw him falling again into a sombre mood. Lurking behind his grief for his mother, there was a revival of his terror of death. Now that the lapse of time was beginning to mitigate his original sorrow, this terror of death asserted all its old sway over him, heightened by the fear of hereditary disease. He felt sure that he too would succumb to some derangement of his heart, and he brooded over the certainty of a speedy and tragic end. He was constantly listening to the sounds of life within him, observing, in a state of nervous excitement, the working of his stomach, kidneys, and liver; but it was particularly his heart-beats which absorbed him. If he laid his elbow upon the table, he heard his heart beating in his elbow; if he rested his neck against the back of a chair, he heard it throbbing there; if he sat down, if he went to bed, he heard it beating in his thighs, his sides, his stomach; and ever and ever its throbbing seemed to him to be telling out his life like a clock that is running down. Dazed by this constant study of his organism, he perpetually alarmed himself with the fear that he was on the point of breaking down. All his organs were worn out, he fancied, and his heart, which disease had distended to a monstrous size, was about to rend his frame in pieces by its hammer-like beating.

In this way Lazare's mental sufferings went on increasing. For many years, every night as he lay down in bed the thought of death had frozen him to the marrow, and now he dared not go to sleep, racked as he was with the fear of never awaking. Sleep was hateful to him, and he experienced all the horror of dying as he felt himself growing drowsy, falling into the unconsciousness of slumber. His sudden waking gave him still a greater shock, dragging him out of black darkness, as though some giant hand had clutched him by the hair and hurled him back into life again, shivering and stammering with horror of the mysterious unknown through which he had passed. He clasped his hands convulsively, more desperate and panic-stricken than ever at the thought that he must die. He suffered such torture every night that he preferred not to go to bed. He found that he could lie down on the sofa and sleep in the daytime in perfect peace, and it was probably that heavy slumber during the day which made his nights so terrible. By degrees he gave over going to bed at night at all, preferring his long siestas of the after-noon, and afterwards only dozing off towards daybreak, when the fear of darkness was driven away.

He had, however, intervals of calmness, and at times he would remain free from his haunting fears of death for two or three nights in succession. One day Pauline found an almanack in his room, dotted over with red ink. She asked him the meaning of the marks.

'What have you marked it for like this? Why are all those days dot-ted?'

'I haven't marked anything,' he stammered. 'I know nothing about it.'

Then his cousin said gaily: 'I thought it was only girls who trusted to their diaries things that they wouldn't tell anyone else. If you have been thinking about us on all the days you have marked, it is very nice of you indeed. Ah! I see you have secrets now!'

However, as she saw him become more and more disturbed, she was good-natured enough to press him no further. On the young man's pale brow she saw the shadow which she knew so well, the shadow left by that secret trouble which she seemed powerless to alleviate.

For some time past he had also been astonishing her by fresh eccen-tricities. Possessed by a firm conviction that his end was close at hand, he never left a room, or closed a book, or used anything without think-ing that it was the last time he would do so, and that he would never again see the thing he had used, the book he had closed, or the room he had left; and he had thus contracted a habit of bidding continual farewells, yielding to a morbid craving to take up and handle different objects that he might see them once more. With all this were mingled certain ideas of symmetry. He would take three steps to the right and then as many to the left, and touch the different articles of furniture on either side of a window or door the same number of times. And beneath this there lurked the superstitious fancy that a certain number of touch-ings, some five or seven, for instance, distributed in a particular fashion, would prevent the farewell from being a final one. In spite of his keen intelligence and his denial of the supernatural, he carried out these foolish superstitious practices with animal-like docility, though trying to hide them as though they were some shameful failing. This was the revenge taken by the deranged nervous system of this pessimist and positivist, who declared that he believed only in what was actually known. He was becoming quite a nuisance, though.

'Why are you pacing up and down like that?' Pauline cried at times. 'That's three times you've gone up to that cupboard and touched the key. It won't run off!'

In the evening it seemed as though he would never be able to get away from the dining-room. He arranged all the chairs in a certain order, tapped the door a particular number of times, and then entered the room again to lay his hands, first the right and then the left, on his grandfather's masterpiece. Pauline, who waited for him at the foot of the stairs, at last broke out into a peal of laughter.

'What idiotic behaviour for a man of twenty-four! Where is the sense, I should like to know, in touching things in that way?'

But after a time she ceased to make a jest of him, for she felt much distressed by his disquietude. One morning she surprised him kissing—seven times in succession—the framework of the bed on which his mother had died. The sight filled her with alarm, and she began to guess the torments which embittered his existence. When she saw him turn pale as he came upon a reference to the twentieth century in a newspaper, she gave him a compassionate glance which made him turn his head aside. He recognised that she understood him, and he rushed off and hid himself in his own room, all shame and confusion. Over and over again did he upbraid himself as a coward, and swear that he would resist the influence of this weakness. He would argue with himself and bring himself to look death in the face, and then in a spirit of bravado, instead of passing the night awake on his couch, he would quickly undress and jump into bed. Death, he would then say to himself, might come and would be welcome; he would await it there as deliverance. But immediately the throbbing of his heart drove all his oaths away, an icy breath seemed to freeze his bones, and he frantically stretched out his hands as he broke into a despairing cry of 'O God! God!' It was these terrible backslidings which filled him with shame and despair. His cousin's tender pity, too, only served to overwhelm him. The days grew so heavy that as he saw them begin he scarcely dared to hope that they would ever end. In this gradual decay of his vitality, his cheerfulness had been the first to depart, and now physical strength seemed to be failing him in its turn.

Pauline, however, in the pride of her self-devotion, was determined to gain the victory. She recognised the source of her cousin's disease, and tried to impart to him some of her own courage by giving him a love of life. But her compassionate kindliness seemed to receive a continual check. At first she made open attacks upon him with her old jests and jokes about 'that silly, stupid pessimism.' 'What!' she said, 'was it she now who had to chant the praises of the great Saint Schopenhauer, while he, like all the humbugging pessimists, was quite willing to see the world blown to pieces, but refused to be blown up himself?' These jests wrung a constrained smile from the young man, but he seemed to suffer from them so much that she did not persist in them. She next tried the effect of such caressing consolations as might be lavished upon a child, and encompassed him with cheerful amiability and placid laughter. She always let him see her beaming with happiness and revelling in the pleasantness of life. The house seemed full of sunshine. There was nothing more required of him than to take advantage of it and let his life flow quietly on, but this he could not do; the happiness that was offered to him only made his feeling of horror at what was to come hereafter all the keener. Then Pauline tried stratagem, and racked her brain to promote enthusiasm in something or other which might have the effect of making him forget himself. But his idleness had become a sort of disease; he had no inclination for anything whatever, and found even reading too great an exertion, so that he spent his whole time in gnawing at himself.

For a moment Pauline had a glimpse of hope. They had gone one day for a short walk on the sands, when Lazare, as they reached the ruins of the stockades, a few of the beams of which were still standing upright, began to explain a new system of protective works which, he assured her, could not fail to prove successful. The collapse of the former ones had been caused by the weakness of the supporting timbers. It would only be necessary to double their thickness and to give a greater inclination to the central beams. His voice vibrated and his eyes lighted up with all his old enthusiasm as he spoke, and his cousin besought him to take up the task again and make another effort. The village was gradually being destroyed; every high tide swept away a further portion of it; and there could be no doubt that, if he went to see the Prefect, he would succeed in obtaining the subvention, while she herself would be only too glad to make further advances in order to assist such a noble work. She was so anxious to spur him into action that she would willingly have sacrificed the remains of her fortune to bring about that end. But he only shrugged his shoulders. What would be the good of it, he asked? He turned pale as the thought struck him that, if he were to commence the work, he would be dead before he could finish it; and, to hide the perturbation which this reflection caused him, he began to inveigh against the Bonneville fishermen.

'A pack of grinning idiots, who jeered at me when that wolfish sea swept everything away! No! no! they may do things for themselves now! I won't give them another chance of laughing at my "bits of sticks," as they called them.'

Pauline tried to soothe him. The poor folk were in a terrible state of wretchedness. Since the sea had carried off the Houtelards' house, the most solidly built of all the village, together with three others, cottages of the poorer fishermen, their misery had increased. Houtelard, who had once been the rich man of the district, had now taken up his quarters in an old barn, some twenty yards behind his former dwelling; but the others, who had no such refuge, were housing themselves in clumsy huts made out of the shells of old boats. They were living in a miserable state of nudity and promiscuousness; the women and children were wallowing in vice and vermin. All that was bestowed upon them in charity went in drink. The wretched creatures sold all the food that was given them, with their clothes, pots, and pans, and what little furniture they had left, in order to buy drams of the terrible 'calvados,' which stretched them on the ground across their doorways like so many corpses. Pauline was the only one who still continued to say a word for them. Abbé Horteur had given them up, and Chanteau talked of sending in his resignation, being unwilling to remain any longer the Mayor of such a drove of swine. Lazare, too, when his cousin tried to excite his pity on behalf of that little colony of drunkards, beaten down by the fierceness of the elements, only repeated his father's eternal refrain:

'No one compels them to remain here. All that they have to do is to go elsewhere. Only a pack of idiots would come and stick themselves right under the waves.'

This was the general feeling of the neighbourhood, and everyone looked upon the Bonneville folk as obstinate fools. The villagers, on the other hand, were mistrustfully unwilling to go elsewhere. They had been born there, they said, and why should they have to leave the place? The same sort of thing had been going on for hundreds and hundreds of years, and there was nothing for them to do anywhere else. Prouane, when he was exceptionally tipsy, always concluded by saying that wherever they might go they would always be devoured by something or other.

Pauline used to smile at this and nod her head in approval, for happiness, in her opinion, depended neither upon people nor circumstances, but on the more or less reasonable way in which people conformed themselves to their circumstances. She redoubled her care and attention, and distributed still larger doles and alms than before. At last she was able to induce Lazare to associate himself with her in her charities; she hoped that she might thereby rouse him from his gloomy broodings, and lead him to forget his own troubles by awaking in him pity for those of others. Every Saturday afternoon he remained at home with her, and from four o'clock till six they received the young folk from the village, the ragged draggle-tail urchins whom their parents sent up to get what they could out of Mademoiselle Pauline. It was an invasion of snivelling little lads and dirty little girls.

One Saturday it was raining, and Pauline could not distribute her alms on the terrace, as was her custom. Lazare had to fetch a bench and place it in the kitchen.

'Good gracious, sir!' Véronique exclaimed. 'Surely Mademoiselle Pauline isn't going to bring all that dirty lot in here? It's a nice idea, indeed; if they do come, I won't answer for the state of the soup.'

At that moment the girl entered the kitchen with her bag of silver and her medicine-chest. She merrily replied to Véronique's indignant outburst:

'Oh! a turn of your broom will make things all right again; and, besides, it's raining so heavily that they will have had a good washing before they come in, poor little things!'

And, indeed, the cheeks of the first to enter were quite bright and rosy from the downpour. They were so soaked that pools of water trickled from their ragged clothes on to the tiles of the kitchen-floor, thereby increasing the servant's wrath, which was by no means diminished when Pauline told her to light a faggot of wood to dry them a little. The bench was carried near the fire, and was soon occupied by a shivering row of impudent, leering brats, who cast greedy eyes at what was lying about—some half-emptied wine-bottles, the remains of a joint, and a bunch of carrots lying on a block.

'Children indeed!' Véronique went on growling. 'Children that are grown up and ought to be earning their own living. They'll go on pretending to be children till they're five-and-twenty, if only you'll let them!'

But Pauline bade her be silent.

'There! have you done now? Talking like that won't fill their mouths or help them to grow up.'

The girl sat down at the table, with her money and the other articles she intended to distribute in front of her; and she was just about to call the children to her in turn, when Lazare, who had remained standing, caught sight of Houtelard's boy amongst the other youngsters, and shouted out:

'Didn't I forbid you to come here again, you young vulture? Your parents ought to be ashamed of themselves for sending you here, for they are quite able to feed you, whereas there are so many others who are dying of hunger.'

Houtelard's son, an overgrown lad of fifteen, with a timid and sad expression, began to cry.

'They beat me if I don't come,' he said. 'The missis got hold of the rope and father drove me out.'

He turned up his sleeve to show a big violet bruise on his arm which had been caused by a blow from a piece of knotted rope. The 'missis' was the old servant whom the lad's father had married, and who was gradually killing the boy by her ill-treatment. Since the loss of their house, their harshness and miserly filthiness had increased, and now their home was a perfect pigsty, where they tortured the lad, as if to revenge themselves for their misfortunes on him.

'Put an arnica compress on his arm,' said Pauline softly to Lazare.

Then she herself gave the lad a five-franc piece. 'Here! give them this so that they shan't beat you any more, and tell them that if they strike you again, and if there are any bruises on your body next Saturday, they will never get another sou out of me.'

All along the bench the other children, cheered by the warming blaze, were now tittering and digging each other in the ribs with their elbows. One tiny little thing had stolen a carrot and was munching it furtively.

'Come here, Cuche!' said Pauline. 'Have you told your mother that I hope to get her admitted very soon into the Hospital for Incurables at Bayeux?'

Cuche's wife, a miserable abandoned woman, had broken her leg in July, and had remained infirm ever since.

'Yes, I told her,' the lad replied in a hoarse voice; 'but she says she won't go.'

He had grown into a strong young fellow, and was now nearly seventeen years old. With his hands hanging at his sides, he swayed about in an awkward manner.

'What! She won't go!' cried Lazare. 'And you won't come, either; for I told you to come up this week and help a little in the garden, and I'm still waiting for you.'

The lad still swayed himself about. 'I haven't had any time,' he replied.

At this Pauline, seeing her cousin about to lose his temper, interposed and said to the lad:

'Sit down again now, and we will speak about it presently. Just reflect a little or you will make me angry too.'

It was next the turn of the Gonins' little girl. She was thirteen years old, and still had a pretty rosy face beneath a mop of fair hair. Without waiting to be questioned, she poured out a flood of prattle, telling them how her father's paralysis was ascending to his arms and even his tongue, and that he could now only grunt like an animal. Cousin Cuche, the sailor who had deserted his wife and installed himself in Gonin's house, had made a violent attack upon the old man that very morning, in the hope of finishing him off.

'Mother sets on him too. She gets up at night and empties bowls of cold water over father, because he snores so loud and disturbs her. If you could only see what a state they have left him in, Mademoiselle Pauline! He is quite naked, and he wants some sheets very badly, for all his skin is getting grazed and peeling off!'

'There! That will do; hold your tongue!' said Lazare, interrupting her chatter; while Pauline, moved to pity, sent Véronique off to look out a pair of sheets.

Lazare considered the girl much too wide-awake for her age, and he believed that, although she did perhaps sometimes ward off a blow meant for her father, she treated him in the long run no better than the others did. Moreover, he felt quite sure that whatever was given to her, whether it was money, or meat, or bed-linen, instead of being of any service to the infirm old man, would only serve for the gratification of his wife and cousin Cuche.

He began to question her sternly, for he had seen her gadding about with several lads of the neighbourhood. However, Pauline laid her hand upon his arm, for the other children, even the youngest amongst them, were sniggering and smiling with all the impudence of precocious vice. How was it possible to arrest that spreading rottenness when the men and women set so bad an example? When Pauline had given the girl a pair of sheets and a bottle of wine, she whispered to her for a moment or two, trying to frighten her as to the consequences which might result from misbehaviour. Warnings of this kind were the only ones that might hold her in check.

Meantime Lazare, wishing to hasten the distribution, the length of which was beginning to disgust and irritate him, called up Prouane's daughter.

'Your father and mother were tipsy again last night,' he said, 'and I hear that you were worse than either of them.'

'Oh! no, sir! I had a very bad headache.'

He placed before her a plate in which were a few pieces of raw meat.

'Eat that!'

She was devoured with scrofula again, and her nervous disorders had reappeared. Drunkenness increased her precocious infirmities, for she had acquired the habit of drinking with her parents. When she had swallowed three lumps of the meat, she stopped and made a grimace of disgust.

'I've had enough; I can't eat any more.'

But Pauline had taken up a bottle.

'Very well,' she said!' if you don't eat the meat, you shan't have your glass of quinine wine.'

On hearing this, the girl fixed her glistening eyes on the glass, which Pauline filled, and overcame her repugnance against the meat. Then she seized the glass and tossed its contents down her throat with all a drunkard's knowing readiness. But she did not then retire; she begged Pauline to let her take the bottle away with her, saying that it interfered too much with what she had to do to come up to the house every day; and she promised to take the bottle to bed with her, and to keep it so securely hidden that her father and mother would never be able to find it and drink the wine. Pauline, however, refused to let her have it.

'You'd swallow every drop of it before you got to the bottom of the hill,' said Lazare. 'It's yourself that we suspect now, you little wine-cask!'

One by one the children left the bench to receive money, or bread, or meat. Some of them, after receiving their share of the distribution, seemed inclined to linger before the blazing fire, but Véronique, who had just noticed that half her carrots had been devoured, drove them off pitilessly into the rain. 'Had anyone ever seen anything like it before?' she cried. 'Carrots, too, that still had all the earth sticking to them!'

Soon there was no one left but young Cuche, who looked very depressed in the expectation of receiving a severe lecture from Pauline. She called him to her, spoke to him for a long time in low tones, and finished by giving him his loaf and the hundred sous which he received from her every Saturday. Then he went off, with his clumsy swaying, having duly promised to work, but having no intention whatever of doing anything of the kind.

The servant was just giving a sigh of relief when she suddenly exclaimed:

'Hallo! they haven't all gone yet, then! There's one of them over there in the corner still!'

It was the Tourmals' little girl, the little abortion of the high roads, who, notwithstanding her ten years, was still quite a dwarf. It was only in shamelessness and effrontery that she seemed to grow, and she groaned more miserably and seemed more wretched than ever, trained for the profession of begging from her cradle, just as some infants have their bones manipulated in order that they may become acrobats. She crouched between the dresser and the fireplace, as though she had stowed herself in that corner for fear of being surprised in some wrongdoing.

'What are you up to there?' Pauline asked her.

'I am warming myself.'

Véronique cast an anxious glance round her kitchen. On previous Saturdays, even when the children had assembled on the terrace, various little articles had disappeared. That day, however, everything seemed in its place, and the little girl, who had hurriedly risen to her feet, began to deafen them with her shrill voice:

'Father is in the hospital, and grandfather has hurt himself at his work, and mother hasn't a gown to go out in. Please have pity upon us, kind young lady—'

'Do you want to split our ears, you little liar?' Lazare cried angrily. 'Your father is in gaol for smuggling, and when your grandfather sprained his wrist he was robbing the oyster-beds at Roqueboise, and, if your mother hasn't got a dress, she must manage to go out stealing in her chemise, for she is charged with having strangled five fowls belonging to the innkeeper at Verchemont. Do you think you can befool us with your lies about matters that we know more of than you do yourself?'

The child did not even appear to have heard him. She went on immediately with all her impudent coolness:

'Have pity upon us, kind young lady! My father and grandfather are both ill, and my mother dare not leave them. God Almighty will bless you for it.'

'There! that will do! Now go away and don't tell any more lies!' Pauline said to her, giving her a piece of money to get rid of her.

She did not want telling twice, but hurried from the kitchen and through the yard as quickly as her little legs would carry her. Just at that moment the servant uttered a cry:

'Ah! the cup that was on the dresser! She's gone off with your cup, Mademoiselle Pauline!'

Then she bolted off in pursuit of the young thief, and a couple of minutes afterwards dragged her back into the kitchen with all the stern ferocity of a gendarme. It was as much as they could do to search the child, for she struggled and bit and scratched and screamed as though they were trying to murder her. The cup was not in her pocket, but they discovered it next to her skin, hidden away in the rag which served her as a chemise. Thereupon ceasing to weep, she impudently asserted that she did not know it was there, that it must have dropped into her clothes while she was sitting on the floor.

'His reverence was quite right when he said she would rob you!' Véronique exclaimed. 'If I were you I would send for the police.'

Lazare, too, began to speak about sending her to prison, provoked as he was by the demeanour of the girl, who perked herself up like a young viper whose tail had been trodden upon. He felt inclined to smack her.

'Hand back the money that was given to you!' he cried. 'Where is it?'

The child had already raised the coin to her lips in order to swallow it, when Pauline set her free, saying:

'Well, you may keep it this time, but you can tell them at home that it is the last they will get. In future I shall come myself to see what you are in need of. Now, be off with you!'

They could hear the girl's naked feet splashing through the puddles, and then all became silent. Véronique pushed the bench aside and stooped down to sponge away the pools of water that had trickled from the children's rags. Her kitchen was in a fine state, she grumbled; it reeked of all that filth to such a degree that she would have to keep all the windows and doors open. Pauline, who seemed very grave, gathered up her money and drugs without saying a word, while Lazare, with an air of disgust and *ennui,* went out to wash his hands at the yard tap.

It was great grief to Pauline to see that her cousin took but little interest in her young friends from the village. Though he was willing to help her on the Saturday afternoons, it was only out of mere complaisance; his heart was not in the work. Whereas neither poverty nor vice repelled her, their hideousness depressed and annoyed Lazare. She could remain cheerful and tranquil in her love for others, whereas he could not cease to think of himself without finding fresh reasons for gloomy broodings. Little by little, those disorderly, ill-behaved children, in whom all the sins of grown-up men and women were already fermenting, began to cause him real suffering. The sight of them proved like an additional blight to his existence, and when he left them he felt hopeless, weary, full of hatred and disgust of the human species. The hours that were spent in good works only hardened him, made him deny the utility of almsgiving and jeer at charity. He protested that it would be far more sensible to crush that nest of pernicious vermin under foot than to help the young ones to grow up. Pauline listened to this, surprised by his violence, and pained to find how different were their views.

That Saturday, when they were alone again, the young man revealed all his suffering by a single remark.

'I feel as though I had just come out of a sewer,' said he. Then he added: 'How can you care for such horrible monsters?'

'I care for them for their own good and not for mine,' the girl replied. 'You yourself would pick up a mangy dog in the road.'

Lazare made a gesture of protest. 'A dog isn't a man,' he said.

'To help for the sake of helping, is not that something?' Pauline resumed. 'It is vexing that they don't improve in conduct, for, if they did, perhaps they would suffer less. But I am content when they have got food and warmth; that is one trouble less for them, at any rate. Why should you want them to recompense us for what we do for them?'

Then she concluded sadly:

'My poor boy, I see that all this only bores you, and it will be better for you not to come and help me in future. I don't want to harden your heart and make you more uncharitable than you already are.'

Thus Lazare eluded all her attempts, and she felt heartbroken at finding how utterly powerless she was to free him from his fear and *ennui*. When she saw him so nervous and despondent, she could scarcely believe that it was the result merely of his secret trouble she imagined there must be other causes for his sadness, and the idea of Louise recurred to her. She felt sure that he must still be thinking about the girl, and suffered from not seeing her. A cold chill came upon her at this thought, and she tried to recover her old feeling of proud self-sacrifice, telling herself that she was quite capable of spreading sufficient brightness and joy about her to make them all happy.

One evening Lazare made a remark that hurt her cruelly.

'How lonely it is here!' he said, with a yawn.

She looked at him. Had he got Louise in his mind? But she had not the courage to question him. Her kindliness struggled within her, and life became a torture again.

There was another shock awaiting Lazare. His old dog, Matthew, was far from well. The poor animal, who had completed his fourteenth year in the previous March, was getting more and more paralysed in his hind-quarters. His attacks left him so stiff that he could scarcely crawl along; and he would lie out in the yard, stretching himself in the sun, and watching the members of the family with his melancholy eyes. It was the old dog's eyes, now dimmed by a bluish cloudiness, blank like those of a blind man, that especially wrought upon Lazare's feelings.

The poor animal, however, could still see, and used to drag himself along, lay his big head on his master's knee, and look up at him fixedly with a sad expression that seemed to say that he understood all. His beauty had departed. His curly white coat had turned yellowish, and his nose, once so black, was becoming white. His dirtiness, and a kind of expression of shame that hung about him—for they dared not wash him any more on account of his great age—rendered him yet more pitiable. All his playfulness had vanished; he never now rolled on his back, or circled round after his tail, or showed any impulses of pity for Minouche's kittens when Véronique carried them off to drown in the sea. He now spent his days in drowsing like an old man, and he had so much difficulty in getting up on his legs again, and dragged his poor soft feet so heavily, that often one of the household, moved to pity at the sight, stooped to support him for a moment or two in order that he might be able to walk a little.

He grew weaker every day from loss of blood. They had sent for a veterinary surgeon, who burst out laughing on seeing him. What! were they making a fuss about a dog like that? The best thing they could do was to put him out of the way at once. It was all very well to try and keep a human being alive as long as possible, but what was the good of allowing a dying animal to linger on in pain? At this they quickly bustled the vet out of the house, after paying him his fee of six francs.

One Saturday Matthew lost so much blood that it was found necessary to shut him up in the coach-house. A stream of big red drops trickled after him. Doctor Cazenove, who had arrived rather early, offered to go and see the dog, who was treated quite as a member of the family. They found him lying down, in a state of great weakness, but with his head raised very high, and the light of life still shining in his eyes. The Doctor made a long examination of him, with all the care and thoughtfulness which he displayed at the bedside of his human patients. At last he said:

'That abundant loss of blood denotes a cancerous degeneration of the kidneys. There is no hope for him, but he may linger for a few days yet, unless some sudden haemorrhage carries him off.'

Matthew's hopeless condition threw a gloom over the dinner-table. They recalled how fond Madame Chanteau had been of him, all the wild romps of his youth, the dogs he had worried, the cutlets he had stolen off the gridiron, and the eggs that he gobbled up warm from the nest. But at dessert, when Abbé Horteur brought out his pipe, they grew lively again, and listened with attention to the priest as he told them about his pear-trees, which promised to do splendidly that year. Chanteau, notwithstanding certain prickings which foreboded another attack of gout, finished off by singing one of the merry songs of his youth. Thus the evening passed away delightfully, and even Lazare himself grew cheerful.

About nine o'clock, just as tea was being served, Pauline suddenly cried out:

'Oh look! There's poor Matthew!'

And, in truth, the poor dog, all bleeding and shrunken, was dragging himself on his tottering legs into the dining-room. Then immediately afterwards they heard Véronique, who was rushing after him with a cloth. She burst into the room, crying:

'I had to go into the coach-house, and he made his escape. He still insists upon being where the rest of us are, and one can't take a step without finding him between one's legs. Come! come! you can't stop here.'

The dog lowered his old trembling head with an expression of affectionate entreaty.

'Oh! let him stop, do!' Pauline cried.

But the servant seemed displeased.

'No! indeed, not in such a state as that. I have had quite enough to do, as it is, with wiping up after him. It's really quite disgusting. You'll have the dining-room in a nice state if he goes dragging himself all over the place in this way. Come along! Come along! Be a little quicker, do!'

'Let him stay here, and you go away!' said Lazare.

Then, as Véronique furiously banged the door behind her, Matthew, who seemed to understand the situation perfectly well, came and laid his head on his master's knee. Everyone wanted to lavish dainties on him; they broke up lumps of sugar, and tried to brighten him up into liveliness. In times past they had been accustomed every evening to amuse themselves by placing a lump of sugar upon the table on the opposite side to that at which the dog was stationed, and then as Matthew ran round they caught up the sugar and deposited it on the other side, in such wise that the dog went rushing round the table in pursuit of the dainty which was ever being removed from him, till at last he grew quite dizzy with the perpetual flitting, and broke out into wild and noisy barking. Lazare tried to set this little game going again, in the hope of cheering the poor animal. Matthew wagged his tail for a moment, went once round the table, and then staggered and fell against Pauline's chair. He could not see the sugar, and his poor shrunken body rolled over on its side. Chanteau had stopped humming, and everyone felt keen sorrow at the sight of that poor dying dog, who had vainly tried to summon up the romping energies of the past.

'Don't do anything to tire him,' the Doctor said gently, 'or you will kill him.'

Then the priest, who was smoking in silence, let fall a remark which was probably intended to account for his emotion.

'One might almost imagine,' he said, 'that these big dogs were human beings.'

About ten o'clock, when the priest and the Doctor had left, Lazare, before going to his own room, went to lock Matthew in the coach-house again. He laid him carefully down upon some fresh straw, and saw that his bowl was full of water; then he kissed him and was about to leave him, but the dog raised himself on his feet with a painful effort, and tried to follow the young man. Lazare had to put him back three times, and then at last the dog yielded, but he raised his head with so sad an expression to watch his master depart that Lazare, who felt heart-broken, came back and kissed him again.

When he reached his room at the top of the house the young man tried to read till midnight. Then he went to bed. But he could not sleep; his mind dwelt continually upon Matthew; the image of the poor animal, lying on his bed of straw, with his failing eyes turned towards the door, never ceased to haunt him. On the morrow, he thought, Matthew would be dead. Every minute he caught himself involuntarily sitting up in bed and listening, fancying he heard a bark in the yard. His straining ears caught all sorts of imaginary sounds. About two o'clock in the morning he heard a groaning which made him jump out of bed. Who could be groaning like that? He rushed out on to the landing, but the house was wrapped in darkness and silence, not a breath came from Pauline's room. Then he could no longer resist his impulse to go downstairs. The hope of once more seeing his old dog alive made him hasten his steps; he scarcely gave himself time to thrust his legs into a pair of trousers, before he started off, taking his candle with him.

When he reached the coach-house Matthew was no longer lying on the straw; he had dragged himself some distance away from it, and was stretched upon the hard ground. When he saw his master enter, he no longer had enough strength to raise his head. Lazare placed his candle on some old boards, and was filled with astonishment when he bent down and saw the ground all black. Then a spasm of pain came to him as he knelt and found that the poor animal was weltering in his death-throes in a perfect pool of blood. Life was quickly ebbing from him; he wagged his tail very feebly, while a faint light glistened in the depths of his eyes.

'Oh! my poor old dog!' sobbed Lazare; 'oh! my poor old dog!'

Then, aloud, he said:

'Wait a moment! I will move you. Ah! I'm afraid it hurts you, but you are drenched lying here; and I haven't even got a sponge. Would you like something to drink?'

Matthew still gazed at him earnestly. Gradually the death-rattle shook his sides, and the pool of blood grew bigger and bigger, quite silently, and as though it were fed by some hidden spring.

Various ladders and broken barrels in the coach-house cast great shadows around, and the candle burnt very dimly. But suddenly there came a rustling among the straw. It was the cat, Minouche, who was reposing on the bed made for Matthew, and had been disturbed by the light.

'Would you like something to drink, my poor old fellow?' Lazare repeated.

He had found a cloth, which he dipped in the pan of water and pressed against the dying animal's mouth. It seemed to relieve him; and his nose, which was excoriated through fever, became a little cooler. Half an hour passed, during which Lazare constantly dipped the cloth in the water, while his eyes filled with tears at the painful sight before him, and his heart ached with all the bitterness of grief. Wild hopes came to him at times, as they do to the watchers at a bedside; perhaps, he thought, he might recall ebbing life by that simple application of cold water.

'Ah! what is the matter? What do you want to do?' he cried suddenly. 'You want to get on your feet, eh?'

Matthew, shaken by a fit of shivering, made desperate efforts to raise himself. He stiffened his limbs, while his neck was distended by his hiccoughs. But the end was close at hand, and he fell across his master's knees, with eyes still straining from beneath their heavy lids to catch sight of him. Quite overcome by that glance, so full of intelligence, Lazare held Matthew there on his knees, while the animal's big body, heavy like that of a man, was racked by a human-like death-agony in his sorrowing embrace. It lasted for some minutes, and then Lazare saw real tears—heavy tears—roll down from the dog's mournful eyes, while his tongue showed forth from his convulsed mouth, as though for a last caress.

'Oh! my poor old dog!' cried Lazare, bursting into sobs.

Matthew was dead. A little bloody foam frothed round his jaws. As Lazare laid him down on the floor he looked as though he were asleep.

Then once more the young man felt that all was over. His dog was dead now, and this filled him with unreasonable grief and seemed to cast a gloom over his whole life. That death awoke in him the memory of other deaths, and he had not felt more heart-broken even when walking through the yard behind his mother's coffin. Some last portion of her seemed to be torn away from him; she had gone from him now entirely. The recollection of his months of secret anguish, of his nights disturbed by nightmare visions, of his walks to the little graveyard, and of all his terror at the thought of annihilation, surged up in his mind.

However, he heard a sound, and when he turned he saw Minouche quietly making her toilet on the straw. But the door creaked, and Pauline then entered the coach-house, impelled thither by an impulse similar to that of her cousin. When he saw her his tears fell faster, and he who had carefully concealed all his grief at his mother's death, as though it had been some shameful folly, now cried:

'Oh, God! God! She loved him so dearly! You remember, don't you? She first had him when he was quite a tiny little thing, and it was she who always fed him, and he used to follow her all over the house!'

Then he added: 'There is no one left now, and we are utterly alone!'

Tears sprang up in Pauline's eyes. She had stooped to look at poor Matthew's body lying there beneath the dim glimmer of the candle. And she did not seek to console Lazare. She made but a gesture of despair, for she felt that she was utterly powerless.

VIII

It was *ennui* that lay below all Lazare's gloomy sadness, a heavy continuous *ennui* which rose from everything, like murky waters from some poisoned spring. He was bored both with work and with idleness, and with himself even more than with others. However, he took himself to task for his idleness and felt ashamed of it. It was disgraceful for a man of his age to waste the best years of his life in such a hole as Bonneville. Until now he had had some excuse for doing so, but at present there was no longer anything to keep him at home, and he despised himself for staying there, leading a useless existence, living upon his family, who were scarcely able to keep themselves. He told himself that he ought to be making a fortune for them, and that he was failing shamefully in not doing so, as he had formerly sworn he would. Great schemes for the future, grand enterprises, the idea of a vast fortune acquired by some brilliant stroke of genius, still occurred to him; but when he rose up from his reveries he lacked the energy to turn his thoughts into action. 'I can't go on like this,' he often said to Pauline. 'I must really do something. I should like to start a newspaper at Caen.'

And his cousin always made the same reply:

'Wait till the time of mourning is over. There is no hurry. You had better think matters well over before you launch out into an undertaking like that.'

The truth was that, notwithstanding her desire to see him occupy himself with some kind of work, she was alarmed by this scheme of founding a newspaper. Another failure, she feared, might kill him, and she thought of all his many previous ones—music, medicine, the seaweed works; everything, in fact, that he had ever taken in hand. And, besides, a couple of hours after he had mentioned this last plan to her he had refused even to write a letter, on the ground that he was too tired.

The weeks passed away, and another flood-tide carried off three more houses at Bonneville. When the fishermen now met Lazare they asked him if he had had enough of it. Though it was really quite useless trying to do anything, they said it grieved them to see so much good timber lost. There was a touch of banter in their expressions of condolence and in the manner in which they besought him not to leave the place to the waves, as though with their sailor-natures they felt a savage pride in the sea's destructive blows. By degrees Lazare grew so annoyed with their remarks that he avoided passing through the village. The sight of the ruined piles and stockades in the distance became intolerable to him.

One day, as he was on his way to see the priest, Prouane stopped him.

'Monsieur Lazare,' he said obsequiously, while a mischievous smile played round his eyes, 'you know those pieces of timber which are rotting away down yonder on the shore?'

'Well, what about them?'

'If you're not going to use them again, you might give them to us. They would serve, at any rate, as firewood.'

The young man was carried away by his anger, and, without even thinking of what he was saying, he answered sharply:

'That's quite impossible. I am going to set men to work again next week.'

At this all the neighbourhood shouted. They were going to have all the fun over again, since young Chanteau was showing himself so pig-headed. A fortnight went by, and the fishermen never met Lazare without asking him if he was unable to find workmen; and thus he was goaded into a renewal of his operations, being induced thereto, also, by the entreaties of his cousin, who was anxious that he should have some occupation which would keep him near her. But he entered into the matter without the least spark of enthusiasm, and it was only his revengeful enmity against the sea which kept him saying that he was quite certain to triumph over it this time, and would make it lick the pebbles on the shore as submissively as a dog.

Once again Lazare set to work preparing plans. He planned fresh angles of resistance and doubled the strength of his supports. No excessive expense was going to be incurred, as most of the old timbers could be used again. The carpenter sent in an estimate of four thousand francs; and, as the sum was so small, Lazare made no objection to Louise advancing it, being quite certain, he said, of getting a subvention from the General Council; indeed, he remarked that this was the only means they had of getting their previous expenditure reimbursed, for the Council would certainly refuse to advance a copper so long as the works remained in their present ruinous condition. This consideration seemed to infuse a little warmth into his proceedings, and the operations were pressed on. In other ways, too, he became very busy, and went over to Caen every week to see the Prefect and the influential members of the Council.

While the piles were being laid, an intimation was received that an engineer would be sent to inspect the operations and make a report, on the receipt of which the Council would vote a subvention. The engineer spent a whole day at Bonneville. He was a very pleasant man, and gladly accepted an invitation from the Chanteaus to lunch with them after his visit to the shore. They refrained from making any reference to the subvention, as they were unwilling to appear in any way desirous of influencing his judgment, but he showed himself so polite and attentive to Pauline at table that she began to feel no doubt as to their success in obtaining the grant. And so, a fortnight later, when Lazare returned from one of his visits to Caen, the whole house was thrown into amazement and consternation by the news which he brought back with him. He was bursting with anger. Would they believe it! That silly fop of an engineer had sent in a simply disgraceful report. Yes! he had been polite and civil, but he had made fun of every single piece of timber with a ridiculous lavishness of technical terms. But it was only what they might have expected, for those official gentlemen didn't believe that any one could put even a rabbit-hutch together without their advice and assistance! However, the worst of the matter was that the Council, after reading the report, had refused to vote any grant at all.

This blow was a source of fresh despondency to the young man. The works were finished, and he swore that they would resist the heaviest tides, and that the whole Engineering Department would go wild with angry jealousy when they saw them. All this, however, would not repay Pauline the money that she had advanced, and Lazare bitterly reproached himself for having led her into that loss. She herself, however, rising victorious over the instincts of her economical nature, claimed the entire responsibility for the course she had taken, impressing upon him that it was she who had insisted upon making the advances. The money had gone in a charitable purpose, she said, and she did not regret a sou of it, but would have gladly given more for the sake of saving the unhappy village. However, when the carpenter sent in his bill, she could not suppress a gesture of grievous astonishment. The four thousand francs of the estimate had grown to nearly eight thousand. Altogether, those piles and stockades, which the first storm might completely sweep away, had cost her more than twenty thousand francs.

By this time Pauline's fortune was reduced to forty thousand francs, which produced a yearly income of two thousand francs, a sum on which she would be barely able to live, should she ever find herself homeless and friendless. Her money had trickled away in small sums in the household expenses, which she still continued to defray. But she now began to exercise a strict supervision over all the outlay of the house. The Chanteaus themselves no longer had even their three hundred francs a month, for, after Madame Chanteau's death, it was found that a certain amount of stock had been sold without there being any clue as to how the amount realised by its sale had been applied. When her own income was added to that of the family, Pauline had little more than four hundred francs a month with which to keep the house going. The expenses of the establishment were heavy, and she had to perform miracles of economy in order to save the money that she needed for her charities. Doctor Cazenove's trusteeship had terminated during the winter, and Pauline, being now of age, her money and herself were entirely at her own disposal; though indeed the Doctor during the term of his authority had never refused to let her have her own way. That authority had legally ceased for some weeks before either of them remembered the fact. But, although Pauline had been practically her own mistress for some time, she felt more thoroughly independent, more like a fully-grown woman, now that she was the uncontrolled mistress of the house, with no accounts to render to anybody, for her uncle was ever entreating her to settle everything, and Lazare, like his father, also hated having anything to do with money matters.

Thus Pauline held the common purse and stepped entirely into her aunt's place, performing her duties as mistress of the house with a practical common-sense that sometimes quite amazed the two men. It was only Véronique who made any complaints, thinking that Mademoiselle

Pauline was very stingy, and grumbling at being restricted to a single pound of butter a week.

The days succeeded each other with monotonous regularity. The perpetual sameness, the unvarying habits of the household, which constituted Pauline's happiness, only tended to increase Lazare's feeling of *ennui*. Never had the house affected him with such uneasy disquietude as now, when every room seemed basking in cheerful peace. The completion of the operations on the shore had proved a great relief, for enforced attention to anything had become intolerable to him, and he had no sooner fallen back into idleness than he once more became the prey of shame and anxiety. Every morning he made a fresh set of plans for the future. He had abandoned the idea of starting a newspaper as unworthy of him, and he inveighed against the poverty which prevented him from quietly devoting himself to some great literary work. He had lately become enamoured of the notion of preparing himself for a professorship, and so earning a livelihood and enabling himself to carry out his literary ambition. There no longer seemed to exist between himself and Pauline anything beyond their old feeling of comradeship, a quiet affection which made them, as it were, brother and sister. The young man never made any reference to their marriage, either because he never thought of it, or, perhaps, because he took it for granted and considered any discussion of the matter unnecessary while the girl herself was equally reticent on the subject, feeling quite certain that her cousin would willingly acquiesce in the first suggestion of their union. And yet Lazare's passion for her was gradually diminishing; a fact of which she was quite conscious, though she did not understand that it was this alone which rendered her powerless to free him from his *ennui*.

One evening, when she had gone upstairs in the dusk to tell him that dinner was ready, she surprised him in the act of hastily hiding something which she could not distinguish.

'What's that?' she asked, with a laugh. 'Some verses for my birthday?'

'No!' he replied, with much emotion and in wavering tones. 'It's nothing at all.'

It was an old glove which Louise had left behind her, and which he had just discovered behind a pile of books. The glove had retained a strong odour of the original skin of which it was made, and this was softened to a musky fragrance by Louise's favourite perfume, heliotrope. Lazare, who was very susceptible to the influence of odours, was violently agitated by that scent, and in a state of emotion had lingered with the glove pressed to his lips, draining from it a draught of sweet recollections.

From that day onward he began to yearn for Louise over the yawning chasm which his mother's death had left within him. He had never indeed forgotten the girl; her image had been dimmed somewhat by his grief, but it only wanted that little thing that had once belonged to her to bring her back to his mind. He took up the glove again, as soon as he was alone, kissed it, inhaled its scent, and fancied that he was still holding the girl in his embrace with his lips seeking hers. His nervous excitement, the mental feverishness which resulted from his long-continued inactivity, tended to intensify this species of intoxication. He felt vexed with himself on account of it, but he succumbed to it again and again, carried away by a passion which quite overpowered him. All this, too, increased his gloomy moodiness, and he even began to get snappish and surly with his cousin, as though she were in some way to blame for his passionate trances. Often, in the midst of some tranquil conversation, he would suddenly rush off and shut himself up in his room and wallow in his passionate recollections of the other girl. Then he would come downstairs again, weary and disgusted with life.

At the end of a month he had so completely changed that Pauline grew quite hopeless and spent nights of torment. In the daytime she forced herself to assume a brave face, and kept herself perpetually busy in the house of which she was now the mistress. But at night, when she had closed the door of her room behind her, she dwelt upon her troubles, gave way completely, and wept like a child. She had no hope left; all her kindliness only met with an increasingly chilling reception. Could it really be, she wondered, that kindness and affection were insufficient, and that it was possible to love a person and yet cause him unhappiness? For she saw that her cousin was really unhappy, and she began to fear that it might somehow be her own fault. And then, beneath her doubts of herself, there lurked increasing fears of a rival influence. She had for a long time explained Lazare's gloomy moodiness to herself as springing from grief at his mother's death; but now she was again haunted by the idea of Louise, an idea which had occurred to her on the very day after Madame Chanteau's death, but which she had then scornfully dismissed amidst her pride in the power of her own affection, though every night now it forced itself upon her as she found the efforts of her love so unavailing.

The girl was haunted by it all. As soon as she had put down her candle after entering her room she threw herself upon her bed, without having the energy to undress. All the gaiety of spirit which she had shown during the day, all her calmness and restraint, weighed upon her like a too heavy gown. The day, like those which had preceded it, and like those which would follow, had passed away amidst that feeling of hopelessness with which Lazare's moody *ennui* contaminated the whole house. What was the use of striving to appear bright and cheerful, when she was unable to cast a gleam of sunshine on him she so dearly loved? Lazare's former cruel remark still rankled in her heart. They were too lonely, and it was her jealousy that was to blame for it; it was she who had sent their friends away. She would not name Louise to herself, and she tried not to think about her; but she could not succeed in banishing the memory of that girl, with the winning ways and coquettish airs which had amused Lazare, who grew bright at the mere rustling of her gown. The minutes glided on, and still Pauline could not drive Louise from her thoughts. She felt sure it was for her that Lazare was anxiously longing, that all that was wanted to set him right again was to send for the girl. And every evening when Pauline went upstairs and threw herself wearily on her bed she relapsed into those same thoughts and visions, and was tortured by the idea that the happiness of her dear ones depended perhaps upon another than herself.

Now and then her spirit would rise within her in rebellion, and she would spring from her bed, rush to the window and open it, feeling suffocated. And there, gazing out into the far-spreading darkness, above the ocean, whose moaning rose to her ear, she would remain for hours, leaning on her elbows, unable to sleep, while the sea-air played upon her burning breast. No; never could she be vile enough, she told herself, to tolerate that girl's return! Had she not surprised them together? Was it not an act of treason—treason of the basest kind—that they had committed? Yes; it was an unpardonable offence, and she would only be making herself their accomplice if she did anything to bring them together again. She grew feverish and excited with angry jealousy at the ideas which she called up, and shook with sobs as she hid her face with her bare arms. The night sped on, and the breezes fanned her neck and played with her hair without calming the angry pulsing of her blood. But even in those moments when indignation most mastered her, her natural kindliness still made its voice heard and struggled against her passion. It whispered to her in gentle tones of the blessedness of charity, of the sweetness of sacrificing one's self for others. She tried to hush that inner voice, telling herself that to carry self-sacrifice to the point of baseness was idiotic; but she still heard its pleading, which refused to be silenced. By degrees she grew to recognise it as the voice of her own better nature, and she began to ask herself what, after all, would suffering matter, if she could only secure the happiness of those who were dear to her? Then she sobbed less loudly as she listened to the moans of the sea ascending through the darkness, weary and ill the while, and not yet conquered.

One night, after long weeping at her window, she at last got into bed. As soon as she had blown out her candle and lay staring into the darkness she came to a sudden resolution. The very first thing in the morning she would get her uncle to write to Louise and invite her to stay at Bonneville for a month. It all seemed quite natural and easy to her just then, and she quickly fell into sound sleep, a deeper and calmer sleep than she had known for weeks. But when she came down to breakfast the next morning and saw herself sitting between her uncle and cousin at the family table, there came a sudden choking sensation in her throat, and she felt all her courage and resolution forsaking her.

'You are eating nothing,' said Chanteau. 'What's the matter with you?'

'Nothing at all,' she replied. 'On the contrary, I have had a remarkably good sleep.'

The mere sight of Lazare brought her back to her mental struggle. He was eating in silence, weary already of the new day that had begun, and the girl could not bring herself to yield him to another. The thought of another taking him from her, and kissing him to console and comfort him, was intolerable to her. Yet when he left the room she made an effort to carry out her resolution.

'Are your hands any worse to-day?' she asked her uncle.

He gazed at his hands, where tophus was again appearing, and he painfully bent the joints.

'No,' he answered. 'My right hand is even more supple than usual. If the priest comes, we'll have a game at draughts.'

Then, after a moment's silence, he added:

'What makes you ask?'

She had been hoping that he would not be able to write, and now she blushed deeply, and, like a coward, determined to defer the letter till the morrow.

'Oh! I only wanted to know!' she stammered.

From that day forward all rest deserted her. Up in her own room at nights, after her fits of tears, she used to gain the mastery over herself, and vow that she would dictate to her uncle a letter in the morning; but when the morning came, and she again joined in the family life amongst those she loved, all her resolution failed her. The most trivial little details sent a pang through her heart; the bread that she cut for her cousin, his shoes which she gave to Véronique to be cleaned, and all the petty incidents of the daily routine. They might surely still be very happy by themselves in their old way, she thought. What was the use of calling in a stranger? Why disturb the affectionate life which they had been living for so many years past? The thought that it would no longer be she herself who would cut the bread and mend the linen made her choke with grief, as if she saw all happiness crumble away. This torture, which lurked in every little homely detail of her work, made all her duties as mistress a torment.

'What can be wrong?' she would sometimes ask herself aloud. 'We love each other, and yet we are not happy. Our affection for each other only seems to make us wretched.'

It was a problem she was constantly trying to solve. Perhaps all the trouble arose from the fact that her own character and that of her cousin did not harmonize. But, though she would willingly have adapted herself, have abdicated all personal will, she found it impossible to do so, for her sense of reason prevented her. Her patience often gave way, and there were days of sulking. She would have liked to be merry and drown all petty wretchedness in gaiety, but she could no longer do so; she, in her turn, was growing moody and despondent.

'It's very nice and pleasant this!' Véronique began to repeat from morning till night. 'There are only three of you now, and you'll end by eating each other up! Madame used to have her bad days, but, at any rate, while she was alive, you managed to keep off banging things at each other's heads.'

Chanteau himself also began to suffer from the influence of this slow and, to him, inexplicable disintegration of the family affections. Whenever he now had an attack of the gout, he bellowed, as the servant said, more loudly than before, and his caprices and violence tormented everyone in the place. The whole house was becoming a hell once more.

At last Pauline, in the last throes of her jealousy, began to ask herself if she was to impose her own ideas of happiness on Lazare. Certainly before everything else it was his happiness that she desired, even at the cost of grief to herself. Why, then, should she go on keeping him in this seclusion, in a solitude which seemed to make him suffer? He must, and doubtless he did, still love her, and he would come back to her when he was better able to appreciate her after comparison with that other girl. But, any way, she ought to let him make his own choice. It was only just, and the idea of justice remained paramount within her.

Every three months Pauline repaired to Caen to receive the dividends. She started in the morning and returned in the evening, after attending to a list of purchases and errands which she compiled during the previous quarter. On her visit to Caen in June that year, however, the family vainly awaited her return, putting off dinner till nine o'clock. Chanteau, who had become very uneasy, sent Lazare off along the road, fearing that some accident had occurred; whereas Véronique, with an air of perfect tranquillity, said that it was foolish of them to distress themselves, for Mademoiselle Pauline, finding herself behindhand, and being anxious to complete her purchases, had doubtless determined to stay at Caen all night. Nevertheless, they spent a very uneasy time at Bonneville, and next morning, as soon as breakfast was over, their anxiety returned. About noon, when Chanteau could scarcely keep himself any longer in his chair, and Lazare had just determined to set off to Arromanches, Véronique, who had been standing on the road, suddenly rushed into the room exclaiming:

'Here she is! Mademoiselle is coming!'

Chanteau insisted upon having his chair wheeled on to the terrace, and the father and son waited there together, while Véronique gave them particulars of what she had seen.

'It was Malivoire's coach. I could tell it was Mademoiselle Pauline by her crape ribbons. But what I couldn't understand was that there seemed to be somebody with her. What can that broken-winded old hack be doing, I wonder?'

At last the coach drove up to the door. Lazare had stepped towards it, and had already opened his mouth to question Pauline, who had sprung down lightly, when he remained as if thunderstruck. Behind his cousin there appeared another young woman, dressed in striped lilac Bilk. Both girls were laughing together in the most friendly fashion. The young man's surprise was so great that he returned to his father, crying:

'She has brought Louise with her!'

'Louise! Ah, that's a capital idea!' Chanteau exclaimed.

And when the girls stood side by side before him, the one still in her deep mourning and the other in her gay summer toilette, he continued, delighted with this new distraction:

'Ah, so you have made peace! Well, I never quite understood what was the matter—some nonsense, I suppose. How naughty it was of you, my poor Louisette, to keep estranged from us during all the trouble we've been through! Well; it's all at an end now, eh?'

A feeling of embarrassment kept the girls silent. They blushed and avoided looking at each other. Then Louise stepped forward and kissed Chanteau to bide her confusion. But he wanted some explanations.

'You met each other, I suppose.'

Thereupon Louise turned towards her friend, while her eyes filled with tears.

'It was Pauline who came to see us. I was just going back into the house myself when she arrived. You mustn't scold her for staying the night with us, for it was my fault. I made her stay. And, as the telegraph

goes no further than Arromanches, we thought we should get here ourselves as soon as any message. Do you forgive me?'
She kissed Chanteau again with all her old caressing manner. He
inquired no further. When what happened contributed to his pleasure,
he had no fault to find with it.

'But there's Lazare,' he added; 'aren't you going to speak to him?'
The young man had kept in the background, with an embarrassed
smile on his face. His father's remark completed his confusion, the
more especially as Louise only blushed again and made no step towards him. Why was she there, he asked himself? Why had his cousin
brought back this rival, whom she had so violently driven away? He
had not yet recovered from his confusion at the sight of her.

'Kiss her, Lazare!' said Pauline softly, 'since she is too timid to kiss
you.'

Her face was quite white, as she stood there in her deep mourning, but her expression was perfectly peaceful, and her eyes clear and
untroubled. She looked at them both with the maternal, serious expression which she assumed in her graver moments of household responsibility, and only smiled when the young man took courage to let his lips
just touch the cheek which Louise offered him.

When Véronique saw this, she rushed away and shut herself up
in her kitchen, perfectly thunderstruck. It was altogether beyond her
comprehension. After all that had passed, Mademoiselle Pauline could
have very little heart. She was becoming quite ridiculous in her desire
to please others. It wasn't sufficient to bring all the dirty little drabs of
the neighbourhood into the house and put them in the way of walking
off with the silver, but now she must bring sweethearts for Monsieur
Lazare! The house was getting into a nice state indeed!

When she had vented a little of her indignation in this explosion
over her fire, she went out on to the terrace again, exclaiming, 'Don't
you know that lunch has been ready for more than an hour? The potatoes are fried to cinders!'

They all ate with good appetites, but Chanteau was the only one
whose mirth flowed freely, and fortunately he was too gay to notice
the persistent constraint of the others. Though they showed themselves
very affectionate, still, beneath it all, there lurked a touch of that
uneasy sadness which manifests itself in one who forgives an irreparable insult, but cannot altogether forget it. The afternoon was spent
in installing the newcomer in her room. She again occupied her old
quarters on the first floor. If Madame Chanteau could only have come
downstairs to dinner, with her quick, short step, nothing would have
appeared changed in the house.

For nearly a week longer this uneasy constraint lasted amongst the young people. Lazare, who did not dare to question Pauline, was altogether unable to understand what he considered her most extraordinary caprice; for any idea of a sacrifice, of a determination deliberately and magnanimously taken, never occurred to him. He himself, amidst the desires fanned by his listless idleness, had never thought of marrying Louise; and so now, on being all three placed together again, they found themselves in a false position, which caused them much distress. There were pauses of silent embarrassment, and sentences that remained half unspoken from fear of conveying any allusion to the past. Pauline, surprised at this unexpected state of affairs, was obliged to exaggerate and force her gaiety, in the hope of bringing back a semblance of the careless merriment of former days. At first she felt a wave of joy rising in her heart, for she thought that Lazare was coming back to her. The presence of Louise had calmed him; he almost avoided her, and shunned being alone with her, horrified at the thought that he might even yet be weak enough to betray his cousin's confidence. Tortured by a feverish affection for Pauline, he attached himself to her, and in tones of emotion proclaimed her to be the best of girls, a true saint, of whom he was utterly unworthy. And so she felt very happy, and rejoiced greatly in what she thought was her victory, when she saw her cousin pay such little attention to Louise. At the end of the week she even began to reproach him for his want of amiability towards her rival.

'Why do you always run off and leave us? It really quite vexes me. She isn't here for us to be rude to her.'

Lazare avoided replying, making only a vague gesture. Then his cousin ventured to make an allusion to what had previously happened:

'I brought her here so that you might know that I have long ago forgiven you. I wanted to wipe out every remembrance of it, as though it were all some horrid dream. It is done with now. I am no longer afraid, you see. I have perfect confidence in you both.'

At this he caught her in his arms. Then he promised to be courteous and amiable with Louise.

From that moment they spent their days in delightful intimacy. Lazare no longer seemed to suffer from *ennui*. Instead of shutting himself up in his room at the top of the house, like a recluse, and making himself ill with very loneliness, he invented amusements and arranged long walks, from which they came back home glowing, invigorated by the fresh air. And it was now that Louise by slow degrees began to recover all her old sway over him. The young man grew quite at his ease with her again, and once more offered his arm, and allowed himself to be thrilled afresh by that disturbing perfume which every fold of the girl's lace seemed to exhale. At first he struggled against her growing influence over him, and tried to escape from her as soon as he found himself becoming intoxicated with her witchery. But Pauline herself bade him go to the girl's assistance when they had to leap over a pool as they skirted the shore. She herself jumped over it boldly, like a boy, disdaining all help; whereas Louise, with a soft cry like that of a wounded lark, surrendered herself to the young man's arms. Then, as they returned home again, and he supported her, all the low laughter and whispered confidences of former days began anew. But Pauline was, as yet, in no way distressed by this; she maintained her brave expression, without guessing that she was risking her happiness by never feeling weary or requiring the assistance of her cousin's arm. It was with a kind of smiling bravado that she made the others walk in front of her, arm-in-arm, as though she wanted to show them how great was her confidence.

Neither Lazare nor Louise, indeed, had the slightest idea of taking advantage of the trust she reposed in them. Though the young man was again bewitched by Louise, he perpetually struggled against her influence and made a point of showing himself more affectionate than before to his cousin. In Louise's society, whilst ever finding some charm by which he allowed himself to be deliciously beguiled, he was always protesting to himself that this time the game should not go beyond the limits of permissible flirtation. Why, he asked himself, should he deny himself some pleasant little amusement, since he was quite determined to go no further? Louise, too, felt more scruples than formerly; not that she accused herself of previous coquetry, for she was naturally of a caressing disposition, but now she would neither have done nor said anything that she thought might be in the least degree distasteful to Pauline. Her friend's forgiveness of what had passed had moved her to tears. She wanted to show that she was worthy of it, and seemed to regard her with that exuberant feminine adoration which finds expression in vows and kisses and all kinds of passionate caresses. She kept a constant watch upon her, so that she might run up to her at the first appearance of displeasure. At times she would abruptly leave Lazare's arm for Pauline's, and try to enliven her, and even pretend to sulk with the young man. Never before had Louise appeared so charming as she did now in this constant state of emotion, which arose from the necessity she felt of pleasing both Pauline and Lazare; and the whole house seemed alive with the rustle of her skirts and her pretty wheedling ways.

Little by little, however, Pauline became quite wretched again. Her temporary hope and momentary feeling of triumph only served to increase her pain. She no longer experienced the violent paroxysms and wild outbursts of jealousy which had once quite distracted her. Hers was rather a sensation of having life slowly crushed out of her, as though some heavy mass had fallen on her with a weight which bore her down more and more each passing minute. She felt that everything was over, that hope was no longer possible for her. And yet she had no reasonable ground of complaint against the two others. They showed the greatest thoughtfulness and affection for her, and struggled earnestly against the influences which attracted them towards each other. But it was this very show of affection which especially tortured her, for she began to see that they were prompted by a desire to prevent her from feeling pained by their love for one another. The pity of those young lovers was unendurable to her. When she left them together, were there not soft confessions and rapid whisperings, and then, when she joined them again, a sudden relapse into silence, after which Louise lavished kisses upon her and Lazare evinced affectionate humility? She would have preferred to know that they were really in the wrong, for all those honourable scruples and compensatory caresses, which plainly told her the real truth, left her quite disarmed, with neither the will nor the energy to try to win back her own happiness. On the day when she had brought her rival to Bonneville she had intended to hold her own against her, if she found any struggle necessary; but what could she do against a couple of children whose love for each other was such a source of distress to them? It was her own doing, too; she might have married Lazare, had she chosen, without troubling herself about his possible preference for someone else. But, in spite of her jealous torments, her heart rebelled against the idea of exacting from him the fulfilment of his promise—a promise which he no doubt now regretted. Though it should kill her to do so, she would give him up rather than marry him if he loved another. Meanwhile she still went on playing the part of mother to her little family; nursing Chanteau, who was not going on very satisfactorily, soothing Véronique, whose sense of propriety was seriously offended, to say nothing of pretending to treat Lazare and Louise as a pair of disorderly children in order that she might be able to smile at their escapades. She succeeded in forcing herself to laugh even more loudly than they did, with that clear, ringing laugh of hers, whose limpid notes testified to her healthy courage. The whole house seemed gay and animated. She herself affected a bustling activity from morning till night, refusing to accompany the young couple in their walks, on the pretence that she had to undertake a general cleaning of the house, or see after the washing, or superintend the making of preserves. It was, however, more particularly Lazare who had now become noisy and energetic. He went whistling up and down the stairs, drummed on the doors, and found the days too short and uneventful. Although he did not actually do anything, his new passion seemed to find him more occupation than he had either time or strength for. Once more he intended to conquer the world, and every day at dinner he expounded fresh extraordinary schemes for the future. He had already grown disgusted with the idea of literature, and had abandoned all notion of reading for the examinations which he had intended to pass in order to enable him to take up a professorship. For a long time he had made this intention of studying an excuse for shutting himself up in solitude in his room; but he had there felt so discouraged that he had never opened a book, and now he began to scoff at his own foolishness in ever contemplating such a thing. Could anything be more idiotic than to chain himself down to a life like that in order to be able at some future time to write a lot of plays and novels? No! Politics alone were worthy of his ambition; and he had now quite made up his mind. He had a slight acquaintance with the Deputy for Caen, and he would go with him to Paris as his secretary, and, doubtless, in a few months' time he would make his way. The Empire was in great want of intelligent young men.

When Pauline, whom this wild whirl of ideas made uneasy, tried to calm his ambitious fever by advising him to look out for some smaller but safer berth, he scoffed at her prudence and jokingly called her 'an old grandmother.'

One day, when Lazare and Louise had gone by themselves to Verchemont, Pauline had need of a recipe for freshening some old velvet, and she went upstairs to search for it in her cousin's big wardrobe, where she thought she recollected having seen it on a scrap of paper between the pages of a book. While she was looking for it she discovered amongst some pamphlets Louise's old glove, that forgotten glove, the contemplation of which had so often filled Lazare with intoxication. It proved a ray of light to Pauline. She recognised in it the object which her cousin had hidden from her with such emotion that evening when she had suddenly entered his room to tell him that dinner was ready. She fell upon a chair, quite overcome by the revelation. Ah! he had been longing for that girl before ever she had returned to the house; he had lived on his recollections of her, and he had worn that glove away with his lips because it retained some scent of her person! Pauline's whole body was shaken by sobs, while her streaming eyes remained fixed upon the glove, which she held in her trembling hands.

'Well, Mademoiselle, have you found it yet?' called Véronique, who had just come upstairs from the landing.

'The best thing you can do is to rub the stuff with a piece of bacon-rind.'

She came into the room, and seemed quite amazed at finding Pauline in tears, with her angers clutching the old glove. But as she glanced round the room she at last guessed the cause of the girl's despair.

'Well! well!' she said, in the rough way that was becoming more and more habitual to her, 'you might have expected it! I warned you how it would be, long ago. You brought them together again, and now they amuse themselves. And perhaps my mistress was right, after all; that kitten of a girl brightens him up more than you do.'

Then she shook her head, and added in a grave voice, as though she was speaking to herself:

'Ah! my mistress had a very clear eyesight, in spite of her faults. For my part, I can't bring myself to think that she is really dead.'

That evening, when Pauline had locked herself in her room and placed her candlestick on the chest of drawers, she threw herself upon her bed, repeating that she must get Louise and Lazare married. All day long a buzzing sensation had made her head throb and prevented her from thinking clearly; and it was only now, in the quiet night-time, when she was able to suffer without witnesses of her trouble, that the inevitable consequence of what had happened presented itself clearly to her mind. It was absolutely necessary that Lazare and Louise should marry. The thought rang through her like an order, like the voice of reason and justice, to which she could no longer turn a deaf ear. For a moment she, who was so courageous, gave way to terror, fancying she heard her dead aunt calling out to her to obey. Then, all dressed as she was, she turned over and covered herself with the bedclothes to drown the sound of her sobs. Oh! to have to surrender him to another! To know that another's arms would be clasped round him and would keep him from her for ever! To lose all hope of ever winning him back! No! she could never have enough courage for it; she would prefer to continue leading her present life of wretchedness. No one at all should have him, neither herself nor that other girl; and Lazare should grow old and withered with waiting! For a long time she lay struggling with herself, racked by jealous fury. Her impetuous temperament, which neither years nor reflection had been able to subdue, always asserted itself at the first moment of a difficulty. Then, however, she became prostrate, physically exhausted.

Too tired and weary to undress, Pauline lay for a long time on her back, debating the question. She succeeded in proving to herself that Louise could do more to secure Lazare's happiness than she ever could. Had not that girl, so weak and puny, already roused him from his *ennui* with her caresses? Doubtless it was necessary for him to have her continually clinging to his neck, that she might drive away with kisses all his gloomy thoughts, his terror of death. Then Pauline fell to depreciating herself, repeating that she was too cold and had none of the amorous graces of a woman, but only kindliness, which was not sufficient allurement. One other consideration, too, brought her complete conviction. She was ruined, and her cousin's plans for the future, those plans which had caused her so much anxiety, would require a large amount of money for accomplishment. Would it be right for her to impose on him the narrow, sordid life which they were now obliged to lead, condemn him to mediocrity, which she could see was painful to him? Their life together would be unhappy, poisoned by continual regret, the querulous bitterness of disappointed ambition. She could only give him a rancorous life of poverty; whereas Louise, who was wealthy, could open out to him the great career of which he dreamed. It was said that the girl's father was keeping some good berth vacant for his future son-in-law, probably some lucrative position in the bank; and, though Lazare affected to despise financiers, matters would no doubt be satisfactorily arranged. She felt that she could hesitate no longer, now that it seemed clear to her that she would be committing an unworthy action if she did not marry them together. And as she lay awake on her bed, that union of Lazare and Louise seemed to her to be a necessity, which she must hasten if she wanted to preserve her own self-respect.

The whole night passed while she was thus wrestling with herself. When the day broke, she at last undressed. She was perfectly calm now, and enjoyed profound repose, though still unable to sleep. She had never before felt so easy, so satisfied with herself, so free from all anxiety. All was ending; she had just severed the bonds of egotism, she had no hopes now centred in any person or thing, and within her lurked all the subtle pleasure that comes of self-sacrifice. She did not even experience any longer her old craving to prove all-sufficient for the happiness of her people. The pride of abnegation had vanished, and she was willing that those she loved should be happy through other instrumentality than her own., It was the loftiest height which love for others can reach, to suppress one's self, to give up everything and still think one has not given enough, to love so deeply as to rejoice in a happiness which one has neither bestowed nor shares. The sun was rising when she at last dropped off into a deep sleep.

Pauline came downstairs very late that morning. When she awoke, it made her happy to find that all the resolutions she had taken during the night remained fixed and unwavering within her. But she began to reflect that she had forgotten what would become of herself, and that she must make some plans for her future altered circumstances. Though she might have the courage to bring about the marriage of Lazare and Louise, she would certainly never be brave enough to remain with them and watch their happiness. Self-devotion has its limits, and she was afraid of some return of her violent outbursts, some terrible scene which would kill her. Besides, was she not really doing all that could possibly be demanded of her, and could anyone have the cruelty to impose useless torture upon her? She came to an immediate and irrevocable decision. She would go away, leave the house, which was so full of disquieting associations. This would mean a complete change in her life, but she did not shrink from it.

At breakfast she showed a calm cheerfulness, which she henceforth maintained. She bravely endured the sight of Lazare and Louise, sitting side by side, whispering and smiling, without any other feeling of weakness than a chilly coldness at her heart. As it was Saturday, she made up her mind to send them out for a long walk together in order that she might be alone when Doctor Cazenove came. They went off, and Pauline then took the precaution of going out into the road to meet the Doctor. As soon as he caught sight of her he wanted her to get up into his gig and drive to the house with him. But she begged him to alight, and they walked along slowly together, while Martin, a hundred yards in the rear, brought on the empty vehicle.

In a few simple words Pauline unbosomed herself to the Doctor. She told him everything—her plan of giving Lazare to Louise and her determination to leave the house. This confession had seemed necessary to her; she was unwilling to act upon mere inspiration, and the old doctor was the only person who could understand her.

Cazenove suddenly halted in the middle of the road and clasped the girl in his long bony arms. He was trembling with emotion, and he kissed her on the hair, as he said affectionately:

'You are quite right, my dear; you are quite right. And it pleases me very much to hear it, for matters might have had a much worse ending. For months past I have been feeling grieved, and I was longing to come and talk to you, for I knew you were very unhappy. Ah! they have plundered you and stripped you nicely, those good folks! First your money and now your heart!'

The young girl tried to stop him.

'My dear friend, I beg you—You are judging them unfairly.'

'Perhaps so, but that does not prevent me from being glad on your account. Yes, yes! Give up your Lazare! It is not a very valuable present that you are making to the other one! I daresay that he is a very charming fellow, and that he has the best intentions in the world; but I prefer that the other should be unhappy with him, and not you. Those fine fellows who grow bored with everything are far too heavy even for broad shoulders like yours to support. I would rather see you marry some sturdy butcher-lad—yes, I mean it—some butcher-lad who would shake his sides day and night with honest, merry laughter.'

Then, as he saw her eyes fill with tears, he added:

'Ah, well! you love him, I suppose, and so I won't say anything more. Give me a kiss again, since you are brave enough to act so sensibly. Ah! what a fool he is not to see what he is doing!'

He took her arm and drew her close to his side. Then they began to talk seriously together as they resumed their walk. The Doctor told her that she would certainly do best to leave Bonneville, and he undertook to find her a situation. He happened, he said, to have a rich old relative living at Saint-Lô, who was looking for a young lady companion. Pauline would be perfectly happy with her, and very likely the old lady, who had no children of her own, would grow much attached to her and subsequently adopt her. They arranged everything between themselves, and the Doctor promised Pauline a definite reply from his relative in a few days' time.

Meanwhile it was settled she should say nothing about her determination to leave the Chanteaus. She was afraid that if she did it might seem to be in some way a threat, and she was anxious to bring the marriage to an issue and then immediately leave the house like one who could no longer be of use there.

On the third day Pauline received a letter from the Doctor. She was expected at Saint-Lô as soon as she could get away. It was on this same day, during Lazare's absence, that she led Louise to an old seat beneath a clump of tamarisks at the bottom of the kitchen-garden. In front of them, above the low wall, they could see nothing but the sea and sky—a measureless expanse of blue, intersected by the far-stretching line of the horizon.

'My dear girl,' said Pauline to Louise with her maternal air, 'let us talk as though we were two sisters. You love me a little, don't you?'

Louise threw one arm round her friend's waist as she exclaimed:

'Indeed I do! You know I do!'

'Well, then, since you love me, it was very wrong of you not to tell me everything. Why do you keep secrets from me?'

'Indeed, I have no secrets.'

'Ah! yes; think again now. Come, open your heart to me.'

Each looked into the other's face so closely for a moment that they

felt the warmth of one another's breath. And the eyes of one gradually grew troubled beneath the clear, unruffled gaze of the other. The
silence was growing painful.

'Tell me everything. When things are discussed openly it is possible to arrange them satisfactorily, but dissimulation is apt to have an
unhappy ending. Isn't that so, eh? It would be very painful for us to
disagree again and to have a repetition of what caused us so much grief
and trouble.'

At this Louise burst into a violent fit of sobbing. She clasped
Pauline round the waist convulsively, and hid her face against her
friend's shoulder while stammering amidst her tears:

'Oh! it is very unkind of you to speak of that again! You ought
never to have mentioned it again, never! Send me away at once, rather
than pain me like this!'

It was in vain that Pauline tried to soothe her.

'No, no!' the weeping girl went on; 'I understand it all. You still
suspect me. Why do you speak to me of secrets? I have no secret at
all. I do everything quite openly, so that you may have no cause to find
fault with me or reproach me. I am not to blame because things happen
which disturb you—I who am even careful how I laugh, though you
don't know it—But, if you don't believe me, I had better go away at
once. Let me go! Let me go!'

They were quite alone in that far-reaching space. The kitchen-garden, scorched by the west wind, lay at their feet like a piece of waste
land, while, further away, the calm sea spread out in its immensity.

'But listen to what I have to say,' Pauline cried. 'I am not reproach-
ing you at all; on the contrary, I want to encourage you.'

Then, taking Louise by the shoulders and forcing her to raise her
eyes, she said to her gently, like a mother questioning her daughter:

'You love Lazare? And he, too, loves you, I am sure.'

The blood surged to Louise's cheeks. She trembled yet more violently, and tried to liberate herself and escape.

'Good gracious! How clumsily I must express myself if you can't
understand me!' Pauline resumed. 'Do you think I should talk to you
on such a subject only to torture you? You love each other, don't you?
Well, I want to get you married to one another! It's very simple!'

Louise, distracted, ceased to struggle. Stupor checked the flow of
her tears, rendered her motionless, with her hands hanging inertly beside her.

'What! And yourself?' she gasped.

'I, my dear? Well, I have been questioning myself very seriously for
some weeks past, at night-time especially, during those waking hours

when one's mind sees things in a clearer light. And I have recognised that I only feel sincere friendship for Lazare. Haven't you been able to see as much for yourself? We are comrades, chums; like a couple of boys, in fact. We do not feel those loving transports—'

She hesitated, trying to find some suitable phrase which would give an appearance of probability to her falsehoods. But her rival still gazed at her with fixed eyes, as though she had discovered the meaning which was hidden beneath her words.

'Why do you tell me untruths?' she murmured at last. 'Is it possible for you to cease to love where you have once loved?'

Pauline grew confused.

'Well! well!' she said; 'what does that matter? You love each other, and it is quite natural that he should marry you. I—I was brought up with him, and I shall continue to be a sister to him. One's ideas alter when one has been waiting so long—And, then, there are several other reasons—'

She was conscious that she was growing more confused, and, carried away by her frankness, she went on:

'Oh! my dear, let me have my way. If I still love him sufficiently to want to see him your husband, it is because I now believe that you are necessary to his happiness. That doesn't vex you, does it? You would do the same if you were in my place, would you not? Come, let us talk it over quietly. Will you join in the little plot? Shall we come to an understanding together to force him into being happy? Even if he seems vexed about it and persists in believing that he is yet bound to me, you must help me to persuade him, for it is you whom he loves, and it is you who are necessary to him. Be my accomplice, I beg you, and let us get everything arranged at once, now, while we are alone.'

But Louise, seeing how she trembled, how heart-broken she was in making those entreaties, persisted in rebelling.

'No, no! I couldn't think of such a thing! It would be abominable. You still love him; I am sure of it, and you are only planning your own torment. Instead of helping you, I will tell him everything. Yes, as soon as he comes back—'

Then Pauline threw her kindly arms round her again to prevent her from continuing, and drew her face close to her breast.

'Hold your tongue, you wicked child! It must be so. It is he whom we have to think about.'

Silence fell again, while they lingered in that embrace. Her powers of resistance already exhausted, Louise gave way, yielded with affectionate languor, while tears mounted to her eyes—happy tears that trickled slowly down her cheeks. She spoke no word, but pressed her friend to her, as though she could find no discreeter or more sincere way of expressing her gratitude. She recognised that Pauline was so much above her, so lofty, so self-sacrificing, that she dared not raise her eyes to meet her gaze. However, after a few minutes, she ventured to lift her head in smiling confusion, and then, protruding her lips, gave her friend a silent kiss. In the distance the sea stretched out beneath the cloudless sky without a single wave breaking on its blue immensity.

When Lazare returned to the house, Pauline went up to him in his room, that big and well-loved chamber where they had grown up together. She was anxious to finish her task that very day. With her cousin she sought no preliminary remarks, but went straight to the point. The room teemed with associations of their old life. Pieces of dry seaweed still lay about there, the models of the stockades littered the piano, and the table was strewn with scientific treatises and scores of music.

'Lazare,' she began, 'I want to talk to you. I have something serious to say to you.'

He seemed surprised, and then took his stand before her.

'What is the matter? Is my father threatened with another attack?'

'No, listen. It is necessary that the subject should now be mentioned; keeping silence about it cannot do any good. You know that my aunt intended we should be married. We have frequently spoken about it, and for months past it has been considered a settled matter. Well, I think that it would now be better if all thought of it were abandoned.'

The young man had turned pale, but he did not allow his cousin to finish; he exclaimed excitedly:

'What? What nonsense are you talking? Are you not already my wife? We will go to-morrow, if you like, and ask the priest to put the finishing-stroke to the matter. And this is what you call something serious!'

The girl replied in her tranquil voice:

'It is very serious; and, though it displeases you, I repeat that it is certainly necessary we should speak about it. We are two old friends and comrades, but I am afraid we should never be two lovers. So what is the good of obstinately persisting in an idea which would probably never result in happiness for either of us?'

Then Lazare burst out into a torrent of ejaculations. Was she trying to quarrel with him? She couldn't expect him to spend his whole time clinging round her neck! And, though the marriage had been put off from month to month, she knew quite well that it wasn't his fault. It was unjust of her, moreover, to say that he no longer loved her. He had loved her so warmly, and in that very room too! At this reference to the past a blush mounted to Pauline's cheeks. Her cousin was right.

She recollected his passing gusts of passion, and his hot breath fanning her neck. But, ah! how far off were those delicious thrilling moments; and what an unimpassioned, brotherly friendship he manifested for her now! So it was with an expression of sadness that she replied to him:

'My poor fellow, if you really loved me, instead of arguing with me as you are doing, you would be clasping me in your arms and sobbing, and finding some very different way of persuading me.'

He turned still paler, and threw up his hands with a vague gesture of protest as he let himself fall upon a chair.

'No!' the girl went on; 'it is quite clear that you love me no longer. But it can't be helped. We are, no doubt, not suited to each other. When we were shut up here together, you were driven into thinking about me. But all your fancy vanished later on; it did not last, because there was nothing in me that could keep you to me.'

A final paroxysm of exasperation carried him off, and he swayed about in his chair as he stammered:

'Well! what do you want? What is the meaning of all this? I quietly return home, and come up here to put on my slippers, and then you suddenly fall on me, and without the least warning launch out into an extravagant harangue—"I don't love you any longer"—"We are not made for one another"—"The wedding must be broken off." Once more I ask you, what is the meaning of it all?'

Pauline, who had drawn near him, slowly answered:

'It means that you love someone else, and that I advise you to marry her.'

For a moment Lazare remained silent. Then he began to sneer. Good! They were going to have the old scenes over again. Everything was going to be turned topsy-turvy once more by her idiotic jealousy! She couldn't bear to see him cheerful even for a single day without wanting to banish everyone away from him.

Pauline listened with an expression of profound grief; then she suddenly laid her trembling hands upon his shoulders, and an involuntary cry burst from her heart:

'Oh! my dear, can you believe that I want to distress you? Can't you see that my only desire is to make you happy? I would endure anything to win you a single hour's happiness. You love Louise; is that not so? Well, I tell you to marry her. Understand me. I am in the way no longer. Marry her; I give her to you!'

Her cousin looked at her in amazement. With his nervous, ill-balanced nature his feelings rushed to extremes at the slightest impulse. His eyelids quivered, and he burst into sobs.

'Oh, don't talk like that!' he cried. 'I am utterly worthless! Yes, indeed, I despise myself bitterly for all that has happened in this house for years past. I am deeply in your debt. Don't say I am not! We took your money, I squandered it like a fool, and now I have sunk so low that you make me alms of my word and promise, and give them back to me out of sheer pity, as to a man destitute of courage and honour!'

'Lazare! Lazare!' she murmered, quite frightened.

But he sprang furiously to his feet and began striding about the room, drumming on his breast with his fists.

'Leave me! I should kill myself straight off if I treated myself as I deserve. Do I not owe you my love? Isn't it a disgrace and an abomination for me to wish for that other girl, who was not meant for me and isn't nearly so good or so pretty as you are? When a man descends to conduct like this, there must be mud in his soul! You see that I am hiding nothing from you, that I am not attempting to defend myself. Listen to me! Rather than accept your sacrifice, I would myself turn Louise out of the house, and then go off to America and never see either of you again!'

For a long time Pauline tried to calm him and reason with him. Couldn't he try for once, she asked, to take life as it was, without any exaggeration? Couldn't he see that the advice she offered him was good advice, resolved upon after long deliberation? The marriage she advocated would be good for everyone. She was able to speak of it in such calm tones because, far from the thought of it paining her, she now sincerely wished it. Then, carried away by her desire to convince him, she unfortunately made an allusion to Louise's fortune, and hinted that Thibaudier, when the marriage had taken place, would certainly find some post for his son-in-law.

'Ah! that's it!' he broke out violently. 'You want to sell me now! Say plainly that I can no longer care for you, because I have ruined you, and that it only remains for me to be base enough to marry a rich girl. No, no, indeed; that is too mean and degrading! Never will I do it—never! Do you hear me? Never!'

Pauline, whose strength was exhausted, ceased her entreaties. Silence reigned. Lazare had thrown himself on the chair again, while the girl paced slowly up and down the big room, lingering before each piece of furniture. Those old familiar things, the table which she had worn away with the pressure of her elbows, the wardrobe where her childish playthings were still stowed away, all the old souvenirs littered about the room, made a feeling of hope, which she strove to dismiss, spring up in her heart—a hope whose sweetness, in spite of herself, gradually thrilled her. Suppose he did really love her sufficiently to refuse to take another! But she knew too well the weak morrows that followed his passionate outbursts of sentiment. Besides, it was very weak of her to harbour hope, and she must guard against allowing herself to yield to his nerveless vacillating nature.

'You must think it all over,' she said in conclusion, as she stopped short before him. 'I won't bother you any more at present. I am sure you will be more reasonable in the morning.'

The next day, however, was passed in painful constraint. The house once more seemed to be under the depressing influence of a vague bitter sorrow. Louise's eyes were red, and Lazare avoided her and spent whole hours by himself in his room. But again the days went on; the constraint began to disappear, and laughter and whispering once more came back. Pauline still waited, indulging in foolish hopes even against her own convictions. Backed by uncertainty, she thought that she had never before really known what suffering was. But, at last, as she was going down to the kitchen one evening in the dusk to get a candle, she found Lazare and Louise kissing each other in the passage. Louise made her escape laughing; while Lazare, emboldened by the darkness, caught hold of Pauline and imprinted two brotherly kisses on her cheeks.

'I have thought it over,' he murmured. 'You are better and wiser than she is; and I still love you, but I love you as I loved my mother.'

She had just strength to say:

'It is settled, then. I am very glad.'

She felt that she had turned so pale, and her face was so cold, that she dared not go into the kitchen for fear she should faint. Without waiting to get a candle, she went upstairs again, saying that she had forgotten something. When she had shut herself up in the darkness, she thought she was going to die, for she felt suffocated, and could not shed a single tear. What had she done, she cried to herself, that he should have been cruel enough to make her torture still greater? Why couldn't he have accepted her sacrifice on the day when she proposed it to him, when she had possessed all her strength, unweakened by any false hope? Now the sacrifice had become a double one. She had lost him a second time, and all the more painfully since she had allowed herself to hope that she was winning him back. Ah, Heaven! She would be brave and bear it, but it was wicked to make her task such torture.

Everything was speedily arranged. Véronique, quite aghast, could make nothing out of it. She thought that things had got turned upside down since her mistress's death. It was, however, Chanteau who was most surprised by the news. He, who usually took no interest in anything and just nodded his head in approval of any scheme that was mentioned to him, as though he were completely absorbed in the selfish enjoyment of the calm moments which he stole from his tormenting pain, burst into tears when Pauline herself announced the new arrangement to him. He gazed at her, and stammered incoherent protests and confessions. It wasn't his fault: he had wanted to do very differently long ago, both about the money and about the marriage, but, as she knew, he was too ill. However, the girl kissed him, protesting that it was she herself who was making Lazare marry Louise for very good reasons. At first he could scarcely believe her, and, blinking his eyes sadly, he asked her:

'Is that really the truth? Really?'

Then, when he saw her smile, he quickly consoled himself and grew quite gay. It was a great relief to have things settled, for the matter had long been distressing him, though he had never dared to open his mouth about it. He kissed Louise on the cheeks, and in the evening, over the dessert, he sang a merry song. Just as he was going to bed, however, he was troubled by a last disquieting thought.

'You will stay with us, eh?' he asked Pauline.

The girl hesitated for a moment, and then, blushing at her falsehood, she answered, 'Oh! no doubt.'

A whole month was required for the completion of the necessary formalities. Thibaudier, Louise's father, had, however, at once consented to the proposal of Lazare, who was his godson. There was only one dispute between them, a couple of days before the wedding, when the young man roundly refused to go to Paris and manage an Insurance Company, in which the banker was the principal shareholder. He intended remaining for a year or two longer at Bonneville and writing a novel, which was to be a masterpiece, before he started off to bring Paris to his feet. At this Thibaudier just shrugged his shoulders, and in a friendly way called him a big simpleton.

It was arranged that the marriage should take place at Caen. During the previous fortnight there were continual comings and goings, a perfect fever of journeyings. Pauline went about with Louise, seeking to divert her thoughts with all the bustle, and returning home quite exhausted. As Chanteau was not able to leave Bonneville, she had to promise to attend the ceremony, at which she would be the only representative of her cousin's family. The near approach of the day filled her with terror. She had arranged that she would not spend the night at Caen, for she thought she would suffer less if she returned to sleep at Bonneville. She pretended that her uncle's health made her very uneasy, and that she was unwilling to remain long away from him. Chanteau himself vainly pressed her to spend a few days at Caen. He wasn't ill at all, he urged. On the contrary, he was very much excited by the idea of the approaching wedding and the thought of the banquet at which he would not be present; and he was craftily planning to make Véronique supply him with some forbidden dish, such as a young truffled partridge, which he could never eat without the absolute certainty of a fresh attack of gout. However, in spite of all that could be urged, the girl declared that she would return home in the evening. She thought that this course would allow her greater facilities for packing her trunk the next morning and disappearing.

A drizzling rain was falling, and midnight had just struck as Malivoire's old coach brought Pauline back to Bonneville on the evening of the wedding. Wearing a blue silk gown, and ill protected by a little shawl, she was pale and shivering though her hands were hot. In the kitchen she found Véronique sitting up for her and dozing beside the table. The tall flame of the candle made the girl's eyes blink, full as they still were of the darkness of the journey, during which they had remained wide open all the way from Arromanches. She could only drag a few incoherent words from the drowsy servant: the master had been very foolish, but he was asleep now, and nobody had called. Then Pauline took a candle and went upstairs, chilled by the emptiness of the house, heart-sick amidst all the gloom and silence which seemed to weigh upon her shoulders.

When she reached the second floor she wished to take immediate refuge in her own room, but an irresistible impulse, at which she felt surprised, led her to open Lazare's door. She raised her candle to enable her to see, as though she fancied the room was full of smoke. Nothing was changed. Every piece of furniture was in its accustomed place, but she felt conscious of calamity, annihilation; it was a vague terror, as though she were in some chamber of death. She slowly walked up to the table and looked at the inkstand, the pen, and an unfinished page of manuscript still lying there. Then she went away. All was over, and the door closed on the echoing emptiness of the room.

When she reached her own chamber, the same vague sensation of strangeness that she had felt in Lazare's again affected her. Could this indeed be her room, with its wallpaper of blue roses and its little muslin-curtained iron bed? Was it really here that she had lived so many years? Still keeping her candle in her hand, she, who was usually so courageous, made a minute inspection of the apartment, pushed the curtains aside, looked under the bed and behind the furniture. She felt overcome by a strange kind of stupor, which kept her standing in front of the different things. She could not have believed that such keen anguish could ever have possessed her beneath that ceiling, whose every stain was familiar to her; and she now began to regret that she had not stayed at Caen. For she felt frightened in that old house, which was so empty and yet so full of memories of the past, and so cold, too, and so dark that stormy night. The thought of going to bed was intolerable to her. She sat down without even taking off her hat, and for several minutes remained motionless, her eyes fixed upon the candle-flame, which dazzled them. Suddenly, however, she started up in astonishment. What was she doing there, with her head throbbing wildly, with a violence that quite prevented her from thinking? It was one o'clock. She ought to be in bed. And she began to undress with slow, feverish hands.

Her orderly habits showed themselves even in this crisis of her life. She carefully put away her hat, and glanced anxiously at her boots to see if they had sustained any damage. She had folded her dress and laid it over the back of a chair, when her glance fell upon her bosom. Gradually a flush crimsoned her cheeks. In her troubled brain arose the thought of those two others over yonder. Alas! the harvest of love was not for her! To another were given the embraces of that husband for whose coming she herself had looked forward for so many years! Never would she be a wife or mother; the years would come and go, and she would age in utter loneliness. Then wild jealousy came upon her. She yearned to live, to live to the full, to drain the joys of life, she who loved life so dearly! She was more beautiful than that scraggy, fair-haired girl; she was stronger and healthier, and yet her cousin had not chosen her. Never now would he be hers; never, as in the past, might she again wait for him, expect him. She was tossed aside like an old rag. It was, no doubt, her own doing; and yet how awful was the thought of the others being together while she was all alone, shivering with fever in that cold, gloomy house!

Suddenly she threw herself on her bed. She seized the pillow with desperate hands, and bit it with her teeth to stifle her sobs. Long convulsive shivers shook her from head to heels. It was in vain that she closed her eyelids, seeking to shut out all sight; she saw just the same, and ever endured torture. Oh! what was she to do? Even if she were to tear her eyes out she would still see—see perhaps for ever.

The minutes glided on, and she was only conscious of everlasting torment. A paroxysm of fear made her spring to her feet. Some one must be in the room, for surely she had heard the sound of laughter. But she found that it was only her candle, which, having nearly burnt out, had broken the glass socket. Yet if anyone really had seen her! That imaginary laugh still coursed through her wildly. Then at last she slipped on a night-dress and hastily buried herself in bed, pulling up the clothes to her chin, and drawing her shivering body as closely together as possible. When the candle died out, she lay perfectly still, exhausted and overcome with shame for her wild conduct.

In the morning Pauline packed her trunk, but she could not summon up courage to tell Chanteau of her departure. In the evening, however, she was obliged to inform him of it, for Doctor Cazenove was to come the next day and take her to his relative's house. When her uncle grasped the situation he was quite overcome, and stretched out his poor, weak hands with a wild gesture as though to detain her, while in broken, stammering sentences he besought her to stay with him. She could surely never really think of such a thing, he cried; she could not possibly desert him; it would be a murder, for it would certainly kill him. Then, seeing her gently resolute and divining her reasons, he confessed his wrong-doing of the previous day in eating a partridge. He already experienced sharp burning pains in his joints. It was always the same old story. He had yielded once more in the struggle. He knew what the consequences would be if he ate, but he ate all the same, in a state of mingled pleasure and terror, quite certain that agony would ensue. Surely, however, Pauline would never desert him in the midst of one of his attacks.

And indeed it happened that about six o'clock in the morning Véronique came upstairs to inform Mademoiselle that she could hear her master bellowing in his bedroom. The woman was in a very bad temper, and went growling about the house that if Mademoiselle were going she would certainly be off as well, as she had grown quite tired of looking after such an unreasonable old man.

Thus Pauline was once more obliged to take up her position by her uncle's bedside; and when the Doctor arrived to take her away with him, she showed him the sick man, who triumphed, bellowing his loudest, and crying to her to leave him, if she could find it in her heart to do so. Everything had to be postponed.

Every day the young girl trembled at the thought of seeing Lazare and Louise come back. Their new room, the former guest-chamber, had been specially fitted up, and had been waiting ready for them ever since their marriage. They were lingering on at Caen, however, and Lazare wrote to say that he was making notes on the financial world before returning to Bonneville and shutting himself up there to start on a great novel, in which he should reveal the truth about company promoters and speculators. At last he arrived one morning without his wife, and unconcernedly announced that he was going to settle with her in Paris. His father-in-law, he said, had prevailed upon him to accept that post in the Insurance Company, on the ground that he would thus have a good opportunity for making his notes from actual observation. Later on, he added, he might perhaps come back and devote himself to literature.

When Lazare had filled a couple of trunks with the various articles he required, and Malivoire's coach had come to fetch him and his luggage, Pauline went back into the house, feeling quite dazed and destitute of her former energy. Chanteau, still in great pain, turned to her and exclaimed:

'You will stop now, I hope! Stay and see me buried!'

She was unwilling to make an immediate reply. Her trunk was still packed in her bedroom. She sat gazing at it for hours. Since the others were going to Paris, it would be wrong of her, she thought, to desert her uncle. She had but little confidence in her cousin's resolutions, but, at any rate, if he and his wife should come back, she would then be free to take her departure. And when Cazenove angrily told her that she was throwing away a splendid position for the sake of ruining her life amongst people who had lived upon her ever since her childhood, she virtually made up her mind.

'Be off with you!' Chanteau now repeated. 'If you are to gain so much money and become so happy that way, I won't keep you here bothering about an old cripple like me. Be off with you!'

One morning, however, she replied to him:

'No, uncle, I am going to stay with you.'

The Doctor, who was present, went off, raising his arms to heaven.

'Ah! there is no doing anything with that child! And what a hornets' nest she has got into! She will never get free of it—never!'

IX

ONCE more did the days glide by in the house at Bonneville. After a very cold winter there had come a rainy spring, and the sea, beaten by the downpour, looked like a huge lake of mud. Then the tardy summer had lasted into the middle of autumn, with heavy, oppressive suns, beneath whose overwhelming heat the blue immensity slumbered. And then the winter came round again, and another spring, and yet another summer, slipping away minute by minute, ever at the same speed, as the hours pursued their rhythmical march.

Pauline, as if her heart were regulated by that clock-like motion, had recovered all her old calmness. The placid sameness of her days, which were passed in the same unvarying occupations, lulled the keenness of her sorrow. She came downstairs in the morning and kissed her uncle, said much the same things to the servant as she had said the day before, sat down twice at table, spent the afternoon in sewing, and then, early in the evening, went to bed. The next day the same programme was gone through, without ever any unexpected incident breaking the monotony of her life. Chanteau, who was becoming more and more disfigured by gout, which had puffed out his legs and warped and deformed his hands, sat silent, when he was not bellowing, quite absorbed in the delight of being free from pain. Véronique, who seemed almost to have lost her tongue, had fallen into a state of gloomy surliness. Only the Saturday dinners brought any relief. Cazenove and Abbé Horteur dined there with great regularity, and chatter was heard till ten o'clock or so, when the priest's wooden shoes clattered away over the stones of the yard, and the Doctor's gig started off at the slow trot of the old horse. Pauline's gaiety—that gaiety which she had so bravely maintained during all her troubles—had assumed a subdued character. Her ringing laughter no longer echoed through the rooms and the staircase, though she still remained all kindliness and activity, and every morning displayed fresh courage and zest for life. By the end of a year her heart had fallen asleep, and she had come to believe that the days would now flow on in that peaceful monotony, without anything ever happening to awake her slumbering sorrow.

For some time after Lazare's departure every letter from him had troubled the girl, though it was only for his letters that she lived, looking out for them with impatience, reading them over and over again, and even adding to them something from her own imagination beyond what they actually contained. For three months Lazare had written very regularly, sending, every fortnight, a very long letter, full of detail and breathing the liveliest hopes. Once more he was wildly enthusiastic. He had launched out into business and was dreaming of a colossal fortune in the immediate future. According to his account, the Insurance Company could not fail to return enormous profits. He was not, however, confining himself to that venture, but was engaging in all kinds of speculations. He appeared to have become quite charmed with the financial and mercantile world, which he now reproached himself for having judged so absurdly. All his literary schemes seemed quite abandoned. Then, too, he was never tired of writing about his domestic joys, and related all sorts of things about his wife—the kisses he had given her, and the life they led together—setting forth at length all his happiness by way of expressing his gratitude to her, whom he called his 'dear sister.' It was those details, those familiar passages, which made Pauline's fingers tremble feverishly. The odour of love which the paper diffused, the perfume of heliotrope, Louise's favourite scent, which clung to it, seemed to stupefy her. But the letters gradually became fewer and shorter. Lazare ceased to write about business, and in other respects confined himself to sending his wife's love to Pauline. He offered no explanations, but simply ceased to tell her everything. Was he discontented with his position and already sick of finance? Was his domestic happiness compromised by misunderstandings? Pauline was afraid it must be so, and she was saddened by the evidence of her cousin's weariness, which she thought she could detect in certain passages that seemed to have been reluctantly written. About the end of April, after a six weeks' silence, she received a short note of four lines, in which her cousin told her that Louise was *enceinte*. Then silence fell again, and she had no further news.

May and June passed away. A heavy tide swept away one of the stockades, an incident which for a long time afforded subject for talk. All the Bonneville folk jeered and grinned, and the fishermen stole the broken timbers. Then came another scandalous affair. The Gonin girl, young as she was, had a baby. And afterwards all the old monotony returned, and the village vegetated at the foot of the cliffs as lifelessly as a tract of seaweed. In July it became necessary to repair the terrace-wall and one of the gable ends of the house. As soon as the workmen began to remove the first stones, the rest threatened to fall, and they were kept at work for an entire month, an expense of nearly ten thousand francs being incurred.

It was still Pauline who had to find the money. Thus another big hole was made in her little hoard in the chest of drawers, her little fortune being reduced to about forty thousand francs. She made the family's few hundred francs a month go as far as possible by economical housekeeping, but she was obliged to sell some of her own stock, in order to avoid encroaching upon her uncle's capital. The latter told his niece, as his wife had done before, that it would all be paid back to her some day. The girl would not have hesitated to part with all she had, for the gradual crumbling away of her fortune had destroyed all tendency to cupidity in her, and her only effort now was to keep a sufficient sum in hand for her charities. The thought that she might possibly be compelled to discontinue her Saturday distributions greatly distressed her, for they constituted her chief pleasure of the week. Since the previous winter she had begun to knit stockings, and all the young urchins in the neighbourhood now went about with warm feet.

One morning towards the end of July, as Véronique was sweeping up the rubbish left by the workmen, Pauline received a letter which quite upset her. It was written from Caen, and contained only a few words. In it Lazare informed her that he should arrive at Bonneville on the evening of the next day, but gave no explanation of his coming. She ran off to tell the news to her uncle. They both looked at each other. Chanteau's eyes expressed the fear that his niece would leave him should Lazare and his wife contemplate a long stay in the house. He dare not question her on the subject, for he could read in her face her firm resolution to go. In the afternoon she even went upstairs to look over her clothes; still, she did not wish to have the air of taking flight.

It was about five o'clock, and lovely weather, when Lazare stepped out of a trap at the door of the yard. Pauline hastened to meet him, but, before even kissing him, she stopped short in astonishment.

'What! Have you come alone?'

'Yes,' he replied quietly.

And then he kissed her on. both cheeks.

'But where is Louise?'

'At Clermont, with her sister-in-law. The doctor has recommended her to go to a mountainous neighbourhood. Her state of health has made her weak and languid.'

As he spoke he walked on to the house, casting long glances about the yard. He scrutinised his cousin, too, and his lips quivered with an emotion which he struggled to restrain. He showed great surprise as a dog rushed out of the kitchen and barked round his legs.

'What dog is that?' he asked.

'Oh! that's Loulou,' Pauline replied. 'He doesn't know you yet, you see. Down! Loulou! You mustn't bite your master.'

The dog went on growling.

'He is dreadfully ugly, my dear. Where did you pick up such a fright?'

The dog was indeed a wretched mongrel, under-sized and mangy. And he had, too, an abominable temper, and was perpetually snarling, and melancholy like an outcast.

'Oh! when he was given me I was told that he would grow up into a huge, magnificent animal, but he has always kept like that. It is the fifth one that we have tried to rear. All the others have died, and this is the only one that has managed to go on living.'

Loulou by this time had sulkily made up his mind to lie down in the sun, and turned his back upon Pauline and her cousin. Then Lazare thought of the old days and of the dog that was dead and of the new and ugly one that now occupied his place. He glanced round the yard once more.

'My poor old Matthew!' he murmured very softly.

On the steps of the house Véronique received him with a nod of her head, without ceasing to pare carrots. Then he walked straight on to the dining-room, where his father, excited by the sound of voices, was anxiously waiting. Pauline called from the threshold:

'You know he has come by himself? Louise is at Clermont.'

Chanteau, whose anxious eyes brightened, began to question his son even before he had kissed him.

'Are you expecting her to follow you? When will she join you here?'

'Oh no! She's not coming here at all,' Lazare replied. 'I'm going to join her at her sister-in-law's before I return to Paris. I shall stay a fortnight with you, and then I shall be off.'

Chanteau's eyes expressed his extreme satisfaction at what he heard, and when at last Lazare embraced him he returned the salute with two hearty kisses. However, he considered that it behoved him to express some regret.

'It is a great pity that your wife could not come. We should have been delighted to have her here. However, I hope we shall see her some other time. You must certainly bring her,'

Pauline kept silent, and concealed her feeling of uneasiness beneath an affectionate smile of welcome. For the second time were her plans being altered; she would not have to go away. She scarcely knew whether she was glad or sorry, so entirely had she now become the property of others. Whatever pleasure she felt in seeing Lazare was tinged with sadness as she noticed his aged appearance. His eyes were dull, and a bitter expression rested on his lips. The lines across his brow and cheeks had been there before, but they were deeper wrinkles now, and she guessed that his *ennui* and terror had increased. The young man scrutinized his cousin with equal care. She appeared to him to have developed, to have gained additional beauty and vigour, and with a smile he muttered:

'Well, you certainly don't seem to have been any the worse for my absence. You are, all of you, looking quite plump. Father is growing young again, and Pauline is superb. And, really, it is very funny, but the house certainly seems bigger than it used to be.'

He glanced round the dining-room, as he had previously done round the yard, with an appearance of surprise and emotion. His eyes at last rested upon Minouche, who lay upon the table, with her feet tucked under her, in such a state of restful beatitude that she had not moved.

'Even Minouche doesn't seem to have grown any older,' the young man resumed. 'Well, you ungrateful animal, you might rouse yourself to welcome me!'

He stroked her as he spoke, and she began to purr, but still without moving.

'Oh! Minouche is only interested in herself,' Pauline said merrily. 'The day before yesterday five more of her kittens were drowned, and, you see, she doesn't seem to mind it at all.'

The dinner was hastened, as Lazare had made an early breakfast. In spite of all the girl's attempts, the evening proved a gloomy one.

The efforts they made to avoid certain subjects interfered with the conversation, and there were awkward intervals of silence. Pauline and Chanteau refrained from questioning Lazare, as they saw that it embarrassed him to reply; they made no attempt to ascertain either how his business at Paris was getting on, or how it came about that his letter to them had been written from Caen. With a vague gesture he put aside all direct questions, as though he meant to reply to them later on. When the tea was brought into the room, a great sigh of satisfaction escaped him. How happy and peaceful they must all be here, said he, and what an amount of work one could get through when all was so quiet! He dropped a word or two about a drama in verse upon which he had been engaged for the last six months. His cousin felt amazed when he added that he intended finishing it at Bonneville. Twelve days would be sufficient, said he.

At ten o'clock Véronique entered to say that Monsieur Lazare's room was ready. But when they had reached the first floor, and she wanted to instal him in the former guest-chamber, which had been subsequently fitted up for the occupation of himself and his wife, he flew into a tantrum.

'You're quite mistaken,' said he, 'if you suppose that I am going to sleep there! I'm going up to the top of the house to my old iron bedstead.'

Véronique began to grumble and growl. Why couldn't he sleep there? The bed had been got ready for him, and, surely, he wasn't going to give her the trouble of preparing another.

'Very well,' he said, 'I will sleep in an easy-chair.'

While Véronique angrily tore off the sheets and carried them up to the top floor, Pauline experienced a sudden delight which impelled her to throw her arms round her cousin's neck, in an outburst of the old chummish feeling of their youth, as she wished him good-night. He was occupying his big room once more, and he was so close to her that for a long time she could hear him pacing about, as though brooding over the recollection which were keeping her awake also.

It was only the next morning that Lazare began to take Pauline into his confidence. Even then he made no clear statement; she had to guess what she could from a few short sentences which he let slip in the course of conversation. By-and-by she took courage and questioned him with an expression of affectionate concern. Were he and Louise still getting on as happily as ever? He replied in the affirmative, but complained about certain little domestic disagreements and other trifling matters which had led to quarrels. Without having come to a definite rupture, they were suffering from the perpetual jarring of two highly-strung temperaments, which were incapable of equilibrium either in joy or sorrow. There existed between them a sort of unconfessed bitterness, as though they were surprised and angry at having mistaken each other, at having discovered each other's real feelings so soon, after all the passionate love of the first days. For a moment Pauline thought she could discover that it was pecuniary troubles that had embittered them; but in this she was mistaken, for their income of ten thousand francs a year had remained almost undiminished. Lazare had simply become disgusted with business, just as he had previously grown disgusted with music and medicine and industrial enterprise; and on this subject he launched out in strong language. Never, he said, never had he come across such a stupid, rotten sphere as that of the financial world. He would prefer anything, the dulness of country life and the mediocrity of small means, to perpetual worries about money, the brain-softening tangle of figures. He had just retired from the Insurance Company, he said, and he was going to try what he could do as a play writer when he returned to Paris in the following winter. His drama would avenge him; he would portray money in it as a festering sore eating away modern society.

Pauline did not distress herself much about this new failure, which she had already inferred from Lazare's embarrassed expressions in his last letters. What grieved her most was the gradually increasing misunderstanding between her cousin and his wife. She strove to find out the real cause of it, how it happened that those young people of ample means and with nothing to do but to be happy had so quickly reached discomfort. She returned to the subject again, and only ceased to question her cousin about it when she saw the embarrassment she was causing him. He stammered and grew pale, and turned his face away from her as she interrogated him. She well knew that expression of shame and fear, that terror of the idea of death, which he had formerly struggled to conceal as though it were some disgraceful disease; but could it be possible, she asked herself, that the cold shadow of nothingness had already fallen between the young couple so soon after their nuptials? For several days she lingered in a state of doubt, and then, without any further confession from him on the subject, she one evening read the truth in his eyes as he rushed downstairs from his room in the dark, as though he were pursued by ghosts.

In Paris, amidst his love-fever, Lazare had at first forgotten all about death. He had found a refuge in Louise's embraces. But satiety came at last, and then in that wife of his, for whom life centred in caressing endearments, he found no sustaining, no courage-prompting influence whatever. Passion was fugitive and deceitful—powerless, he found, to give a semblance of happiness to life. One night he awoke with a start, chilled by an icy breath that made his hair stand on end. He shivered and wailed out his cry of bitter anguish: 'O God! God! oh! to have to die!' Louise was sleeping by his side. It was death that he had found again at the end of their kisses.

Other nights followed, and all his old torture came on him again. It seized him suddenly as he lay sleepless in bed, without ability on his part to foresee or prevent it. All at once, while he was lying there perfectly calm, a fearful shudder would convulse him; whereas, on the other hand, when he was irritable and weary, he perhaps escaped altogether. It was more than the mere shock of earlier times that he experienced now; his nervous excitement increased, and his whole being was shaken by each fresh attack. He could not sleep without a night-light, for the darkness increased his anxiety, in spite of his constant fear that his wife might discover his secret suffering. This very fear, indeed, increased his distress and aggravated the effects of his attacks; for in the old days, when he lay alone, he had been able to vent his dread, but now the presence of another at his side was a source of additional disquietude. When he started in terror from his pillow, his eyes heavy with sleep, he instinctively glanced at her, fearing he might find her eyes wide open and fixed upon his own. But she never moved, and by the glimmer of the night-light he could watch her quiet slumber, her placid face, thick lips, and little, blue-veined eyelids. And as she never awoke, he at last grew less disturbed on her account, until one night what he had so long feared really happened, and he saw her staring at him. But she said not a word when she saw him all pale and trembling. She, like himself, must have been thrilled by the horror of death, for she seemed to understand what was passing in his mind, and threw herself against him like a frightened woman seeking protection. Then, still desiring to deceive each other, they pretended that they had heard the sound of footsteps, and got out of bed to look under the furniture and behind the curtains.

Thenceforward they were both haunted with nervous fear. Never a word of confession escaped the lips of either. They felt that it was a shameful secret of which they must not speak; but as they lay in bed, with their eyes staring widely into space, they knew quite well what each was thinking of. Louise had become as nervous as Lazare; they must have infected each other with this dread, even as two lovers are sometimes carried off by the same fever. If he awoke, while she continued to sleep, he grew alarmed at her very slumber. Was she still breathing? He could not hear the sound of any respiration. Perhaps she had suddenly died! He would then peer into her face for a moment and touch her hands; but, even when he had satisfied himself that she was alive and well, he could not get to sleep again. The thought that she would certainly die some day plunged him into a mournful reverie. Which of them would go first, he or she? Then his mind dwelt at length on the alternative suppositions; and scenes of death, with the last torturing throes, the hideous shrouding and laying-out, the final heartbreaking separation, presented themselves to his mind. That thought of never seeing each other again, when they had lived together thus as man and wife, drove him to distraction, filled him with revolt; he could not endure the thought of such horror. His very fear made him wish that he himself might be the first to go. Then his heart ached with bitter grief for Louise, as he pictured her as a widow, still carrying on the old routine of life, doing this and that, when he should no longer be there. Sometimes, to free himself from those haunting thoughts, he would gently pass his arms about her without awaking her; but this he could not long endure, for he became still more terrified as he felt the pulsations of her life within his embrace. If he rested his head upon her breast and listened to her heart, he could not hear it beating without alarm, without feeling that all action might suddenly cease. And even love was powerless to drive away that great dread which still hovered around their curtains after every transport.

About this time Lazare began to grow weary of business. He fell back into his old state, and spent whole days in idleness, excusing himself on the ground of the contempt and dislike he felt for money-grubbing. The real truth was that constant brooding over the thought of death was daily depriving him of the desire, the strength to live. He came back to his old question, 'What was the good of it all?'

Since it would all end in complete extinction sooner or later, perhaps to-morrow, or even to-day, or a single hour hence, what was the use of troubling and exciting one's self and bothering about one thing more than another? It was all quite purposeless. His existence itself had become a slow, lingering death, continuing day after day, and he strained his ears to listen to the sounds of its progress, even as he had done before in earlier times, and thought that he could detect the mechanism of his life quickly running down. His heart, he fancied, no longer beat so strongly as before, the action of every other organ was becoming feebler, and all would doubtless soon come to a dead stop. He noted with a shudder that gradual diminution of vitality which growing age was bringing in its train. His very frame was perishing; its component parts were constantly disappearing. His hair was falling off, he had lost several teeth, and he could feel his muscles and sinews shrinking away, as though they were already returning to dust. The approach of his fortieth year filled him with gloomy melancholy; old age would soon be upon him now and make a speedy end of him. He had already begun to believe that his system was quite deranged, and that some vital part would very soon give way. Thus his days were spent in a morbid expectation of some catastrophe. He took anxious note of those who died around him, and every time he heard of the death of an acquaintance he received a fresh shock. Could it be possible that such an one was really dead? Why, he was three years younger than himself and had seemed likely to last a hundred years! And then that other man he knew so well, had he, too, really gone? A man who was so careful of himself, and who even weighed the very food he ate! For a couple of days after occurrences like these he could think of nothing else, but remained stupefied by what had happened; feeling his pulse, carefully observing all his own symptoms, and then falling foul of the poor fellows who had gone. He felt a craving to reassure himself, and accused the departed of having died from their own fault. One had been guilty of inexcusable imprudence, while another had succumbed to so rare a disease that the doctors did not even know its name.

But it was in vain that he tried to banish the importunate spectre; he never ceased to hear within himself the grating of the wheels which he fancied had so nearly run down; he felt that he was helplessly descending the slope of years, and the thought of the deep, black pit that lay at the bottom of it threw him into an icy perspiration and made his hair stand on end with horror.

When Lazare ceased going to his office, quarrels broke out at home. He manifested excessive irritability, which flared up at the slightest opposition. His increasing mental disorder, which he tried so carefully to conceal, revealed itself in angry snappishness, fits of moody sulking, and wild, mad actions. At one time he was so possessed by the fear of fire that he removed from a third-floor flat to one on the ground floor, in order that he might more easily escape whenever the house should burn. A perpetual anticipation of coming evil completely poisoned the present, and prevented him from deriving any enjoyment from it. Every time a door was opened rather noisily he started up in fear; and his heart throbbed violently whenever a letter was put into his hand. He suspected everybody. His money was hidden in small sums in all sorts of places, and he kept his simplest plans and intentions secret. He felt embittered, too, against the world, thinking that he was misunderstood and underrated, and that all his successive failures were the result of a general conspiracy against him. But ever-growing boredom dominated everything else—the *ennui* of a man whose mind was unhinged and to whom the incessant idea of death made all action distasteful, so that he dragged himself idly through life on the plea of its nothingness and worthlessness. What was the use of troubling? The powers of science were miserably limited; it could neither prevent nor foresee. He was possessed by the sceptical *ennui* of his generation, not the romantic *ennui* of Werther or René, who regretfully wept over the old beliefs, but the *ennui* of the new doubters, the young scientists who worry themselves and declare that the world is unendurable because they have not immediately found the secret of life in their retorts.

In Lazare the unavowed terror of ceasing to be was, by a logical contradiction, blended with a ceaseless braggart insistence upon the nothingness of things. It was his very terror, the want of equilibrium in his morbid temperament, that drove him into pessimistic ideas and a mad hatred of life. As it could not last for ever, he looked upon it as a mere fraud and delusion. Was not the first half of one's days spent in dreaming of happiness and the latter half in regrets and fears? He fell back again upon the theories of 'the old one,' as he called Schopenhauer, whose most violent passages he used to recite from memory. He expatiated on the desirability of destroying the wish to live, and so bringing to an end the barbarous and imbecile exhibition of existence, with the spectacle of which the master force of the world, prompted by some incomprehensible egotistical reason, amused itself. He wanted to do away with life in order to do away with fear. He always harped upon the great deliverance; one must wish nothing for fear of evil, avoid all action since it meant pain, and thus sink entirely into death. He occupied himself in trying to discover some practical method of general suicide, some sudden and complete disappearance to which all living creatures would consent. This was perpetually recurring to his mind, even in the midst of ordinary conversation, when he freely and roughly gave vent to it. The slightest worry was sufficient to make him cry that he was sorry he was not yet annihilated; a mere headache set him raging furiously at his body. If he talked with a friend, his conversation immediately turned upon the woes of life, and the luck of those who were already fattening the dandelions in the cemeteries. He had a perfect mania for mournful subjects, and he was much interested in an article by a fanciful astronomer who announced the arrival of a comet with a tail which would sweep the earth away like a grain of sand. Would not this indeed prove the expected cosmical catastrophe, the colossal cartridge destined to blow the world to bits like a rotten old boat? And this desire of his for death, this constant theorizing about universal annihilation, was but the expression of his desperate struggle with his terror, a mere vain hubbub of words, by which he tried to veil the awful fear which the expectation of his end caused him.

The knowledge that his wife was *enceinte* gave him a fresh shock. It caused him an indefinable sensation, compounded of joy and an increase of disquietude. Notwithstanding the contrary views of 'the old one,' the thought of becoming a father thrilled him with pride—indeed, a vain wonder, as though he were the first person whom such a thing had befallen. But his joy quickly became poisoned; he tormented himself with forebodings of a disastrous issue; already making up his mind that his wife would die, and that the child would never *be* born. And, indeed, it happened that Louise's health became very bad, for she was far from strong; and then the confusion of the household and the upsetting of their usual habits, together with their frequent bickerings, soon made them both thoroughly miserable. The expectation of a child, which ought to have brought the husband and wife more closely together, only served, indeed, to increase the misunderstanding between them. Thus, when Louise's doctor suggested a visit to the mountains, Lazare was delighted to take her to her sister-in-law's and secure a fortnight's freedom for himself on the plea of going to see his father at Bonneville. At the bottom of his heart he really felt ashamed of this flight; but, after arguing the matter with his conscience, he persuaded himself that a short separation would have a tranquillising effect upon both of them, and that it would be quite sufficient if he joined his wife before the expected event.

On the evening when Pauline at last learned the whole history of the past eighteen months she remained for a moment unable to speak—quite overcome, indeed, by the pitiable story. They were sitting in the dining-room; she had put Chanteau to bed, and Lazare had just finished making his confession in front of the cold tea-pot, beneath the lamp which was now burning dimly.

After an interval of silence Pauline at last exclaimed:

'Why, you don't love each other any longer!'

Her cousin rose to go upstairs, and replied, with an uneasy smile:

'We love each other as much as is possible, my dear girl. You don't understand things, shut up here in this hole. Why should love fare better than anything else?'

As soon as she had closed the door of her own room Pauline fell into one of those fits of despondency which had so often tortured her and kept her awake, on the very same chair, while all the rest of them were sleeping. Was there going to be a renewal of trouble? She had hoped it was all done with, both for others and herself, when she had torn her heart asunder and given Lazare to Louise; and now she found how useless her sacrifice had been. They had already ceased to love each other; it was all to no purpose that she had wept bitter tears and martyred herself. To this wretched result had she come, to fresh trouble and strife, the thought of which added to her grief. There seemed to be no end to suffering!

Then as, with her arms hanging listlessly in front of her, she sat watching her candle burn away, the oppressive thought arose from her conscience that she alone was guilty. She tried, but in vain, to struggle against the facts. It was she alone who had brought about that marriage, without understanding that Louise would never prove the wife that her cousin needed. She saw it now clearly enough. She recognised that the other was much too nervously inclined herself to be able to steady him, for she lost her head at the merest trifle, and her only charm lay in her caressing nature—a charm of which Lazare had already tired. Why did all this only occur to her now? Were not these, indeed, the very reasons which had determined her to let Louise take her place? She had thought that Louise possessed a more loving nature than her own; she had believed that Louise, with her kisses and caresses, would be able to free Lazare from his gloomy despondency. Ah! the pity of it all! To have brought about evil when she had striven to accomplish good, and to have shown such ignorance of life as to have brought ruin upon those she yearned to save! Yet she had felt so sure that she was right and was perfecting her good work on the day when their happiness had cost her such bitter tears! Now she felt contempt for her kindliness, since kindliness did not always create happiness.

The house was wrapped in sleep. In the quiet of her room she could hear nothing but the throbbing of her temples. Within her was gradually surging a rebellious regret. Why had she not married Lazare herself? He had been hers; she had had no right to give him to another. Perhaps he might have been wretched and despondent at first, but by-and-by she would have restored his courage and protected him from his insane fancies. She had always felt foolishly doubtful of herself, and from that alone all the unhappiness had arisen. The consciousness of her own robust health and strength and all her power of affection forced itself upon her again. Was she not superior in every way to that other girl? How foolish she had been in weakly effacing herself! She loved her cousin sufficiently well to disappear if the other girl could make him happy; but since she knew not how to keep his love, was it not her duty to act and break that wicked union? And her anger grew apace; she felt that she was both braver and more beautiful than the other. Conviction flashed upon her mind; it was she who ought to have married Lazare.

Then she was overwhelmed with regret. The hours of the night passed, one by one, yet she did not think of seeking her bed. She sat there, staring at the tall flame of the candle without seeing it, in a vivid waking dream. She was no longer in her old bedroom. She thought she had married Lazare, and their life unrolled itself before her eyes in a series of pictures of love and delight. They were at Bonneville, by the edge of the blue sea, or in Paris, in some busy street. They were in a peaceful little room, with books lying about it and sweet roses on the table; the lamp gave out a soft, clear light, while the ceiling was steeped in shadow. Every moment their hands sought each other. Lazare had recovered all the careless gaiety of his early youth, and she loved him so much that he had again come to believe in the eternity of existence. Just now they were sitting at table; now they were going out together; to-morrow she would go over the week's accounts with him. She loved those little domestic details; she made them the foundation of their happiness, which knew no break from the laughing toilet in the morning until the last kiss at night. In the summer they travelled. Then one day she discovered that she was likely to become a mother. But just then a shivering shudder dissipated her dream, and she was no longer far away, but in her own room at Bonneville, staring at her expiring candle. A mother! Ah! the misery of it! It was that other who would be one; never would any of those things happen to herself, never would those joys be hers! The shock was so painful that tears gushed from her eyes, and she wept distractedly, sobbing like one heart-broken. At last the candle burnt out, and she had to seek her bed in darkness.

That feverish night left Pauline with a feeling of deep emotion and charitable pity for the disunited husband and wife, and for herself. Her grief melted into a kind of affectionate hope. She could not have told on what she was reckoning; she dared not analyse the confused sentiments which agitated her heart. But, after all, why should she trouble herself in this way? Hadn't she at least ten days before her? It would be time enough to think of matters by-and-by. What was of immediate importance was to tranquillise Lazare, so that he might derive some benefit from his stay at Bonneville. And she assumed her old gaiety of demeanour, and soon they plunged afresh into their life of former days.

At first it seemed a renewal of the old comradeship of early youth. 'Don't bother about that tiresome play of yours. It will only get hissed. Come and help me to look whether Minouche has carried her ball of thread on to the top of the cupboard,' said Pauline.

He held a chair for her, while she mounted upon it, and, standing on tip-toes, looked for the missing thread. The rain had been falling for the last two days and they could not leave the big room. Their laughter rang out as they kept on unearthing some relic of old days.

'Oh, see! here is the doll which you made out of two of my old collars. Ah! and this—don't you remember?—is the portrait of you that

I drew the day when you made yourself so frightfully ugly by getting into a rage and crying, because I wouldn't lend you my razor.'

Then Pauline wagered that she could still jump at a single bound on to the table; Lazare, too, jumped, quite glad at being drawn out of himself. His play was already lying neglected in a drawer. One morning when they came across the great symphony on Grief she played portions of it to him, accentuating the rhythm in a comical fashion. He made fun of his composition and sang the notes to support the piano, whose weak tones could scarcely be heard. But one little bit, the famous March of Death, made them both serious; it was really not bad, and must be preserved. Everything pleased them and struck a chord of tenderness in their hearts: a collection of *floridae* which Pauline had once mounted, and which they now discovered behind some books; a forgotten jar containing a sample of the bromide of potassium which they had extracted from the seaweed; a small broken model of a stockade, which looked as though it had been wrecked by a storm in a teacup. Then they romped over the house, chasing each other like schoolboys at play. They were perpetually rushing up and down the stairs and scampering through the rooms, banging the doors noisily. It seemed as if the old days had come back again. She was ten years old once more, and he was nineteen; and she again felt for him all the enthusiastic friendship of a little girl. Nothing was changed. In the dining-room there still remained the sideboard of bright walnut, the polished brass hanging-lamp, the view of Vesuvius, and the four lithographs of the Seasons, while the grandfather's masterpiece still slumbered in its old place. There was only one room which they entered with silent emotion—that which Madame Chanteau had occupied, and which had been unused since her death. The secrétaire was never opened now, but the hangings of yellow cretonne, with their pattern of flower-work, were fading from the bright sunlight which was occasionally allowed to enter the room. It so happened that the anniversary of Madame Chanteau's birth came round about this time, and they decked the room with big bunches of flowers.

Soon, however, as the wind rose and dispersed the rain-clouds, they betook themselves out of doors on to the terrace, into the kitchen-garden and along the cliffs, and their youth began anew.

'Shall we go shrimping?' Pauline cried to her cousin one morning, through the partition, as she sprang out of bed. 'The tide is going down."

They set off in bathing costumes, and once more found the old familiar rocks on which the sea had wrought no perceptible change during the past weeks and months. They could have fancied that they had been exploring that part of the coast only the day before.

'Take care!' cried Lazare; 'there is a hole there, you know, and the bottom of it is full of big stones.'

'Oh, yes, I know; don't be frightened—Oh! do come and look at this huge crab I have just caught!'

The cool waves splashed round their legs and the fresh salt breezes from the sea intoxicated them. All their old rambles were resumed—the long walks, the pleasant rests on the sands, the hasty refuge sought in some hollow of the cliffs at the approach of sudden showers, and the return home at nightfall along the dusky paths. Nothing seemed changed; the sea, with its ceaselessly varying aspect, still stretched out into the boundless distance. Little forgotten incidents returned to their memory with all the vividness of present facts. Lazare seemed to be still six-and-twenty and Pauline sixteen. When he casually happened to pull her about with his old playful familiarity, she seemed greatly embarrassed, however, and was thrilled with delicious confusion. But she in no way tried to avoid him, for she had no thought of the possibility of evil. Fresh life began to animate them; there were whispered words, causeless laughter, long intervals of silence which left them quivering. The most trivial incidents—a request for some bread, a remark about the weather, the good-nights they wished each other as they went to bed—seemed full of a new and strange meaning. All their past life was reviving within them and thrilling them with the tenderness that comes of the remembrance of former happiness. Why should they have felt anxious? They did not resist the spell; the sea, with its ceaseless monotonous voice, seemed to lull and fill them with pleasant languor.

And so the days quietly passed by. The third week of Lazare's visit was already commencing. He still stayed on, though he had received several letters from Louise, who felt very lonely, but whom her sister-in-law wished to keep with her some time longer. In his replies he had strongly advised her to stay where she was, even telling her that Doctor Cazenove, whom he had consulted on the matter, recommended her to do so. Gradually he fell again into the quiet routine of the house, accustoming himself once more to the old times for meals, for getting up and going to bed, which he had changed in Paris, as well as to Véronique's grumpy humour and the incessant suffering of his father, who remained immutable, ever racked by pain, while everything around him altered. Lazare was confronted, too, by the Saturday dinners, and the familiar faces of the Doctor and the Abbé, with their eternal talk of the last gale or the visitors at Arromanches. Minouche still jumped upon the table at dessert as lightly as a feather, or rubbed her head caressingly against his chin, and the gentle scratching of her teeth seemed to carry him back long years. There was nothing new amongst all those old familiar things save Loulou, who lay rolled up under the table, looking mournful and hideous, and growling at everyone who came near him. It was in vain that Lazare gave him sugar; when he had swallowed it, the wretched beast only showed his teeth more surlily than before. They were obliged to leave him entirely to himself; he led quite a lonely life in the house, like an unsociable being who only asks of men and gods to be allowed to spend his time in quiet boredom.

However, Pauline and Lazare sometimes had adventures when they were out walking. One day, when they had quitted the path along the cliffs to avoid passing the works at Golden Bay, they came across Boutigny at a bend of the road. He was now a person of some importance, for he had grown rich by the manufacture of soda. He had married the woman who had shown herself so devoted as to follow him into that deserted region, and she had recently given birth to her third child. The whole family, attended by a manservant and a nurse, were driving in a handsome break, drawn by a pair of big white horses, and the two pedestrians had to squeeze themselves against the bank to escape being caught by the wheels. Boutigny, who was driving, checked the horses into a walking pace. There was a moment's embarrassment. They had not spoken for years, and the presence of the woman and the children made the embarrassment still more painful. At last, as their eyes met, they just bowed to each other, without a word.

"When the carriage had passed on, Lazare, who had turned pale, said with an effort:

'So he's living like a prince now!'

Pauline, whom the sight of the children had affected, answered gently:

'Yes; it seems he has made some enormous profits lately. He has begun to try your old experiments again.'

That, indeed, was the sore point with Lazare. The Bonneville fishermen, who with their pertinacious banter seemed bent on making themselves disagreeable to him, had informed him of what had taken place. Boutigny, assisted by a young chemist in his employment, was again applying the freezing treatment to seaweed ashes, and, by practical and prudent perseverance, had obtained marvellous results.

'Of course!' Lazare growled, in a low voice; 'every time that science takes a step forward, it is some fool that helps her on through sheer accident.'

Their walk was spoilt by that meeting, and they went on in silence, gazing into the distance and watching the grey vapour rise from the sea and spread palely over the sky. When they returned home at nightfall, they were shivering; however, the cheerful light of the hanging-lamp streaming down upon the white cloth warmed them again.

Another day, as they were following a path through a field of beet in the neighbourhood of Verchemont, they stopped in surprise at seeing some smoke rising from a thatched roof. The place was on fire, but the brilliance of the sun's rays streaming from overhead prevented the blaze from being seen. The house, which had its doors and windows closed, was apparently deserted, its peasant owners doubtless being at work in the neighbourhood. Pauline and Lazare at once left the path, and ran up shouting, but with no other effect than that of disturbing some magpies who were chattering in the apple-trees. At last a woman with a handkerchief round her head appeared from a distant field of carrots, glanced about her for a moment, and then rushed on over the ploughed land as fast as her legs could carry her. She gesticulated and shouted something which the others could not catch, for flight interfered with her utterance. After tripping and falling she got up, then fell again, and started off once more, with her hands torn and bleeding. Her kerchief had slipped off her head, and her hair streamed in the sunlight.

'What was it she said?' asked Pauline, feeling frightened.

The woman was rushing up to them, and at last they heard her hoarse scream, like the wail of an animal:

'The child! the child! the child!'

Her husband and son had been at work since the morning some couple of miles away in an oat-field which they had inherited. She herself had only lately gone out to get a basketful of carrots, leaving the child asleep, and, contrary to her habit, fastening up the house. The fire had probably been smouldering some time, for the woman was stupefied, and swore she had extinguished every ember before going out. At all events the thatched roof was now aglow, and flames shot up athwart the golden sunlight.

'Is the door locked, then?' cried Lazare.

The woman did not hear him. She was quite distraught, and rushed without any apparent reason round the house, as though she were trying to discover some opening, some means of entrance which she must have known did not exist. Then she fell again. Her legs no longer had the strength to support her, and her ashy face showed all the agony of despair and tenor, while she continued screaming:

'The child! the child!'

Big tears rose to Pauline's eyes; but Lazare was even more painfully affected by the woman's cry, which completely unnerved him. It was becoming more than he could bear, and he suddenly exclaimed:

'I'll go and fetch your child!'

His cousin looked at him in wild alarm. She grasped his hands and tried to hold him back.

'You! you mustn't go! The roof will fall in!'

'We'll see about that,' he replied quietly.

Then he shouted in the woman's face:

'Your key! You've got your key with you, haven't you?'

The woman still remained agape, but Lazare hustled her and at last wrung from her the key. Then, while the woman remained screaming on the ground, he stepped quietly towards the house. Pauline followed him with her eyes, rooted to the ground with fear and astonishment, but making no further attempt to detain him, for it seemed by his demeanour as though he were about to attend to some very ordinary business. A shower of sparks rained on him, and he had to squeeze himself closely against the door, for handfuls of burning straw fell from the roof, like water streaming down during a storm. Moreover, he found himself hindered by an annoying obstacle. The rusty key would not turn in the lock. But he manifested no irritation; coolly taking his time, he at last succeeded in opening the door. Then he lingered for a moment longer on the threshold, in order to let out the first rush of smoke, which blew in his face. Never before had he known such calmness; he moved as though he were in a dream, with all the assurance, skilfulness, and prudence which the danger he was encountering inspired. At last he lowered his head and disappeared within the cottage.

'O God! O God!' stammered Pauline, who was choking with anguish.

She clasped her hands involuntarily, almost crushing them together as she moved them up and down, like one racked by great agony. The roof was cracking, and was already collapsing in places. Never would Lazare have time to make his escape. It seemed an eternity to her since he had entered. The woman on the ground had ceased crying; the sight of the gentleman rushing into the fire seemed to have stupefied her.

But a piercing cry broke through the air. It had come involuntarily from Pauline, from the very depths of her being, as she saw the thatch fall in between the smoking walls:

'Lazare!'

He was at the door, his hair scarcely singed and his hands but slightly scorched; and when he had tossed the child, who was struggling and crying, into the woman's arms, he almost became angry with his cousin:

'What's the matter with you? What are you going on like this for?'

She threw her arms round his neck and burst out sobbing in such a state of nervous excitement that, fearing she might faint, he made her sit down on an old moss-covered stone by the side of the house well. He himself was now beginning to feel faint. There was a trough full of water there, and he steeped his hands in it with a sensation of acute relief. The coldness restored him to himself, and he then began to experience great surprise at what he had done. Was it possible that he had gone into the midst of those flames? It was as if he had had a double; he could distinctly see himself showing incredible agility and presence of mind amidst the smoke, as though he were looking at some wonderful feat performed by a stranger. A remnant of mental exaltation filled him with a subtle joy which he had never known before.

Pauline had recovered a little, and examined his hands, saying:

'No! there's no great harm done. The burns are only slight ones. But we must go home at once, and I will attend to them. Oh! how you did frighten me!'

She dipped her handkerchief in the water and bound it round his right hand, which was the more severely burnt of the two. Then they rose and tried to console the woman, who, after showering wild kisses on the child, had laid it down near her, and was now not even looking at it. She had begun to grieve about the house, wailing pitiably as she asked what would her men say and do when they came back and found their home in ruins. The walls were still standing, and black smoke was pouring out of the brazier within them, amidst a loud crackling of sparks which could not be seen.

'Come! my poor woman,' Pauline said to her; 'don't be so down-hearted. Come and see us to-morrow.'

Some neighbours, attracted by the smoke, now ran up, and Pauline led Lazare away. Their return home was a very pleasant one. Though Lazare suffered but little pain, his cousin insisted upon giving him her arm to support him. They still felt too much emotion to speak, and they looked at each other smiling. Pauline felt a kind of happy pride. He must really be brave, then, in spite of his pallor at the thought of death! As they made their way along she became absorbed in astonishment at the inconsistencies of the only man whom she knew well. She had seen him spend whole nights at his work, and then give himself up to idleness for months. She had known him exhibit the most uncompromising truthfulness after lying unblushingly. She had received a brotherly kiss from him on her brow, and she had felt his hands, hot and feverish with passion, burn her wrists with their grasp; and now to-day he had proved himself a hero. She had done right, then, in not despairing of life, in not judging that everyone must be altogether good or altogether bad. When they arrived at Bonneville their emotion and silence found relief in a torrent of rapid talk. They went over every little detail again, recounting the story a score of times, and remembering at each repetition some little incident that had been previously forgotten. The affair was indeed talked about for a long time afterwards, and help was sent to the burnt-out peasants.

Lazare had been nearly a month at Bonneville when a letter arrived from Louise, complaining that she was utterly overwhelmed with *ennui*. In his reply to it he told her that he would fetch her at the beginning of the following week. There had been some tremendous falls of rain, those violent deluges which so frequently swept down upon the district, and shrouded earth, sea, and sky beneath a pall of grey vapour. Lazare had spoken seriously of finishing his play, and Pauline, whom he wished to have near him that she might encourage him, took her knitting—the little stockings which she distributed among the village children—into her cousin's room. But it was very little work he did when she had taken her place by the table. They were constantly talking to each other in low tones, repeating the same things over and over again, without ever seeming to weary of them, while their eyes never strayed from one another. Nothing seemed to them more delightful than that languid quiet, that feeling of drowsiness which glided over them, while the rain pattered down upon the slates of the roof. An interval of silence would at times make them flush, and they unconsciously put a caress in every word they addressed to each other, impelled thereto by that influence which had brought a renewal of those old days which they had thought had passed away for ever.

One evening Pauline had sat up knitting in Lazare's room till nearly midnight, while her cousin, whose pen had dropped idly from his fingers, slowly told her about what he intended to write in the future—dramas peopled with colossal characters.

The whole house was asleep. Véronique had gone to bed long ago, and the deep stillness of the night, through which only broke the familiar wail of the high tide, gradually permeated them with tenderness. Lazare, unbosoming himself, confessed that his life hitherto had been a failure; if literature also failed him, he had made up his mind to retire to some secluded spot and live the life of a recluse.

'Do you know,' he added with a smile, 'I often think that we ought to have emigrated after my mother's death?'

'Emigrated! Why?'

'Yes; have taken ourselves very far away—to Oceania, for instance, to one of those islands where life is so sweet and pleasant.'

'But your father? Should we have taken him with us?'

'Oh! it's only a fancy, a dream, that I'm talking of. One may indulge in pleasant dreams, you know, when the actual truth is not very cheerful.'

He had risen from the table and had sat down upon one of the arms of Pauline's chair. She let her knitting drop, that she might laugh at ease over the ceaseless flow of the young man's imagination.

'Are you mad, my poor fellow?' she asked. 'What should we have done out there?'

'We should have lived! Do you remember that book of travels that we read together a dozen years ago? There is a perfect paradise out there. There is no winter, the sky is always blue, and life is passed beneath the sun and the stars. We should have had a cabin and have lived upon delicious fruits, with nothing to do and never a trouble to vex us.'

'Ah! then we should soon have become a pair of savages, with rings through our noses and feathers on our heads!'

'Well, why not? We should have loved each other from one end of the year to the other, taking no count of the days. Ah! it would have been delightful!'

She looked at him. Her eyelids were quivering and her face turned pale. That thought of love had filled her with delicious languor. He had playfully taken hold of her hand and was smiling in an embarrassed manner. At first Pauline felt no disquietude. It was nothing more than a revival of their old intimacy. But she slowly grew disturbed; her strength seemed to ebb from her, and her very voice faltered as she said:

'Nothing but fruit would make rather a spare diet. We should have had to hunt and fish, and cultivate a piece of land. If it is true, as they say, that the women do the work out there, would you have set me to dig the ground?'

'You! With those tiny hands of yours! Oh! we could have made capital servants out of the monkeys, you know!'

She smiled languidly at this pleasantry, while he added:

'Besides, they would have been no longer in existence, those little hands of yours! I should have eaten them up—like this!'

He kissed her hands and pretended to bite at them, while the blood surged to his face in a sudden thrill of passion. They neither of them spoke. They were affected by a common madness—a vertigo which threw them both into dizzy faintness. Pauline seemed on the point of swooning; her eyes closed; but at last, as Lazare's lips suddenly met hers, the thrill she felt made her raise her eyelids, and she awoke like one who has just passed through a terrible dream. Then she sprang to her feet, and, faint though she still felt, she found courage to resist both Lazare and her own passion. The struggle was short, but violent. She repulsed him again and again, and at last, profiting by a brief respite, she fled across the landing into her own room. He followed, and she could hear him speaking to her, but in spite of the passionate promptings of her own heart she kept silent. He sobbed and her own tears fell, yet she gave him no response. When at last she heard him close his door behind him she gave full rein to her grief. It was all over and she had conquered, but her victory filled her with distress. It was impossible for her to sleep; she lay awake till morning. What had happened took complete possession of her thoughts. That evening had been a sin at which she now shuddered with horror. She felt that she could no longer find excuse for herself, that she must acknowledge the duplicity of her affections. Her motherly love for Lazare and her condemnation of Louise were but a hypocritical revival of her old passion for her cousin. She had let herself glide into falsehood, for, as she analysed more closely the secret sentiments of her heart, she became conscious that the rupture between Lazare and his wife had pleased her rather than otherwise, and that she had hoped in some way to profit by it. Was it not she, too, who had brought about between her cousin and herself a renewal of the intimacy of former days? Ought she not to have known that the result must be disastrous? Now matters had reached a terrible pass, and they were threatened with ruin. She had given him to another, while she herself loved him passionately, and he, too, longed for her. This thought careered through her brain and beat upon her temples like a peal of bells. At first she made up her mind to run away from the house in the morning. Then she thought that such flight would be cowardly. Since Lazare was leaving very shortly, why should she not remain? Her pride, too, awoke within her; she resolved to conquer herself, for she felt that she could never again carry her head erect should the occurrence of that night inspire her with remorse.

The nest morning she came downstairs at her accustomed hour. There was nothing about her to reveal the night of torture she had spent except the heaviness of her eyes. She was pale and quite calm. When Lazare appeared in his turn, he explained his air of weary lassitude by telling his father that he had sat up late, working. The day passed in the usual way. Neither Pauline nor Lazare made any reference to what had occurred between them, even when they found themselves alone and free from all observation. They made no attempt to avoid each other; they appeared quite confident of themselves. But in the evening, when they wished each other good-night on the landing near their rooms, they fell into each other's arms, and their lips met in a kiss. Then Pauline, full of alarm, hastily escaped and locked herself in her room, while Lazare, too, rushed away, bursting into tears.

It was thus that they continued to bear themselves towards each other. The days slowly glided away, and the cousins lived on together in constant anxiety of possible backsliding. Though they never spoke of such a thing, and never referred to that terrible night, they thought of it continually and were filled with fear. Their sense of what was right and honourable remained undimmed, and every sudden little lapse, any embrace or stolen kiss, left them full of anger with themselves. But neither had the courage to take the only safe step, that of immediate separation. Pauline, believing that it would be cowardly for her to flee, persisted in remaining in the presence of danger; while Lazare, absorbed in his transports, did not even reply to the pressing letters he received from his wife. He had now been six weeks at Bonneville, and he and Pauline had begun to believe that this existence of alternate pain and sweetness would go on for ever.

One Sunday, at dinner, Chanteau became quite gay, after venturing to drink a glass of Burgundy, a luxury for which he had to pay very dearly each time that he indulged in it. Pauline and Lazare had spent some delightful hours together by the sea under the bright blue sky, exchanging looks full of tenderness, though marked with that haunting fear of themselves which infused such passion into their intimacy.

They were all three smiling, when Véronique, who was just about to bring in the dessert, called from the door of the kitchen:

'Here comes Madame!'

'Madame who?' cried Pauline, with a feeling of stupefaction.

'Madame Louise!'

They all broke out into exclamations. Chanteau, quite scared, gazed at Pauline and Lazare, who had turned very pale. But the latter rose excitedly from his seat and stammered angrily:

'What! Louise? She never told me she was coming, and I had forbidden her to do so. She must be mad!'

The twilight was falling, soft and clear. Lazare threw down his napkin and rushed out of the room. Pauline followed him, struggling to regain her cheerful serenity. It was indeed Louise who was alighting with difficulty from old Malivoire's coach.

'Are you mad?' her husband cried to her across the yard. 'Why have you done such a foolish thing without writing to me?'

Then Louise burst into tears. She had been so poorly at Clermont, she said, and had felt so depressed and weary. And as her two last letters had remained unanswered, she had felt an irresistible impulse to set off, a yearning desire to see Bonneville again. If she had not sent him word of her intention, it was because she feared that he might have prevented her from satisfying her whim.

'And to think I was pleased with the idea of taking you all by surprise!' she concluded.

'It is idiotic! You will go back again to-morrow!' her husband cried.

Louise, quite overcome, crushed by this reception, fell into Pauline's arms. The latter had again turned pale. And now, when she felt this woman, so soon to be a mother, pressing against her, both horror and pity came upon her. However, she succeeded in conquering her jealousy and in silencing Lazare.

'Why do you speak to her so unkindly? Kiss her! You did quite right to come, my dear, if you thought you would be better at Bonneville. You know very well that we all love you, don't you?'

Loulou was barking furiously at all the hubbub which disturbed the usual quiet of the yard. Minouche, having poked her head out of the door, had retired again, shaking her feet as though she had just escaped mixing herself up in some compromising incident. The whole party went into the house, and Véronique laid another cover at the table and began to serve the dinner over again.

'Hallo! is it really you, Louisette?' Chanteau exclaimed, with an uneasy smile. 'You wanted to take us by surprise? You have almost made my wine go the wrong way!'

However, the evening passed off pleasantly. They had all regained their self-possession, and avoided making any reference to the immediate future. There was a momentary revival of embarrassment at bedtime, when Véronique inquired if Monsieur Lazare was going to sleep in his wife's room.

'Oh no! Louise will sleep better alone,' Lazare replied, looking up instinctively and catching Pauline's glance.

'Yes, that will be better,' said the young wife; 'sleep at the top of the house, for I'm dreadfully tired, and like that I shall have the whole bed to myself.'

Three days passed. Then Pauline at last came to a determination. She would leave the house on the following Monday. Lazare and Louise had already begun to talk of remaining till after the birth of the expected baby, and Pauline thought she could see that her cousin had had enough of Paris, and would settle down altogether at Bonneville, weary and sick of his perpetual failures. The best thing she could do, therefore, was to give the place up to them at once, for she had not been able to conquer herself, and she more than ever lacked the courage to live beside them and witness all the intimacy of man and wife. Besides, this course seemed the best means of escaping from all the perils threatened by the reviving passion from which she and Lazare had just suffered so cruelly. Louise alone expressed some astonishment on learning Pauline's decision, but she was supplied with undeniable reasons for it. Doctor Cazenove told her that his relation at Saint-Lô had made Pauline unusually favourable offers, that the girl could not really refuse them any longer, and that her friends must insist upon her accepting a position which would make her future safe. Chanteau, too, with tears in his eyes, expressed his consent.

On the Saturday came a farewell dinner, with the priest and the Doctor. Louise, who suffered greatly, could scarcely drag herself to the table, and this threw additional gloom over the meal, in spite of the efforts of Pauline, who had cheerful smiles for everyone, though in reality she grieved bitterly at the thought of leaving that house, which she had animated and brightened for so many years with her ringing laughter. Her heart was aching with pain, and Véronique served the dinner with a tragic air. Chanteau refused to touch a single drop of Burgundy, having become all at once almost superfluously prudent, for he trembled at the thought of being so soon deprived of a nurse whose mere voice seemed able to lull his pains. Lazare, for his part, was feverish, and wrangled with the Doctor about a new scientific discovery.

By eleven o'clock the house had once more subsided into silence. Louise and Chanteau were already asleep, while Véronique was tidying up her kitchen. Then, at the top of the house, by the door of his old room, which he still occupied, Lazare detained Pauline for a moment, according to his wont.

'Good-bye!' he murmured.

'No! not good-bye,' she said, forcing herself to smile. '*Au revoir,* since I am not going away till Monday.'

They gazed at each other, and as their eyes grew dim they fell into each other's arms, while their lips met passionately in a last kiss.

X

THE next morning, as they sat down to their coffee at the early breakfast, they were surprised that Louise did not make her appearance. The servant went upstairs to knock at her door, and when the young woman at last came down it was evident that she was in a state of great suffering. She took but a few sips of coffee; and all the morning she dragged herself about the house, rising from one chair to go and sit down upon another. They did not venture to speak to her, for she grew irritable and seemed to suffer the more when any notice was taken of her. She experienced no relief until a little before noon, when she was able to sit down at the table again and take some soup. Between two and three o'clock, however, she was again unable to remain still, and dragged herself about between the dining-room and the kitchen, finally going, with great difficulty, upstairs, but only to come down again immediately.

At the top of the house Pauline was now packing her trunk. She was to leave Bonneville the next morning, and she had only the needful time to empty her drawers and get everything ready for departure; nevertheless, she every minute went out on to the landing and looked over the banisters, distressed by the other's evident suffering. About four o'clock, as she heard Louise becoming still more agitated, she resolved to speak to Lazare, who had locked himself up in his room, full of nervous exasperation at the troubles with which he accused Fate of overwhelming him.

'We cannot leave Louise like this,' insisted Pauline. 'We must go and talk to her. Come with me.'

They found her half-way on the first flight of stairs, lacking the strength to go either up or down.

'My dear girl,' said Pauline tenderly, 'we are quite distressed about you. We are going to send for Madame Bouland.'

At this Louise grew angry. 'Why do you torment me like this,' she cried, 'when all that I want is to be left alone? I shan't need Madame Bouland for a long time yet. Leave me alone and don't torture me!'

Louise showed herself so obstinate and displayed so much temper that Lazare, in his turn, grew angry; however, Pauline was compelled to promise that she would not send for Madame Bouland. This person was an *accoucheuse* of Verchemont, who possessed an extraordinary reputation throughout the district for skill and energy. She was considered to have no equal at Bayeux or even at Caen. It was on account of this great reputation of hers that Louise, who was very timid and had a presentiment of disaster, had resolved to place herself in her hands. None the less she experienced a great fear of Madame Bouland—the same irrational fear, indeed, with which patients contemplate a dentist whom it is necessary they should visit, though they defer doing so as long as possible.

At six o'clock Louise felt much better again, and showed herself very triumphant in consequence. But she was worn out, and, when she had eaten a cutlet, she went back to her room. She would be all right, she said, if she could only get to sleep. Thus she obstinately refused to let anyone sit upstairs with her, and insisted upon being left alone. The others then sat down to a stew and a piece of roast veal. The dinner began in silence, for Louise's illness increased the gloom which was caused by

Pauline's approaching departure. They made as little noise as possible with their spoons and forks, for fear it might reach the ears of the invalid and still further distress her. Chanteau, however, grew very loquacious by degrees, and had begun relating some wonderful stories, when Véronique, as she was handing round the veal, suddenly exclaimed:

'I'm not quite sure, but I fancy I can hear Madame Lazare groaning upstairs.'

Lazare sprang from his seat and opened the door. They all gave over eating, and strained their ears to listen. At first they could hear nothing, but soon the sound of prolonged groaning reached them.

Pauline thereupon threw down her napkin and ran upstairs, followed by Lazare. And now Louise, whom they found seated on her bed in a dressing-gown, rather peevishly consented to let them send for Madame Bouland. When Lazare, however, suggested that they had better send for Doctor Cazenove as well, on the chance of complications arising, his wife burst into tears. Hadn't they the least pity for her, she cried? Why did they go on torturing her? They knew very well that the idea of being attended by a doctor was intolerable to her. She would have nobody but Madame Bouland.

'If you send for the Doctor,' said she, 'I'll get into bed and turn my face to the wall and refuse to say another word to anybody.'

'At any rate, go for Madame Bouland,' said Pauline to Lazare by way of conclusion. 'She may be able to give her some relief.'

They both went downstairs again, and found Abbé Horteur, who had come to pay a short visit, standing in silence before the alarmed Chanteau. An attempt was made to persuade Lazare to eat a little veal before starting, but he declared that a single mouthful would choke him, and forthwith he set off at a run to Verchemont.

'I think I hear her calling me!' Pauline exclaimed a moment later, hastening towards the staircase. 'If I want Véronique I will knock, on the floor. You can finish your dinner without me, can't you, uncle?'

The priest, much embarrassed at finding himself in the midst of this confusion, could not summon up his customary consolatory phrases, and he also soon retired, promising, however to return after he had been to the Gonins', where the crippled old man was very ill. Thus Chanteau was left alone before the disordered table. The glasses were half full, the veal was growing cold on the plates, and the greasy forks and half-eaten pieces of bread still lay where they had been dropped in the sudden alarm which had come upon the diners. As Véronique put a kettle of water on the fire, by way of precaution, in case it might be wanted, she began to grumble at not knowing whether she ought to clear the table or leave things in their present state of confusion.

Two anxious hours went by; nine o'clock came, and still Madame Bouland did not arrive. Louise was now anxiously longing for her to come, and bitterly complained that they must want her to die, since they left her so long without assistance. It only took twenty five minutes to get to Verchemont, and an hour ought to have been sufficient to fetch the woman. Lazare must be amusing himself somewhere, or, perhaps, an accident had happened, and no one would ever come at all. Then, however, the young wife ceased complaining, for an attack of sickness came upon her, and the whole house was once more in a state of alarm.

Eleven o'clock struck, and the delay became intolerable. So Véronique in her turn set off for Verchemont. She took a lantern with her, and was instructed to search all the ditches. Meantime Pauline remained with Louise, unable to assist her in spite of her desire to do so.

It was nearly midnight when the sound of wheels at last impelled the girl to rush downstairs.

'Why, where is Véronique?' she cried out from the steps, as she recognised Lazare and Madame Bouland. 'Haven't you met her?'

Lazare replied that they had come by the Port-en-Bessin road, after encountering all sorts of hindrances. On reaching Verchemont he had found that Madame Bouland was eight miles away attending to another woman. He could procure no horse or vehicle to go after her, and had been obliged to make the whole journey on foot, running all the way. And, besides, there had been endless other troubles. Fortunately, however, Madame Bouland had a trap with her.

'But the woman!' exclaimed Pauline. 'She has been attended to all right, I suppose, since Madame Bouland has been able to come with you?'

Lazare's voice trembled as he replied hoarsely:

'The woman is dead.'

They went into the hall, which was dimly lighted by a candle placed on the stairs. There was an interval of silence while Madame Bouland hung up her cloak. She was a short, dark woman, very thin, and as yellow as a lemon, with a large prominent nose. She spoke loudly, and had an extremely authoritative manner, which caused her to be much respected by the peasantry.

'Will you be good enough to follow me?' Pauline said to her. 'I have been quite at a loss to know what to do; she has never ceased complaining since the beginning of the evening.'

Louise still stood before a chest of drawers in her room, pawing the floor with her feet. She burst into tears as soon as she saw Madame Bouland, who forthwith began to question her. But the young wife turned a glance of entreaty towards Pauline, which the latter well understood. She therefore led Lazare from the room, and they both remained on the landing, unable to take themselves further away. The candle, which was still burning below, threw a dim light, broken by weird shadows, up the stairs, and the two cousins stood, Lazare leaning against the wall and Pauline against the banisters, gazing at each other in motionless silence. They strained their ears to catch the sounds that came from Louise's room; and when Madame Bouland at last opened the door they would have entered, but she pushed them back, came out, and closed the door behind her.

'Well?' Pauline murmured.

She signed to them to go downstairs, and it was not till they had reached the ground floor that she opened her mouth. It was a premature and very difficult case.

'It seems likely to be extremely serious,' she said. 'It is my duty to warn the family.'

Lazare turned pale. An icy breath passed over his brow. Then in stammering accents he asked for particulars.

Madame Bouland gave them, adding: 'I cannot undertake the responsibility. The presence of a doctor is absolutely necessary.'

Silence fell once more. Lazare was overcome with despair. Where were they to find a doctor at that time of night? His wife might die twenty times before they could get the surgeon from Arromanches.

'I don't think there is any immediate danger,' said Madame Bouland; 'still, you had better lose no time. I myself can do nothing further.'

And as Pauline besought her, in the name of humanity, to try something, at any rate, to alleviate the sufferings of Louise, whose groans echoed through the house, she replied in her clear sharp voice: 'No, indeed; I can do nothing of that kind. That other poor woman over yonder is dead, and I would rather not be responsible for this one.'

Again did Lazare shudder. At this moment, however, a tearful call was heard from Chanteau in the dining-room.

'Are you there? Come in! No one has been to tell me anything. I have been waiting to hear something ever so long.'

They entered the room. They had forgotten all about poor Chanteau since the interrupted dinner. He had remained at the table, twisting his thumbs and patiently waiting with all the drowsy resignation which he had acquired during his long periods of lonely quiescence. This new catastrophe, which was revolutionising the house, had greatly saddened him; he had not even had heart enough to go on eating, his food still remained untouched on his plate.

'Is she no better?' he inquired.

Lazare ragefully shrugged, his shoulders. But Madame Bouland, who retained all her accustomed calmness, pressed the young man to lose no further time.

'Take my trap!' she said. 'The horse is tired out; still, you will be able to get back in two hours or two hours and a half. I will stay here and look after her.'

Then with sudden determination Lazare rushed out of the room, feeling convinced that he would find his wife dead upon his return. They could hear him shouting and lashing the horse with his whip as the conveyance clattered noisily away.

Madame Bouland went upstairs again, and Pauline followed her, after briefly replying to her uncle's questions. When she had offered to put him to bed he had refused to go, insisting on staying up in order that he might know how things went on. If he felt drowsy, he said, he could sleep very well in his easy-chair, for he often slept in it the whole afternoon. He had only just been left alone again when Véronique returned with her lantern extinguished. She was boiling over with rage. For two years she had never poured forth so many words at one time.

'Of course they took the other road!' she cried. 'And there have I been looking into all the ditches and nearly killing myself to get to Verchemont! And I waited, too, for a whole half-hour down there in the middle of the road!'

Chanteau looked at her with his big eyes.

'Well, my girl, it was scarcely likely that you would meet each other.'

'And then, as I was coming back,' she continued, 'I met Monsieur Lazare galloping on like a madman in a crazy gig. I shouted out to him that they were anxiously waiting for him, but he only whipped his horse the more violently and nearly ran over me. I've had quite enough of these errands, of which I can make neither head nor tale. To make matters worse, too, my lantern went out.'

She hustled her master about, and tried to make him finish eating his food, so that she might, at any rate, get the table cleared. He was not at all hungry, but he ate a little of the cold veal for the sake of doing something. He was worried now by the Abbé's failure to return that evening. What was the use of the priest promising to come and keep him company if he had made up his mind to stay at home? However, priests certainly cut a comical figure on such occasions as the present; and, this idea amusing Chanteau, he set himself cheerfully to take his supper in solitude.

'Come, sir, make haste!' cried Véronique. 'It is nearly one o'clock, and it won't do to have the plates and dishes and things lying about like this till to-morrow. There's always something going wrong in this awful house!'

She was just beginning to clear the table when Pauline called to her from the staircase. Then Chanteau was once more left alone and forgotten in front of the table, and nobody came again to give him any news.

Louise was in quite a desperate condition, and her strength seemed to be rapidly ebbing away, when, about half-past three o'clock, Véronique privately warned Pauline of Lazare's arrival with Doctor Cazenove. Madame Bouland insisted on remaining alone with the Doctor beside the patient, while the others betook themselves to the dining-room, where Chanteau was now fast asleep. And then there again came a long, weary, and very anxious wait. When the Doctor joined them his voice betrayed his emotion.

'I have done nothing yet,' said he; 'I wouldn't do anything without consulting you.'

And thereupon he passed his hand over his forehead, as if to drive away some irksome thought.

'But it is not for us to decide, Doctor,' said Pauline, for Lazare was incapable of speech; 'we leave her in your hands.'

He shook his head. 'I must tell you,' said he, 'that both mother and child seem to me lost. Perhaps I might save one or the other.'

Lazare and Pauline rose up shuddering. Chanteau, aroused by the conversation, opened his heavy eyes and listened with an expression of amazement.

'Which of the two must I try to save?' repeated the Doctor, who trembled as much as those of whom he asked the question—'the child or the mother?'

'Which, o God?' cried Lazare. 'Do I know? Can I say?'

Tears choked him once again, whilst his cousin, ghastly pale, remained silent in presence of that awful alternative.

But Cazenove went on giving explanations. 'It is a case of conscience,' he concluded. 'I beg of you, decide yourselves.'

Sobs now prevented Lazare from answering. He had taken his handkerchief and was twisting it convulsively whilst striving to recover a little of his reason. Chanteau still looked on in stupefaction. And only Pauline was able to say, 'Why did you come down? It is cruel to torture us like this, when you alone know the best course, and alone are able to act.'

Just then Madame Bouland herself descended the stairs to say that matters were becoming much worse. 'Have you decided?' she inquired. 'The lady is sinking.'

Thereupon, with one of those sudden impulses which disconcerted people, Cazenove threw his arms about Lazare, kissed him, and exclaimed: 'Listen, I will try to save them both.... And if they succumb—well, I shall be yet more grieved than yourself, for I shall take it to be my own fault.'

Excepting Chanteau, who in his turn embraced his son, they all went upstairs together. Cazenove desired it. Louise was fully conscious, but very low. She offered no objection to a doctor now; her sufferings were too great. When he began to speak to her she simply answered: 'Kill me; kill me at once.'

There came a cruel and affecting scene. It was one of those dread hours when life and death wrestle together, when human science and skill battle to overcome and correct the errors of Nature. More than once did the Doctor pause, fearing a fatal issue. The patient's agony was terrible, but at last science triumphed, and a child was born. It was a boy.

Lazare, who had turned his face to the wall, was sobbing, and burst out into tears. He had been a prey to the keenest mental torture during the progress of the operations, and he thought despairingly that it would be preferable for them all to die rather than to continue living if such intense agony was to be mingled with life.

But Pauline bent over Louise and kissed her on the forehead.

'Come and kiss her!' she said to her cousin.

He came and stooped down over his wife; but he shuddered when his lips touched her brow, which was moist with icy perspiration. Louise lay there with her eyes closed, and seemed to be no longer breathing. Lazare leaned against the wall at the foot of the bed, trying to stifle his sobs.

'I am afraid the child is dead,' said the Doctor.

The baby, indeed, had given utterance to none of the usual shrill calls. It was a very small infant of a deathly hue.

'We might try the effect of friction and inflation,' the Doctor continued; 'but I'm afraid it would only be time wasted. And the mother stands in need of all my attention.'

Pauline heard him.

'Give me the child!' she exclaimed. 'I will try what I can do. If I don't manage to make it breathe, it will be that I have no more breath left myself.' Thereupon she carried the infant into the next room, the room which had once been Madame Chanteau's, taking with her a bottle of brandy and some flannel. She laid the poor wee creature in an arm-chair before a blazing fire; and then, having steeped a piece of flannel in a saucer of brandy, she knelt down and rubbed it without a pause, quite regardless of the cramp that gradually stiffened her arm. It was so small a child, and looked so wretched and fragile, that she feared lest she might kill it by rubbing it too hard. And so she passed the flannel backwards and forwards with a gentle, almost caressing motion, like the constant brushing of a bird's wing. Then she turned the child over, and tried to recall each of its tiny limbs to life. But it still lay there motionless. Though the friction seemed to impart a little warmth, the infant's chest remained shrunken, uninflated, and it even seemed to grow darker in colour.

Then, without evincing any repugnance, Pauline pressed her mouth to its tiny, rigid lips, and drawing long, slow breaths she strove to adapt the force of her lungs to the capacity of those little compressed organs into which the air had been unable to make its way. She was obliged to stop every now and then, when her breath grew exhausted; but, after inhaling a fresh supply, she turned to her task again. Her blood mounted to her head, and her ears began to buzz; she even became a little giddy. Nevertheless she still persevered, striving to inflate the baby's lungs for more than half an hour, without being encouraged by the least result. She vainly tried to make the ribs play by pressing them very gently with her fingers. But nothing seemed to do the least good, and anyone else would have abandoned in despair this apparently impossible resurrection. Pauline, however, brought maternal perseverance to her task, the obstinate insistence of a mother who is determined that her child shall live, and at last she felt that the poor wee body was stirring, that its tiny lips moved slightly beneath her own.

For nearly an hour she had remained alone in that room, absorbed in the anguish of that struggle with death, and forgetful of all else. That faint sign of life, that transitory tremor of the little lips, filled her with fresh courage. She had recourse to friction again, and every other minute she resumed her attempt at inflation, employing the two processes alternately without any regard for her own exhaustion. She felt a growing craving to conquer and produce life. For a moment she feared she had been mistaken, for it again seemed that her lips were only pressing lifeless ones. But she became conscious of another rapid contraction. Little by little the air was forcing its way into the child's lungs; she could feel it being sucked from her and returned, and she even fancied she could detect the little heart beginning to beat. Her mouth never left the tiny lips; she shared her life with that little creature; they had only one breath between them in that wonderful resurrection, a slow, continuous exchange of breath going from one to the other as if they had a common soul. Pauline's lips were soiled, for the child had scarcely been cleansed, but her joy at having saved it prevented any feeling of disgust. She began to inhale a warm pungency of life, which intoxicated her; and when, at last, the baby broke out into a feeble, plaintive wail, she fell back from the chair on to the floor, stirred to the depths of her being.

The big fire was blazing brightly, filling the room with cheerful light. Pauline remained on the floor in front of the baby, whom she had not yet examined. What a poor, frail mite it was! All her own robust vigour rose up in rebellious protest as she thought what a wretched puny son Louise had given to Lazare. She felt keen regret for her own wasted life. She herself would never be a mother! She was young and strong, and healthy and beautiful, but of what avail was all that? The fulness of life was not for her. And she wept for the child that she would never have.

Meantime the poor, frail little creature that she had revived to existence was still wailing and writhing on the chair, and Pauline began to fear that it might fall upon the floor. Her pity was aroused at the sight of such uncomeliness and weakness. She would at least do what she could for it; she would help it to continue living, as she had had the happiness of helping it into life. So she took it upon her knees and did what she could for it, while still shedding tears, in which were mingled sorrow for her own lonesome fate and pity for the misery of all living creatures.

Madame Bouland, whom she called, came to help her to wash the baby. They wrapped it in warm flannels and then laid it in the bed, till the cradle should be prepared for it. Madame Bouland was astonished to find it alive, and examined it carefully. It seemed well formed, she said, but its frailty would make it difficult to rear. Then she hurried off again to Louise, who still remained in a very critical condition.

As Pauline was again taking up her position at the baby's side Lazare, who had been informed of the miracle his cousin had accomplished, entered the room.

'Come and look at him!' said Pauline, with much emotion. But as he drew near he began to tremble, and exclaimed:

'What! you have laid him in that bed!'

He had shuddered as he entered. That room, so long unused, so full of mournful associations and so rarely entered, was now warm and bright, enlivened by the crackling of the fire. Each article of furniture was still in its accustomed position, and the clock still marked twenty-three minutes to eight. No one had occupied that chamber, now prepared for Madame Bouland, since his mother had died there. And it was in that very bed where she had passed away—in that sacred, awful bed—that he saw his own son restored to life, looking so tiny as he lay among the spreading coverings.

'Does it displease you?' Pauline asked in surprise.

He shook his head. He could not speak for emotion. At last he stammered:

'I was thinking of mamma. She has gone, and now here is another who will go away as she went. Why, then, did he come?'

His words were cut short by a burst of sobbing. His terror and his disgust of life broke out in spite of all the efforts he had made to restrain himself since Louise's terrible delivery. When he had touched his baby's brow with his lips, he hastily stepped back, for he had fancied that he could feel the infant's skull giving way beneath his touch. He was filled with remorseful despondency at the sight of the poor, frail little thing.

'Don't distress yourself!' said Pauline, by way of cheering him. 'We'll make a fine young fellow of him. It doesn't at all matter that he is small now.'

He looked at her, and, utterly upset as he was, a full confession escaped from his heart:

'It is again to you that we owe his life! Am I destined, then, to be always under obligations to you?'

'To me!' she exclaimed. 'I have done nothing more than Madame Bouland would have done if I hadn't happened to be here.'

He silenced her with a wave of his hand.

'Do you think,' he said, 'that I am so base that I cannot understand that I owe everything to you? Ever since you first came into this house you have never ceased to sacrifice yourself. I will say nothing now about your money, but you still loved me yourself when you gave me to Louise. I know it now quite well. Ah! if you only knew the shame I feel when I look at you and recollect! You would have given your very life-blood, you were always kind and cheerful, even at the very time when I was crushing down your heart. Ah, yes! you were right; cheerfulness and kindliness are everything; all else is mere delusion!'

She tried to interrupt him, but he continued in a louder voice:

'What a fool I made of myself with all my disbelief and boasting, and all the pessimism which I paraded out of vanity and fear! It was I who spoilt our lives—yours and my own, and those of the whole family. Yes! you were the only sensible one amongst us! Life becomes so easy when everyone in a family is cheerful and affectionate, and each lives for the others. If the world is to die of misery, at any rate let it die cheerfully, and in sympathy with itself!'

Pauline smiled at the violence of his language, and caught hold of his hands.

'Come! come!' she said, 'don't excite yourself! Now that you see I was right, you are cured, and all will go well.'

'Ah! I don't know that! I am talking like this just now, because there are times when the truth will force itself out, even in spite of one's self. But to-morrow I shall slip back into all my old torment. One can't change one's nature! No, no! Things will go no better. On the contrary, they will gradually get worse and worse. You know that as well as I do. It is my own stupidity that enrages me.'

She drew him gently towards her, and said to him in her grave way:

'You are neither foolish nor base; you are unfortunate. Kiss me, Lazare.'

They exchanged a kiss before that poor little babe, who seemed to be asleep. It was the kiss of brother and sister, untainted by the slightest breath of the passion which had glowed within them only the day before.

The dawn was breaking, a soft grey dawn. Cazenove came to look at the baby, and was astonished to find it doing so well. He determined to take it back into the other room, for he felt that he could now answer for Louise. When the little creature was brought to its mother, she looked at it with a feeble smile, then closed her eyes and fell into deep and restorative slumber. The window had been slightly opened, and a delicious freshness, like a very breath of life, streamed in from the sea. They all stood for a moment motionless, worn out, but very happy, beside the bed in which the young mother was sleeping. Then, with silent tread, they left the room, leaving Madame Bouland to watch over her.

The Doctor, however, did not go away till nearly eight o'clock. He was very hungry, and Lazare and Pauline themselves were famished, so Véronique prepared some coffee and an omelet. Downstairs they found Chanteau, whom they had all forgotten, sleeping soundly in his chair. Nothing had been touched since the previous evening, and the room reeked with the acrid smoke of the lamp, which was still burning. Pauline jokingly remarked that the table, on which the plates and dishes had remained, was already laid for them. She swept up the crumbs and made the things a little tidier. Then, as the coffee took some little time to prepare, they attacked the cold veal, joking the while about the dinner that had been so unpleasantly interrupted. Now that all danger was over, they were as merry as children.

'You will hardly believe it,' Chanteau exclaimed, beaming, 'but I slept without being asleep. I was very angry that nobody came down to give me any news, but I felt no uneasiness, for I dreamt that all was going on well.'

His delight increased when he saw Abbé Horteur enter the room. The priest had come across after saying Mass. Chanteau joked him merrily.

'Ah! here you are at last! You deserted me in a nice way last night! Are you frightened of babies, then?'

The priest defended himself from this charge by telling them how he had one night delivered a poor woman on the high-road and baptized her child. Then he accepted a small glass of curaçoa.

Bright sunshine was gilding the yard when Dr. Cazenove at last took his departure. As Lazare and Pauline walked with him to the gate, he whispered to the latter:

'You are not going away to-day?'

She remained for a moment silent, then raised her big dreamy eyes, and seemed to be looking far away into the future.

'No!' she answered; 'I must wait.'

XI

AFTER an abominable month of May, June set in with very warm weather. Westerly gales had been blowing for the last three weeks, storms had devastated the coast, swept away masses of the cliffs, swallowed up boats, and killed many people; but now the broad blue sky, the satiny sea, and the bright hot days were infinitely pleasant and enjoyable.

One glorious afternoon Pauline had wheeled Chanteau's chair on to the terrace, and near him, on a red woollen rug, she had deposited little Paul, who was now eighteen months old. She was his godmother, and she spoilt the child as much as she did the grandfather.

'Are you sure the sun won't inconvenience you, uncle?' she asked.

'Oh dear no! I should think not, indeed! It is so long since I saw it. Are you going to leave little Paul asleep there?'

'Yes. The fresh air will do him good.'

She knelt down on the edge of the rug and gazed at him. He was dressed in a white frock, with bare legs and arms peeping beyond it. His eyes were fast closed, and his quiet little rosy face was turned up towards the sky.

'He has dropped off to sleep at once,' she said softly. 'He tired himself out with rolling about. Don't let the animals bother him.'

She shook her finger at Minouche, who sat at the dining-room window making an elaborate toilet. Some distance off Loulou lay stretched out on the gravel, opening his eyes every now and then with a glance of suspicion, and ever ready to snarl and bite.

As Pauline rose to her feet again, a low groan came from Chanteau.

'Ah! has your pain returned?'

'Returned! Ah! it never leaves me now. I groaned, eh? Well, it's funny, but I do so without even being aware of it.'

He had become a most pitiable object. By degrees his chronic gout had led to the accumulation of cretaceous matter at all his joints, and great chalk-stones had formed and pushed out through his skin. His feet, which were hidden out of sight in his slippers, were contracted inwards like the claws of a sickly bird. But his hands openly displayed all their horrible deformity, swollen as they were at every joint with gleaming red knots, the fingers warped by swellings which forced them apart, and the left hand being rendered especially hideous by a secretion as big as a small egg. On the left elbow, too, a more voluminous deposit had brought on an ulcer. Ankylosis was now complete; Chanteau could no longer make use of his hands or feet, and the few joints which could still slightly bend cracked with as much noise as though a bag of marbles were being shaken. His whole body seemed to have become petrified in the position which he had adopted as the least painful—that is, a somewhat forward one, with an inclination to the right; and he had so completely shaped himself to his easy-chair that even when he was put to bed he remained twisted and bent. His pain never left him now, and the least change in the weather, or a drop of wine, or a mouthful of meat in excess of his usual diet, brought on inflammation.

'Would you like a glass of milk?' Pauline asked him. 'It would refresh you perhaps.'

'Ah! milk indeed!' he replied, between two groans. 'That's another pretty invention of theirs, that milk-cure! I believe they finished me off with that! No, no! I won't take anything; that's the treatment that does me the most good.'

He asked her, however, to change the position of his left leg, for he could not move it himself.

'The villain is all on fire to-day. Put it further away; push it. There, that will do, thank you. What a lovely day! Oh dear! oh dear!'

With his eyes turned towards the far-spreading panorama, he continued to groan quite unconsciously. His moan of pain had now become quite as natural to him as breathing itself. He was wrapped in a heavy blue woollen rug, and his poor deformed hands, that looked so pitiable in the bright sunshine, lay helpless on his knees. It pleased him to sit and look at the sea with its infinite azure, over which white sails flitted as over a boundless highway, open there before him who could no longer put one foot before another.

Pauline, feeling anxious at the sight of Paul's little naked legs, knelt down again and covered them up with part of the rug. For three months past she had always been intending to take her departure on the following Monday. But the child's feeble hands held her back with a force she could not resist. For the first month of the boy's life they had each morning feared that he would not live to see the evening. It was Pauline who had kept him alive from day to day, for his mother was long confined to her bed, and the nurse, whom they had been obliged to procure, simply gave him the breast, evincing the gentle stupidity of a cow. The most devoted, constant care and attention were needed, and Pauline had to keep perpetual watch over the child. By the end of the first month, however, the boy had happily acquired the strength of a child born in due season, and gradually developed. Still, he was but a little creature, and Pauline never left him for a minute, more especially since the weaning, which had been attended by much trouble.

'There!' she said, 'he can't take cold now. See, uncle, how pretty he looks in this crimson rug! It makes him quite rosy.'

Chanteau painfully turned his head, which was now the only part of his body which he was able to move.

'If you kiss him,' he murmured, 'you will wake him. Don't disturb the little cherub. Do you see that steamer over there? It is coming from Havre. How fast it is cutting along!'

Pauline watched the steamer in order to please him. It looked like a black speck on the boundless waters; a slight streak of smoke just blurred a point of the horizon. For a short time the girl stood there, perfectly still, gazing at that sea which slumbered so peacefully beneath the clear sky, and enjoying the beauty of the day.

'But, while I'm stopping here, the stew is getting burned!' she exclaimed at last, hurrying off towards the kitchen.

Just as she was about to enter the house a voice called from the first floor:

'Pauline!'

It was Louise, who was leaning out of the window of what had once been Madame Chanteau's room, but which was now occupied by herself and Lazare. She wore a loose jacket, and her hair was hanging down. In querulous tones she went on: 'If Lazare's down there, tell him to come upstairs.'

'No, he isn't here. He hasn't come back yet,' Pauline replied.

At this Louise broke out angrily:

'I knew quite well that we shouldn't see him again till this evening, even if he condescends to come back then. He stayed away all night in spite of his express promise. Ah! he's a nice fellow. When he once gets to Caen, there's no getting him away from it!'

'He has so few amusements,' Pauline gently urged. 'And then this business about the manure would keep him some time. No doubt he will take advantage of the Doctor's gig, and come back in it.'

Since Lazare and Louise had settled down at Bonneville they had lived a life of perpetual misunderstanding and bickering. There were no open quarrels between them, but constant signs of ill-temper, the lives of both being rendered unhappy by want of harmony. Louise, after a long and painful convalescence, was now leading an empty, aimless existence, manifesting the greatest distaste for domestic matters, and spending her time in novel-reading and protracted toilets. Lazare had again fallen a prey to overwhelming *ennui;* he never opened a book, but spent his time in gazing abstractedly at the sea, just escaping to Caen at long intervals, though only to return home more weary than ever. Pauline, who had been obliged to retain the management of the house, had become quite indispensable to them, for she patched up their quarrels several times a day.

'Be quick and finish dressing!' added the girl. 'The Abbé will be here directly, and you must come and sit with him and my uncle. I have too much to do myself.'

But Louise could not rid herself of her rancour.

'How *can* he do it? Keeping away from home all this time! My father wrote to me yesterday and told me that the remainder of our money would go the same way as the rest.'

Lazare had, indeed, allowed himself to be swindled in a couple of unfortunate speculations, and Pauline had become so anxious on the child's account that, as his godmother, she had made him a present of two-thirds of what she still possessed, taking out in his name a policy which would assure him a hundred thousand francs on the day he reached his majority. She now had only an income of five hundred francs herself, but her sole regret in the matter was the necessity she was under of curtailing her customary charities.

'A fine speculation that manure business is!' Louise continued. 'I am sure my father will have made him give it up, and he's only stopping away to amuse himself. Oh, well! I don't care! He may be as dissolute as he likes!'

'Then what are you getting so angry for?' Pauline retorted. 'But you know that's all nonsense; the poor fellow never thinks of anything wrong. Do hurry down, won't you? What can have happened to Véronique, I wonder, that she should disappear in this way on a Saturday, and leave me all her work to do?'

In fact, a most extraordinary thing had happened—one which had been puzzling the whole house since two o'clock. Véronique had prepared the vegetables for the stew, and plucked and trussed a duck; and then she had disappeared as suddenly and completely as if the earth had swallowed her up. Pauline, quite astounded by this sudden disappearance, had at last resolved to undertake the cooking of the stew herself.

'She hasn't come back, then?' asked Louise, recovering from her anger.

'No, indeed!' Pauline replied. 'Do you know what I am beginning to think? She bought the duck for forty sous of a woman who happened to be passing, and I remember telling her that I had seen much finer ones for thirty sous at Verchemont. She tossed her head directly, and gave me one of her surly looks. Well, I'll be bound that she has gone to Verchemont to see if I wasn't telling a lie.'

She smiled, but there was a touch of sadness in her smile, for the surliness which Véronique was again manifesting pained her. The servant's gradually increasing ill-will against Pauline since Madame Chanteau's death had now brought her back to the virulence of the very early days.

'We've none of us been able to get a word out of her for a week or more,' said Louise. 'Any sort of folly may be expected from a person with such a disposition.'

'Well,' said Pauline charitably, 'we must excuse her whims. She is sure to come back again, and we shan't die of hunger this time.'

But the baby now began to move about on the rug, and she ran up and bent over it.

'Well! what is it, my dear?'

The mother, who was still at the window, glanced out for a moment and then disappeared within the room. Chanteau, quite absorbed in his own reflections, just turned his head as Loulou began to bark, and then called out to his niece:

'Here are your visitors, Pauline!'

Two ragged young urchins, the advanced guard of the troop which she received every Saturday, now came up. Little Paul had quickly dropped off to sleep once more, and she rose and said:

'It's a nice time for them to come! I haven't a minute to spare. Well, never mind; stay, since you're here. Sit down on the bench. And, uncle, if any more of them come, please make them sit down by the side of these. I must just go and glance at my stew.'

When she returned, at the end of a quarter of an hour, two boys and two girls were already seated on the bench; they were some of her little beggars of former days, but had now grown much bigger, though they still retained their mendicant habits.

Never before had there been so much distress in Bonneville. During the storms in May the three remaining houses had been crushed against the cliffs. The destruction was now complete; the flood-tides had made a clean sweep of the village after centuries of attack, during which the sea had each year devoured one or another part of the place. On the shingle one now only saw the conquering waves, which effaced even all trace of the ruins. The fishermen, expelled from the nook where for generation after generation they had obstinately persisted in struggling against the ceaseless onslaught, had been compelled to migrate further up the ravine, where they were camping in companies. The richer ones had built cabins for themselves, while the poorer ones were taking refuge under rocks, all combining to found a new Bonneville, from which their descendants would in turn be ejected after fresh centuries of contest. Before it could complete its work of destruction, the sea had found it necessary to sweep the piles and stockades away. On the day of their overthrow the wind had blown from the north, and such huge mountains of water had clashed up that the church itself had been shaken by the violence with which they broke against the shore. Lazare, though he was told of what was happening, would not go down. He had remained on the terrace, watching the waves sweep up, while the fishermen rushed off to view the desperate onslaught. They were thrilled with mingled pride and awe. Ah! how the hussy was howling! Now she was going to make a clean sweep of it all! And in less than twenty minutes, indeed, everything had disappeared, the stockades were broken down, and the timbers were smashed into matchwood. And the fishermen roared with the waves, and gesticulated and danced like so many savages, intoxicated by the wind and the sea, and glutting themselves with the sight of all that destruction. Then, while Lazare angrily shook his fist at them, they had fled for their lives, closely pursued by the wild rush of the waves, which nothing more held in check. Now they were perishing of starvation, and groaning as of old in their new Bonneville, accusing the hussy of their ruin and commending themselves to the charity of the 'kind young lady.'

'What are you doing there?' cried Pauline, as she saw Houtelard's son. 'I forbade you ever to come here again!'

He was a great strapping fellow, now nearly twenty years old. His former sad and timid expression, that told of bad treatment at home, had turned into a sly, crafty look. He lowered his eyes as he replied:

'Please take pity upon us, Mademoiselle Pauline. We are so miserable and wretched now that father is dead!'

Houtelard had gone off to sea one stormy evening and had never returned. His body had never been found, nor had that of his mate, nor even a single plank of their boat. Pauline, however, obliged as she was to exercise strict supervision over her charities, had sworn that she would never give a single sou to either son or widow, for they lived together in open shame.

'You know quite well why I won't have you coming here,' Pauline replied. 'When you behave differently, I will see what I can do for you.'

Thereupon the young fellow began to plead his cause in a whining voice: 'It is all her fault; she brought it about. She would have gone on beating me otherwise. Please give us a trifle, kind young lady. We have lost everything. I could get on well enough myself, but it is for her that I'm asking you, and she is very ill—indeed she is; I swear it.'

Pauline ended by taking pity on him and sending him away with a loaf of bread and some stew; and she even promised to call on the sick woman and take her some medicine.

'Medicine, indeed!' muttered Chanteau. 'Just you try to get her to swallow it!'

But Pauline had already turned her attention to the Prouane girl, one of whose cheeks was gashed.

'How have you managed to do that?'

'I fell against a tree, Mademoiselle Pauline.'

'Against a tree? It looks more like a cut from the corner of a table.'

She was a big girl now, with prominent cheek-bones, but she still had the great haggard eyes of a weak-witted child, and she made vain efforts to remain standing in a respectful attitude. Her legs shook under her, and she could scarcely articulate her words.

'Why! you have been drinking, you wicked girl!' cried Pauline, scrutinizing her keenly.

'Oh, Mademoiselle! how can you say so?'

'You were drunk and you fell down! Isn't it so? I know very well what you are all given to. Sit down, and I will go and get some arnica and a bandage.'

She attended to the girl's cheek, and tried to make her feel ashamed of herself. It was disgraceful, she told her, for a girl of her age to intoxicate herself with her father and mother, a couple of drunkards who would be found dead some morning, poisoned by calvados. The girl listened drowsily, and when her cheek was bandaged she stammered out:

'Father is always complaining of pains, and I could rub him well if you would give me a little camphorated brandy.'

Neither Pauline nor Chanteau could keep from laughing.

'No, no! I know very well what would become of the brandy. I will give you a loaf, though I'm afraid you will go and sell it and spend the money in drink. Stay where you are, and Cuche shall take you home.'

Young Cuche got up from the bench in his turn. His feet were bare; indeed, the only clothes he wore were some old breeches and a ragged shirt, through which showed parts of his skin, browned by the sun and torn by brambles. He was to be met running about the high-roads, leaping over hedges with the agility of a wolf, living like a savage, to whom hunger makes every sort of prey acceptable. He had reached the lowest depths of misery and destitution, such an abyss of wretchedness that Pauline looked at him with remorse, as though she felt guilty for allowing a human being to go on living in such a state. But whenever she had attempted to rescue him, he had always fled, hating all thought of work or service.

'Since you have come here again,' she said to him gently, 'I suppose you have thought over what I said to you last Saturday. I hope that your return here is a sign that you are not lost to all sense of what is right. You cannot go on leading your present vagabond life; I am no longer as rich as I was, and I cannot support you in idleness. Have you made up your mind to accept my offer?'

Since the loss of her fortune Pauline had tried to make up for her lack of money by interesting other charitable people in her pensioners. Doctor Cazenove had at last succeeded in obtaining the admission of Cuche's mother into the hospital for incurables at Bayeux, and Pauline herself held in reserve a sum of one hundred francs to provide an outfit for the son, for whom she had found a berth among the workmen employed on the railway line to Cherbourg. He bent his head as she spoke, and listened to her with an expression of distrust.

'It's quite settled, isn't it '?' she continued. 'You will accompany your mother, and then you will go to your post.'

But as she stepped towards him he sprang back. His eyes, though downcast, never left her, and he seemed to think that she was going to seize him by his wrists.

'What is the matter?' she asked in surprise.

Then, with a wild animal's uneasy glance, the lad murmured: 'You are going to take me and shut me up. I don't want to go.'

All further attempts at persuasion were useless. He let her continue talking, and appeared to admit the force of her reasoning; but as soon as ever she moved he sprang towards the gate, and with an obstinate shake of the head refused her offers for his mother and for himself, preferring freedom and starvation.

'Take yourself off, you lazy impostor!' Chanteau cried at last in indignation. 'It is kindness thrown away, troubling one's self about such a vagabond.'

Pauline's hands trembled as she thought of her wasted charity, her failure to effect anything for this lad, who insisted on remaining in misery.

'No, no! uncle,' she said, with an expression of despairing tolerance, 'they are starving, and they must have some food in spite of everything.'

She called Cuche back to her to give him, as on other Saturdays, a loaf of bread and forty sous. But he backed away from her, saying:

'Put it down on the ground and go away, and I will come and pick it up.'

She did as he told her. Then he cautiously stepped forward, casting suspicious glances around him. As soon as he had picked up the forty sous and the loaf he ran off as fast as his bare feet could carry him.

'The wild beast!' cried Chanteau. 'He will come and murder us all one of these nights. It's just like that little gaol-bird's daughter there. I would swear it was she who stole my silk handkerchief the other day.'

He was speaking of the Tourmal girl, whose grandfather had lately joined her father in gaol. She was now the only one who was left on the bench with the little Prouane, who was stupefied with drink. She got up, without any sign that she had heard the charge of theft brought against her, and she began to whine: 'Have pity upon us, kind young lady! There is nobody but mother and me at home now. The gendarmes come and beat us every night. My body is all one big bruise, and mother is dying. Oh! kind young lady, do give us some money and some good meat-soup and some wine—'

Chanteau, quite exasperated by the girl's string of lies, moved restlessly in his chair, but Pauline would have given the chemise off her back.

'There! there! That will do,' she muttered. 'You would get more if you talked less. Stay where you are, and I will make up a basket for you.'

When she came back, bringing with her an old fish-hamper, in which she had put a loaf, two litre-bottles of wine, and some meat, she found another of her pensioners on the terrace, the Gonin girl, who had brought her child with her, a girl now some twenty months old. The mother, who was sixteen years of age, was so fragile and slight of figure that she seemed more like the child's elder sister. She was scarcely able to carry the infant, but she nevertheless brought it to the house, as she knew that Mademoiselle Pauline was very fond of children and could refuse them nothing.

'Good gracious! How heavy she is!' cried Pauline, as she took the child in her arms. 'And to think that she is not six months older than our Paul!'

Despite herself, her eyes turned sadly towards the little boy, who was still lying asleep upon the rug. However, the young mother began to complain:

'If you only knew how much she eats, Mademoiselle Pauline! And I've no bed-linen, and nothing to dress her with. And then, since father is dead, mother and the other one are always ill-using me. They treat me like the lowest of the low, and say that if I have a baby I ought to provide what it costs to keep it.'

'Poor little thing!' Pauline murmured. 'I am knitting her some socks. You must bring her to see me oftener; there is always milk here, and she might have a few spoonfuls of gruel. I will go and see your mother, and I'll try to frighten her, as she still behaves unkindly to you.'

The girl took up her daughter again, while Pauline began to prepare a parcel.

However, Abbé Horteur now appeared upon the terrace.

'Here come Monsieur Lazare and the Doctor,' he announced.

At the same moment they heard the wheels of the gig, and while Martin, the ex-sailor with the wooden leg, was leading the horse to the stable, Cazenove came round from the yard, crying:

'I am bringing you back the rake who stopped away from home all night. You won't be very hard on him, I hope!'

Lazare now appeared, smiling feebly. He was quickly ageing; his shoulders were bent and his face was cadaverous, devastated by the mental anguish which was destroying him. He was no doubt on the point of explaining the reason of his delay when the window of the first floor, which had remained open, was violently closed.

'Louise hasn't quite finished dressing yet,' Pauline explained. 'She will be down in a minute or two.'

They all looked at one another, and there was a feeling of embarrassment. That angry banging of the window portended a quarrel. After taking a step or two towards the stairs, Lazare checked himself and determined to wait where he was. He kissed his father and little Paul; and then, to conceal his disquietude, he tackled his cousin, saying to her in a querulous voice:

'Bid us of all this vermin! You know I can't bear to see them anywhere near me.'

He was referring to the three girls who were still on the bench. Pauline hastened to tie up the parcel which she had made for the Gonin girl.

'There! you can go now,' she said. 'You two just take your companion home, and mind she doesn't fall any more. And, you, look well after your baby, and try not to forget it or leave it anywhere on the road.'

As they were at last setting off Lazare insisted upon examining the Tourmal girl's hamper. She had already contrived to stow away in it an old coffee-pot, which had been thrown aside in a corner and which she had managed to steal. Then all three of the little hussies were driven away, the young drunkard tottering along between the two others.

'What a dreadful lot they are!' exclaimed the priest, sitting down by Chanteau's side. 'God has certainly abandoned them. Some have children directly after their first Communion, and others take to drinking and thieving like their parents. Ah, well! I've warned them of what will happen to them some day!'

'I say, my dear fellow,' then began the Doctor, addressing Lazare in an ironical tone, 'are you thinking of building those famous stockades of yours over again?'

Lazare made an angry gesture. Any allusion to his defeat in his struggle with the sea exasperated him.

'No indeed!' he cried. 'I would let the sea sweep into our own house, without even putting a broom-handle across the road to stay its course. No, no! indeed. I've been very foolish as it is, but one doesn't commit that kind of folly again. I actually saw those scoundrels dancing with delight on the day of the catastrophe! Do you know what I begin to think? I feel sure they had sawn through the beams on the day before the flood-tide, for they would never have given way as they did if they had not been tampered with.'

He tried in this way to salve his wounded pride as an engineer. Then, stretching his hand towards Bonneville, he added:

'Let them all go to smash! I will take my turn at dancing then!'

'Don't say such wicked things!' Pauline observed in her quiet manner. 'Only the poor may be excused for being wicked. You ought to build up the stockade again in spite of everything.'

Lazare had already calmed down, as though his last burst of passion had exhausted him.

'No, no!' he muttered, 'it would bore me too much. But you are right; there is nothing for one to make oneself angry about. Whether they're drowned or not, what does it matter to me?'

Silence fell again. Chanteau had fallen back into a posture of dolorous immobility after raising his head to receive his son's kiss. The priest was twirling his thumbs, and the Doctor paced about, with his hands behind his back. They all began to look at little Paul, whom Pauline defended even from his father's caresses, to prevent him from being wakened. Since the others had come she had begged them to lower their voices and not to tread so heavily about the rug, and she now shook a whip at Loulou, who still continued to growl at the noise he had heard when the horse was led to the stable.

265

'You don't suppose that that will quiet him, do you?' said Lazare. 'He'll make that row for an hour. He's the most disagreeable brute I ever came across. He begins to snarl directly one moves, and one might as well be without a dog at all, he is so completely absorbed in himself. The only good the sulky beast does is to make us regret our poor old Matthew.'

'How old is Minouche now?' Cazenove inquired. 'I have seen her about here as long as I can remember.'

'She is turned sixteen,' Pauline answered, 'and she keeps very well yet.'

Minouche, who was still at her toilet on the dining-room window-sill, raised her head as the Doctor pronounced her name. For a moment she held her foot suspended in the air, then again began to lick her fur delicately.

'She isn't deaf yet, you see,' Pauline said; 'but I fancy her sight is not so good as it was. It is scarcely a week ago since seven kittens of hers were drowned. It is really quite terrible to think of the number she has had during the last sixteen years. If they had all been allowed to live they would have eaten up the whole neighbourhood.'

'Well, well, she at any rate keeps neat and clean,' said the priest, glancing at Minouche as she continued washing herself with her tongue.

Chanteau, who, like the others, was looking towards the cat, now began to moan more loudly with that incessant involuntary expression of pain which had become so habitual to him that he had grown unconscious of it.

'Are you feeling worse?' the Doctor asked him.

'Eh? What? Why do you ask?' he said, suddenly seeming to awake. 'Ah, it's because I'm breathing heavily. Yes, I am in great pain this evening. I thought that the sun would do me good, but I feel as though I were being suffocated, and I haven't a joint that isn't burning.'

Cazenove examined his hands. They all shuddered at the sight of those poor deformed stumps. The priest made another of his sensible remarks.

'Such fingers as those are not adapted for playing draughts. That's an amusement which you can't have now.'

'Be very careful about what you eat and drink,' the Doctor urged. 'Your elbow is highly inflamed, and the ulceration is increasing.'

'How can I be more careful than I am?' Chanteau wailed hopelessly. 'My wine is all measured out and my meat is weighed! Must I give up taking anything at all? Indeed, it isn't living to go on like this, and one might as well die at once. I can't eat even without assistance—how is it likely with such things as these at the end of my arms?—and you may be quite sure that Pauline, who feeds me, takes care that I don't get anything that I oughtn't to have.'

The girl smiled.

'Ah! yes, indeed,' she said, 'you ate too much yesterday. It was my fault, but I couldn't refuse when I saw how your appetite was distressing you.'

At this they all pretended to grow merry, and began to tease him about the junketings in which they declared he still indulged. But their voices trembled with pity as they glanced at that remnant of a man, that inert mass of flesh, which now only lived enough to suffer. He had fallen back into his usual position, with his body leaning to the right and his hands lying on his knees.

'This evening now, for instance,' Pauline continued, 'we are going to have a roast duck—'

But she suddenly checked herself to ask:

'By the way, did you see anything of Véronique as you came through Verchemont?'

Then she told Lazare and the Doctor the story of Véronique's disappearance. Neither of them had seen anything of her. They expressed some astonishment at the woman's strange whims, and ended by growing merry over the subject. It would be a fine sight, they said, to see her face when she came back and found them already round the table with the dinner cooked and served.

'I must leave you now,' said Pauline gaily, 'for I have to attend to the kitchen. If I let the stew get burnt, or serve the duck underdone, my uncle will give me notice!'

Abbé Horteur broke out into a loud laugh, and even Doctor Cazenove himself seemed tickled at the idea, when the window on the first floor was suddenly thrown open with a tremendous clatter. Louise did not show herself, but merely called in a sharp voice:

'Come upstairs, Lazare!'

At first Lazare seemed inclined to rebel and to refuse obedience to a command given in such a voice. But Pauline, anxious to avoid a scene before visitors, gave him an entreating look, and he went off to the house, while his cousin remained for a moment or two longer on the terrace to do what she could to dissipate the awkwardness of the situation. No one spoke, and they all looked at the sea in embarrassment. The westering sun was now casting a sheet of gold over it, crowning the little blue waves with quivering fires. Far away in the distance the horizon was changing to a soft lilac hue. The lovely day was drawing towards its close in perfect serenity, and not a cloud or a Bail flecked the infinite stretch of sky and sea.

'Well, as he never came home last night,' Pauline at last ventured to say with a smile, 'I suppose it is necessary to lecture him a little.'

The Doctor looked at her, and on his face also appeared a smile, in which Pauline could read his prediction of former days, when he had told her that she wasn't making them a very desirable present in bestowing them on one another. And at this she walked away towards the kitchen.

'Well, I must really leave you now,' she said. 'Try to amuse yourselves. Call for me, uncle, if Paul wakes up again.'

In the kitchen, when she had stirred the stew and got the spit ready, she knocked the pots and pans about impatiently. The voices of Louise and Lazare reached her more and more distinctly through the ceiling, and she grew distressed as she thought that they would certainly be heard on the terrace. It was very absurd of them, she said to herself, to go on shouting as though they were both deaf, and letting everybody know of their disagreements. But she did not care to go up to them, partly because she had to get the dinner ready, and partly because she felt ill at ease at the thought of interfering with them in their own room. It was generally downstairs, amid the common life of the family, that she played her part of reconciler.

She went into the dining-room for a few moments and busied herself with laying the table. But the shouting still continued, and she could no longer bear the thought that they were making themselves unhappy. So, impelled by that spirit of active charity which made the happiness of others the chief thought of her life, she at last went upstairs.

'My dear children,' she exclaimed, as she abruptly entered the room, 'I daresay you will tell me it is no business of mine, but you are really making too much noise. It is very foolish of you to excite yourselves in this way and disturb the whole house.'

She had hastily stepped across the room, and at once closed the window, which Louise had left open. Fortunately neither the priest nor the Doctor had remained on the terrace. With one quick glance she had seen that there was nobody there except the drowsing Chanteau and little Paul, who was still asleep.

'We could hear you out there as plainly as if you had been in the dining-room,' she resumed. 'Come, now, what is the matter this time?'

But, their tempers aroused, they continued quarrelling without taking any notice of Pauline. She now stood there, still and silent, feeling ill at ease again in that room. The yellow cretonne with its green pattern, the old mahogany furniture and the red carpet, had been replaced by heavy woollen hangings and furniture more in harmony with Louise's delicacy of taste. There was nothing left to remind one of the dead mother. A scent of heliotrope arose from the toilet-table, on which lay some damp towels, and the perfume somewhat oppressed Pauline. She involuntarily glanced round the room, in which every object spoke of the familiar life of husband and wife. Though, as her rebellious thoughts calmed down, she had at last prevailed upon herself to continue living with them, she had never previously entered their room, where all things suggested conjugal privacy. And thus she quivered almost with the jealousy of former times.

'How can you make each other so unhappy?' she murmured, after a short interval of silence. 'Won't you ever be sensible?'

'Well, no, I've had quite enough of it!' cried Louise. 'Do you think he will ever allow that he is in the wrong? I merely told him how uneasy he had made us all by not coming home last night, and then he flew at me like a wild beast and accused me of having ruined his life, and threatened that he would go off to America!'

Lazare interrupted her in furious tones:

'You are lying! If you had chided me for my absence in that gentle fashion, I should have kissed you, and there would have been an end of the matter. But it was you who accused me of making you spend your life in tears. Yes, you threatened to go and throw yourself into the sea, if I continued to make your life unbearable.'

Then they flew at each other again, and gave vent to all the bitterness which the continual jarring of their temperaments aroused in them. The slightest little differences set them bickering, and brought them to a state of exasperated antipathy which made the rest of the day wretched. Whenever her husband interfered with her enjoyment Louise, despite her gentle face, proved as malicious as a fawning cat, that loves to be caressed, but strikes out with its claws at the slightest irritation; and Lazare, finding in these quarrels a relief from his besetting *ennui,* frequently persisted in them for the sake of the excitement they brought.

However, Pauline continued, listening to the quarrel. She was suffering greater unhappiness than they themselves were. That fashion of loving one another was beyond her comprehension. Why couldn't they make mutual allowances and accommodate themselves to each other, since they had to live together? She was deeply pained, for she still regarded the marriage as her own work, and she longed to see it a happy and harmonious one, so that she might feel compensated for the sacrifice she had made by knowing that she had, at any rate, acted rightly.

'I never reproach you for squandering my fortune,' Louise continued.

'There was only that accusation wanting!' Lazare cried. 'It wasn't my fault that I was robbed of it.'

'Oh! it's only stupid folks who allow their pockets to be emptied, who are robbed. But, any way, we are now reduced to a wretched income of four or five thousand francs, barely sufficient to enable us to live in this hole of a place. If it were not for Pauline, our child would have to go naked one of these days, for I quite expect that you will squander all that we have left, what with all your extraordinary fads and speculations that come to grief one after the other.'

'There! there! Prate away! Your father has already paid me similar pretty compliments. I guessed you had been writing to him. I've given up that speculation in manure in consequence; though I know it was a perfectly safe thing, with cent per cent to be gained. But now I'm like you, and I've had enough of it, and the deuce take me if I bestir myself any more. We will go on living here.'

'A pretty life, isn't it, for a woman of my age? It's nothing but a gaol, with never an opportunity of going out or seeing anybody; and there's that stupid sea for ever in front of one, which only seems to increase one's *ennui*—Oh! If I had only known! If I had only known!'

'And do you suppose that I enjoy myself here? If I were not married, I should be able to go away to some distant place and try my fortune. I have longed to do so a score of times. But that's all at an end now; I'm nailed down to this lonely wilderness, where there's nothing to do but to go to sleep. You have done for me; I feel that very clearly.'

'I have done for you! I!—I didn't force you to marry me, did I? It was you who ought to have seen that we were not suited to each other. It is your fault if our lives are wrecked.'

'Ah! yes, indeed, our lives are certainly wrecked, and you do all you can to make them more intolerable every day.'

Pauline, though she had resolved not to interfere between them, could no longer restrain herself.

'Oh! do give over, you unhappy creatures! You seem to take a pleasure in marring a life which might be such a happy one. Why will you goad each other into saying things which you cannot recall and which make you so wretched? Hold your tongues, both of you! I won't let this go on any longer.'

Louise had fallen into a chair in a fit of tears, while Lazare, in a state of wild excitement, strode up and down the room.

'Crying won't do any good, my dear,' Pauline continued. 'You are really not tolerant; you have too many grievances. And you, my poor fellow, how can you treat her in this unkind fashion? It is abominable of you. I thought that, at any rate, you had a kind heart. You are, both of you, a couple of overgrown children, and are equally in fault, making yourselves wretched without knowing why. But I won't have it any longer, do you hear? I won't have unhappy people about me. Go and kiss each other at once!'

She tried to laugh; she no longer felt that tremor which had at first so disquieted her. She was only thrilled by a glow of kindliness, a desire to see them in each other's arms, so that she might be sure their quarrel was at an end.

'Kiss him, indeed! I should just think so!' exclaimed Louise. 'He has insulted me too much!'

'Never!' exclaimed Lazare.

Then Pauline broke into a merry laugh.

'Come, come!' she said; 'don't sulk with each other. You know, I am very determined about having my own way. The dinner is getting burnt, and our guests are waiting. If you don't do as I tell you, Lazare, I shall come and make you. Go down on your knees before her, and clasp her affectionately to your heart. No, no! you must do it better than that!'

She made them twine their arms closely and lovingly about each other, and watched them kiss, with an air of joyful triumph, without the least sign of trouble in her clear, calm eyes. Within her glowed warm, thrilling joy, like some subtle fire, which raised her high above them. Lazare pressed his wife to his heart in remorse; and Louise, who was still in her dressing-wrap, with her neck and arms bare, returned his caresses, her tears streaming forth more freely than before.

'There! that's much nicer, isn't it, than quarrelling?' said Pauline. 'I will be off, now that you no longer need me to make peace between you.'

She sprang to the door as she spoke, and quickly closed it upon that chamber of love, with its perfume of heliotrope, which now thrilled her with soft emotion, as though it were an accomplice perfume which would complete her task of reconciliation.

When she got downstairs to the kitchen, Pauline began to sing as she stirred her stew. Then she threw a bundle of wood on the fire, arranged the turnspit, and began to watch the duck roast with a critical eye. It amused her to have to play the servant's part. She had tied a big white apron round her, and felt quite pleased at the thought of waiting upon them all and undertaking the most humble duties, so that she might be able to tell them that they were that day indebted to her for their gaiety and health. Now that, thanks to her, they were smiling and happy, she wanted to serve them a festive repast of very good things, of which they would partake plentifully while growing bright and mirthful round the table.

She thought, however, of her uncle and the child again, and hastily ran out on to the terrace, where she was greatly astonished to find her cousin seated by the side of his little son.

'What!' she exclaimed, 'have you come down already?'

He merely nodded his head in answer. He seemed to have fallen back into his former weary indifference; his shoulders were bent, and his hands were lying listlessly in front of him. Then Pauline said to him with an expression of uneasy anxiety:

'I hope you didn't begin again as soon as my back was turned?'

'No, no!' he at last made up his mind to reply. 'She will be down as soon as she has put on her dress. We have quite forgiven each other and made it up. But how long will it last? To-morrow there will be something else; every day, every hour! You can't change people, and you can't prevent things happening.'

Pauline became very grave, and her saddened eyes sought the ground. Lazare was right. She could clearly foresee a long series of days like this in store for them, the same incessant quarrels, which she would have to smooth away. And she was no longer quite sure that she was altogether cured herself, and might not again give way to her old outbursts of jealousy. Ah! were these daily troubles never to have an end? But she had already raised her eyes again; she remembered how many times she had won the victory over herself; and as for those other two, she would see whether they would not grow tired of quarrelling before she did of reconciling them. This thought brightened her, and she laughingly repeated it to Lazare. What would be left for her to do, if the house became perfectly happy? She would fall a victim to *ennui* herself, if she hadn't some little worries to smooth away.

'Where are the priest and the Doctor?' she asked, surprised to see them no longer there.

'They must have gone into the kitchen garden,' said Chanteau. 'The Abbé wanted to show our pears to the Doctor.'

Pauline was going to look from the corner of the terrace, when she stopped short before little Paul.

'Ah! He has woke up again!' she cried. 'Just look at him! He's already trying to be off on the loose!'

Paul had just pulled himself up on to his little knees in the midst of the rug, and was beginning to creep off slyly upon all fours. Before he reached the gravel, however, he tripped over a fold in the rug, and rolled upon his back, with his frock thrown back and his little legs and arms in the air. He lay kicking about and wriggling amidst the poppy-like brilliance of the rug.

'Well! he's kicking in a fine way!' cried Pauline merrily. 'Look, and you shall see how he has improved in his walking since yesterday.'

She knelt down beside the child and tried to set him on his feet. He had developed so slowly that he was very backward for his age, and they had for a time feared that he would always be weak on his legs.

So it was a great joy to the family to see him make his first attempts at walking, clutching at the air with his hands, and tumbling down over the smallest bit of gravel.

'Come now! give over playing,' Pauline called to him. 'Come and show them that you are a man. There now, keep steady, and go and kiss papa, and then you shall go and kiss grandfather.'

Chanteau, whose face was twitching with sharp shooting pains, turned his head to watch the scene. Lazare, notwithstanding his despondency, was willing to lend himself to the fun.

'Come along!' he cried to the child.

'Oh! you must hold out your arms to him,' Pauline explained. 'He won't venture if you don't. He likes to see something that he can fall against. Come, my treasure, pluck up a little courage!'

There were three steps for him to take. There were loving exclamations and unbounded enthusiasm when Paul made up his mind to go that little distance, with all the swaying of a tight-rope walker who feels uncertain of his legs. He fell into the arms of his father, who kissed him on his still scanty hair, while he smiled with an infant's vague delighted smile, widely opening his moist and rosy little mouth. Then his godmother wanted to make him talk, but his tongue was still more backward than his legs, and he only uttered guttural sounds in which his relatives alone could distinguish the words 'papa' and 'mamma.'

'Oh! but there's something else yet,' Pauline resumed. 'He promised to go and kiss his grandfather. Go along with you! Ah! it's a fine walk you've got before you this time!'

There were at least eight steps between Lazare's chair and Chanteau's. Paul had never ventured so far out into the world before, and so there was considerable excitement about the matter. Pauline took up a position half-way in order to prevent accidents, and two long minutes were spent in persuading the child to make a start. At last he set off, swaying about, with his hands clutching the air. For an instant Pauline thought that she would have to catch him in her arms, but he pushed bravely forward and fell upon Chanteau's knees. Bursts of applause greeted him.

Then they made him repeat the journey half a score of times. He no longer showed any signs of fear; he started off at the first call, went from his grandfather to his father, and then back again to his grandfather, laughing loudly all the time, and quite enjoying the fun, though he always seemed on the point of tumbling over, as if the ground were shaking beneath him.

'Just once again to father!' Pauline cried.

Lazare was beginning to get a little tired. Children, even his own, quickly bored him. As he looked at his boy, so merry and now out of danger, the thought flashed through his mind that this little creature would outlive him and would doubtless close his eyes for the last time, an idea which made him shudder with agony. Since he had come to the determination to continue vegetating at Bonneville, he was constantly occupied with the thought that he would die in the room where his mother had died; and he never went up the stairs without telling himself that one day his coffin would pass that way. The entrance to the passage was very narrow, and there was an awkward turning, which was a perpetual source of disquietude to him, and he worried himself with wondering how the bearers would be able to carry him out without jolting him. As increasing age day by day shortened his span of life, that constant dwelling upon the thought of death hastened his breaking-up, annihilated his last shreds of manliness. He was 'quite done for,' as he often told himself; he was of no further use at all, and he would ask himself what was the good of bestirring himself, as he fell deeper and deeper into the slough of boredom.

'Just once more to grandfather!' cried Pauline.

Chanteau was not able to stretch out his arms to receive and support his grandson, and, though he set his knees apart, the clutching of the child's puny fingers at his trousers drew sighs of pain from him. The little one was already used to the old man's ceaseless moaning, and probably imagined, in his scarcely awakened mind, that all grandfathers suffered in the same way. That day, however, in the bright sunshine, as he came and fell against him, he raised his little face, checked his laugh, and gazed at the old man with his vacillating eyes. The grandfather's deformed hands looked like hideous blocks of mingled flesh and chalk; his face, dented with red wrinkles, disfigured by suffering, seemed to have been violently twisted towards his right shoulder; while his whole body was covered with bumps and crevices, as if it were that of some old stone saint, damaged and badly pieced together. Paul appeared quite surprised to see him looking so ill and so old in the sunshine.

'Just once more! Just once more!' cried Pauline again.

She, full of health and cheerfulness, kept sending the little lad to and fro between the two men, from the grandfather, who obstinately lived on in hopeless suffering, to the father, who was already undermined by terror of the hereafter.

'Perhaps his generation will be a less foolish one than this,' she suddenly exclaimed. 'He won't accuse chemistry of spoiling his life; he will believe that it is still possible to live, even with the certainty of having some day to die.'

Lazare smiled in an embarrassed way.

'Bah!' he muttered, 'he will have the gout like my father, and his nerves will be worse strung than mine. Just see how weak he is! It is the law of degeneration.'

'Be quiet!' cried Pauline. 'I will bring him up, and you'll see if I don't make a man of him!'

There was a moment's silence, while she clasped the child to her in a motherly embrace.

'Why don't you get married, as you're so fond of children?' Lazare asked.

She looked at him in amazement.

'But I have a child! Haven't you given me one? I get married! Never! What an idea!'

She dandled little Paul in her arms, and laughed yet more loudly as she declared that Lazare had quite converted her to the doctrines of the great Saint Schopenhauer, and that she would remain unmarried in order to be able to work for the universal deliverance. And she was, indeed, the incarnation of renunciation, of love for others and kindly charity for erring humanity.

The sun was sinking to rest in the boundless waters, perfect serenity fell from the paling sky, the immensity of air and sea alike lay wrapped in all the mellow softness of the close of a lovely day. Par away over the water one single little white sail gleamed like a spark, but it vanished as the sun sank beneath the long line of the horizon; then there was nothing to be seen save the gradual deepening of the twilight over the motionless sea. And Pauline was still dandling the child, and laughing with brave gaiety as she stood between her despairing cousin and her moaning uncle, in the middle of the terrace, which was now growing bluish in the shadowy dusk. She had stripped herself of everything, but happiness rang out in her clear laugh.

'Aren't we going to dine this evening?' asked Louise, making her appearance in a coquettish dress of grey silk.

'I'm quite ready,' Pauline replied. 'I can't think what they can be doing in the garden.'

At that moment Abbé Horteur came back, looking very much distressed. In reply to their anxious questions, after seeking for some phrase which would soften the shock, he ended by bluntly saying:

'We have just discovered poor Véronique hanging from one of your pear-trees.'

They all raised a cry of surprise and horror, and their faces paled beneath the passing quiver of death.

'But what could make her do such a thing?' cried Pauline. 'She could have had no reason, and she had even to prepare the dinner. It can scarcely be because I told her that they had made her pay ten sous too much for her duck!'

In his turn Doctor Cazenove now came up. For the last quarter of an hour he had been vainly trying to restore animation to the poor woman's body in the coach-house, whither Martin had helped him to carry it. One could never tell, he said, what such whimsical old servants would do. She had never really got over her mistress's death.

'It didn't take her long,' he added. 'She just strung herself up by the strings of one of her kitchen aprons.'

Lazare and Louise, frozen with terror, said not a word. Chanteau, after listening in silence, felt a pang of disgust as he thought of the compromised dinner. And that wretched creature without hands or feet, who had to be put to bed and fed like a child, that pitiable remnant of a man, whose almost vanished life was nothing more than one scream of pain, cried out in furious indignation:

'What a fool one must be to go and kill oneself!'

THE END

Other books published by Mondial

Emile Zola: The Fortune of the Rougons
(ISBN 1595690107 / ISBN 9781595690104)

Emile Zola: A Love Episode (A Page of Love)
(ISBN 1595690271 / ISBN 9781595690272)

Emile Zola: The Fat and the Thin (The Belly of Paris)
(ISBN 1595690522 / ISBN 9781595690524)

Emile Zola: Abbé Mouret's Transgression (The Sin of the Abbé Mouret)
(ISBN 1595690506 / ISBN 9781595690500)

Emile Zola: The Dream
(ISBN 1595690492 / ISBN 9781595690494)

Emile Zola: A Love Episode
(ISBN 1595690271 / ISBN 9781595690272)

Emile Zola: The Conquest of Plassans
(ISBN 1595690484 / ISBN 9781595690487)

Emile Zola: The Joy of Life (Zest for Life)
(ISBN 1595690476 / ISBN 9781595690470)

Emile Zola: Doctor Pascal
(ISBN 1595690514 / ISBN 9781595690517)

Emile Zola: His Excellency
(ISBN 1595690557 / 9781595690555)

Emile Zola: Fruitfulness
(ISBN 1595690182 / 9781595690180)

Victor Hugo: The Man Who Laughs (By Order of the King)
(ISBN 1595690131 / 9781595690135)

Victor Hugo: History of a Crime
(ISBN 1595690204 / 9781595690203)

Honoré de Balzac: Ursula (Ursule Mirouët)
(ISBN 1595690530 / 9781595690531)

Honoré de Balzac: Maître Cornelius
(ISBN 1595690174 / 9781595690173)

Anatole France: Penguin Island
(ISBN 1595690298 / 9781595690296)

Gustave Flaubert: Salammbo (Salambo)
(ISBN 1595690352 / 9781595690357)

Jules Verne: An Antarctic Mystery (The Sphinx of the Ice Fields)
(ISBN 1595690549 / 9781595690548)

Agatha Christie: Two Novels (The Mysterious Affair at Styles. The Secret
Adversary.) (ISBN 1595690417 / 9781595690418)

Frederick (Friedrich) Engels: Socialism: Utopian and Scientific
(Appendix: The Mark; Preface: Karl Marx)
(ISBN 1595690468 / 9781595690463)

Karl Marx: The Eighteenth Brumaire of Louis Bonaparte
(ISBN 1595690239 / 9781595690234)

Johann Wolfgang von Goethe: The Sorrows of Young Werther
(ISBN 159569045X / 9781595690456)

Jack London: War of the Classes. Revolution. The Shrinkage of the Planet.
(ISBN 1595690409 / 9781595690401)

Jack London: Before Adam. Children of the Frost.
(ISBN 1595690395 / 9781595690395)

Jack London: The Iron Heel
(ISBN 1595690379 / 9781595690371)

Oscar Wilde, Anonymous: Teleny or The Reverse of the Medal
(ISBN 1595690360 / 9781595690364)

Martin Andersen Nexo: Pelle the Conqueror
(ISBN 159569028X / 9781595690289)

Susan Coolidge: Clover
(ISBN 1595690263 / 9781595690265)

Jerome K. Jerome: Idle Thoughts of an Idle Fellow
(ISBN 1595690247 / 9781595690241)

Gertrude Stein: Three Lives. With an introduction by Carl Van Vechten
(ISBN 1595690425 / 9781595690425)

Malama Katulwende: Bitterness (An African Novel from Zambia)
(ISBN 159569031X / 9781595690319)

Sigmund Freud: Dream Psychology (Psychoanalysis for Beginners) (ISBN
1595690166 / 9781595690166)

Theodor Storm, Adelbert von Chamisso, Adalbert Stifter: Famous German
Novellas of the 19th Century (Immensee. Peter Schlemihl. Brigitta)
(ISBN 159569014X / 9781595690142)

James Baldwin: Fifty Famous People (Illustrated Book of Short Stories)
(ISBN 1595690301 / 9781595690302)

Printed in the United States
128431LV00003B/15/A